SILVER BAY

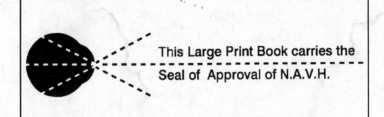

This Large Print Book carries the
Seal of Approval of N.A.V.H.

SILVER BAY

JOJO MOYES

THORNDIKE PRESS
A part of Gale, Cengage Learning

GALE
CENGAGE Learning·

Farmington Hills, Mich • San Francisco • New York • Waterville, Maine
Meriden, Conn • Mason, Ohio • Chicago

GALE
CENGAGE Learning®

LIBRARY OF CONGRESS CATALOGING-IN-PUBLICATION DATA

Moyes, Jojo, 1969-
  Silver Bay / by Jojo Moyes. — Large print edition.
    pages cm. — (Thorndike Press large print core)
  ISBN 978-1-4104-8215-0 (hardcover) — ISBN 1-4104-8215-4 (hardcover)
  1. Hotels—Conservation and restoration—Australia—Fiction. 2. Whales—Conservation—Australia—Fiction. 3. Large type books. 4. Domestic fiction. I. Title.
PR6113.O94S57 2015
823'.92—dc23   2015026362

Published in 2015 by arrangement with Penguin Books, an imprint of Penguin Publishing Group, a division of Penguin Random House LLC

Printed in the United States of America
1 2 3 4 5 6 7 19 18 17 16 15

FOR LOCKIE, FOR EVERYTHING HE IS,
AND EVERYTHING HE WILL BE

ACKNOWLEDGMENTS

Thank you, in no particular order, to Meghan Richardson, Matt Dempsey and Mike the Skipper of the *Moonshadow V,* the Nelson Bay whale-watching community and to all the crew members who gave up their time during August 2005 to talk to me about whale behavior and life out on the waves. Thanks also to the New South Wales police for explaining to me which particular seaborne offenses they were likely "to get picky" about.

Thank you to Hachette Livre (formerly Hodder) Australia and New Zealand, whose efforts helped prompt this book in the first place: particularly Raewyn Davies, Debs McInnes of Debbie McInnes PR, Malcolm Edwards, Mary Drum, Louise Sherwin-Stark, Kevin Chapman and Sue Murray, as well as Mark Kanas of Altour, none of whom were fazed by having to transport a particularly chaotic family of five through the Antipodes on a tight schedule.

Thank you, as ever, to Carolyn Mays, my editor, who managed not to sound panicked when I decided to ditch the book she had been expecting in favor of this one, and to Sheila Crowley, my agent, for her usual enthusiasm and selling abilities. Thanks to Emma Knight, Lucy Hale, Auriol Bishop, Hazel Orme, Amanda O'Connell and the whole team at Hodder UK for their continued hard work and support, and to Linda Shaughnessy, Rob Kraitt and everyone at AP Watt for the same.

Closer to home, thanks to Clare Wilde, Dolly Denny, Barbara Ralph and Jenny Colgan for their practical help and friendship in a difficult year. I hope you know how much it was appreciated.

Thank you also to: Lizzie and Brian Sanders, Jim and Alison Moyes, Betty McKee, Cathy Runciman, Lucy Ward, Jackie Tearne, Monica Hayward, Jenny Smith, and everyone at Writersblock.

Most of all thanks to Charles, Saskia and Harry, the motors for my spluttering engine. And to Lockie, for showing us that perfection is a relative term.

Jojo Moyes
July 2006

PROLOGUE:
KATHLEEN

My name is Kathleen Whittier Mostyn, and when I was seventeen I became famous for catching the biggest shark New South Wales had ever seen: a gray nurse with an eye so mean it still looked like it wanted to rip me in two several days after we'd laid it out. That was back in the days when all of Silver Bay was given over to game fishing, and for three straight weeks all anyone could talk about was that shark. A newspaper reporter came all the way from Newcastle and took a picture of me standing next to it (I'm the one in the bathing suit). It's several feet taller than I am, in that picture, and the photographer made me wear my heels.

What you can see is a tall, rather stern-seeming girl, better-looking than she knew, shoulders broad enough to be the despair of her mother, and a waist trim enough from reeling and bending that she never needed a corset. There I am, unable to hide my pride, not yet aware that I would be tied to that beast for the rest of my days as surely as if we had been married. What you can't see is that he is held up by two wires, supported by my father and his business partner Mr. Brent Newhaven — hauling it ashore had ripped several tendons in my right shoulder and by the time the photographer arrived I couldn't lift a mug of tea, let alone a shark.

Still, it was enough to cement my reputation. For years I was known as the Shark Girl, even when my girlhood was well over. My sister Norah always joked that, given the state of my appearance, they should have called me the Sea Urchin. But my success, my father always said, made the Bay Hotel. Two days after that picture appeared in the newspaper we were booked solid, and stayed booked solid until the west wing of the hotel burned down in 1962. Men came because they wanted to beat my record. Or because they assumed that if a *girl* could land a creature like that, why, what was possible for a *proper* fisherman? A few came to ask me to marry them, but my father always said he could smell them before they'd hit Port Stephens and sent them packing. Women came because until then they had never thought it possible that they could catch game fish, let alone compete with the men. And families came because Silver Bay, with its protected bay, endless dunes and calm waters, was a fine place to be.

Two more jetties were hurriedly constructed to cope with the extra boat traffic, and every day the air was filled with the sound of clipped oars and outboard motors as the bay and the sea around it was virtually dredged of aquatic life. The night air was filled with the revving of car engines, soft bursts of music and glasses clinking. There was a time, during the 1950s, when it is not too fanciful to say that we were *the* place to be.

Now we still have our boats, and our jetties, although we only use one now, and what people are chasing is pretty different. I haven't picked up a rod in almost twenty years. I don't much care for killing things anymore. We're pretty quiet, even in the summer. Most of the holiday traffic heads to the clubs and high-rise hotels, the more obvious delights of Coffs Harbour or Byron Bay and, to tell the truth, that suits most of us just fine.

I still hold that record. It's noted in one of those doorstop-sized books that sell in huge numbers, and no one you know ever buys. The editors do me the honor of ringing me now and then to let me know my name will be included for another year. Occasionally the local schoolchildren stop by to tell me they've found me in the library, and I always act surprised, just to keep them happy.

But I still hold that record. I tell you that not out of any desire to boast, or because I'm a seventy-six-year-old woman and it's nice to feel I once did something of note, but because when you're surrounded by as many secrets as I am, it feels good to get things straight out in the open occasionally.

One:
Hannah

If you stuck your hand in right up to the wrist, you could usually uncover at least three different kinds of biscuit in *Moby One*'s jar. Yoshi said that the crews on the other boats always skimped on biscuits, buying the cheapest arrowroot in value packs at the supermarket. But she reckoned that if you'd paid nearly a hundred and fifty dollars to go out chasing dolphins, the least you could expect was a decent biscuit. So she bought all-butter Anzacs — thick, oaty, double-layered with chocolate — Scotch Fingers, Mint Slices wrapped in foil and very occasionally, if she could get away with it, home-baked cookies. Lance, the skipper, said she got decent biscuits because they were pretty well all she had to eat. He also said that if their boss ever caught her spending that much on biscuits he'd squash her like a Garibaldi. I stared at the biscuits, as *Moby One* headed out into Silver Bay, holding up the tray as Yoshi offered the passengers tea and coffee. I was hoping they wouldn't eat all the Anzacs before I had a chance to take one. I'd snuck out without breakfast, and I knew it was only when we headed into the cockpit that she'd let me dip in.

"*Moby One* to *Suzanne,* how many beers did you sink last night? You're steering a course like a one-legged drunk."

Lance was on the radio. As we went in, I dropped my hand straight into the biscuit jar and pulled out the last Anzac. The ship-to-ship radio crackled, and a voice muttered something I couldn't make out. He tried again: "*Moby One* to *Sweet Suzanne.* Look, you'd better straighten up, mate . . . you've got four passengers up front hanging over the rails. Every time you swerve they're decorating your starboard windows."

Lance MacGregor's voice sounded like it had been rubbed down with wire wool, like the boat's sides. He took one hand off the wheel and Yoshi gave him a mug of coffee. I tucked myself in behind her. The spray on the back of her navy blue uniform sparkled like sequins.

"You seen Greg?" Lance asked.

She nodded. "I got a good look before we set off."

"He's so done in he can't steer straight." He pointed out of the droplet-flecked window toward the smaller boat. "I tell you, Yoshi, his passengers will be asking for refunds. The one in the green hat hasn't lifted his head since we passed Break Nose Island. What the hell's got into him?"

Yoshi Takomura had the prettiest hair I'd ever seen. It hung in black clouds around her face, never tangling despite the effects of wind and saltwater. I took one of my own mousy locks between my fingers; it felt gritty, although we had been on the water only half an hour. My friend Lara said that when she hit fourteen, in four years' time, her mum was going to let her put streaks in hers. It was then that Lance had caught sight of me. I guess I'd known he would.

"What are you doing here, Squirt? Your mum'll have my guts for garters. Don't you have school or something?"

"Holidays." I stepped back behind Yoshi, a little embarrassed. Lance always talked to me like I was five years younger than I was.

"She'll stay out of sight," Yoshi said. "She just wanted to see the dolphins."

I stared at him, pulling my sleeves down over my hands.

He stared back, then shrugged. "You gonna wear a life jacket?"

15

I nodded.

"And not get under my feet?"

I tilted my head. As if, my eyes said.

"Be nice to her," said Yoshi. "She's been ill twice already."

"It's nerves," I said. "My tummy always does it."

"Ah . . . Hell. Look, just make sure your mum knows it was nothing to do with me, okay? And listen, Squirt, head for *Moby Two* next time — or, even better, someone else's boat."

"You never saw her," said Yoshi. "Anyway, Greg's steering's not the half of it." She grinned. "Wait till he turns and you see what he's done to the side of his prow."

It was, Yoshi said, as we headed back out, a good day to be on the water. The sea was a little choppy, but the winds were mild, and the air so clear that you could see the white horses riding the little breakers miles into the distance. I followed her to the main restaurant deck, my legs easily absorbing the rise and fall of the catamaran beneath me, a little less self-conscious now that the skipper knew I was onboard.

This, she had told me, would be the busiest part of today's dolphin-watching trip, the time between setting off and our arrival at the sheltered waters around the bay where the pods of bottlenoses tended to gather. While the passengers sat up on the top deck, enjoying the crisp May day through woolen mufflers, Yoshi, the steward, was laying out the buffet, offering drinks and, if the water was choppy, which it was most days now that winter was coming, preparing the disinfectant and bucket for seasickness. It didn't matter how many times you told them, she grumbled, glancing at the well-dressed Asians who made up most of the morning's custom, they *would* stay belowdecks, they *would* eat and drink too quickly and they *would* go into the tiny lavatories to be sick, rather than hanging over the edge, thereby making them unusable by anyone else. And if they were Japanese, she added, with a hint of malicious pleasure, they would spend the rest of the voyage in a silent frenzy of humiliation, hiding behind dark glasses and raised collars, their ashen faces turned resolutely to sea.

"Tea? Coffee? Biscuits? Tea? Coffee? Biscuits?"

I followed her out on to the foredeck, pulling my windbreaker up around my neck. The wind had dropped a little but I could still feel the chill in the air, biting at my nose and the tips of my ears. Most of the passengers didn't want anything — they were chatting loudly, to be heard above the engines, gazing out at the distant horizon, and taking pictures of each other. Now and then I dipped my hand into the biscuits until I'd taken what I thought they would have eaten anyway.

Moby One was the biggest catamaran — or "cat," as the crews called them — in Silver Bay. It was usually a two-steward vessel, but the tourists were tailing off as the temperature dropped, so it was just Yoshi now until trade picked up again. I didn't mind — it was easier to persuade her to let me aboard. I helped her put the tea and coffeepots back in their holders, then stepped back out onto the narrow side deck, where we braced ourselves against the windows, and gazed across the sea to where the smaller boat was still making its uneven path across the waves. Even from this distance we could see that more people now were hanging over *Suzanne*'s rails, their heads lower than their shoulders, oblivious of the spattered red paint just below them. "We can take ten minutes now. Here." Yoshi cracked open a can of cola and handed it to me. "You ever heard of chaos theory?"

"Mmm." I made it sound like I might.

"If only those people knew," she wagged a

finger as we felt the engines slow, "that their long-awaited trip to go see the wild dolphins has been ruined by an ex-girlfriend they will never meet and a man who now lives with her more than two hundred and fifty kilometers away in Sydney and thinks that purple cycling shorts are acceptable daywear."

I took a gulp of my drink. The fizz made my eyes water and I swallowed hard. "You're saying the tourists being sick on Greg's boat is down to chaos theory?" I'd thought it was because he'd got drunk again the night before.

Yoshi smiled. "Something like that."

The engines had stopped, and *Moby One* quieted, the sea growing silent around us, except for the tourist chatter and the waves slapping against the sides. I loved it out here, loved watching my house become a white dot against the narrow strip of beach, then disappear behind the endless coves. Perhaps my pleasure was made greater by the knowledge that what I was doing was against the rules. I wasn't rebellious, not really, but I kind of liked the idea of it.

Lara had a dinghy that she was allowed to take out by herself, staying within the buoys that marked out the old oyster beds, and I envied her. My mother wouldn't let me roam around the bay, even though I was nearly eleven. "All in good time," she would murmur. There was no point arguing with her about stuff like that.

Lance appeared beside us: he'd just had his photograph taken with two giggling teenagers. He was often asked to pose with young women, and hadn't yet been known to refuse. It was why he liked to wear his captain's peaked cap, Yoshi said, even when the sun was hot enough to melt his head.

"What's he written on the side of his boat?" He squinted at Greg's cruiser in the distance. He seemed to have forgiven me for being onboard.

"I'll tell you back at the jetty."

I caught the eyebrow cocked toward me. "I *can* read what it says, you know," I said. The other boat, which had until yesterday described itself as the *Sweet Suzanne,* now suggested, in red paint, that "Suzanne" do something Yoshi said was a biological impossibility. She turned to him, lowering her voice as far as possible — as if she thought I couldn't hear her. "The missus told him there was another man after all."

Lance let out a long whistle. "He said as much. And she denied it."

"She was hardly going to admit it, not when she knew how Greg was going to react. And he was hardly an innocent . . ."

She glanced at me. "Anyway, she's off to live in Sydney, and she said she wants half the boat."

"And he says?"

"I think the boat probably says it all."

"Can't believe he'd take tourists out with it like that." Lance lifted his binoculars better to study the scrawled red lettering.

Yoshi gestured at him to pass them to her. "He was so ill this morning I'm not sure he's even remembered what he's done."

We were interrupted by the excited yells of the tourists on the upper deck. They were jostling toward the pulpit at the front.

"Here we go," muttered Lance, straightening up and grinning at me. "There's our pocket money, Squirt. Time to get back to work."

Sometimes, Yoshi said, they could run the whole bay but the bottlenoses would refuse to show, and a boat full of unsatisfied dolphin-watchers was a boat full of free second trips and fifty-percent refunds, both guaranteed to send the boss into meltdown.

At the bow, a group of tourists were pressed together, cameras whirring as they tried to catch the glossy gray shapes that were now riding the breaking waves below. I checked the water to see who had come to play. Belowdecks, Yoshi had covered a wall with photographs of the fins of every dolphin in the area. She had given them all names: Zigzag, One Cut, Piper . . . The other crews had laughed at her, but now they could all recognize the distinctive fins — it was the second time they'd seen Butterknife that week, they'd murmur. I knew the name of every one by heart.

"Looks like Polo and Brolly," Yoshi said, leaning over the side.

"Is that Brolly's baby?"

The dolphins were silent gray arcs, circling the boat as if they were the sightseers. Every time one broke the surface the air was filled with the sound of clacking camera shutters. What did they think of us gawping at them? I knew they were as smart as humans. I used to imagine them meeting up by the rocks afterward, laughing in dolphin language about us — the one in the blue hat, or the one with the funny glasses.

Lance's voice came over the PA system: "Ladies and gentlemen, please do not rush to one side to see the dolphins. We will slowly turn the ship so that everyone can get a good view. If you rush to one side we are likely to capsize. Dolphins do not like boats that fall over."

Glancing up, I noticed two albatross; pausing in midair, they folded their wings and dived, sending up only the faintest splash as they hit the water. One rose again, wheeling in search of some unseen prey, then the other rejoined it, soaring above the little bay and disappeared. I watched them go. Then, as *Moby One* slowly shifted position, I leaned over the side, sticking my feet under the bottom rail to see my new trainers. Yoshi had promised she'd let me sit in the boom nets when the weather got warmer, so that I could touch the dolphins, perhaps even swim with them. But only if my mother agreed. And we all knew what that meant.

I stumbled as the boat moved unexpectedly. It took me a second to register that the engines had started up. Startled, I grabbed the handrail. I had grown up in Silver Bay and knew there was a way of doing things around dolphins. Shut down engines if you want them to play. If they keep moving, hold a parallel course, be guided by them. Dolphins made things pretty clear: if they liked you they came close, or kept an even distance. If they didn't want you around they swam away. Yoshi frowned at me, and as the catamaran lurched, we grabbed the lifelines. My confusion was mirrored in her face.

A sudden acceleration sent the boat shooting forward, and, above, squealing tourists collapsed onto their seats. We were flying.

Lance was on the radio. As we clambered into the cockpit behind him, *Sweet Suzanne* was scudding along some distance away, bouncing over the waves, apparently heedless of the increasing numbers of miserable people now hanging over her rails.

"Lance! What are you doing?" Yoshi grabbed at a rail.

"See you there, bud . . . Ladies and gentlemen —" Lance pulled a face and reached for the PA system button. *I need a translation,* he mouthed. "We have something a bit special for you this morning. You've already enjoyed the magical sight of our Silver Bay dolphins, but if you hold on tight, we'd like to take you to something *really* special. We've had a sighting of the first whales of the season, a little further out to sea. These are the humpbacked whales who come past our waters every year on their long migration north from the Antarctic. I can promise you that this is a sight you won't forget. Now, please sit down, or hold on tight. Things may get a little choppy as, from the south, there's a little more size in the swell, but I want to make sure we get you there in time to see them. Anyone who wants to stay at the front of the boat, I suggest you bor-

24

row a raincoat. There are plenty inside at the back."

He spun the wheel and nodded to Yoshi, who took the PA system. She repeated what he had said in Japanese, then in Korean for good measure. It was entirely possible, she said afterward, that she had simply recited the previous day's lunch menu: she had been unable to focus since Lance had made his announcement. One word sang through, as it did in my own mind: *whale!*

"How far?" Yoshi's body was rigid as she scanned the glinting waters. The earlier relaxed atmosphere had disappeared completely. My stomach was in knots.

"Four, five miles? Dunno. The tourist helicopter was flying over and said they'd seen what looked like two a couple of miles off Torn Point. It's a little early in the season, but . . ."

"Fourteenth of June last year. We're not that far out," said Yoshi. "Bloody hell! Look at Greg! He's going to lose passengers if he carries on at that pace. His boat's not big enough to soak up those waves."

"He doesn't want us to get there before him." Lance shook his head and checked the speed dial. "Full throttle. Let's make sure *Moby One*'s first this year. Just for once."

Some crew members were doing the job to make up their shipping hours, on course for bigger vessels and bigger jobs. Some, like Yoshi, had begun as part of their education and had simply forgotten to go home. But, whatever reason they might have for being there, I had grasped long ago that there was magic in the first whale sighting of the migration season. It was as if, until that creature had been seen, it was impossible to believe they would be back.

To be the first to see one didn't mean much — once the whales were known to be out there, all five boats that operated off Whale Jetty would switch their business from dolphins to whale-watching. But it was of importance to the crew. And, like all great passions, it made them mad. Boy, did it make them mad.

"Look at that great idiot. Funny how he can hold a straight course now," Lance spat. Greg was portside of us, but seemed to be gaining.

"He can't bear the thought of us getting there before him." Yoshi grabbed a raincoat and threw it at me. "There! Just in case we go out front. It's going to get pretty wet."

"I don't bloody believe it." Lance had spied another boat on the horizon. He must have forgotten I was there, to be swearing.

26

"There's Mitchell! I bet you he's been sitting on the radio all afternoon and now he swans up, probably with a cabinful of passengers. I'm going to swing for that bloke one of these days."

They were always moaning about Mitchell Dray. He never bothered to look for the dolphins, like the others: he would just wait until he overheard a sighting on the ship-to-ship radio and go where everyone else was headed.

"Am I really going to see a whale?" I asked. Beneath our feet, the hull smacked noisily against the waves, forcing me to hang on to the side. Through the open window, I could hear the excited shouts of the tourists, the laughter of those who had been hit by rogue waves.

"Fingers crossed." Yoshi's eyes were trained on the horizon.

A real whale. I had only once seen a whale, with my aunt Kathleen. Usually I wasn't allowed this far out to sea.

"There . . . There! No, it's just spray." Yoshi had lifted the binoculars. "Can't you change course? There's too much glare."

"Not if you want me to get there first." Lance swung the boat to starboard, trying to alter the angle of the sun on the waves.

"We should radio ashore. Find out exactly

where the chopper saw it."

"No point," said Lance. "It could have traveled two miles by now. And Mitchell will be listening in. I'm not giving that bugger any more information. He's been stealing passengers from us all summer."

"Just watch for the blow."

"Yeah. And the little flag that says, 'Whale.' "

"Just trying to help, Lance."

"There!" I could just make out the shape, like a distant black pebble dipping below the water. "North-northeast. Heading behind Break Nose Island. Just dived." I thought I might be sick with excitement. I heard Lance start counting behind me. "One . . . two . . . three . . . four . . . *whale*!" An unmistakable plume of water rose joyously above the horizon. Yoshi let out a squeal. Lance glanced toward Greg, who, from his course, hadn't seen it. "We got her!" Lance hissed. All whales were "her" to Lance, just as all kids were "squirt."

Whale. I took the word into my mouth, rolled it around and savored it. My eyes did not leave the water. *Moby One* shifted course, the huge catamaran slapping hard as it bounded over each wave. Behind the island I imagined the whale breaching, displaying its white belly to the world in an unseen display of buoyancy. "Whale," I whispered.

"We're going to be first," muttered Yoshi, excitedly. "Just for once we're going to get there first."

I watched Lance swing the wheel, counting under his breath to mark the number of times the whale blew. More than thirty seconds apart and it was likely to dive deep. Then we would have lost it. Closer together meant it had already dived, and we would have a chance to follow.

"Seven . . . eight . . . She's up. *Yessss.*" Lance hit the wheel with his palm, then grabbed the PA system. "Ladies and gentlemen, if you look over to your right, you might make out the whale, which is headed behind that piece of land there."

"Greg's realized where we're headed." Yoshi grinned. "He'll never catch us now. His engine isn't powerful enough."

"*Moby One* to *Blue Horizon.* Mitchell," Lance yelled into his radio, "you want to see this baby you're going to have to get off my coattails."

Mitchell's voice came over the radio: "*Blue Horizon* to *Moby One.* I'm just here to make sure there's someone to pick up Greg's overboards."

"Oh, nothing to do with the big fish?"

Lance responded tersely.

"*Blue Horizon* to *Moby One*. Big old sea, Lance. Plenty of room for everyone."

I gripped the wooden rim of the chart table so tightly that my knuckles turned white as I watched the scrubby headland grow. I wondered whether the whale would slow there, allow us to come closer. Perhaps it would lift its head and eye us. Perhaps it would swim up to the side of the boat and reveal its calf.

"Two minutes," said Lance. "We'll be around the head in about two minutes. Hopefully get up close."

"Come on, girlie. Give us a good show." Yoshi was talking to herself, binoculars still raised.

Whale, I told it silently, *wait for us, whale.* I wondered whether it would notice me. Whether it could sense that I, of all the people on the boat, had a special empathy with sea creatures. I was pretty sure I did.

"I don't — bloody — believe — it." Lance had taken off his peaked cap, and was scowling out of the window.

"What?" Yoshi leaned toward him.

"Look."

I followed their gaze. As *Moby One* came around the headland, all of us fell silent. A short distance from the scrub-covered landmass, half a mile out to sea in aquamarine waters, the stationary *Ishmael* sat, its newly painted sides glinting under the midday sun.

At the helm stood my mother, leaning over the rail, her hair whipping around her face under the bleached cap she insisted on wearing out to sea. She had her weight on one leg and Milly, our dog, lay apparently asleep across the wheel. She looked as if she had been there, waiting for this whale, for years.

"How the bloody hell did she do that?" Lance caught Yoshi's warning glare and shrugged an apology at me. "Nothing personal, but — Jeez . . ."

"She's always there first." Yoshi's response was half amused, half resigned. "Every year I've been here. She's always first."

"Beaten by a bloody Brit. It's as bad as the cricket." Lance lit a cigarette, then tossed away the match in disgust.

I stepped out onto the deck.

At that moment the whale emerged. As we gasped, it lobtailed, sending a huge spray of water toward *Ishmael.* The tourists on *Moby One*'s top deck cheered. It was enormous, close enough that we could see the barnacled growths along its body, the corrugated white belly; near enough that I

31

could look briefly into its eye. But ridiculously swift — something of that bulk had no right to be so agile.

My breath had stalled in my throat. One hand clutching the lifelines, I lifted the binoculars with the other and gazed through them, not at the whale but at my mother, hardly hearing the exclamations about the creature's size, the swell it sent before the smaller boat, forgetting briefly that I should not allow myself to be seen. Even from that distance I could make out that Liza McCullen was smiling, her eyes creased upward. It was an expression she rarely, if ever, wore on dry land.

Aunt Kathleen walked to the end of the veranda to put a large bowl of prawns and some lemon slices on the bleached wooden table with a large basket of bread. She's actually my great-aunt but she says that makes her feel like an antique, so most of the time I call her Auntie K. Behind her the white weatherboard of the hotel's frontage glowed softly in the evening sun, eight fiery red peaches sliding down the windows. The wind had picked up a little, and the hotel sign whined as it swung back and forth.

"What's this for?" Greg lifted his head from the bottle of beer he'd been nursing.

He had finally taken off his dark glasses, and the shadows under his eyes betrayed the events of the previous evening.

"I heard you needed your stomach lined," she said, thwacking a napkin in front of him.

"He tell you four of his passengers asked for their money back when they caught sight of his hull?" Lance laughed. "Sorry, Greg mate, but what a damn fool thing to do. Of all the things to write."

"You're a gent, Kathleen." Greg, ignoring him, reached for the bread.

My aunt gave him one of her looks. "And I'll be something else entirely if you write those words where young Hannah can see them again."

"Shark Lady's still got teeth." Lance mimed a snapping motion at Greg.

Aunt Kathleen ignored him. "Hannah, you dig in now. I'll bet you never had a bite to eat for lunch. I'm going to fetch the salad."

"She ate the biscuits," said Yoshi, expertly undressing a prawn.

"Biscuits." Aunt Kathleen snorted.

We were gathered, as the Whale Jetty crews were most evenings, outside the hotel kitchens. There were few days when the crews wouldn't share a beer or two before they headed home. Some of the younger members, my aunt often said, shared so many that they barely made it home at all.

As I bit into a juicy tiger prawn, I noticed that the burners were outside; few guests at the Silver Bay Hotel wanted to sit out in June, but in winter the whale-watching crews congregated here to discuss events on the water, no matter the weather. Their members changed from year to year, as people moved on to different jobs or went to uni, but Lance, Greg, Yoshi and the others had been a constant in my life for as long as I had lived there. Aunt Kathleen usually lit the burners at the start of the month and they stayed on most evenings until September.

"Did you have many out?" She had returned with the salad. She tossed it with brisk, expert fingers, then put some onto my plate before I could protest. "I've had no one at the museum."

"*Moby One* was pretty full. Lot of Koreans." Yoshi shrugged. "Greg nearly lost half of his over the side."

"They got a good sight of the whale." Greg reached for another piece of bread. "No complaints. No refunds necessary. Got anymore beers, Miss M?"

"You know where the bar is. You see it, Hannah?"

"It was enormous. I could see its barnacles." For some reason I'd expected it to be smooth, but the skin had been lined, ridged, studded with fellow sea creatures, as if it were a living island.

"It was close. I've told her we wouldn't normally get that close," said Yoshi.

Greg narrowed his eyes. "If she'd been out on her mother's boat she could have brushed its teeth."

"Yes, well, the least said about that . . ." Aunt Kathleen shook her head. "Not a word," she mouthed at me. "That was a one-off."

I nodded dutifully. It was the third one-off that month.

"That Mitchell turn up? You want to watch him. I've heard he's joining those Sydney-siders with the big boats."

They all looked up.

"Thought the National Parks and Wildlife Service had frightened them off," said Lance.

"When I went to the fish market," Aunt Kathleen said, "they told me they'd seen one all the way out by the heads. Music at top volume, people dancing on the decks. Like a discothèque. Ruined the night's fishing. But by the time the Parks and Wildlife people got out there they were long gone.

Impossible to prove a thing."

The balance in Silver Bay was delicate: too few whale-watching tourists and the business would be unsustainable; too many, and it would disturb the creatures it wanted to display.

Lance and Greg had come up against the triple-decker catamarans from around the bay, often blaring loud music, decks heaving with passengers, and were of similar opinion. "They'll be the death of us all, that lot," Lance said. "Irresponsible. Money-mad. Should suit Mitchell down to the ground."

I hadn't realized how hungry I was. I ate six of the huge prawns in quick succession, chasing Greg's fingers around the empty bowl. He grinned and waved a prawn head at me. I stuck out my tongue at him. I think I'm a little bit in love with Greg, not that I'd ever tell anybody.

"Aye aye, here she is. Princess of Whales."

"Very funny." My mother dumped her keys on the table and gestured to Yoshi to move down so that she could squeeze in next to me. She dropped a kiss onto my head. "Good day, lovey?" She smelt of sun-cream and salt air.

I shot a look at my aunt. "Fine." I bent to fondle Milly's ears, grateful that my mother could not see the pinking in my face. My head still sang with the sight of that whale. I thought it must radiate out of me, but she was reaching for a glass and pouring herself some water.

"What have you been doing?" my mother asked.

"Yeah. What have you been doing, Hannah?" Greg winked at me.

"She helped me with the beds this morning." Aunt Kathleen glared at him. "Heard *you* had a good afternoon."

"Not bad." My mother downed the water. "God, I'm thirsty. Did you drink enough today, Hannah? Did she drink enough, Kathleen?" Her English accent was still pronounced, even after so many years in Australia.

"She's had plenty. How many did you see?"

"She never drinks enough. Just the one. Big girl. Lobtailed half a bath of water into my bag. Look." She held up her checkbook, its edges frilled and warped.

"Well, there's an amateur's mistake." Aunt Kathleen sighed in disgust. "Didn't you have anyone out with you?"

My mother shook her head. "I wanted to try out that new rudder, see how well it worked in choppier waters. The boatyard warned me it might stick."

"And you just happened on a whale," said Lance.

She took another swig of water. "Something like that." Her face had closed. *She* had closed. It was as if the whale thing had never happened.

For a few minutes we ate in silence, as the sun sank slowly toward the horizon. Two fishermen walked past, and raised their arms in greeting. I recognized one as Lara's dad, but I'm not sure he saw me.

My mother ate a piece of bread and a tiny plateful of salad, less even than I eat and I don't like salad. Then she glanced up at Greg. "I heard about *Suzanne*."

"Half of Port Stephens has heard about *Suzanne*." Greg's eyes were tired and he looked as if he hadn't shaved for a week.

"Yes. Well. I'm sorry."

"Sorry enough to come out with me Friday?"

"Nope." She stood up, checked her watch, stuffed her sodden checkbook back into her bag and made for the kitchen door. "That rudder's still not right. I've got to ring the yard before they head off. Don't stay out without your sweater, Hannah. The wind's getting up."

I watched as she strode away, pursued by

the dog.

We were silent until we heard the slam of the screen door. Then Lance leaned back in his chair to gaze out at the darkening bay, where a cruiser was just visible on the far horizon. "Our first whale of the season, Greg's first refusal of the season. Got a nice kind of symmetry to it, don't you think?"

He ducked as a piece of bread bounced off the chair behind him.

Two:
Kathleen

The Whalechasers Museum had been housed in the old processing plant, a few hundred yards from the Silver Bay Hotel, since commercial whaling was abandoned off Port Stephens in the early 1960s. It didn't have much to recommend it as a modern tourist attraction: the building was a great barn of a place, the floor a suspiciously darkened red-brown, wooden walls still leaching the salt that had been used on the catch. There was an outhouse at the back, and a fresh jug of lemon squash made up daily for the thirsty. Food, a sign observed, was available in the hotel. I'd say that the "facilities," as they're now known, are probably twice what they were when my father was alive.

Our centerpiece was a section of the hull of *Maui II,* a commercial whalechaser, a hunting vessel that had broken clean in two in 1935 when a minke had taken exception to it, and had risen beneath the boat, lifting it on its tail until it flipped and snapped. Mercifully a fishing trawler had been nearby and had saved the hands and verified their story. For years local people had come to see the evidence of what nature could wreak on man when it felt man had harvested enough.

I had kept the museum open since my father died in 1970, and had always allowed visitors to climb over the remains of the hull, to run their fingers over the splintered wood, their faces coming alive as they imagined what it must have been like to ride on the back of a whale. Long ago I had posed for pictures, when the sharp-eyed recognized me as the Shark Girl of the framed newspaper reports, and talked them through the stuffed game fish that adorned the glass cases on the walls.

But there weren't too many people interested now. The tourists who came to stay at the hotel might pass a polite fifteen minutes walking around the museum's dusty interior, spend a few cents on some whale postcards, perhaps sign a petition against the resumption of commercial whaling. But it was usually because they were waiting for a taxi, or because the wind was up and it was raining and there was nothing doing out on the water.

That day, behind the counter, I thought perhaps I couldn't blame them. *Maui II* was more and more like a heap of driftwood, while there were only so many times people could handle a whalebone or a bit of baleen — the strange plasticky filter from a humpback's mouth — before the delights of minigolf or the gaming machines at the surf club became more inviting. For years people had been telling me to modernize, but I hadn't paid much heed. What was the point? Half the people who walked around the museum looked a little uncomfortable to be celebrating something that is now illegal. Sometimes even I didn't know why I stayed open, other than that whaling was part of Silver Bay's history, and history is what it is, no matter how unpalatable.

I adjusted *Maui II*'s old harpoon, known for reasons I can't recall as Old Harry, on its hooks on the wall. Then, from below it, I took a rod, ran my duster up its length and wound the reel, to confirm that it still worked. Not that it mattered anymore, but I liked to know things were shipshape. I hesitated. Then, perhaps seduced by the familiar feel of it in my hand, I tilted it backward, as if I were about to cast a line.

"Won't catch much in here."

I spun around, lifting a hand to my chest. "Nino Gaines! You nearly made me drop my rod."

"Fat chance." He removed his hat and walked from the doorway into the middle of the floor. "Never saw you drop a catch yet." He smiled, revealing a row of crooked teeth. "I got a couple of cases of wine in the truck. Thought you might like to crack open a bottle with me over some lunch. I'd value your opinion."

"My order's not due till next week, if I remember rightly." I replaced the rod on the wall and wiped my hands on the front of my moleskin trousers. I'm old enough to be beyond such considerations, but it bugged me that he'd caught me in my work trousers with my hair all over the place.

"As I said, it's a good batch. I'd appreciate your opinion." He smiled. The lines on his face told of years spent in his vineyards, and a touch of pink around his nose hinted at the evenings afterward.

"I've got to get a room ready for a guest coming tomorrow."

"How long's it going to take you to tuck in a sheet, woman?"

"Not too many visitors this deep in winter. I don't like to look a gift horse . . ." I saw the disappointment in his face and relented.

43

"I should be able to spare a few minutes, long as you don't expect too much in the way of food to go with it. I'm waiting on my grocery delivery. That darned boy's late every week."

"Thought of that." He lifted up a paper bag. "Got a couple of pies, and a couple of tamarillos for after. I know what you career girls are like. It's all work, work, work . . . Someone's got to keep your strength up."

I couldn't help laughing. Nino Gaines had always got me like that, as long ago as the war, when he'd first come and announced his intention to set up here. Then the whole of the bay had been taken over by Australian and American servicemen, and my father had had to make pointed references to his accuracy with a shotgun when the young men whooped and catcalled at me behind the bar. Nino had been more gentlemanly: he had always removed his cap while he waited to be served, and he had never failed to call my mother "ma'am." "Still don't trust him," my father had muttered, and, on balance, I thought he had probably been right.

Out at sea it was bright and calm, a good day for the whale crews, and as we sat down, I watched *Moby One* and *Two* heading out for the mouth of the bay. My eyes weren't as good as they had been, but from here it looked like they had a good number of passengers. Liza had headed out earlier; she was taking a group of pensioners from the Returned and Services League (RSL) club for nothing, as she did every month, even though I told her she was a fool.

"You shutting this place up for the winter?"

I shook my head, and took a bite of my pie.

"Nope. The *Moby*s are going to try out a deal with me — bed, board and a whaling trip for a fixed sum, plus admission to the museum. A bit like I do with Liza. They've printed some leaflets, and they're going to put something on a New South Wales tourism website. They say it's big business that way."

I'd thought he would mutter something about technology being beyond him, but he said, "Good idea. I sell maybe forty cases a month online now."

"You're on the Internet?" I gazed at him over the top of my glasses.

He lifted a glass, unable to hide his satisfaction at having surprised me. "Plenty you don't know about me, Miss Kathleen Whittier Mostyn, no matter what you might think. I've been out there in cyberspace for a good eighteen months now. Frank set it up for me. Tell you the truth, I quite like having a little surf around. I've bought all sorts." He gestured at my glass — he wanted me to taste the wine. "Bloody useful for seeing what the big growers in the Hunter Valley are offering too."

I tried to concentrate on my wine, unable to admit quite how thrown I was by Nino Gaines's apparent ease with technology. I felt wrong-footed, as I often did when talking to young people, as if some vital new knowledge had been dished out when I'd had my back turned. I sniffed the glass, then sipped, letting the flavor flood my mouth. It was a little green, but none the worse for that. "This is very nice, Nino. A hint of raspberry in there." At least I still understand wine.

He nodded, pleased. "Thought you'd pick up on that. And you know you get a mention?"

"A mention of what?"

"The Shark Girl. Frank typed you into a search engine and there you are — picture and all. From newspaper archives."

"There's a picture of me on the Internet?"

"In your bathing suit. You always did look fetching in it. There's a couple of pieces of writing about you too. Some girl at university in Victoria used you in her thesis on the role of women and hunting, or somesuch. Quite an impressive piece of writing — full of symbolism, classical references and goodness knows what else. I asked Frank to print it out — must have forgotten to pick it up. I thought you could put it in the museum."

Now I felt very unbalanced indeed. I put my glass down on the table. "There's a picture of me in my bathing suit on the Internet?"

Nino Gaines laughed. "Calm down, Kate — it's hardly *Playboy* magazine. Come over tomorrow and I'll show you."

"I'm not sure if I like the idea of this. Me being out there for anyone to look at."

"It's the same photograph as you've got in there." He waved toward the museum. "You don't mind people gawping at that."

"But that's — that's different." Even as I said it, I knew the distinction made little sense. But the museum was my domain. I could dictate who entered it, who got to see what. The thought of people I didn't know being able to dip into my life, my history, as casually as if they were scanning the betting pages . . .

"You should put up a picture of Liza and her boat. You might get a few more visitors. Forget advertising the hotel with the *Moby*s

— a fine-looking girl like her could be quite a draw."

"Oh, you know Liza. She likes to pick who she takes out."

"No way to run a business. Why don't you focus on your own boat? Bed, board and a trip out on *Ishmael* with Liza. She'd get inquiries from all over the world."

"No." I began to tidy up. "I don't think so. Very kind of you, Nino, but it's really not for us."

"You never know, she might find herself a bloke. About time she was courting."

It was a couple of minutes before he realized that the atmosphere had changed. Halfway through his pie, he saw something in my expression that gave him pause. He was disconcerted, trying to work out what he'd said that had been so wrong. "Didn't mean to offend you, Kate."

"You haven't."

"Well, something's wrong. You're all twitchy."

"I have not gone all twitchy."

"There! Look at you." He pointed to my hand, which was playing restlessly up and down the bleached wood.

"Since when was tapping my fingers a crime?" I placed my hand firmly on my lap.

"What's the matter?"

"Nino Gaines, I have a room to make up. Now, if you'll excuse me, I've already wasted half the day."

"You're not going in? Aw, come on, Kate. You haven't finished your lunch. What's the matter? Is it what I said about your picture?"

No one except Nino Gaines calls me Kate. For some reason this intimacy just about finished me off. "I've got things to do. Will you stop going on?"

"I'll e-mail them, ask them to take it down. Perhaps we can say it's copyright."

"Oh, will you stop wittering on about that darned photograph? I'm going in. I really have to get that room finished. I'll see you soon." I brushed imaginary crumbs from my trousers. "Thank you for the lunch."

He watched as I — the woman he had loved and been perplexed by for more than half a century — stood up, less heavily than age should have allowed, and began to walk briskly toward the kitchen, leaving him with two half-eaten pies and a barely touched glass of his best vintage. I felt his eyes burn into my back all the way back to the house.

Just for once, I imagined, he might have felt a bubble of frustration at the unfairness, at the arbitrary manner in which, once again, he had apparently been judged. Because I heard him stand and his voice on

49

the soft wind. He was unable, just this once, to contain himself. "Kathleen Whittier Mostyn — you're the most contrary woman I ever met," he yelled after me.

"No one's asking you to come," I shot back. To my shame, I didn't even bother to turn my head.

A long time ago, back when my parents died and I was left in charge of the Silver Bay Hotel, plenty of people told me I should take the opportunity to modernize, install en-suite bathrooms and satellite television, as they had at Port Stephens and Byron Bay, that I should advertise more to spread the word about the beauty of our little stretch of coast. I paid them heed for all of two minutes — our lack of custom had long since ceased to worry me, as I suspect it had most of Silver Bay. We had watched our neighbors up and down the coast grow fat on their profits, but then have to live with the unexpected results of success: heavy traffic, drunken holidaymakers, an endless round of updating and installation. The loss of peace.

In Silver Bay I liked to think we had the balance about right — enough visitors to provide us with a living, not so many that anyone was likely to start getting ideas. For years now I had watched Silver Bay's population rise and double during the summer peak, drifting down in the winter months. The growth of interest in whale-watching had caused the odd peak now and then, but in general it was steady business, likely neither to make us rich nor cause too many upsets. It was just us, the dolphins and the whales. And that suited most of us fine.

Silver Bay had never been particularly hospitable to strangers. When the first Europeans arrived in the late eighteenth century, it was dismissed at first as uninhabitable, its rocky outcrops, its bushland and shifting dunes too barren to support human life. (I guess back then the Aboriginals weren't considered human enough.) The coastal shoals and sandbars put paid to too much interest, grounding and wrecking visiting ships until the first lighthouses were erected. Then, as ever, greed did what curiosity could not: the discovery of lucrative timber forests up and down our volcanic hills, and the vast beds of oysters below did for the bay's solitude.

The trees were logged until the hillsides were near-barren. The oysters were harvested for lime and, later, for eating, until that was banned before they, too, were depleted. If I'm honest, when my father first landed here he was no better: he saw the seas leaping with game fish — marlin and tuna, sharks and spearfish — and he saw profit in what nature had provided. An endless array of prizes on his doorstep. And so, on this last rocky outcrop of Silver Bay, our hotel was built with every last penny of his and Mr. Newhaven's savings.

Back then, my family lived in quarters completely separate from the rest of the Silver Bay Hotel. My mother didn't like to be seen by guests in what she called "domestic mode" — I think that meant without her hair done — while my father liked to know that there were limits on how much access my sister and I had to the world outside (not that that stopped Norah: she was off to England before she hit twenty-one). I always suspected they wanted to be sure that they could argue in private.

Since the west wing burned down we — or, for the most part, I — had lived in what remains as if it were a private house and our guests boarders. They slept in the rooms off the main corridor, while we had the rooms on the other side of the stairs, and anyone was welcome to use the lounge. Only the kitchen was sacred, a rule we made when the girls first came to live with me a few years ago. They were complete opposites. When Liza was not outside with the crews, she spent all her time in the kitchen. She disliked casual conversation, and avoided the lounge and the dining room. She liked to have a closed door between her and the unexpected. Hannah, with the conviviality of youth, spent most of her time draped across the sofa in the lounge, Milly at her feet, watching television, reading or, more often now, on the telephone to her friends — goodness knows what they found to talk about having already spent six hours together at school.

"Mum? Have you ever been to New Zealand?" As she entered the kitchen, I saw a deep indent running down the side of her cheek from the binding of the sofa cushion where her face must have been resting on it.

Liza reached out absently to try to smooth it away. "No, sweetheart."

"I have," I said. I was darning an old pair of socks, which Liza told me was a waste of my energy when the supermarket sold them for a few dollars a pack. But I'm not the kind of person who can sit and do nothing. "I went to Lake Taupo a few years ago on a fishing trip."

"I don't remember that," said Hannah.

I calculated. "Well . . . I suppose it was

about twenty years ago, so that would be fourteen years before you came."

Hannah looked at me with the blank incomprehension of a child who cannot imagine anything existing before they were born, let alone any period of time that long ago. I couldn't blame her — I can just about remember being that age, when an evening without one's friends seemed to stretch to the length of a prison sentence. Now whole years flash by.

"Have you been to Wellington?" She sat down at the table.

"Yup. Got a lot of houses built into the hills around the harbor. Last time I went I couldn't imagine how they stayed up there."

"Were they on stilts?"

"Something like that. Foolish, though — I heard the whole town was built on a fault line. I wouldn't want to be in a house on stilts when the earth moved."

For a moment Hannah digested this.

"Why do you ask, sweetheart?" Liza patted her legs for the dog to jump up. Milly never had to be asked twice.

Hannah twisted a strand of hair in her fingers. "There's a school trip. After Christmas. I was wondering if I could go." She looked from one of us to the other, as if she'd guessed what we would say. "It's not that expensive. We'll be staying in hostels — and you know what the teachers are like. We'd never be allowed to go anywhere without them." Her voice got a little quicker. "And it's meant to be very educational. We'd be learning about Maori culture and volcanoes . . ."

It's a terrible thing to watch the face of a child who knows she is asking the impossible.

"I could help out with my savings if it costs too much."

"I don't think it's possible." Liza reached out a hand. "I'm really sorry, lovey."

"Everyone else is going."

She was too good a child to get angry. It was more a plea than a protest. Sometimes I would have preferred it if she had got angry.

"Please."

"We don't have the money."

"But I've got nearly three hundred dollars saved up — and there's ages to go. We could all save up."

Liza looked at me and shrugged. "We'll see," she said, in a tone that suggested even to me that she clearly wouldn't.

"I'll make a deal with you, Hannah." I put down my darning. I was doing a terrible job anyway. "I've got some investments that are due to come in around spring next year. I thought I might pay for us all to take a trip up to the Northern Territory. I've always fancied a look around Kakadu National Park, maybe a wrestle with the crocodiles. What do you think?"

I could see from her face what she thought: that she didn't want to be traveling around Australia with her mum and an old woman, that she would rather be headed for a foreign country, flying on an airplane with her friends, giggling, staying up late and sending homesick postcards. But that was the one thing we couldn't give her.

I tried, Lord knows I tried. "We could take Milly too," I said. "Perhaps if we've got enough money we could even ask Lara's mother if Lara would like to come with us."

Hannah was staring at the table. "That would be nice," she said eventually, and then, with a smile that wasn't very much like one, she added, "I'm going next door. My program's on in a minute."

Liza looked at me. Her eyes said everything we both knew: Silver Bay is a beautiful little town, but even a stretch of Paradise will become ugly if you're never allowed to leave it.

"There's no point blaming yourself," I said, when I was sure Hannah couldn't hear.

"There's nothing you can do. Not for now."

I have seen many times over the past few years the doubt that flickered across her face. "She'll get over it," I said. I laid a hand on hers, and she squeezed it gratefully.

I'm not sure either of us was convinced.

THREE:
MIKE

Tina Kennedy was wearing a violet brassiere, edged with lace and four, possibly five, mauve rosebuds at the top of each cup. It was not an observation I would normally have made in my working day. Tina Kennedy's lingerie was not something I wanted to think about — and especially not now. But as she paused by my boss's shoulder to hand him the file of documents he had requested, she bent low and looked straight at me in a manner I could only describe afterward as challenging.

That violet brassiere was sending me a message. That, and the moisturized, lightly tanned flesh it contained, was a souvenir of my promotion night two and a half weeks previously.

I do not scare easy, but it was the most terrifying thing I had ever seen.

In an involuntary gesture, I felt in my pocket for my phone. Vanessa, my girlfriend, had texted me three times in the past half hour, even though I had told her that this meeting was of vital importance and not to be interrupted. I had read the first message, and tried to ignore the insistent vibration of those that followed:

"Don't forget to get Men's Vogue re suit on page 46. You would look great in the dark one XXX"

"Swtie pls call me we need 2 talk about seat plans"

"Imp U call b4 2p.m. as I hv to give Gav answer about shoes. AM WAITING XXX"

I sighed, feeling the peculiar mix of nagging anxiety and stasis that two hours spent in a stuffy boardroom surrounded by other men in suits can bring.

"The bottom line, as with all such ventures, is unit capacity. We think we have put together a development plan that will give us the growth potential of the longer-term luxury-stay market, with the benefits of a more fluid short-term market, both designed to maximize revenue streams not just throughout the summer months but the whole year."

The phone buzzed against my thigh, and I wondered absently if it was audible over the sound of Dennis Beaker's voice. I had to hand it to Nessa. She wouldn't give in.

She'd seemed barely to hear me this morning when I explained that leaving work mid-afternoon or, for that matter, calling her would be difficult. But, then, she didn't seem to hear much these days, except "wedding." Or, perhaps, "baby."

Below, the gray, lead-tarnished length of Liverpool Street stretched away toward the City. I could just see, if I tilted my head, the figures on the pavement: men and women dressed in blue, black or gray, marching smartly along below the sooty masonry to get plastic-boxed lunches that they would gobble at their desks. Some people thought of it as a rat race, but I had never felt like that: I had always felt comforted by the uniformity, the shared sense of purpose. Even if that purpose was money. On quiet days, Dennis would point out of the window and demand, "What do you think he earns, eh, or her?" And we would value them, depending on such variables as cut of jacket, type of shoes and how straight they stood as they walked. Twice, he had sent the office junior running downstairs to see if he had guessed right, and both times, to my surprise, he had.

Dennis Beaker says that nothing and nobody on God's earth is without a monetary value. After four years' working with him, I'm inclined to agree.

On the slickly polished table in front of me sat the bound proposal, its glossy pages testament to the weeks Dennis, the other partners and I had spent clawing this deal back from the brink. Nessa had complained last night, as I checked it yet again for errors, that I was devoting far more energy to that one document than to what she considered our more pressing concerns. I protested, but mildly. I knew where I was with those pages. I was far more comfortable with revenue streams and income projections than with her amorphous, ever-shifting desires for this flower arrangement or that color-coordinated outfit. I couldn't tell her I preferred to leave the wedding to her — on the few occasions I'd got properly involved, as she had requested, I'd reduced her to hysterics with things I'd apparently got wrong. I couldn't help it — it was as if we were speaking different languages.

"So, what I'd like to do now is get my colleague to make a short presentation. Just to give you a flavor of what we consider a very exciting opportunity."

Tina had crossed to the other side of the boardroom. She stood next to the coffee table, her stance deceptively relaxed. I could still glimpse that violet strap. I closed my eyes, trying to force away a sudden memory of her breasts, pushed up against me in the men's toilets at Bar Brazilia, the fluid ease with which she had removed her blouse.

"Mike?"

She was staring at me again. I glanced up, then away, not wanting to encourage her.

"Mike? You still with us?" There was the faintest edge to Dennis's voice. I rose from my seat, shuffling my notes. "Yes," I said. And, more firmly, "Yes." I raised a smile for the row of Vallance Equity's flint-eyed venture capitalists around the table, trying to convey some of Dennis's own confidence and bonhomie. "Just — ah — mulling over a couple of points you made." I took a deep breath and gestured across the room. "Tina? Lights?"

I took hold of the remote-control device for my presentation, and as my phone vibrated again, wished I had thought to remove it. I fumbled in my pocket to try to turn it off. Unfortunately, glancing up through the dimmed light at Tina, I realized she thought this had been for her benefit. She responded with a slow smile, her eyes dropping to my groin.

"Right," I said, letting out a breath and refusing resolutely to look at her. "I'd like to show you lucky gentlemen a few images of what we modestly consider to be the investment opportunity of the decade." There was a low rumble of amusement. They liked me. There they sat, primed by Dennis's raw enthusiasm, ready for my sonorous list of facts and figures. Receptive, attentive, waiting to be reassured. My father often said I was ideally suited to a business environment. He meant business in the gray-suited sense, rather than the hyper-sexy megadeal sense. Because, although I had somehow ended up at the latter end, I had to admit that I was not a natural risk-taker. I was Mr. Due Diligence, one of life's careful, considered deliberators, who researched everything not just to the nth degree but several degrees beyond.

As a child, before I spent my carefully saved pocket money, I would spend hours in a shop, weighing up the benefits of Action Man against his compatriots, fearful of the crushing disappointment that came when you made the wrong choice. Offered a choice of puddings, I would pit the potential infrequency of lemon meringue pie against the solid comfort of chocolate sponge, and double-check that raspberry jelly wasn't among the options.

None of this meant I was unambitious. I knew exactly where I wanted to be, and had long since learned that taking the quiet path was the key to my success. While colleagues' more incendiary careers crashed and burned, I had become financially secure, due to my dogged monitoring of interest rates and investments. Now, six years into my tenure at Beaker Holdings, my promotion to junior partner apparently nothing to do with my engagement to the boss's daughter, I was valued as someone who would accurately assess the benefits of any choice — geographical, social or economic — before making it. Two big deals and I would be senior partner. Another seven years until Dennis retired, and I would be ready to step into his shoes. I had it all planned.

Which was why my behavior that night had been so out of character.

"I think you're having your teenage rebellion late," my sister Monica had observed, two days previously. I had taken her to lunch, in the smartest restaurant I knew, as a birthday treat. She worked on a national newspaper but earned less per month than I spent in expenses.

"I don't even like the girl," I said.

"Since when did sex have anything to do with liking someone?" She sniffed. "I think I'll have two puddings. I can't choose between the chocolate and the crème brûlée." She had ignored my look. "It's a reaction against the wedding. You're trying unconsciously to impregnate someone else."

"Don't be ridiculous." I almost winced. "God! The thought of —"

"All right. But it's obvious you're bucking against something. *Bucking.*" She grinned. My sister's like that. "You should tell Vanessa you're not ready."

"But she's right. I'll never be ready. I'm not that kind of bloke."

"So you'd rather she made the decisions?"

"In our personal life, yes. It works well for us like that."

"So well that you felt the need to shag someone else?"

"Keep your voice down, okay?"

"You know what? I'll just have the chocolate. But if you have the crème brûlée I'll try it."

"What if she says something to Dennis?"

"Then you're in big trouble — but you must have known that when you slept with his secretary. Come on, Mike, you're thirty-four years old, hardly an innocent."

I dropped my head into my hands. "I don't know what the hell I was doing."

Monica had been suddenly buoyant. "God, it's nice to hear you say that. You don't know how cheering it is for me to

65

know that *you* can mess up your life just like the rest of us. Can I tell Mum and Dad?"

Now, filled with a sudden picture of my sister's triumph, I forgot where I was and had to glance at my notes. I breathed out slowly, and looked up again at the expectant faces around me. It seemed to have become uncomfortably warm in the boardroom. I let my gaze settle on their team — no one was even remotely flushed. Dennis always said that venture capitalists had ice in their blood. Perhaps he was right.

"As Dennis has explained," I continued, "the emphasis in this project is on the quality end of the market. The consumers we'll be targeting in this development are hungry for experiences. They are people who have spent the last decade acquiring material goods, which haven't made them happy. They are possession-rich, time-poor, and are searching for other ways to spend their money. And the real growth area, according to our research, is in their sense of well-being.

"To that end, this development will not just offer accommodation of a quality that will ensure it a slot at the top end of the market, but a variety of leisure opportunities suited to the surroundings." I clicked the remote control, bringing up the images that the artist had only delivered that morning, leaving Dennis turbocharging what barely remained of his blood pressure. "It will have a state-of-the-art spa, with six different pools, a full-time therapeutic staff and a range of the newest holistic treatments. If you turn to page thirteen you will see the space itself in more detail, as well as a menu of the kind of thing it will offer. And for those who prefer to get their sense of well-being from something a little more active — and, let's face it, that's usually the men . . ." here I paused for the amused nods of recognition . . . "we have the pièce de résistance of the whole complex — an integrated center devoted entirely to watersports. This will include jet-skis, waveboards, speedboats and waterskiing. There will be game-fishing. There will also be PADI-trained instructors to take clients on tailor-made diving trips further out to sea. We believe a combination of top-class equipment with a highly skilled team will give clients a never-to-be-forgotten trip and offer them the chance to learn new skills."

"All while staying in a resort that will be a byword for service and luxury," Dennis put in. "Mike, bring up the architect's pictures. As you can see, there are three levels of accommodation, to suit both the affluent singles and families, with a special penthouse for VIPs. You'll notice we have avoided the budget option. We've already had interest from —"

"I heard you lost the site for this." The voice had come from the back.

The room fell quiet. Oh, Christ, I thought.

"Tina, bring up the lights." It was Dennis's voice, and I wondered if he was about to answer, but he was looking at me.

I made my expression bland. I'm good at that. "I'm sorry, I didn't catch that, Neville. Did you have a question?"

"I heard this was planned for South Africa and that you lost your site. There's nothing on this document about where it's going to be now. You can hardly expect us to consider investing in a holiday resort that has yet to find a site."

The flicker in Dennis's jaw betrayed his own surprise. How the hell had they found out about South Africa?

My voice cut through the air even before I knew what I was saying: "I'm not quite sure where your information has come from, but South Africa was only ever an option for us. Having examined our potential location there in some detail, we decided that it couldn't provide our clients with the kind of holiday we had in mind. We're looking at a very specialized market and we —"

"Why?"

"Why what?"

"Why was South Africa unsuitable? My understanding is that it's one of the fastest-growing holiday destinations in the world."

My Turnbull and Asser shirt was sticking to the small of my back. I hesitated, wondering if Neville had any knowledge of the failure of our previous financing deal.

"Politics," interjected Dennis.

"Politics?"

"It would have been an hour-and-a-half transfer from the airport to the resort. And whatever route we took would have brought us through some of the . . . shall we say less . . . *affluent* areas? Our research tells us that when they have paid a premium for a luxury holiday, clients don't want to be confronted by abject poverty. It makes them . . ." Please don't smile sympathetically at their secretary, I pleaded silently. Too late. Dennis's empathetic beam was as treacly as it was misjudged. ". . . uncomfortable. And that is the last emotion we want clients to feel at this resort. Joyous, yes. Excited, yes. Satisfied, of course. Guilty, or uncomfortable, at the plight of their . . . colored cousins, no."

I closed my eyes. I felt, rather than saw, the black secretary do the same.

"No, Neville, politics and luxury holidays just do not mix." Dennis shook his head, sagely, as if delivering some oracle. "And that is the kind of detailed research on which we at Beaker Holdings pride ourselves before we embark on a major project."

"So you have an alternative site in mind?"

"Not just in mind but signed and sealed," I said. "It's a bit of a departure, but it avoids all the potential minefields of South Africa, and other parts of the third world. It's full of English-speakers, it has a superb climate and it is, I can truly say, one of the most beautiful spots I have ever seen. And in this line of work, Neville, you know as well as I do that there are some very beautiful destinations indeed."

RJW Land had stolen the site from under our noses. Someone there must have tipped off Vallance. My mind raced: if RJW was attempting a similar development, would their people also have approached Vallance for funding? Were they attempting to sabotage our deal?

"I can't go into more detail," I said smoothly. "But I can tell you — in confidence — that there were other things we discovered about the South African site that suggested much lower future revenues. And, as you know, we're all about maximizing profit here."

In truth, I knew almost nothing about the new site. Out of desperation we had used a land agent, some old mate of Dennis's, and the deal had been closed only two days previously. I hated the sensation of flying blind.

"Tim," I smiled, "you know I'm a boring sod when it comes to research, that there's nothing I like better for my bedtime reading than a pile of analysis. Believe me, if I'd thought the South African site was going to work better in the long run, I wouldn't have been so glad to let it go. But I like to go a layer deeper —"

"Your bedtime reading is all very interesting, Mike, but it would be useful if —"

"— and it's really all about the margins. That's the bottom line."

"No one cares about the margins more than us, but —"

Dennis held up a pudgy hand. "Tim. No. Not a word — because there's something else I'd like to show you before we go any further. In fact, gentlemen, if you'd like to follow me through to the next room, we have a bit of fun lined up before we tell you exactly where it is."

Venture capitalists, I mused, as we followed them, didn't look as though fun was a high priority on their agenda. Some were positively disgruntled at having been uprooted from their comfort zone of boardroom table and leather-backed chair, muttering uneasily to each other. Then again, having come in half an hour late, I wasn't sure what Dennis had in mind. Please don't let him have asked Tina to dress up in a bikini, I prayed. I was still haunted by memories of the Hawaiian Hula Proposal.

But what Dennis had planned was quite different. Boardroom Two had been emptied of its table, chairs and pull-down screen. There was no two-way video link, or a tea cart in the corner. What sat, huge, squat and foreboding, in the center of the floor was a large piece of machinery, surrounded by inflatable blue tubing, its centerpiece a florid yellow surfboard.

We were all stunned into immobility by the sheer unlikeliness of the thing.

"Gentlemen. Remove your shoes, and prepare to hang ten!" Dennis held out an arm toward the machine. "It's a simulator," he announced, when nobody said anything. "You can all have a go."

The room was silent, bar the low hum of the surf simulator. It sat, an alien creature in this sea of gray, its flashing buttons gamely advertising that, should they want it, their surf experience could be accompanied by a Beach Boys tune.

I registered their expressions, and decided that the best way to rescue the situation was to divert them. "Perhaps the ladies and gentlemen would like a bite to eat first? A drink, perhaps? Tina, would you mind?"

"Whatever you say, Mike," she said, catching my eye lazily. I could have sworn there was a sway to her walk as she left the room, but Dennis didn't notice.

"I just want to give you gentlemen an idea of how irresistible our proposal is. I had a little go earlier," he said, kicking off his shoes. "It really is quite good fun. If no one else is brave enough, I'll show you how it works. You stand on here and . . ." He had removed his jacket and the barely restrained bulk of his stomach hung over the waistband of his trousers. I was grateful, not for the first time, that Vanessa had inherited her mother's genes. "I'll start off with some little waves. See? It's easy."

To the strains of "I Get Around," my boss, who in the past three years had overseen seventy million pounds' worth of property investment, and has on his desk photographs of himself shaking hands with Henry

Kissinger and Alan Greenspan, stood on the surfboard. His arms were raised in a parody of athleticism to reveal two dark patches of sweat. His buffoonish exterior was renowned for masking a razor-sharp business brain — although sometimes I had to wonder.

"Switch it on, Mike."

I glanced at the men behind me, trying to smile. I wasn't sure that this was a good idea. It wasn't the image I thought we should portray.

"Just switch it on at the plug, Mike, and I'll do the rest. Come on, Tim, Neville, you can't pretend you don't want to have a go."

With a low whine, the surfboard jolted slowly into life. Dennis bent his knees and stuck one hand forward, wiggling his fingers. "What — I — haven't — told — you, gentlemen, is that simulators will also — be — whoops!" He struggled to keep his balance. "There we go . . . The simulators will be on-site for clients to learn on before they go out on the water. It's a complete — package."

Even those who had never been on the water in their lives, he said, gasping with the effort, would be able to practice in private before exposing themselves to the gaze of their fellow holidaymakers. I don't know if it was the bizarre improbability of this machine forming part of the proposal, or Dennis's evident enjoyment, but within a few minutes even I had to admit that he was winning them over. I watched as Tim and Neville crept closer to the machine, sipping the champagne that Tina had handed to them.

Their finance man, a florid heavyweight called Simons, had already taken off his shoes, to reveal surprisingly threadbare socks, and the two junior members of their team were quoting at each other from the pages of surfing slang that Tina had prepared.

Dennis had imagination, I had to hand it to him.

"What happens if we turn it up, Dennis?" Neville was smiling. I wondered if that was a good sign.

"Tina has given you — a — list," he said breathlessly. "I believe — I'll be — whoops! 'Catching a pounder.' "

Neville had moved closer. He took off his jacket and handed his glass to his secretary. "What level will you go to, Dennis?"

He was, I had guessed, one of nature's competitors.

But so was Dennis. "Any you want, Nev. Turn her up," he cried, his face beaded with sweat. "We'll see who can catch the biggest wave, eh?"

"Go on, Mike," Neville urged. I smiled. They were all enjoying themselves. As Dennis had guessed, the simulator had drawn away their attention from the South African rumors.

"I've always fancied a bit of the old surf," said Tim, removing his jacket too. Before them, the simulator whined and shuddered under Dennis's weight. "What level you on there, old chap?"

"Three," I said, glancing at the dial. "I really don't think —"

"Come on, we can do better than that. Turn him up, Mike. Let's see who can stay on longest."

"Yes, turn him up," the gray suits of Vallance Equity Financing chanted, the veneer of restraint peeled away by amusement.

I looked at Dennis, who nodded, then motioned toward the dial. "Come on, Mike old boy, bring on the waves."

"You're stoked, Dennis!" Tim was checking the surfing terminology. "The waves are gnarly, but you're stoked!"

Despite his apparent gaiety, Dennis was now sweating profusely. He tried to smile, but I saw a hint of desperation in his eyes as he tried to stay aloft the now rapidly undulating board. "Want me to take you down a notch, Dennis?" I offered.

"No! No! I'm — stoked! How long have I been at level four, chaps?"

"Take him to five!" yelled Neville, stepping forward and grasping the dial. "Let's see how he rides the — ah, the crunchers!"

"I'm not —" I began.

Afterward, no one was sure how it had happened. Dennis was one of the few people in the room who had not drunk any champagne. But somehow the simulator was booted up to its highest level at the moment when Dennis's balance failed him. With a terrible cry he was hurled clear of the surrounding inflatable cushions and across the boardroom, more swiftly than someone his size should have been, to land heavily on his hip.

It broke, of course. Those who hadn't guessed that the impact would do it heard the sickening crunch. I don't think I'll ever forget that sound. It removed, for me, even the slender desire I'd felt to try the machine. As I've mentioned, I'm not one of nature's risk-takers.

There was pandemonium. Everyone crowded around. Over the exclamations of concern and cries of "Call an ambulance!" the surfboard gyrated and the Beach Boys sang on.

"Australia, eh?" said Neville, as Dennis was stretchered toward the lift. "Unforgettable presentation. We're definitely interested. When you're out of hospital we'll talk more about the site."

"Mike will send you a copy of the site report. Won't you, Mike?" Dennis spoke through clenched teeth, his face gray with pain.

"Sure." I tried to look as confident as he had sounded.

As he was loaded into the ambulance, he beckoned me closer. "I know what you're thinking," he whispered. "You'll have to compile one."

"But the timing — the wedding —"

"I'll square it with Vanessa. Best you're out of the way for most of the planning anyway. Book yourself a flight this afternoon. And for God's sake, Mike, come back with a plan that's going to make this site work."

"But we haven't even —"

"I'll stall them as long as it takes for you to pull it together. But this is our biggest ever development. I want to know I was right to promote you, that you can bring it in."

It didn't occur to him that I might refuse.

That I might put my personal life before the needs of the company. But, then, he was probably right. I'm a company man. A safe pair of hands. I booked the flight that afternoon. Business class in one of the Asian carriers was cheaper than economy in both my initial choices.

FOUR:
GREG

What's an okay time of day to start on the beer? According to my old man, any time after midday. He used to sink them like my mother sank cups of tea, cracking open a Toohey's every couple of hours or so when he took a break from whatever house he was building.

He was a big bloke, and you'd never have known he was drinking that much. My mum reckons that was because he was permanently drunk; cheerful in the afternoons, ebullient at tea, a little muzzy in the mornings from the night before. We never had the misfortune to deal with him stone-cold sober.

I believe the right time is around two p.m., unless I'm working, in which case it's whatever time I bring *Sweet Suzanne* back in. You wouldn't catch me drunk at the helm — whatever my faults, I'd never put my boat or my passengers at risk. But a cold beer at

Kathleen's, with the sun high in the sky and a few chips on the table, that'll do me. Can't see how anyone could object to that. Apart from my ex.

According to Suzanne, there's never a good time for me to drink beer. She said I was a mean drunk, an ugly drunk, and drunk too often to make up for it. She said that was why she could no longer stand the sight of me. She said that was why I was losing my looks. She said that was why we'd never had kids — although she'd refused point-blank when I suggested she and I head for the doc to see if he could work it out. And I told her — I might not be an angel and I'm the first to admit I'm not the easiest bloke to be hitched to — there's not a lot of men in Australia would volunteer to have their tackle tampered with, especially by another bloke.

But that was how bad I wanted kids. And that was why, as I left my solicitor's office at eleven twenty-five — amazing how you keep track of time when you're paying by the hour and it's Saturday rates — I decided that, as far as I was concerned, eleven twenty-five a.m. was the perfect time to crack open a cold can of VB, even though it was chilly enough for me to be wearing my sweater, and the wind was too high to sit outside without turning blue.

I guess that beer must have been like giving her the finger, as much as anything. Her and her bloody fitness-instructor bloke and her half share of everything and her stupid demands. Because, to be honest, it didn't taste that great. I was going to drink one at the pub but somehow, when I thought about it, sitting in a pub by yourself at eleven twenty-five in the morning seemed a little . . . sad. Even on a Saturday.

So I sat in the front of my truck, drinking my beer with a little less speed than I might have done, waiting for the point when it would stop feeling like an effort, and start easing the hours along from the inside. I had no customers that day. I'd had to admit my numbers had dropped a lot since I'd graffitied the boat. Liza had helped me paint over it at the weekend, and told me briskly that if I kept my mouth shut everyone would have forgotten about it in a week or two. And I did — I was going to have to work like a bloody dog to pay the kind of settlement that that ex of mine was demanding.

"A clean break," they called it. The same phrase doctors use when they talk about a snapped limb. And that was how it felt, I can tell you. So painful that if I thought about it too hard it made me feel physically sick.

But for now I sat in my cab in the car park thinking of how I had watched the tourists totter down Whale Jetty in their high heels, clutching their video cameras and their whalesong CDs, and eye *Suzanne* warily, as if she might jump out of the water to reveal some other blasphemy.

If I hadn't had other plans that day, I would have taken her out by myself. Even after a beer. I'd found that sometimes just sitting in the bay watching the bottlenose made me feel better. They stick their heads up with those stupid old smiles as if they're having a joke with you, and sometimes you can't help but laugh, even on days when you want to slit your wrists. I guess we were all a bit like that, the crews. We knew that was the best bit — just you and those creatures, out in the silence of the water.

"At least you didn't have kids," the solicitor had remarked, checking out the joint account. She'd no idea what she'd said.

I'd finished the second beer when I saw him. I'd crumpled the tin in my fist and was about to chuck it into the passenger footwell when I noticed him. You couldn't miss him. He stood there in his dark blue pen-pusher's suit, flanked by two oversized matching suitcases, gazing back toward the main street. I stared at him until he noticed me back, then stuck my head out of the window. "You all right, mate?"

He hesitated, then picked up his cases and stepped forward. His black lace-up shoes had been polished to within an inch of their lives. Not the kind of bloke I'd normally have got chatting to, but he looked dead beat, and I guess I felt sorry for him. One deadbeat to another, like.

When he reached my window, he dropped the cases and fished a piece of paper out of his pocket. "I think my taxi's dropped me at the wrong place. Can you tell me if there's a hotel near here?"

A Brit. I might have guessed. I squinted at him. "There's a few, mate. Which end of Silver Bay you after?"

He glanced at his piece of paper again. "It just says the . . . ah . . . Silver Bay Hotel."

"Kathleen's place? It's not a hotel as such. Not anymore."

"Is it much of a walk?"

I guess curiosity got the better of me. You don't often see men dressed up like a dog's dinner in this neck of the woods. "She's a way up the road. Hop in. Got a bit of business over there myself. You can sling your bags in the back."

I saw doubt pass over his face, as if an offer of a lift was to be mistrusted. Or perhaps he didn't want his smart luggage touching my seaweedy gear in the back. This bugged me a little, and I nearly changed my mind. But he dragged his cases around to the tailgate and I watched him haul them over the side. Then he opened the door and climbed in, struggling as his feet made contact with the pile of empties.

"Mind your shoes on those cans," I said, as I pulled off. "The beer should be long gone, but I can't promise."

As a name "Silver Bay" is a little misleading. It's not really one bay at all but two, separated by Whale Jetty, which sticks out on the piece of land that cuts through them. From above, I used to say, the sea looks like a giant blue backside. (Suzanne would raise her eyebrows at that but, then, she raised her eyebrows at almost everything I said.)

Kathleen's place sat on one of the bays, the furthest, right at the end, near the point that took you out to the open sea. All that remained on her side, really, was the old Bullen house, the museum and the sand dunes. The other side of Whale Jetty was MacIver's Seafood Bar and Grill, the fish market, and then, as you moved further from Kathleen's, the growing spread of the town.

He told me his name was Mike, and I forget his surname. He didn't say much else. I asked him if he was here on business, and he said, "Pleasure, mainly." I remember thinking, What the hell kind of bloke dresses like that on his holidays? He said he'd just got off the plane that morning and he should have had a rental car but the company had screwed up and said they'd deliver one to him up here from Newcastle tomorrow.

"Long flight, but," I said.

He nodded.

"Been here before?"

"Sydney. Once. I wasn't there very long."

I figured he was in his midthirties. He looked at his watch a lot, for someone who wasn't working. I asked him how he came to be booked into Kathleen's. "It's not the busiest," I said, glancing pointedly at his expensive suit. "I thought someone like you'd want to be somewhere . . . you know . . . smarter."

He looked straight ahead, as if he was working out his answer. "I heard the area was nice," he said. "It was the only hotel I could find listed."

"You really want to be over at the Blue

Shoals up the coast there," I said. "Pretty nice place, that. En suites, Olympic-sized pool, all that jazz. Monday to Thursday they do a pretty good all-you-can-eat buffet too. Fifteen dollars a head, I think it is. Fridays the price goes up a bit." I swerved to avoid a dog that loped across the road. "And there's the Admiral, in Nelson Bay. Satellite telly in every room, the decent channels, not the crap. You'd get a good deal this time of year — I happen to know there's hardly anyone in there."

"Thank you," he said eventually. "If I decide to move, that may come in useful."

After that there wasn't much we said to each other. I drove, feeling a bit irritated that the guy hadn't made more of an effort. I'd picked him up, driven him all the way — a cab ride would have cost him a good ten bucks — given him the low-down on the area, and he made barely any effort to talk to me.

I was half thinking of saying something — I guess the beer had warmed me up a little — but then I realized he'd fallen asleep. Out cold. Not even a sharp-suited businessman looks like a winner when he's drooling on his shoulder. For some reason this made me feel better and I found myself whistling all the way along the coast road to Silver Bay.

Kathleen had done up the table something beautiful. I saw the cloth and the balloons long before I saw anything else, the white damask billowing in the brisk winds, the balloons bobbing in a bid to break free for the heavens.

The homemade bunting read "Happy Birthday, Hannah," and below it, the birthday girl and a gang of her mates were squealing at some bloke with a snake wrapped around his arm.

For a minute I forgot about the visitor in my cab. I climbed out and walked along the driveway, remembering with a jolt that the party had started an hour earlier.

"Greg." Kathleen had a way of looking you up and down that told you she knew exactly where you were coming from. "Nice of you to make it."

"Who's that?" I nodded toward the bloke with the snake.

"The Creature Teacher, I believe he calls himself. Every creepy-crawly you can imagine. Giant cockroaches, snakes, tarantulas . . . He lets the kids hold them, stroke them, that kind of thing. It was what Hannah asked for." She shuddered. "Can't think of anything more disgusting."

"In my day you'd stamp on 'em," I agreed, "with your Blundstones on."

There were eight kids, and a few adults, mainly other crew. That didn't surprise me. Hannah was a funny kid, old before her time, and we were all used to her hanging around with us. She had since she was small.

It was good to see her with some kids her own age. Apart from that girl Lara, I hardly ever saw her with one. You'd forget how young she was, half the time. Liza said she was like that, a bit solitary. I sometimes wondered whether she was talking about Hannah or herself.

Kathleen handed me a cup of tea, and I took it, hoping she couldn't smell the beer on my breath. It didn't seem right, somehow, at a child's party. And I was very fond of that kid.

"Your boat's a bit prettier now." Kathleen grinned.

"I suppose you know Liza helped me repaint her name."

"That temper of yours'll get you into trouble." She tutted. "Old enough to know better, I'd say."

"Is this you telling me off, Kathleen?"

"You're not that drunk, then."

"One," I protested. "Just one. Okay, maybe two."

She glanced at her watch. "And it's just after midday. Well, good for you."

You've got to hand it to the Shark Lady. She tells it as she sees it. Always has, always will. Not like Liza. She looks at you as if there's a whole other conversation going on in her head, and when you ask her what she's thinking (like a woman! That's what she reduces you to!) she'll shrug as if nothing's going on at all.

"Hi, Greg." Hannah ran past, beaming. I remember that feeling — when you're a kid and it's your birthday and for one day everyone makes you feel like the most special person in the world. She paused just long enough to notice the little parcel under my arm. She's an angel, that girl, but she's not stupid.

"Oh, this is for your aunt Kathleen," I said.

She stopped right in front of me, mischief in her eyes. "How come it's got kids' wrapping paper?" she said.

"It has?"

"It's for me," she ventured.

"Are you saying your aunt Kathleen's too old for this paper?" I put on my best innocent face.

It had never worked with Suzanne either. She stared at it, trying to work out what it might be. She's not the kind of kid to snatch. She's cautious — thinks before she acts. I couldn't bear making her wait any longer, so I handed it over. I have to admit, I was quite excited myself.

She ripped it open, flanked by her friends. They were all growing up, I noticed, losing the skinny little legs and the chubby cheeks. In a couple you could already see the women they would become. I had to fight my sadness at the thought that some would end up like Suzanne. Dissatisfied, nagging . . . faithless.

"It's a key," she said, puzzled, as she held it aloft. "I don't get it."

"A key?" I said, making myself look confused. "Are you sure?"

"Greg . . ."

"You sure you don't recognize it?"

She shook her head.

"It's the key to my lockup."

She frowned, still not getting it.

"The one by the jetty. Darn — I must have left your present in there. You and your mates might want to scoot down and check."

They were gone before I could say another word, feet kicking up in the sand, all squeals and sneakers. Kathleen gazed at me quizzically, but I said nothing. Sometimes you just want to savor the moment and, these days, I get precious few to savor.

Within minutes they were sprinting back up the path. "Is it the boat? Is it the little boat?" Her cheeks were flushed, her hair mussed around her face. I lost my breath. She was so much like her mother.

"Did you check the name?" I said.

"Hannah's Glory," she told her aunt Kathleen breathlessly. "It's a blue dinghy and it's called *Hannah's Glory.* Is it really for me?"

"Sure is, Princess," I said. That smile nixed my crappy morning. She threw her little arms round me, and I hugged her right back, unable to stop myself beaming.

"Can we take it out? Can I take it out, Auntie K?"

"Not right now, sweetheart. You've got your cake to cut. But I'm sure you can sit in it in the lockup."

I could hear her excited chatter the whole way down the path.

"A boat?" Kathleen turned to me, one eyebrow arched, when Hannah was out of earshot. "You talk to Liza about this?"

"Ah . . . not yet." The kids were skipping back to my lockup. "But I think I'm about to get my chance."

She was striding toward me, holding a plate with the birthday cake on it, the little dog at her heels. She was beautiful. As always she looked like she'd meant to head for somewhere else but at the last minute she'd decided to stop by you, as a favor, you understand.

"Hi. I've been hanging that bit of baleen on her wall — over her bed, she wants it." She nodded a greeting at me. "Stinks to high heaven. She's got four books on dolphins, two on whales and a video. She'll be opening her own museum at this rate. You've never seen a room so full of dolphin kitsch." She straightened. "Where are the kids off to?"

"You might want to talk to Greg about that," said Kathleen. Then she walked off, one hand raised, as if she didn't want to be around for the next bit.

"They're — ah — checking out my present."

She put the plate on the table. "Oh, yes? What did you get?" She began to whip the plastic wrap off the sandwiches.

"Old Carter was selling it. Little sculling craft. I've rubbed it down, given it a lick of paint. It's in perfect condition."

It took her a minute to register what I'd said. She stared at the table for a moment, then looked up at me. "You got her a what?"

"A little boat. Of her own. I thought once she's had a few lessons she can go and see the bottlenoses with her mates." I was a bit unnerved by her expression, so I added, "She's got to have one eventually."

She put her hands up to her mouth — a little like she was praying. She seemed something less than grateful.

"Greg?"

"Yeah?"

"Are you out of your tiny mind?"

"What?"

"You bought my daughter a boat? My daughter who isn't allowed out on the water? What the hell did you think you were doing?" Her voice was blistering.

I stared back at her, unable to believe she was so mad. "I was giving the kid a birthday treat."

"It's not your place to give my kid a birthday treat."

"She lives on the water. All her mates have little boats. Why shouldn't she have one?"

"Because I've told her she can't."

"Why? What harm can it do? She's got to learn, hasn't she?"

"She'll learn when I'm ready for her to learn."

"She's eleven years old! Why are you so

mad? What the hell is this about?" When she didn't answer, I gestured toward Hannah, who was standing at the door of the lockup. "Look at her — she's pleased as punch. I heard her telling her mates it was the best birthday present she'd ever had."

She wouldn't listen, just stood in front of me, yelling, "Yes! So now I've got to be the wicked witch who tells her she can't accept it. Thanks a bunch, Greg."

"So don't. Let her have it. We'll mind her."

"We?"

It was then that Mike appeared. I'd forgotten about him, asleep in my cab, some time ago. But now he was standing there, a little awkward, his suitcases in hand, his face still crumpled from sleep. I could cheerfully have told him to get lost.

Not that Liza noticed. She was still raging. "You should have asked me, Greg, before you butted in trying to buy a little girl's love with a bloody boat — the one thing I've been telling her for the past five years she is not allowed to have."

"It's just a little rowing boat. It's hardly a bloody two-hundred-horsepower speedboat." She was making me mad now. It was as if she was accusing me of trying to harm the kid.

"Excuse me — can I just —"

She held up a hand, still facing me. "Just butt out of my life, okay? I've told you a dozen times I don't want a bloody relationship with you, and you sucking up to my daughter isn't going to change that." We fell silent, as the words settled around us. By God, she'd known that would sting.

"Sucking up?" I could hardly bear to repeat the words. "Sucking up? What bloody kind of man do you take me for?"

"Just go away, Greg —"

"I'm really sorry to interrupt but —"

"Mum?"

Hannah was standing beside the English bloke, her birthday smile wiped clean off her face. She looked from me to her mum and back again. "Why are you shouting at Greg?" She spoke quietly and carefully, her eyes wide, as if we'd frightened her.

Liza took a deep breath.

"I'll — ah — if someone could point me toward Reception?" Mike looked as if he wanted to be there even less than I did.

Suddenly Liza noticed our extra guest. She turned toward him, face still flushed with anger. "Reception? You want to speak to Kathleen, over there. Lady in the blue shirt."

He tried to smile, muttered something about an English accent and, after a brief pause, disappeared.

Hannah was still standing next to me. Her sad little voice, when it came, made me want to give that mother of hers a slap. "I suppose this means I'm not allowed to keep the boat?"

When Liza turned to me, the full force of every bad thought she had ever had hit me square on. It wasn't a pretty feeling.

"We'll talk about it, lovey," she said.

"Liza," I tried to keep my voice nice, for the kid's sake, "I never meant to —"

"I'm not interested," she cut in. "Hannah. Tell your friends it's time for the cake." When Hannah didn't move, she waved an arm. "Go on. And I'll see if we can light some candles. It's not going to be easy in this breeze."

I put my hand on Hannah's shoulder. "Your boat will be waiting for you in the lockup whenever you're ready," I said, hearing the defiance in my voice. And then I walked stiffly away, muttering words I'm not proud of under my breath.

Yoshi met me at the truck. "Don't go, Greg," she said. "You know how worked up she gets about stuff. Don't ruin Hannah's day." She was still holding a party bag — she'd sprinted down from the kitchen to stop me.

It wasn't me ruining it, I wanted to say. It wasn't me determined to stop my little girl doing the one thing she wanted most in all the world. It wasn't me who acted like the kid's childhood was normal but never talked about any family other than Kathleen. It wasn't me who, three or four times a year, would be all over her like a rash and the next day act as if I was something she'd picked up on the back of her shoe. I know when I'm guilty, and I also know that sometimes it simply isn't my fault.

"Tell her I've got a boat to take out," I said, more sourly than I'd intended. I felt bad afterward. It had nothing to do with Yoshi, after all.

But I wasn't going out on the water. I was going to head for the nearest bar and drink until someone was good enough to tell me we'd made it into the next day.

FIVE:
KATHLEEN

It's hard to believe now, given the size of our land, but whaling was once one of Australia's primary industries. From way back in the nineteenth century whaling ships would come from Britain, unload a few convicts on us, then load up with some of our whales and sell them back to us at our ports. Some exchange, as Nino said. The Aussies got wise in the end and caught their own. After all, you could use a whale for just about anything — the oil for lamp fuel, candles and soap, the baleen for corsets, furniture, umbrellas and whips. I guess there was a lot more call for whips in those days. Back then the whalers mainly hunted the southern right whale — they called it "right" because it was so darn easy to catch. That poor beast was about the slowest thing in the southern hemisphere and, once dead, it would float, so that they could tow it into shore. I reckon it could only have made it easier for those whale-chasers if it had harpooned itself and swum to the processing plant.

They're protected now, of course, what remains of them. But I remember, as a girl, seeing one towed into the bay by two small boats. It seemed wrong to me, even then, as I watched the huge, swollen belly hauled inelegantly onto the shore, the blank eye gazing balefully up to the heavens as if despairing at man's inhumanity. I would catch just about anything — even as a little girl, my father would boast, I could hook, land and gut with an efficiency that might have been construed as heartless — but the sight of that southern right made me cry.

Here on the east coast, there hadn't been the whaling madness that we'd heard of out west. Here, fewer whales were taken before the end of the war — except in our little corner. Perhaps because the whales came so close that you could see them from dry land, this bay became a base for whalechas-ers. (Our whale-watching crews have inherited their nickname.) When I was a girl, they had killed them from small boats. It seemed like a fair fight, and it kept the catch down. But then they got greedy.

Between 1950 and 1962 some 12,500 humpbacks were killed and processed at stations like Norfolk Island and Moreton Island. Whale oil and meat made people rich, and the whalechasers used more and more sophisticated weaponry to increase their catch. The ships became bigger and faster, and the haul a plentiful, grim harvest. By the time humpback whaling was banned in Australian waters, they were using sonars, guns and cannon-launched harpoons — the equipment of war, my father said, in disgust.

And, of course, they killed too many. They swept those oceans until there was near none left of the humpbacks and put themselves out of business in the process. One by one the whaling operations closed, the processing plants shut down or converted to seafood processing. The area sank back slowly into shabby solitude, and most of us were relieved. My father, who had loved the romanticism of early whaling, back when it was about man versus whale rather than whale versus penthrite-charge grenade, bought Silver Bay's own whale-processing plant, and turned it into the museum. Nowadays the scientists reckon there might be fewer than two thousand humpbacks come past us on their annual migration, and some say the numbers will never recover.

· I tell this story to the crews, occasionally, when they talk about getting a bigger fleet, or trying to up their passenger numbers, of whale-watching as the tourist attraction of the future, the way to rejuvenate Silver Bay.

There's a lesson in there for us all. But I'm darned if anyone's listening.

"Good afternoon."

"Afternoon?" Michael Dormer hovered in the doorway, wearing the dazed expression of someone whose body clock was insisting he was in the wrong hemisphere.

"I knocked earlier and left a cup of coffee outside your room, but when I found it stone cold an hour later I figured I'd let you sleep." He looked like he wasn't taking in what I was saying. I gave him a minute, and motioned to him to sit at the kitchen table. I don't normally let people sit in the kitchen, but I'd just finished preparing the dining room for that evening. I placed a plate and a knife in front of him. "They say it usually takes a week to sleep through properly. Did you wake up much?"

He rubbed at his hair. He was unshaven, and wearing a shirt and casual trousers — still smarter than we were used to in Silver Bay, but a good step forward from the formal getup he'd arrived in.

"Only once." He smiled, a little ruefully. "But that was for about three hours."

I laughed, and poured him a coffee. He had a good face, Mr. Michael Dormer, the kind that suggested a little self-knowledge, an attribute I find in short supply in many of my guests. "Like some breakfast? I'm happy to fix you something."

"At a quarter to one?" He glanced at the clock.

"We can call it lunch. It'll be our secret." I still had some pancake batter in the fridge. I'd serve them with blueberries, and a side order of eggs and bacon.

He stared at his coffee for a bit, stifling a yawn. I said nothing, but pushed the newspaper toward him, recognizing that his disorientation would ease off after a mug or two of caffeine. I moved quietly, half an ear on the radio, distantly calculating the food I needed to prepare for supper that evening. Hannah was at a friend's house after school, and Liza ate barely enough to feed a fly, so it was only the guests I had to worry about.

The pancakes were done. Mr. Dormer perked up a bit when I put a plate in front of him. "Wow," he said, staring at the stack. "Thank you." I'd bet he didn't get much in the way of home cooking. They're always the most grateful.

But he ate like most men here do, with enthusiasm and a kind of single-mindedness

I don't often see in women. My mother always said I ate like a man, but I don't think it was a compliment. While he had his head down I had the chance to look him over. We don't get many men of his age on their own; usually they're with wives or girlfriends. The single ones stick to the busier resorts. I'm a little embarrassed to admit that I looked at him in the way I always look at men who might be suitable for Liza. No matter how hard she protests, I've not yet given up hope of pairing her off. "Whales don't stick together for life," she would scoff, "and, as you always say, Kathleen, we should learn from the creatures around us."

She had an answer for everything, that girl. The one time I'd remarked that it would be good for Hannah to have a father figure, she'd glared at me with such anguish and reproach that I'd felt instantly ashamed. I'd never brought up the subject again.

But that didn't mean I couldn't live in hope.

"That was delicious. Really."

"A pleasure, Mr. Dormer."

He smiled. "Mike. Please."

Not as formal as he seemed, then.

I sat down opposite him, giving myself a coffee break as I refilled his mug. "Got any plans for today?" I was going to point him toward the leaflets in the front hall, but I wasn't sure he was the amusements-and-day-trip-to-the-tea-gardens type.

He looked down at his coffee. "Just thought I'd get my bearings, really. My rental car should arrive later so there's not much I can do till then."

"Oh, there's lots of places you can go when you've got wheels. But you're right. The bus goes to Port Stephens from up the road, but apart from that you'd be pretty stuck. Did you say you were here on holiday?"

A curious thing: he flushed a little. "Something like that," he said.

I left it there. I know not to pursue someone who doesn't want to talk. He might have his own reasons for being here — a broken relationship, a personal ambition, a decision to be made in solitude. I can't bear those people who rattle on and on with questions. Mike Dormer had paid me for a week in advance, thanked me politely for his breakfast, and those two things alone entitled him to my professional courtesy.

"I'll — erm — leave you to it, then," he said, placing his knife and fork neatly on his plate and rising from the table. "Thank you very much, Miss Mostyn."

"Kathleen."

"Kathleen."

I went to clear his plates without another thought.

I had other guests to worry about that week — namely a middle-aged couple here for their twenty-fifth wedding anniversary. It would have been our first booking through the new Internet advertisement had the *Moby*s not already been fully booked, forcing Liza to take them out instead. That alone would have put her in a bad mood — she had been adamant that she would play no part in the Internet business — but the man complained about everything. The room wasn't big enough, the furnishings were shabby, the shower smelt of mildew. On his first two mornings he finished the box of bran flakes and when I set out a fresh box the next day he complained I hadn't given him a choice. To cap it, he complained that Liza had set off late on their whale-watching trip, even though they'd arrived late at the jetty because he had been determined to look around the Whalechasers Museum, and had made me open it specially. It was included in the price, you see.

His wife, an elegant woman, immaculately put together in the way that makes me wonder about the time and effort people are prepared to devote to such things, followed him around apologizing under her breath to everyone he rubbed up the wrong way. The breathless, conspiratorial ease with which she did this suggested it was not a new experience for her. The trip was her anniversary "treat," she told me apologetically, glancing behind her to where he was pacing toward the hotel, his head sunk into his shoulders. I wondered how many years it had taken for the deep grooves to appear on her forehead. "He's enjoyed it much more than last year's trip," she said, and I laid a hand on her arm in sympathy.

"He was a bully," Liza said, when she came in. "If it hadn't been for her I wouldn't have taken them."

We exchanged a look. "Bet you made her day, though."

"Not really. Not a whale anywhere. I gave them an extra hour but it was like the seas were empty."

"Perhaps they knew."

"I sent out a whale sonar, telling them to bugger off for the day."

Sometimes I can see her mother, my little sister, in Liza. She's there in the way Liza tilts her head when she's thinking, in her thin strong fingers, in her smile when she sees her daughter. That's when I know my niece's presence here, and Hannah's, is a blessing. That there is an elemental pleasure in seeing the continuation of a family line, a joy that we who are childless might not otherwise experience. It's that jolt of recognition when suddenly you see not only her mother but your great-uncle Evan, your grandmother, perhaps even yourself. I have been grateful for this knowledge, these last five years. Those glimpses of familial brow, frown or giggle have made up, in some small way, for the loss of my sister.

Liza, however, has other features — her watchfulness, the ever-present sadness, the faded white scar where her cheekbone meets her left ear — that are entirely her own.

I suppose it should have been of no great surprise to me that Nino Gaines hadn't called by for a few days — not after the way I sent him packing the last time he came. But his unusual show of self-sufficiency got to me. I wouldn't go so far as to say I missed him, but I didn't like the idea that he might be sitting at Barra Creek thinking badly of me. More than anyone, I knew that life was too short for grudges.

After lunch I packed up a lemon cake in

waxed paper, sat it on the passenger seat of my car and headed out to his place. It was a beautiful day, the air so clear you could see the mountains in the distance, and pick out every needle on the pines that lined the road. It had been an especially dry summer, and as I drove inland I glanced at the reddish earth, the bony horses with no grass to graze, killing time by swishing their tails at the never-ending flies. The air was different out here: the pollen and dust motes hung static, the atmosphere unfiltered and sullen. I don't understand how people can live inland. I find that endless brown depressing, the solid outline of hill and valley too unchanging. You get used to the moods of the sea — like those of a spouse, I imagine. Over enough years, you may not always like them but it's what you know.

He was just headed indoors when I pulled up outside. He turned at the sound of my engine, wiping his oversized hands on the back of his trousers, and touched one hand to the brim of his hat when he'd grasped who it was. He was wearing a quilted waistcoat that I swear he'd had back in the 1970s when his two boys were born.

I hesitated before I got out of the car. We had rarely fallen out, and I was not entirely sure of my reception. We stood squinting at each other, and I remember thinking how ridiculous we were: two brittle old skeletons, facing each other like teenagers. "Afternoon," I said.

"Come for your order?" he asked, but there was a twinkle in his eye that made me relax. A twinkle that, if I'm honest, I didn't deserve.

"I brought you a cake," I said, reaching back into the car to get it.

"I hope it's lemon."

"Why? Are you going to send it back if it's not?"

"I might."

"I don't remember you as picky, Nino Gaines. Stubborn, greedy and rude, yes. Picky, no."

"You've got lipstick on."

"Overfamiliar, too."

He grinned at me, and I couldn't quite keep the smile from my face. That's what they don't tell you about old age: it doesn't stop you acting like a young fool.

"Come on in, Kathleen. I'll see if I can get Stubborn, Greedy and Overfamiliar Mark Two to make us both a cup of tea. You look very nice, by the way."

The first time Nino Gaines asked me to marry him I was nineteen years old. The second time I was nineteen and two weeks.

The third time was forty-two years later. This was not due to any lapse in memory or attention on his part, but because in the intervening years, having given up on me, he was married to Jean. He met her two months after I'd turned him down for the second time when she disembarked at Woolloomoolloo from a bride-ship, having changed her mind about the soldier she was due to marry. He had been waiting for an old friend on the docks, found his gaze drawn to her wasp waist and crooked nylons and, like the force of nature she was, she had reeled him in and got a ring firmly on her finger before another two months were out. Many people thought they were a strange couple — they used to fight like crazy! — but he brought her back to his newly purchased vineyard at Barra Creek and they were together until she died at the age of fifty-seven from cancer. It didn't take a fool to see that, for all their arguments, they were a good match.

I don't blame her for her determination. Nino Gaines, it was widely acknowledged back then, was one of the handsomest men in Silver Bay, even wearing a woman's bathing suit. This he did every year, when the servicemen put on a show for the local children. It was a matter of some embarrassment to me that mine was the first he was told to ask for. In the war years I was a strapping lass, tall and square-shouldered; I'm not a lot smaller now. While other women have shrunk, backs bending like question marks, joints knotting with arthritis and osteoporosis, I'm still pretty upright, my limbs strong enough. I say it's the effort of running the old hotel, with its eight bedrooms and only sporadic help. (The crews say that shark cartilage is now famed for its preservative qualities. Their idea of a joke.)

The first time I laid eyes on him I was serving at the hotel bar. He strode in wearing his air-force uniform, appraised me hard enough to make me blush, saw the newspaper picture framed beside the shelves, and asked, "Do *you* bite?"

It wasn't the words that got my father's back up, but the wink that went with them. I was such an innocent that it all flew as swiftly over my head as the warplanes that stacked up over Tomaree Point.

"No," my father said, from behind his newspaper by the till. "But her father does."

"You want to watch that one," he said to my mother later. "Got a mouth as smart as a whip cut." And to me, "You stay away from him, you hear?"

Back in those days, I thought my father's word was gospel. I kept my exchanges with Nino Gaines to the minimum, tried not to blush too hard when he complimented me on my dresses, stifled my giggles when he cracked secret jokes at me from across the bar. I tried not to notice that he came in every night that he wasn't on duty, even though everyone agreed that the best night-life was to be found a good twenty minutes' drive up the coast road. My little sister Norah was just four at the time (it's fair to say her arrival had been something of a surprise to my parents) and she used to gaze up at him like he was a god, largely because he plied her with chocolate and chewing gum.

And then Nino asked me to marry him. Knowing my father's stringent views on servicemen, I had to refuse. We might have been all right, I sometimes think, if the second time he'd asked me he hadn't done it in front of my father.

When Jean died, nearly fifteen years ago now, I thought Nino Gaines might collapse into himself and fade away. I've seen it before with men of that age — their clothes get a little more unkempt, they forget to shave, they start living on packet food. They have a lost quality about them, as if permanently hopeful that someone will step in and take care of them. It was how that generation of men was raised, you see. They never learned to do anything for themselves. But Frank and John John kept him busy, made sure their father was not alone, set up new projects with this grape and that blend. Frank remained at home and John John's wife came twice a week and cooked for them. Yes, Nino Gaines did better than any of us had expected. After a year or so, there was little about him to suggest that he had suffered such a blow. Then one night, over a nice bottle of shiraz merlot, he confided in me that, two weeks before she'd died, Jean had told him she'd celestially box his ears if he moped around by himself when she was gone.

There was a long pause after he said this. When I looked up from my glass he was staring straight at me. That silence burns me now, if I think too hard about it.

"She was quite right," I said, avoiding his eye. "Be silly for you to mope around. Make sure you get out and about. Go see a few friends up north. Best thing for you."

There were other things he said, later, but we didn't talk about those anymore. For many years now Nino had accepted that he and I would never be more than good friends. I treasured his friendship — probably more than he knew — and it was rare that one of us was invited to some event without the other. We had settled into a kind of joke intimacy, a verbal dance that we performed partly because we both enjoyed sparring, partly because neither of us knew how else to hide the slight awkwardness that existed between us. But it was some years since he had talked to me with any intimacy, which suited us both fine.

"Frank was in town yesterday, and bumped into Cherry Dawson," he said.

I had been staring at his place mats, with pencil and watercolor views of London landmarks, which he still put on the table for every meal, as Jean would have asked him to. Her presence was everywhere in that house, even so long after her death. She had favored heavy, ornate furnishings, which were at odds with his personality. I was surprised the house didn't depress him: it was like a funeral home. I had never yet been in his drawing room, with its flock three-piece and antimacassars, without wanting to rip out the whole lot and splash some white paint about.

"She still working for the council?"

"Sure is. She told me the Bullens have sold the old oyster farm. There's a lot of cloak-and-dagger stuff in the town hall about what'll go there instead."

I took a sip of my tea. I hated the fancy floral teacups too. I always wanted to tell him that I'd be happier with a mug, but somehow it would have seemed like a criticism of Jean. "Land as well?"

"A good stretch of the beachfront, including the old hatchery. But it's the oyster beds I'm curious about."

"What can they do with an underwater stretch like that?"

"That's what I'm curious about."

There had been a time, before he got into wine, that Nino had toyed with opening his own oyster farm. He'd considered buying the Bullen place, back when they were struggling against the Japanese imports. He'd asked my father's advice, but Daddy scoffed at him, and said a man who knew as little about the sea as Nino Gaines should leave it well alone. I think he might have changed his mind a little when Nino's vineyards won an award for Australian wine, and again when his turnover headed toward six figures for the first time, but he was not the kind of man to admit it.

"You still got designs on it?"

"Nah. Your old man was probably right." He downed the last of his tea, and looked at his watch. Every evening he climbed onto his quad bike to ride around the estate, inspecting the irrigation system, checking his vines for botrytis bunch rot and powdery mildew, still taking pleasure in the knowledge that he owned all the land he could see.

"The bay's not suitable for much. It could only really be another oyster farm."

"I don't think so." Nino shook his head.

I got the feeling he knew more than he was telling. "Well," I said, when I realized he wasn't going to elucidate, "they'll have to keep the deep-water channel open for the boats to get in and out, so I don't see how it will make too much difference to the crews, whatever they decide to do with it. That reminds me — did I tell you Hannah saw her first whale?"

"Liza finally took her out, did she?"

I grimaced. "No, so keep it under your hat. She went out on *Moby One* with Yoshi and Greg. She was so happy that night I was surprised Liza didn't guess. Went past her door at ten thirty and she was singing along to a whalesong tape."

"She'll have to ease up on that kid eventually," he said. "She's headed for the difficult years. If Liza tries to keep her too close she'll pull right back the other way." He mimed straining at a reel. "But I don't need to tell you that."

I glanced at the clock over the mantelpiece and stood up. I hadn't noticed how late it had got. I'd only meant to bring him a cake.

"Good to see you, Kate." When I made to leave he leaned forward to kiss my cheek, and I held his arm, which might have been a sign of my affection — or a way to keep him at a distance.

My dad had thought he was like all the rest, you see. He swore they were only after my fame and the hotel. It's only now I wonder at a man who couldn't let his daughter believe she was good enough to be loved for herself.

When I got back they were already out at the tables. Liza must have served them, and they sat along the bench, cradling their beer and packets of chips. Yoshi and Lance were playing cards, and all were wrapped in fleeces and hats, muffled against the cool southerly wind. Apparently no one had thought to turn on the burners.

"The butcher's delivery arrived," Liza said, raising a hand. She was studying the local paper. "I wasn't sure what you wanted out so I stuck it all in the fridge."

"I'd better make sure he brought the right order. Last time he got it all wrong," I said.

"Afternoon, all. You're back early."

"One pod, too far off for the customers to see much. Been off with your fancy man, Miss M?"

Greg glanced at my niece as he spoke, but Liza was studiously ignoring him. I guessed she had probably not spoken to him yet and I felt almost sorry. He had meant well, Greg, but sometimes he was his own worst enemy.

When I reached the door I found Mike Dormer in the hallway, flicking through the newspaper I leave out for guests. He looked up when I entered, and nodded.

"Did you get your car?" I was going to remove my coat, then figured I'd probably end up outside again.

"Yup. A . . ." he pulled the keys from his pocket ". . . Holden."

"That'll do you. You feeling anymore human?" He looked weary still. The jet lag, I remembered, would hit in waves.

"I'll get there. I was wondering . . . would it be possible to eat here this evening?"

"Eat now, if you want. I'm about to put some soup out for the crews. Grab your jacket and join us."

I saw his hesitation. I don't know why I pushed him. Perhaps it was because I felt suddenly tired myself and couldn't face the

119

thought of laying out a whole meal for one guest. Perhaps I wanted Liza to see a male face that wasn't Greg's . . .

"This is Mike. He'll be eating with us this evening." They murmured hello. Greg's glance was a little more assessing than the others', and his voice carried a little further after Mike had sat down, his jokes a little more hearty.

Stirring the soup as I listened through the kitchen window, I nearly laughed at his transparency.

I took the food out on two trays. (I don't offer the crews any choice — I'd be there all night.) Each man reached for a bowl and a hunk of bread, hardly looking up as they thanked me. But Mike stood and climbed out of the bench. "Let me help you," he said, taking the second tray.

"Strewth," said Lance, grinning. "Can tell you're not from around here."

"Thank you very much, Mr. Dormer," I said, and sat down beside him.

"Mike. Very kind of you."

"Ah, don't go giving Kathleen ideas," said Greg.

Liza looked up then, and I saw her glance at him.

He seemed embarrassed by all the attention. He sat down, looking somehow out of place in his ironed shirt. He was probably no younger than Greg, but in comparison his skin was curiously unlined. All that time cooped up in an office, I thought.

"Are you not cold in just a shirt?" said Yoshi, leaning forward. "It *is* nearly August."

"It feels quite warm to me," Mike said, glancing around him, as if at the atmosphere.

"You were like that when you first came, Liza." Lance waved a finger at her. "Now she wears her thermals for sunbathing."

"Where do you come from originally?" he asked, but Liza didn't appear to have heard him.

"What do *you* do, Mike?" I said.

"I work in finance," he said.

"Finance," I said a little louder, because I wanted Liza to hear that. I had had a gut feeling that there wasn't anything to worry about.

"A jackeroo rides up to a bar," said Greg, his voice lifting. "As he gets off he walks around the back of his horse, lifts its tail and kisses its arse."

"Greg," I warned.

"Another cowboy stops him as he goes to walk into the bar. He says, 'S'cuse me, mate, did I just see you kiss that horse's arse?'"

"Greg," I said, exasperated.

" 'Sure did,' says the jackeroo. 'Can I ask why?' says the cowboy. 'Sure,' he says. 'I've got chapped lips.' "

He looked around, making sure he had the table's full attention. " 'Does that cure 'em?' " says the cowboy. 'Nope,' says the jackeroo. 'But it sure stops me lickin' em.' " He slapped the table with mirth. As Hannah giggled, I raised my eyes to heaven.

"That's terrible," said Yoshi. "And you told it two weeks ago."

"Wasn't any funnier then," said Lance. I noticed their legs were entwined under the table. They still thought nobody knew.

"D'you know what a jackeroo is, mate?" Greg leaned across the table.

"I can guess. The soup's delicious," said Mike, turning to me. "Do you make it yourself?"

"Probably caught it herself," said Greg.

"How are you finding Silver Bay?" Yoshi was smiling at Mike. "Did you get out at all today?"

He paused while he finished a mouthful of bread. "Didn't get much further than Miss Mostyn — Kathleen's kitchen. What I've seen seems very . . . nice. So . . . ah . . . do you all work on cruise boats?"

"Whalechasers," said Greg. "This time of

year we're out pursuing moving blubber. Of the nonhuman variety."

"But Greg's not fussy."

"You hunt whales?" Mike's spoon stopped in midair. "I thought that was illegal."

"Whale-watching," I butted in. "They take tourists out to look at them. Between now and September the humpbacks travel north to warmer waters, and they pass by not far from here. Then they pass us again on the way back down, a couple of months later."

"We're modern-day whalechasers," said Lance.

Mike looked surprised.

"I hate that phrase," said Yoshi, emphatically. "Makes us sound . . . heartless. We don't chase them. We watch from a safe distance. That phrase gives the wrong impression."

"If it was up to you, Yosh, we'd all be 'licensed marine observers of cetacea whatever-it-is.' "

"*Megaptera novaeangliae,* actually."

"I never thought about it," said Lance. "It's what we've always been called out here."

"I thought that was why you were staying," I said to Mike. "Most people only stop here for the whale-watching."

He glanced down at his bowl. "Well . . .

I'll certainly . . . It sounds like a good thing to do."

"Careful if you go out with Greg, though," said Yoshi, wiping her bread around the edge of her bowl. "He tends to lose the odd passenger. Unintentionally, of course."

"That girl jumped. Bloody madwoman," Greg expostulated. "I had to throw a life belt overboard."

"Ah. But why did she jump?" said Lance. "She was afraid she was about to get — ahem — harpooned by Greg."

Yoshi giggled.

Greg glanced at Liza. "Not true."

"Then how come I saw you taking her number later?"

"I gave her my number," he said slowly, "because she said she might want me to take out a private party."

The table burst into noisy laughter. Liza didn't look up. "Oooh," said Lance. "A private party. Like the private party you gave those two air stewardesses back in April?"

Mike was gazing at my niece. She was saying little, as was common, but her stillness marked her out in the exact opposite way that she had intended. I tried to see her through his eyes: a still-beautiful woman, who was both older and younger than her thirty-two years, her hair scraped back as if she had long since stopped caring what she looked like.

"And you?" he said quietly, leaning toward her across the table. "Do you chase whales too?"

"I don't chase anything," she said, and her face was unreadable, even to me. "I go to where they might be and keep my distance. I find that's generally the wisest course of action."

As their eyes locked, I became aware that Greg was watching. His eyes followed her as she rose from the table, saying she needed to pick up Hannah. Then he turned to Mike, and I hoped that only I could see the wintriness in his smile. "Yup. Generally the best course of action when it comes to Liza," he said, his smile as wide and friendly as that of a shark. "Keep your distance."

Six:
Mike

The bay stretches around an area of four miles between Taree Point and the outlying Break Nose Island, a short drive north from Port Stephens, a large port favored for recreational activities. The waters are clear and protected, perfectly suited to watersports and, in the warmer months, swimming. There is little in the way of a tidal system, making it safe for bathing, and there is a thriving but low-level cottage industry in cetacean-watching.

Silver Bay is three to four hours' drive from Sydney and accessible most of the way by a major highway. The seafront is made up of two half-bays. One, at the northernmost point, is virtually undeveloped, and another, home to Silver Bay proper, is a short drive away, or perhaps a ten-minute walk. This supports a number of small accommodation units and retail outlets, most of whose business comes from residents of Sydney and Newcastle. There is a . . . *I paused, staring at the screen . . .* an existing operation ripe for redevelopment, and numerous buildings with little economic worth. It is highly likely that the owners would see a fair financial settlement as advantageous both to themselves and the local economy.

As far as competition is concerned, there are no local hotels of any size or stature. The only hotel located within the bay is half its original size, having suffered a fire several decades ago. It is run on a bed-and-breakfast basis. There are no recreational facilities, and it would be unlikely to create a problem in terms of competition should the owner be unwilling to sell.

I couldn't present anyone with this, I thought. It was all over the place. And it didn't matter how many facts and figures I had gleaned from the local planning department and chamber of commerce, I still felt as though I was writing about something I knew nothing about.

I had discovered almost as soon as I had arrived that this was not a straightforward site. I was used to square footage in the City; executive apartments, razed seventies office blocks waiting for a new health-and-fitness chain, new prestige headquarters. On such jobs I could go in, look around unobserved, work out the local rental yields against property prices, the disposable income of nearby residents, and, at the end of the day, disappear.

This, I had known from the moment I stepped into Greg's beer-can-filled truck, would be different.

Here, I was acutely aware of my visibility. Even in a sweatshirt and jeans I felt as if my lack of a salt crust gave away my intentions. And considering how empty it was, the area seemed too inhabited somehow, too influenced by its people. It was a new experience for me, but somehow I couldn't see straight.

I sighed, opened a new document and began to type in headlines: Geography, Economic Climate, Local Industry, Competition. I thought, with a little resentment, about my new two-seater sports car, the one I had promised myself on the back of this deal; the car that was waiting for me, paid for and polished, on the dealer's showroom. I consulted my watch. I had been sitting there for almost two hours and strung together three paragraphs. It was time for another tea break.

Kathleen Mostyn had given me what she

described as her "good" room, some other guests having recently departed, and the previous night had brought up a tray with tea- and coffee-making equipment. She wouldn't have given it to the last occupants, she muttered, because they "would no doubt have complained that the water didn't boil fast enough." She was the kind of woman who in England would have been running a school, or perhaps a stately home. The kind who makes you think "Age shall not wither her," sharp-eyed, fiercely busy, wit undimmed. I liked her. I guess I like strong women: I find it easier not to have to think for two. My sister would have other theories, no doubt.

I boiled the kettle and stood at the window, preparing a cup. The room was not luxurious but was oddly comfortable; the polar opposite to most of the executive-class hotel rooms I stay in. The walls were whitewashed, and the wood-framed double bed was made up with white linen and a blue-and white-striped blanket. There was an aged leather armchair and a Persian rug that might once have been valuable. I worked at a small scrubbed-pine desk with a kitchen chair. I had the feeling, when I looked around the Silver Bay Hotel, that Kathleen Mostyn had long since decided that decorating for guests required far too much in the way of imagination, and had chosen instead to whitewash everything. "Easy to clean, easy to paint over," I could imagine her saying.

I realized pretty quickly that I was her only long-term guest. The hotel had the air of somewhere that might once have been pretty smart, but had long since settled for pragmatic, then decided it didn't want much in the way of company anyway. Most of the furniture had been selected for practicality rather than some great aesthetic. Pictures were largely confined to old sepia-tinted photographs of the hotel in its former glory, or generic seaside watercolors. Mantelpieces and shelves, I had discovered, often contained odd collections of pebbles or driftwood, a touch that in other hotels might have signified stylistic pretensions, but here were more likely just the day's finds, needing a home.

My room looked straight out across the bay with not even a road between the house and the beach. The previous night I had slept with the window open, the sound of the waves lulling me into my first decent night's sleep for months, and I had been dimly aware, as dawn broke, of the whalers' trucks, their tires hissing on the wet sand,

and the fishermen heading back and forth across the shingle to the jetty.

When I told Nessa about the setting, she had accused me of being a jammy bugger and said she'd given her father an earful for sending me away. "You wouldn't believe how much I've got to organize," she'd said, her voice half accusing, as if my presence in London had been of any help.

"You know, we could do this differently," I ventured, when she had run out of complaints. "We could fly off somewhere and get married on a beach."

The ensuing silence was lengthy enough for me to wonder what it was costing.

"After all this?" Her voice was disbelieving. "After all the planning I've done you want to just fly off somewhere? Since when did you start having opinions?"

"Forget I said anything."

"Do you know how hard this is? I'm trying to work and do all this and half the bloody guests haven't even replied to their invitations. It's so rude. I'm going to have to chase up everyone myself."

"Look, I'm sorry. You know I didn't ask to be here. I'm working on this deal as hard as I can and I'll be back before you know it."

She was mollified. Eventually. She seemed to cheer up when I reminded her it was winter over here. Besides, Nessa knows I'm not a holiday person. I have never yet managed to lie on a beach for anything resembling a week. Within days I'm scouting inland, looking at the local paper for business opportunities. "Love you," she said, before she rang off. "Work hard so you can come home soon."

But it was hard to work in an environment that conspired to tell even me to do the opposite. The Internet connection, routed through the phone line, was slow and temperamental. The newspapers, with the city pages, didn't arrive until nearly noon. Meanwhile the beach, with its elegant curve and white sand, demanded to be walked on. The wooden jetty called out to be sat on, bare legs dangling into the sea. The long bleached table where the whale crews relaxed on their return spoke of ice-cold beers and hot chips. Even putting on my work shirt that morning hadn't motivated me.

I opened an e-mail and began to type: *"Dennis. Hope you're feeling OK. Went to the planning dept yesterday and met Mr. Reilly, as you suggested. He seemed to like the look of the plans and said the only possible problems were —"*

I jumped at a knock then slammed my

laptop shut.

"Can I come in?"

I opened the door to find Hannah, Liza McCullen's daughter. She was holding out a sandwich on a plate. "Auntie K thought you might be hungry. She wasn't sure if you wanted to come down."

I took it from her. How could it be lunchtime already? "That was kind. Tell her thank you."

She peered around the door and caught sight of my computer. "What are you doing?"

"Sending a few e-mails."

"Is that connected to the Internet?"

"Just about."

"I'm desperate for a computer. Loads of my friends at school have them." She hovered on one leg. "Did you know my aunt is on the Internet? I heard her telling my mum."

"I think lots of hotels are on the Internet," I said.

"No," she said. "*She's* on the Internet. Herself. She doesn't like to talk about it now but she used to be famous around here for catching sharks."

I tried to imagine the old lady wrestling with some *Jaws*-like creature. Oddly, it wasn't as hard as I'd imagined.

The child was hovering in the doorway, plainly in no hurry to leave. She had that light, gangly look that girls get just before they burst into adulthood; the opaque quality where, for a couple of months, or even years, it's impossible to tell whether they're going to be great beauties, or whether hormones and genetics will conspire to pull out that nose a little too far, or make that chin a bit heavy. I suspected in her case that it would be the former.

I looked down, in case she thought I was staring at her. She was very like her mother.

"Mr. Dormer."

"Mike."

"Mike. When you're not too busy — if you're not too busy — one day, can I have a go on your computer? I'd really like to see that picture of my aunt."

The sun had cast the whole bay in radiance, the shadows shrinking, the sidewalks and sand bouncing reflected light back into the air. Since I'd arrived at Kingsford Smith, Sydney's airport, I'd felt like a fish out of water. It was nice to have someone ask me to do something familiar. "Tell you what," I said, "we could have a look now."

We were sitting there for almost an hour, during which time I decided she was a sweet kid. A little young for her age in some ways

— she was much less interested in her appearance than the London kids I knew, or pop culture, music, all that stuff — yet she carried an air of wistfulness, and a maturity that sat awkwardly on such a young frame. I'm not usually great with kids — I find it hard to know what to talk to them about — but I found myself enjoying Hannah McCullen's company.

She asked me about London, about my house, whether I had any pets. She found out pretty quickly that I was due to get married, and fixed her big, dark, serious eyes on me as she asked, with some gravity, "Are you sure she's the right person?"

I was a little taken aback, but I felt she deserved to be answered with equal gravity. "I think so. We've been together a long time. We know each other's strengths and weaknesses."

"Are you nice to her?"

I thought for a minute. "I hope I'm nice to everyone."

She grinned, a more childish grin. "You do *seem* quite nice," she conceded. Then we turned to the important business of the computer. We looked up — and printed out — two different photographs of the young woman in the bathing suit with the shark, and a couple of pieces about her by people she had evidently never met. We visited the website for a well-known boy band, a tourism site for New Zealand, then a string of facts and figures about humpback whales that Hannah said she already knew by heart. I learned that a whale's lungs are the size of a small car, that a newborn calf can weigh up to one and a half tons and that whale milk has the consistency of cottage cheese. I have to admit that I could have done without knowing that last one.

"Do you go out with your mum much to see the whales?"

"I'm not allowed," she said. I heard the twang of an Australian accent, noted the way that her sentence lilted upward at the end. "My mum doesn't like me going out on the water." Suddenly I remembered the fierce exchange between Liza McCullen and Greg when I had arrived. I do my best to stay out of other people's private business, but I vaguely remembered that it had been something about Hannah and a boat.

She shrugged, as if she was trying to convince herself she didn't care. "She's trying to make sure I'm safe. We . . ." She looked up at me, as if wondering whether to say something, then apparently changed her mind. "Can we find some pictures of England on your computer? I sort of remember it, but not very much."

"We certainly can. What was it you wanted to look at?" I began to type in the words.

Liza McCullen appeared. "I was wondering where you were," she said, standing in the open doorway. She looked from one of us to the other, and the way she did so made me feel vaguely guilty, as if I had been caught doing something wrong. A second later, I felt really pissed off.

"Hannah brought me a sandwich," I said, a little pointedly. "Then she asked if she could look at my computer."

"There are twenty-three thousand one hundred Web pages for humpback whales on the Internet," Hannah said triumphantly.

Liza softened. "And I suppose she wanted to check out every one." There was the hint of an apology in her voice. "Hannah, lovey, come and leave Mr. Dormer alone now."

She was wearing the same outfit she had had on the last two times I had seen her: dark green canvas jeans, a fleece and a yellow storm jacket. Her hair, as then, was scraped back into a ponytail, and the ends had been bleached white, although her natural color was much darker. I thought of Nessa, who, for the first year of our relationship, used to get up half an hour earlier than me to do her hair and put on her makeup before I could see her. It had taken me almost six months to work out how she had slept in lip gloss without leaving it all over the pillows.

"I'm sorry if she's been bothering you," she said, without fully meeting my eye.

"She hasn't bothered me in the slightest. It's been a pleasure. If you want, Hannah, I'll bring the computer downstairs and set it up for you to use when I'm out."

Hannah's eyes widened. "Really? By myself? Mum! I could do all the stuff for my project."

I didn't look at her mother. I'd guessed what her response would be — and if I didn't catch her eye, I couldn't acknowledge it. It was no big deal, after all. I unhooked the computer, having first closed all my password-protected files.

"Are you going out now?"

A thought had occurred to me. Something Kathleen had mentioned earlier that morning.

"I am," I said, placing the laptop in Hannah's arms. "If your mother will take me."

Given that Silver Bay's meager economy relied almost entirely on tourism, and that, according to local-government figures, the average monthly wage was equivalent to less than a thousand pounds, you'd have thought that Liza McCullen would be glad to take out a private charter. You'd think that a woman whose boat had just cost nearly two hundred dollars in repairs, who had no trips lined up until Monday and whose aunt had stated several times that she was much happier on the water than she was on land would jump at the chance to take a commercial trip out to sea. Especially when I offered to pay the equivalent of four people's fares — the minimum the boats needed allegedly to make a trip economically viable.

"I'm not going out this afternoon," she said, hands deep in her pockets.

"Why? I'm offering you almost a hundred and eighty dollars. That's got to be worth your while."

"I'm not going out this afternoon."

"Is there a storm coming?"

"Auntie K said it was set fair," said Hannah.

"Have you got some special knowledge about the whales? Have they gone on a day trip somewhere else? I'm not going to ask for my money back if they don't show, Ms. McCullen. I just want to get out on the water."

"Go on, Mum. Then I can use Mike's

computer."

I couldn't quite suppress a smile.

She still wouldn't look at me. "I'm not taking you out. Find someone else."

"The others are big boats, right? Full of tourists. Not my scene."

"I'll ring Greg for you. See if he's going out this afternoon."

"Isn't he the one who loses people off the side of his boat?"

At this point Kathleen had arrived and was standing on the landing, watching the scene in my room with quiet surprise.

"I'll give you a ticket for Monday," Liza said finally. "I've got three other people going out then. You'll have a better time."

For some reason I had started to enjoy myself. "No, I won't," I said. "I'm antisocial. And I want to go this afternoon."

Finally she looked directly at me and shook her head, a little defiantly. "No," she said.

I was aware that something about this scene had struck Kathleen. She was standing behind Liza, saying nothing but watching intently. "Okay . . . three hundred dollars," I said, pulling the money out of my wallet. "That's a full boat, right? I'll pay you three hundred dollars and you can tell me everything there is to know about whales." I heard Hannah's sharp intake of breath.

Liza looked at her aunt. Kathleen raised her eyebrows. I was aware that the atmosphere in the room had become a vacuum. "Three fifty," I said.

Hannah was giggling.

I wasn't about to let go. I'm not sure what had got hold of me by then. Perhaps it was boredom. Perhaps it was her reticence. Perhaps it was because Greg had attempted to warn me off, which had made me curious. But I was going out in that boat if it killed me.

"Five hundred dollars. Here, cash in your hand." I pulled out the other notes. I didn't wave them at her, just held them in my closed hand.

Liza stared at me.

"And I'll expect a lot of coffee and biscuits."

Kathleen snorted.

"Your money," said Liza, eventually. "You'll need soft-soled shoes and a warm sweater, not that townie getup you're wearing. And I'll be leaving in fifteen minutes." She took the money from my fingers and stuffed it into her jeans pocket. Her sideways glance at me said she thought I was insane.

But I knew what I was doing. As Dennis

always says, everyone and everything has its price.

Liza's boat was the only one on the jetty. She walked a couple of steps ahead of me, not indulging in small talk, except with the little dog so I had a chance to look around as we approached it. There was little in Silver Bay, even around the jetty: a café, a souvenir shop, whose turnover was obviously slow — the window display was dusty — and a seafood market, situated toward the main town and housed in the most modern building in the bay. It had its own car park, and was a short walk away, which meant that the customers who stopped for fresh fish were unlikely to walk back to use any other facilities — a poorly thought-out decision. I would have insisted they place it right opposite the jetty.

Although it was a Saturday, few people were about. The tourists, if there were any, must be out on the water in the other whale-watching boats. The few motels I saw dotted along the main road out of town forlornly advertised their available rooms, breakfast included, but the bay had the air of a place that did not expect much out of season. That said, neither did it look particularly troubled. It lacked the peculiarly sullen, abandoned aspect of an English seaside town in winter; the bright sunshine lent it a jovial air, while its inhabitants seemed uncommonly cheerful.

Except Liza.

She had ordered me aboard, made me stand and watch while she ran through a safety checklist in a flat monotone, then rather grudgingly, I thought, asked me if I wanted her to put on the coffee. "Point me toward it, and I'll do it," I said.

"Bend your knees when you walk around, and when you come up," she said, turning her back to me. "Don't feed the gulls. It encourages them to dive-bomb the passengers, and they mess everywhere." Then, bounding up the steps, she was gone.

The lower deck had two tables and chairs, some plastic-covered benches and a glass case, with chocolate, whale videos and tapes and seasickness tablets for sale. A handwritten sign warned customers that it was wise not to make their drinks too hot as spillages often occurred. I found the tea and coffee area and made two coffees, noting the raised edges of the sideboard, the secured tea and coffee holders, presumably to stop the pots tipping off in high seas. I did not want to think too hard about the kind of seas that might send boiling coffeepots flying, the kind that apparently kept Hannah ashore, but then the engines started, and I had to hold on to the side to keep steady. We were headed out to sea at some pace.

I made my way unsteadily up the flight of stairs to the back of the boat. Liza was standing at the wheel, her little dog draped across the helm behind it; obviously a favored post. I handed her a mug and felt the wind on my face, tasted the faint tang of salt on my lips.

This is just part of the job, I thought, trying to justify what I had done. But it would be an interesting one to put through on expenses.

Liza's gaze was fixed on the sea, and I wondered why she had been so determined not to take me out. I wasn't aware that I had offended her in any way. Then again, she seemed like the kind of woman who instinctively rebelled against being corralled. And I had been pretty determined.

"How long have you been doing this?" I had to shout to be heard over the engine.

"Five years. Getting on for six."

"Is it a good business?"

"It does for us."

"Is this your own boat?"

"It used to be Kathleen's, but she gave it to me."

"Generous of her." I can count the times I have been on a boat on one hand so I was interested in everything. I asked her the names of a few parts of the boat, which was port and which starboard (I've always mixed them up), what you called the various instruments. "So what's a boat this size worth?"

"Depends on the boat."

"What's this boat worth?"

"Does everything for you revolve around money?"

It wasn't said in an unfriendly manner, but it gave me pause. I took a sip of my coffee and tried again. "You come from England."

"Is that what Hannah told you?"

"No — it's what the, ah, whale crews said. That afternoon at the table. And I can — you know — hear it."

She thought for a moment. "Yes. We used to live in England."

"Do you miss it?"

"No."

"Did you come out here specially?"

"Specially?"

"To do whale-watching?"

"Not really."

Was she like this with all her customers? Bad divorce, I speculated. Perhaps she just didn't like men.

"Do you see lots of whales?"

"If I go to the right places."

"Is it a good way of life?"

She took her hand off the wheel and faced me, suspicious. "You ask a lot of questions."

I was determined not to bite back. I had the feeling she was not a naturally antagonistic person. "You're a rarity. I don't imagine there are many female English skippers around here."

"How would you know? There could be thousands of us." She allowed a small smile. "Actually, Port Stephens is famous for them." This, I guessed, was the closest she would come to humor.

"Okay, a question for you. Why did you spend so much money just to go on a boat trip?"

Because it was the only way I could get you to take me. But I didn't say it aloud. "Would you have done it for less?" I asked, changing tack.

She grinned. "Of course."

After that something changed. Liza McCullen relaxed, or perhaps decided that I wasn't as objectionable, or as threatening, as she had initially decided, and the *froideur* that had hung over our trip out of the bay dissipated.

We didn't say much. I sat on the wooden bench behind her and gazed out to sea, quietly enjoying someone else's competence at a skill I know nothing about. She spun the wheel, checked the dials, radioed one of the other boats, fed Milly, the dog, the odd biscuit. Sometimes she would point at a stretch of land or a creature that held some interest, and elaborate a little. But I couldn't tell you now what she said. Because although she was not the most beautiful woman I had ever seen, and she appeared to pay no more attention to how she looked than she did to how she spoke, and although half the time she was turned away or scowling at me, I found Liza McCullen oddly compelling. If I hadn't already worked out that she would have been sensitive to it, I would have stared at her. That's not like me at all.

Nessa will tell you I'm no great psychologist. I don't care much what makes people tick if I don't need to know, but I had never met someone so determined to give away so little. Every conversational snippet dragged itself out of her. She seemed to make every personal admission under pain of torture. I asked her how she took her coffee and she frowned as if I had asked about her underwear. When she told me, "No sugar," it was like a confession. And all tinged with a slight . . . melancholy?

"Lance says they've sighted a female about three miles on," she said, after we had been at sea about half an hour. "You happy to keep going?"

"Sure," I said. I'd forgotten we were meant to be searching for whales. If you're not used to being on the ocean, the first thing that strikes you is the sheer bloody scale of it. It's like a landscape in itself. When you're out so far that three-quarters of your view is endless water, your eye becomes lost in its vast movement, drawn by an illuminated patch where the sun shines through cloud, or by the distant area where white horses have sprung up. I can't say I didn't feel nervous — I'm used to dry land — but once I'd got over the instability, the crashing and creaking that came from beneath my feet, I liked the aloneness, the boat's freedom to move unencumbered by other people. I liked seeing Liza's face lose its tense watchfulness to take on the openness of the sea and sky.

"That's where we're headed," she said, spinning the wheel, one hand raised against the glare. I could just make out the birds, dive-bombing in an area where it was impossible to see anything. "That means there are fish. And where there are fish there are often whales."

By then we had seen the others. She pointed out Greg's boat, which looked about the same size as hers, and further away what she described as *Moby Two*.

"There!" she said. "Blow!"

"Blow what?" I queried. That made her laugh.

"There."

I couldn't see where she was pointing and squinted. Perhaps unconsciously she took my arm and drew it toward her. "Look!" she said, trying to get me to focus along it. "We'll go a bit closer."

I couldn't see a thing. It would have been frustrating, except that I was diverted by the childish pleasure on her face. This was a Liza McCullen I had not yet seen in six days of living at the hotel. A wide, ready smile, a lift in her voice.

"Oh, she's a beauty. I bet you there's a calf too. I've got a feeling . . ."

It was as if she had forgotten her earlier chill toward me. I heard her on the radio: *"Ishmael* to *Moby Two* — our girl is port-side to you, about a mile and a half ahead. Got a feeling she may have a calf with her so go steady, okay?"

"Moby Two to *Ishmael.* Spotted her, Liza.

Giving her a wide berth."

"We stay at least a hundred meters away," she explained. "We make that three hundred when calves are involved. It all depends on the mother. Some are curious — they'll bring the babies right up to see us, and that's different. But I always feel . . . I don't like to encourage it." She looked directly at me. "You can't guarantee that the next boat they meet is going to be as friendly. Okay! Here we go!"

I hung on and, as if in some delicately choreographed formation, the three boats moved closer together until we were near enough to make out the waving passengers on board each one. The seas were quiet as the engines were turned off, and I stood next to Liza as we waited for the whale to show herself again.

"Will she definitely come back up?"

I needn't have asked. When that great head come out of the water, not thirty feet from us, an involuntary *"whoa"* escaped me. It's not that I have never seen a picture of a whale, or couldn't have guessed what it looked like. It's just that meeting a creature so huge, so unlikely, in its own environment, throws you in a way I find hard to convey.

"Look!" Liza was shouting. "There it is! Look down!" And just visible, sheltered half under its mother, I saw a flash of gray or blue, which was the calf. They went past our boat twice, then shouts from the other boats told us she had gone to look at them too.

I was grinning like an idiot. When Liza smiled back at me, there was something triumphant in it, as if she were saying, "You see?" as if there was something she knew. When its weirdly long fin appeared, she laughed. "She's waving," she said, then laughed harder when I found myself tentatively waving back.

"She's belly up — it means she's comfortable with us. You know she and the baby use those pectoral fins to stroke each other?"

As we sat, Liza spotted two more in the distance. I was dimly aware of the radio conversation between the three boats, the exclamations of pleasure at this unexpected haul. When she turned back to me, her face was illuminated. "Want to hear something magic?" she said suddenly.

She nipped down into the galley and emerged with a strange-looking thing on a cable. She plugged one end into a box on the side, then threw it into the water. "Listen," she said, flicking a few switches. "Hydrophone. There might be escorts nearby."

For several minutes, there was nothing. I stared out to sea, trying to spot the whale, hearing nothing but the sound of the water meeting the sides of the boat, the wheeling birds overhead, and occasionally, brought over on a soft wind, the other boats' passengers. Then there was a low moan, drawn out, almost eerie. A sound like nothing I had ever heard. It sent shivers up my spine.

"Beautiful, isn't it?"

I stared at her. "That's a whale?"

"A male. They all sing the same song, you know. They've done research into it — it's eighteen minutes long and each year all the whales in the pod sing the same song. If a new whale comes along with a new song, they pick it up instead. Can you imagine them down there teaching each other?" Suddenly I saw Hannah in her, her face lit with excitement at the prospect of using my computer. I had been wrong when I said Liza McCullen wasn't beautiful: when she smiled she was stunning.

The smile evaporated. "What the —"

It was a thumping sound, regular, insistent. For a moment I wondered whether it was someone's engine, but then it grew louder, and I knew it had nothing to do with the microphone. Two large boats came round the headland, strung with bunting, packed with passengers. Loud music emanated from four oversized speakers on the top deck, and even from our distance away, the clink of glasses and the hysterical laughter of the well lubricated were audible.

"Not again," said Liza. "The noise," she said. "It destroys them. They get confused . . . especially the babies. And there are too many boats. She'll be frightened." She got on to the radio, fiddling with the dial. "*Ishmael* to *Disco Ship,* or whatever your name is. Turn your music down. You are too loud. Do you hear me? You're too loud." As we listened to the static of the radio, I stared at the water. Nothing broke the surface now. No sound could be heard above the insistent thud of the beat, drawing closer.

Her brow wrinkling as she realized the speed at which it was approaching. "*Ishmael* to unidentified large cat, east-northeast of Break Nose Island. Turn off your engines and your music. You are close to a whale cow and calf, possibly one male too. You are going too fast, putting you at risk of collision, and your noise is likely to cause them distress. Do you read me?"

I stood there helplessly as she tried twice more to contact them. It was unlikely, I thought, that they could hear anything above the noise of that bass.

"*Ishmael* to *Suzanne* — Greg, can you call the coast guard? The police? See if they can send out a speedboat. They're too close."

"Got you, Liza. *Moby Two* is headed around to see if they can steer them off course."

"*Moby Two* to *Ishmael.* I can't see our whales, Liza. Hope to God they're headed the other way."

"What can I do?" I said. I had no idea of the significance of what she was saying, but the anxiety in the atmosphere was clear.

"Hold this," she said, and handed me the wheel. She started the engines. "Now, steer for *Disco Billy* over there, and I'll tell you when to turn. I'm going to make sure we don't hit anything as we go."

She didn't give me a chance to say no. She ran downstairs, then came up with a load of things under her jacket. I made out a bullhorn, but I was too busy focusing on the wheel to notice much. It felt unfamiliar in my hands, and daunting to be going at such speed, the waves bouncing under us. The little dog had picked up on the tension and stood up, whining.

We were about a hundred feet from the ship when Liza instructed me to keep a parallel course. Then she ran to the front, shouting at me to stay where I was.

She leaned over the rail, a bullhorn in her hand. "*Night Star Two,* you are too loud and traveling too fast. Please turn your music down. You are in an area inhabited by migrating whales."

God knows how they could have been so drunk in the middle of the afternoon. The dancing figures on the top deck reminded me of those holidays for young people where the object of day trips is to get them as inebriated and incapable as possible. Was there an Australian equivalent?

"*Night Star Two,* we have alerted the coast guard and National Parks and Wildlife Service. Turn your music down and leave the area at once."

If there was a skipper, he wasn't listening. One of the stewards — a young guy in a red polo shirt — gave Liza the finger and disappeared. A moment later the music was noticeably louder. There was a faint cheer aboard, as more people began to dance. Liza stared at the boat, then reached down. From where I was I could no longer see what she was doing. I stared at the name on the side of the big boat. Then it hit me.

I pulled my phone from my pocket, as the radio hissed into life: "Liza? Liza? It's Greg. The Parks people are on their way. C'mon, let's head back. The fewer of us moving around the better for the whales."

I put my phone back into my pocket, then stared at the receiver for a moment. I picked it up. I squeezed it tentatively. "Hello?"

"Hello?"

"*Suzanne* to *Ishmael,* do you read me?"

"It's — ah — Mike Dormer."

There was a brief silence, then Greg said, "What's she doing up front?"

"I don't know," I confessed.

I heard him mutter something, which might have been an expletive, and then there was an explosion. I leapt to the side of the boat just in time to see a huge flare headed into the air angled at no more than twenty feet above the disco ship.

Liza was standing at the prow, loading something long and thin into some kind of launcher.

"You're not going to bloody shoot them?" I yelled at her. But she didn't seem to hear me. My heart thumping, I saw people backing away rapidly from the top deck of the other ship, heard the shouts of concern and a man screaming abuse at her. The dog was barking wildly. Then I saw Liza load another flare, point it high into the air and stumble backward as, with a huge *crack,* she sent it into the sky not quite high enough above them.

As my ears rang and the disco ship's engines finally swung it around and propelled it the other way, I heard another voice come over the radio: a gravelly one, filled with disbelief and admiration. "*Moby Two* to *Ishmael. Moby Two* to *Ishmael.* Jesus Christ, Liza. You've really gone and done it now."

Seven:
Liza

By the time we reached the jetty Kathleen was already shouting at me, her rigid, upright body bristling with indignation. I secured *Ishmael,* helped Milly ashore and walked briskly toward her. "I know," I said.

She raised her hands in a gesture of exasperation. "Do you realize what you've done? Are you totally insane, girl?"

I stopped and pushed my hair off my face. "I wasn't thinking."

The anxiety on her face mirrored my own. In fact, I could have kicked myself. I had thought of nothing else for the twenty minutes it had taken us to come back to the bay.

"They were straight on to the Water Police, Liza. For all we know they're on their way over here now."

"But what can they prove?"

"Well, put it this way, you let the second

one off while they were on the marine radio."

I was a fool, I knew it, and Kathleen did too. Against every rule of marine safety, against all common sense, I had loaded those two distress flares into their launchers, and positioned them just close enough to scare the boat's passengers. Flares were notoriously unpredictable. If one had misfired . . . If Search and Rescue had caught sight of the other . . . But while I knew it was a stupid thing to do, how else could I have got those boats away? And how could I tell my aunt that if I had held a gun, instead of a distress flare, I would have shot at them instead?

I closed my eyes. It was only when I opened them again that I remembered I hadn't waited for Mike Dormer to disembark. The crunch of his shoes in the dirt heralded his arrival next to us, his brown hair disheveled and damp from the speed of the journey back. He looked a little shaken. Kathleen's face softened. "Why don't you go inside, Mike? I'll make some tea."

He began to protest.

"Really," she said, and there was something steely in her tone. "We need a few moments alone."

I felt his eyes on me. Then he took a few

reluctant paces away and stroked Milly, as if unwilling to go altogether.

"What do I do?" I whispered.

"Let's not overreact," she said. "They might just caution you."

"But they'll want to take down my details. There might be some kind of database . . ."

I could see from Kathleen's face that she'd already considered this. And hadn't yet been able to find an answer. I felt a rising swell of panic in my chest. I glanced behind me to where the *Suzanne* and *Moby Two* were berthing. "I could just go," I said. I had a sudden wild notion of loading myself, Hannah and Milly into the wagon. But then the sound of a different kind of engine drew my attention to the other end of the bay. Headed up the coast road, bearing its distinctive headlamps and logo, I saw the white pickup truck of the New South Wales Police.

"Oh, Christ," I said.

"Smile," she said. "For God's sake, smile and say it was an accident."

There were two officers, and they climbed out of the cab with the relaxed air that belies serious intent, their badges glinting in the late-afternoon sun. I had always been excessively careful to stay on the right side of Australian law, could not even claim knowledge of a parking ticket, but even I knew that firing a distress flare illegally and at another vessel had not been a good move.

"Afternoon, ladies," said the taller man, tipping his cap as he approached. He looked at us, letting his eyes linger on my storm jacket, the keys in my hand. "Greg," he added.

"Officer Trent," said my aunt, and smiled. "Beautiful afternoon."

"It is," he agreed. The creases in the sleeves of his blue shirt were as sharp as knives. He gestured down the jetty toward *Ishmael*. "That yours?"

"It certainly is," said my aunt, before I could speak. "*Ishmael*. Registered to me. Has been for seventeen years."

He looked at her then back at me. "Had a call from two other vessels who say distress flares were fired at them from a boat matching her description this afternoon. Could you tell me anything about that?"

I wanted to speak, but the sight of that blue uniform had stuck my tongue to the roof of my mouth. I was dimly aware of Mike Dormer, watching from a few feet away, and that the policeman was now standing squarely in front of me, waiting for an answer. "I . . ."

Greg was beside me. "Yes, mate," he said

161

firmly, tipping back the peak of his cap. "That'd be my fault."

The policeman turned to him.

"I was out with a group of whale-watchers. I knew the kids would be trouble, but I wasn't watching them close enough. While I had my back turned, searching for the whales, the little buggers let off two flares."

"Kids?" the officer said skeptically.

"I knew I shouldn't have let them on," Greg said, and paused to light a cigarette. "Liza here said they'd be trouble. But we like to let all the kids see the whales and dolphins. Educate them, you know." He met my eye briefly, and what I saw in it filled me with gratitude, and a little shame.

"Why didn't you notify Marine Rescue, let them know what had happened? You know what would have happened if we'd instituted a search-and-rescue?"

"I'm sorry, mate. I just wanted to get back here soon as possible, so they couldn't do anything else. I had other passengers aboard, you know . . ."

"Which boat is yours again, Greg?"

Greg gestured. Our boats were both forty-eight-foot cruisers. Since I had helped him paint out his homemade graffiti, they bore a band of the same color.

"Okay, so what were the kids' names?"

The policeman took out his notebook.

Kathleen broke in: "We don't keep records. If we wrote down the details of every person we took out on our boats we'd never get out on the water." She placed a hand on Trent's arm. "Look, Officer, you know we're not some fly-by-night operation, working off this jetty. My family's been in this bay for more than seventy years. You're not going to penalize us for one pair of idiots, are you?"

"Why weren't your flares secured, Greg? They should be in a locked box if you've got kids mucking around belowdecks."

Greg shook his head. "Little buggers had my keys from my pocket. I always carry a spare set, see? Just to be on the safe side."

I was sure the policeman didn't believe a word of it: he frowned at the three of us in turn, and I tried hard to look aggrieved rather than terrified. He peered at his notebook again, then up at me. "The caller said a woman was firing at them."

"Long hair," said Greg, quick as you like. "You can't tell them apart, these days. Bloody hippies. Look, Officer, it was my fault. I was minding the wheel and it was my responsibility. I guess I took my eye off the ball. No harm done, though, eh?"

I tried hard to keep my breath steady in

my chest, and began to examine a small cut on my hand. It was something to do.

"You realize the use of a distress flare as a weapon is an offense under the Firearms and Dangerous Weapons Act, leading to a charge of assault under the NSW Crimes Act?"

"That's what I told them," said Greg. "Big mistake, that was. It meant they legged it as soon as we got back here."

"That's two thousand dollars and/or twelve months in jail. And you could be charged under the Maritime Services Act if we wanted to be really picky."

Greg appeared penitent. I had never seen him so conciliatory with a policeman.

"This better not have involved alcohol. I've not forgotten your caution from June," the man went on.

"Officer, you can breathalyze me, if you want. I don't touch a drop while I'm working."

Suddenly I ached for him. I sensed his humiliation — and I was responsible for it.

The two policemen glanced back at their truck. The shorter one turned away to take a message on his radio.

"Tell you what," said Kathleen, "why don't I get some tea and you can decide what you want to do while it's brewing?

Officer Trent, do you still take sugar?"

At that point Mike Dormer approached. My heart leapt into my mouth. Go away, I told him silently. He had no idea what we'd told them. If he opened his mouth and blurted out the truth we'd all be sunk.

"Actually," he said, "can I say something?"

"Not now, Mike," said Kathleen, briskly. "We're a bit busy."

"Go on, Officer," said Greg. He stepped forward, placing himself between Mike and the police. "I'll take any kind of test you want. Blood, breathalyzer, whatever."

"I just wanted to tell the police something," Mike said, louder. I thought, with horror, that I had no idea how he felt about what I'd done. I hadn't spoken a word to him the whole way back, my brain humming with the reality of what I'd done, wanting to get to shore as fast as I could.

The same thought had occurred to Kathleen, I could tell. But it was too late. He was pulling something from his pocket.

"I don't think this is anything you can help with, Mike," she said, firmly. But he appeared not to hear her.

"Mike —" I felt sick.

"While we were out on the water," he said, "some kind of party boat came close by. It was making enough noise and commotion

165

to frighten the whales. I believe there are regulations about such things."

The first policeman crossed his arms. "That'd be right," he said.

Mike allowed himself a small smile. He held up his mobile phone. The Englishness in his voice gave him a kind of gentle authority. "Well, I thought you might like the evidence. I filmed it all on my phone. You can hear the level of noise." As we gaped, his little mobile phone displayed a clip of the *Night Star,* showing the speed at which it had been traveling, revealing the outline of the revelers on deck. You could hear the thump of the music. I had never seen anything like it.

"The whales seemed distressed by it. Not that I'm an expert or anything," Mike said.

"Look," I said, pointing at the little image, "you can see it's around by the headland. We did try to radio the coast guard, but they didn't get out there in time." My voice was squeaky with relief.

"I can send you a copy," said Mike, "if you want to use it to prosecute anyone."

The two policemen examined the image, nonplussed. "Not sure what you'd send it to," said one, "but give us your number and we'll let you know. Who are you?"

"Oh, I'm just a guest," Mike said. "Michael Dormer. Here on holiday from England. I can get my passport, if you like." He held out his hand. I'm not sure that many people offer to shake hands with the police out here. The stunned faces that accompanied the handshake suggested not.

"That won't be necessary just now. Well, we'll be getting on. But make sure you lock up your flares securely, people, or you'll be getting another visit. A less friendly one."

"Two locks," said Greg, waving his keys.

"Thank you, Officers," said Kathleen. She stepped after them. "You take care, now."

I couldn't speak. As they climbed back into the truck and reversed, a long, quivering breath escaped from somewhere high in my chest and I realized my legs were shaking.

"Thank you," I mouthed at Greg, and nodded at Mike. Then I had to bolt for the back of the house because I had run out of words altogether.

There are many things I love about Australia. I'm not about to spout off like a parody of the Brit who never went home, because it's not the usual things — the weather, the light, or the wide-open spaces — although they're a bonus. It's not the good food and wine, or the scenery, or the leisurely pace of life, although those things have made bringing up my daughter here more of a pleasure. For me it's that, in a quiet corner like Silver Bay, you can live out your life without anyone paying you the slightest attention.

Despite our shared heritage Australians, I had quickly discovered, are unlike the British in many ways. They will accept you at face value, perhaps because there's no class thing to measure yourself against, so no careful analysis of where you might stand in relation to someone new. If you're straight with them, by and large, they'll be straight with you. From almost the day I pitched up at Kathleen's, with my exhausted daughter in tow, she was able to introduce me as her niece, and I said hello and they all said hello back. With the barest of explanations, we were drawn into the Silver Bay community.

It helped me to be part of this seafaring community. Half of the crews were transient, used to flitting in and out of people's lives. The others might be there for their own reasons. Either way nobody asked too many questions. And if you chose not to answer those that were asked, well, that seemed okay too. I knew I hadn't always been careful enough to hide my feelings, and I was grateful that the whale crews, with the intuition of all the best hunters, had understood that some things were better left unpursued. In five years, only Greg had grilled me over why I'd left England. I'd been so drunk when we'd had any kind of intimate conversation that, to my shame, I couldn't remember what I'd told him.

I'd guessed instinctively that Mike Dormer would upset that. I'd panicked when I overheard him asking Kathleen all sorts of questions about who worked in the bay, how long people tended to stick around, how long we'd lived there. He'd said he was on holiday, but I'd never known a holiday-maker ask so many focused questions.

When I told Kathleen so afterward she said I was being dramatic. All the years of having us here had lulled her into believing we would always be left alone. She'd said it was all in my imagination, and her unspoken look said she understood why.

But I suspected that Mike wasn't going to respect my boundaries. When I take a group out on *Ishmael,* they talk to each other. When it's just me and one other, they want to talk to me. They want to ask questions, take home part of me, along with their seafaring experience. That's why I don't generally take people out alone.

As Greg well knew. "So, what was your cozy little trip for two about, then, huh?"

He had to go and ruin it. We were sitting on the bench, watching, as Hannah made Milly chase bits of bladder wrack up and down the shore in the fading light. Mike Dormer was in his room, and Kathleen had gone for more beers. He spoke quietly so that Lance and Yoshi couldn't hear.

"Money, mainly."

Evidently Greg thought that saving my bacon gave him the right to ask. He was so transparent. I pulled the wad of notes from my jeans pocket. "Five hundred," I said. "For one trip."

He stared at it. Thought about his words, which was unusual for Greg. "Why would he pay that much to go out with you?"

I didn't need to answer that one. I knew Greg would have done the same.

"So what did you talk about?" he asked.

"Oh, for God's sake."

"I'm just interested," he protested. "He turns up here, looking like some kind of slacker, throws his money around . . . What's it all about?"

I shrugged. "I don't know and I don't care. Let the man be. He'll be gone soon enough."

"He'd better be. I don't like him."

"You don't like anyone new."

"I don't like anyone new who sucks up to you."

Hannah ran up to us, breathless and giggling. Milly flopped down at my feet. "She's been rolling in something disgusting," Hannah said. "She smells. I think it might have been a dead crab."

"Have you got homework?" I reached out to push her hair off her face. Every time I looked at her now she seemed to have grown a little, her face taking on new aspects. It reminded me that one day she would break away from me. Given the ties that bound us, I was not yet sure how that would work.

"Just revision. We've got a science test on Tuesday."

"Go and do it now. Then you'll be free for the rest of the evening."

"What's your test about?" asked Yoshi. "Bring it out and I'll help you, if you like."

Over the years I had discovered that the crews had enough skills between them to provide a whole education for Hannah. Yoshi, for example, had an advanced degree in biology and marine science, while Lance could tell you anything you wanted to know about weather. One or two had given her skills with which I was less impressed, like Scottie, who had taught her to swear and

171

once, while I was out, suggested she take a drag on his cigarette — Lance saw and punched him. She had skills of her own, my daughter. Skills, I suspect, she had inherited from me: how to assess people, how to stand back from them until you're sure of who or what they are, how to make yourself invisible in a large group. How to cope with grief.

She'd learned that lesson way too early.

Yoshi sat with her and, as night fell around us, they plowed through something to do with osmosis, Yoshi explaining things far better than I ever could. But I hadn't had much of an education, a mistake I was determined that Hannah would not repeat.

Greg seemed to recognize that I'd been shaken by the day's events, and tried to make me laugh with stories of the warring couple he'd had on board his boat. He didn't mention his ex or the fate of his boat; I hoped she'd backed off him a little. But my eyes kept wandering down the coast road, as I waited for that truck to reappear, those blue uniforms to climb out of the cab again.

Greg leaned into me. "You fancy coming to my place tonight? I got a whole load of videos off one of the guys at the boatyard. New comedies. Might be something you'd like." He made it sound casual.

"No," I said, "but thanks."

"It's just a film," he said.

"It's never just a film, Greg."

"One day," he said, his eyes lingering on mine.

"One day," I conceded.

Mike Dormer came out as the last of the light disappeared. The burners were on, and Kathleen had made bacon sandwiches, with fat slices of floury white bread. I didn't have much appetite, and picked at a bit of bacon. Hannah was squashed next to me, wrapped in a muffler against the colder air, her straight dark hair pulled into a knot. I could smell the shampoo when I dipped my head to hers.

Kathleen had handed him a plate, and he walked around the side of the table to get to the remaining seat. He appeared to have showered, and had put on a different shirt and sweater from what he had worn on the boat. His clean, well-cut clothes marked him out. Most of us are capable of wearing the same clothes for days on end if storm jackets and raincoats hide them. He glanced at me, then at the others, muttering, "Evening." His accent still made me start. We didn't get many English people in Silver Bay, and it was several years since I'd heard the accent of my own country.

Hannah leaned forward. "Did you see what I wrote?"

He tilted his head.

"On your computer. I left you a note. I was playing around earlier and I did that thing you said for looking people up."

He took a sandwich.

"I looked up Auntie K again. And then I looked you up."

Mike's head shot up.

"There's a picture of you. Of your face. And your company."

He seemed oddly uncomfortable. Mind you, I sympathize with people who don't like to have their lives dug into, and I admonished Hannah for prying.

"So what is it, mate?" said Lance. "Drugs? White-slave trade? We can sell you Squirt here at a good price. Throw in the dog, if you like."

Hannah poked Lance's arm. "Actually, it looks a bit boring," she said, grinning. "I don't think I'd like to work in a city."

"I think," Mike said, recovering slightly, "you have the better deal out here."

"What is it you actually do?" said Greg. His aggressive tone told me that Mike had not been forgiven for the temerity of our boat trip. It made me feel somehow protective of him.

Mike took a big bite of his sandwich. "It's research, mainly. Background information for financial deals." His voice was muffled with food.

"Oh," said Greg, dismissively. "The boring stuff."

"Is it your own company?" said Hannah.

Mike shook his head, his mouth apparently too full to talk.

"Pay well?" said Lance.

Mike finished chewing. "I do all right," he said.

I waited until Hannah had gone in before I spoke to him again. "Listen, I'm sorry about earlier. If I gave you a fright, I mean. I just couldn't work out how to get rid of those boats. But it was stupid. I acted . . . hastily. Especially with a passenger onboard."

He had had a couple of beers and looked about as loosened up as I imagined Mike Dormer got, collar open above the neck of his sweater, sleeves rolled up. He was leaning back in his chair, staring at the black nothing where the sea should have been. The clouds obscured the moon, and I could just make out his smile from the porch light.

"It was a bit of a surprise," he said. "I thought you were going to harpoon them."

That smile made me wonder how I had

ever suspected he would talk to the police about me. But that is how I am: my default position, if you like, is one of suspicion. "Not this time," I said, and he grinned.

He was all right, Mike. And it was a long time since I'd thought that about a man.

My room was at the back of the hotel. I was at the furthest end of the corridor, the furthermost point of the building, if you like, with nothing but glass and timber between the ocean and me. Hannah's room was next door in, and in the small hours still, more frequently than either of us cared to admit, she would pad along the corridor and crawl into my bed as she had when she was small, so that I could wrap myself around her, grateful for her presence and the sweet scent of her warm skin. I only slept soundly when I could feel her against me. I would never have told her so: she had enough burdens to carry without me making her responsible for my only chance of sleep. But from the way she always fell into a deep slumber almost before I had pulled my covers over her, I thought the same might be true for her.

Milly slept between me and the window, stretched out on the rug on the floor, and from the day I had arrived I had slept with it open, lulled by the sound of the sea, comforted by the endless stars in the uninterrupted sky. There had never been a night cold enough for me to close it completely. There, two storeys up, I could be alone with my thoughts, and, when alone, cry without anyone hearing. Those were the only times when I closed my window, so that any sound I uttered did not carry down to the whale crews or to stray listeners below. But the reverse was also true: just as the east wind sent my muffled tears downwind, so the gentle breeze from the west carried their words, their laughter, straight up to me. Which was how, as I hauled my fleece over my head, and stood there half undressed, I heard Greg's voice. It was a little lubricated by drink, its warmth gone. "You won't get anywhere with her," he was saying emphatically. "I've been waiting four years for her, and I tell you, no one's got closer than me."

It was several seconds before I grasped that he was talking about me. And I was so mad at his arrogance, that he could dare to presume any kind of ownership over me, that he could say any of this to a stranger, that I had to fight the urge to get dressed again, go down and say as much.

But I didn't. I was too shaken by the day's events to pick another fight. I just lay awake, cursed Greg Donohoe and tried not to think about things that could be brought back by an English accent.

It was a good hour before I realized I hadn't heard Mike Dormer's reply.

EIGHT:
KATHLEEN

He thought I couldn't tell. He didn't realize it shone out of him like a beacon every time he looked at her. I could have warned him, could have told him that what Greg had said was partially true. But what would have been the point? People hear what they want to hear. And I've never yet met a man who didn't think he could turn the world on its axis if he wanted something badly enough.

That said, the prospect of him making a move on my niece made me look a little harder at Mr. Michael Dormer of London, England. I found myself examining innocent exchanges for signs of character, trying to glean a little more about his history. Hannah had said he worked in the City, and the little more he had told me suggested nothing particularly interesting in that. Some people might have been impressed by the fact that he obviously had money, but that has never meant much here, and certainly not to me. Besides, running this hotel I've seen the effect of money on character, and it's rarely pleasant. No, Mike Dormer seemed kind, was unfailingly polite, always had time to indulge Hannah, no matter how trivial the query, and all these things were in his favor. He was handsome, at least to my eyes — not that that means much, according to Hannah — and despite his quiet, easygoing manner, he was no pushover, as I had observed when, one late evening recently, Greg had tried to warn him off my niece. "Thank you for your advice," he had replied. I had stood back in the doorway, unsure whether to be prepared for an explosion. But he continued, in that clipped accent of his, "You won't mind if I ignore it, since my private life is none of your business." And, to my surprise, Greg — perhaps as wrong-footed as I was — had backed off.

He still looked like a fish out of water, even after the best part of three weeks in Silver Bay. His collars had become a little looser, and he had bought himself a storm jacket. But sitting with the whalers, as he did most evenings, he was still no more at home than I would have been in the boardroom of some City firm.

Oh, he tried: he responded good-naturedly to their jokes, accepted their off-color teasing, bought more than his share of drinks. And when he thought he was not being observed, he gazed at my niece.

But something about Mike bothered me. I had the feeling he wasn't being straight with us. There was an absence at his core that left me uneasy. Why would a single young man spend so long in a quiet little resort like ours? Why did he never talk about his family? He had told me one morning that he wasn't married, and had no children, then politely changed the subject. Most men, I've found, especially successful men, will talk about themselves at the drop of a hat, yet he didn't seem to want to impart to us anything about himself.

Then there was the afternoon I saw him at the council offices. I was in town, picking up a new school dress for Hannah — Liza had had two trips planned that day and couldn't get away. As I stood outside the bank, having drawn some cash to pay for it, I saw him coming down the steps, a big folder under his arm, two at a time.

In itself that wouldn't have bothered me. The tourism office is on the ground floor, and plenty of my guests head there at some point, often at my urging. I can't explain it too clearly, but he seemed more upright, a more dynamic character than the one we saw at home. And his expression when he caught sight of me: I know when someone feels they have been discovered, and it was there in the jolt on his face.

He recovered pretty quickly, came striding across the road and made small talk with me about what he had seen in town, asked the best place to buy postcards. But it shook me a little. I felt, suddenly, that Mike had something to hide.

Nino told me I'd made too much of it. He knew a little of Liza's history — as much as he needed to know — and thought me overprotective. "She's a big girl," he said, "a very different character from the one who arrived here. She's thirty-two, for God's sake." And he was right. In fact, I can chart the truth of Nino's words in the photographs she and my sister sent me, the story of her life over the past fifteen years.

A life told in photographs is not unusual — but what was, was the way Liza's appearance so nakedly reflected her circumstance; you could see it in the size of her eyes after my sister, her mother, died — a year later she was wearing garish, dark makeup that presumably gave her something to hide behind and certainly made her seem alien to me. It was hard to believe that the girl who had written me rambling letters about ponies and the hardships of the fourth form, the child who had visited here and turned cartwheels the length along the jetty, was under that camouflage.

Then a few years later, I saw something else: the softening and vulnerability that comes with motherhood. There she was, proud, exhausted, just hours after giving birth, her hair stuck in sweaty fronds to her face, and later on when Hannah was a toddler, kissing her fat cheeks in some cramped passport-photograph booth. When she met Steven the pictures had stopped coming. In the only one I have from that period I have never wanted to put up, he looks smug, his arm around her shoulders, apparently proud to be a father. Nino thought I'd overreacted there, too. "She looks beautiful," he said. "Groomed, expensively dressed." But to me her eyes are veiled, saying nothing.

We have no pictures of the time when she arrived here. What would have been the point?

And now, five years on, what would a photograph of her show? A wiser, stronger woman. Someone who might not have come to terms with the past, but whose character contains a fierce determination to elude it.

A good mother. A courageous, loving person, but sadder, more guarded than I'd like her to be. That's what her photograph would show. If she'd let us take one.

The following morning, as Hannah and Liza sat at the kitchen table eating breakfast, a delivery man arrived, his van — like all delivery vans — skidding to a halt in the grit outside. Audibly chewing gum, he handed me a box addressed to Mike, which I signed for. By the time Mike came down — he was eating with us in the kitchen most days now — Hannah was in a frenzy of curiosity about it.

"You got a parcel!" she announced, as he appeared. "It came this morning."

He picked up the box and sat down. He was wearing the softest-looking sweater I had ever seen. I fought the urge to ask if it was cashmere. "Quicker than I'd thought," he observed. He handed it to Liza. "For you," he said.

I'm afraid the look she gave him was of deep suspicion.

"What?"

"For you," he said.

"What's this?" she said, staring at it as if she didn't want to touch it. She hadn't yet tied back her hair, and it fell around her cheeks, obscuring her face. Or perhaps that was the point.

"Open it, Mum," said Hannah. "I'll open it, if you want." She reached over, and Liza let it slide from her fingers.

As I sliced bread, Hannah attacked the plastic security wrapping, digging at the stubborn bits with the knife. A few moments later she ripped it off and examined the cardboard box underneath.

"It's a mobile phone!" she announced.

"With a video facility," said Mike, pointing to the image, "like mine. I thought you could use it to film those boats."

Liza stared at the little silver gadget; so exquisitely small, it seemed to me, that you couldn't have dialed a number without a pencil point and a microscope. After an age, she said, "How much did it cost?"

He was buttering a slice of toast. "Don't worry about it."

"I can't accept it," she said. "It must have cost a fortune."

"Can you make films on it?" Hannah was already rifling through the box for the instructions.

Mike smiled. "Really, it cost nothing. I did a deal a while back with the company that manufactures them. They were happy to send it to me." He patted his pocket. "That's how I got mine."

Hannah was impressed. "Do lots of people

send you stuff for free?"

"It's called business," he said.

"Can you get anything you want?"

"You usually only get something if the person giving it thinks they might one day get something in return," he said, and added hurriedly, "In business, I mean."

I thought about that phrase as I put down the milk in front of him, a little harder than I'd intended. I tried not to think of our meeting the previous day.

"Look," he said, when Liza had still not touched the phone, "treat it as a loan, if you like. Take it and use it for the whale-migration season. I didn't like what I saw the other day, and it would be nice to know that you had some more ammo against the bad guys."

I could see that this was a persuasive argument for my niece. I suppose he had guessed that she couldn't have afforded a piece of equipment like that if she'd had two full boats a day for the entire season.

Finally, tentatively, she took the phone from Hannah. "I could send pictures straight to the National Parks," she said, turning it over in her hand.

"The minute you saw anyone doing anything wrong," he said. "May I have some more coffee, Kathleen?"

"Not just the disco boats, but all sorts of things. Creatures in distress, wrapped in fishing lines. I could lend it to other boats if I wasn't using it."

"I could take a film of the dolphins in the bay and show it at school. If you took me out to see them, I mean." Hannah looked at her mother, but Liza was still staring at the little phone.

"I don't know what to say," she said eventually.

"It's nothing," said Mike, dismissively. "Really. You don't have to say anymore about it." As if to underline the point he picked up the newspaper and began to read.

But just as I could tell he wasn't taking in the printed words before him, I had a feeling about that phone, which was confirmed later in the day when, as I was making his bed, I found the receipt. It had been ordered in Australia, through some Internet site, and had cost more than this hotel takes in a week.

The day that Liza and Hannah arrived here, I drove the three hours to Sydney airport to pick them up, and when we got back to the hotel Liza lay down on my bed and didn't get up for nine days.

I was so frightened by day three that I

called the doctor. It was like she was in some kind of coma. She didn't eat, she didn't sleep, she took only occasional sips of the sweet tea that I placed on the bedside table and declined to answer any of my questions. Most of the time she lay on her side and stared at the wall, sweating gently in the midday heat, her pale hair lank, a cut on her face and a huge bruise down the side of her arm. Dr. Armstrong spoke to her, pronounced her basically healthy and said it might be something viral, or possibly a neurosis, and that she should be left to rest.

I guess I was just relieved she hadn't come here to die, but she had brought me enough to cope with. Hannah was only six, anxious and clingy, prone to tearful outbursts and often to be found wandering weeping through the corridors at night. It was unsurprising, considering she had traveled for a day and two nights to a place she didn't know to be looked after by an old lady she had never met. It was high summer, and she came out in a rash from the heat, got bitten half to death by mosquitoes, couldn't understand why I wouldn't let her run around outside. I was afraid of the sun on her fair skin, afraid of letting her too close to the water, afraid of her not coming back. If I wasn't watching her, if I was distracted by some domestic task, she would creep upstairs and hold on to her mother like a little monkey, as if she could hug her into life. The way she cried at night broke your heart. I remember calling up to my sister in the heavens, asking her what the hell I was meant to do with these offspring of hers.

By day nine I had had enough. I was exhausted from looking after the guests and this tearful child, who had not been able satisfactorily to explain what was going on, just as I in return could explain nothing to her. I wanted my bed back, and a moment's peace. I had never had a family of my own, so I wasn't used to the chaos that children bring, their endless morphing needs and demands, and I got snappy.

By that stage I half suspected it was drugs: Liza was so distanced from life, so pale and disengaged. It could have been anything, I had concluded, with some discomfiture — we had had so little contact over the past few years. Fine, I thought. If this was what she was bringing to my doorstep, she would have to address it. She would have to abide by my rules.

"Get up," I yelled at her, opening the window and placing a fresh mug of tea beside her. When she didn't respond, I pulled back the covers, trying not to wince at how painfully thin she was. "C'mon, Liza, it's a beautiful day and it's time for you to get up. Your daughter needs you, and I have to get on."

I remember how she turned her head, her eyes dark with remembered horrors, and how my resolve vanished. I sat down on my musty bed, taking her hand between mine.

"What is it, Liza?" I said softly. "What's going on?"

And when she told me I hauled her into my chest and held her, white-knuckled, my eyes on the distant horizon, as finally, twelve thousand miles and several hundred hours later, she wept.

It was after ten o'clock that evening when we heard that a baby whale had beached. Yoshi had called me on the radio that afternoon to tell me they had seen a female humpback in distress, swimming up and down at the mouth of the bay. She and Lance had come quite close but they hadn't been able to work out what was wrong: she bore no obvious signs of illness, dragged no loose nets that might have cut into her. She just kept swimming, following some strange irregular path. It was abnormal behavior for a migrating whale. That evening, as they took out a night party, a boatload of office workers from an insurance firm in Newcastle, they discovered the beached calf.

"It's the one we saw before," said Liza, as she put down the receiver. "I know it."

We had been sitting in the kitchen; it was a chilly night, and Mike had retreated to the lounge to read a newspaper in front of the fire.

"Can I help?" he said, when he saw us in the main hallway, pulling on our jackets and boots.

"Could you stay here so that Hannah's not alone? Don't tell her what's going on if she happens to wake up."

I was surprised that Liza asked him — she had never so much as employed a sitter since she'd been here — but we had to get out as quickly as possible, and I suppose she had made up her mind about his character as I had. "We may be a while," I said, patting his arm. "Don't wait up. And whatever you do don't let Milly out. The poor whale will have enough on its plate without a dog running around it."

He watched as we climbed into the truck. I had the feeling he would rather have come with us and helped. In my rearview mirror I saw him silhouetted in the doorway the whole way down the coast road.

■ ■ ■ ■

There are few more heartbreaking sights than a beached calf. Thank God I've seen it only twice in all my seventy-odd years. The baby lay in the sand, maybe two meters long, alien and vulnerable, yet oddly familiar. The sea pulled at it gently, as if the waves were trying to persuade it to go home. It could only have been a few months old.

"I've called the authorities," said Greg, who was already there, trying to stop the animal being sucked too deep into the grit of the shore. It was no longer legal to try to move a whale without official help: if it was sick you could do more harm than good. And if well-wishers turned it toward the sea, it might call in an entire pod: the next day they would be beaching themselves in terrifying numbers, as if in sympathy. "He might be sick," Greg said. "Pretty weak, but." His jeans were wet to halfway up his legs where he had been kneeling. "He'll still be nursing, and he's not going to last long without milk. Reckon he could have been here a few hours already."

The calf lay on its side, its nose pointed toward the shore, its eyes half closed as if in contemplation of its misery. It looked piti-ful, somehow too unformed to be alone in this environment.

"He didn't beach because he's sick. It's those bloody boats," hissed Liza, grabbing her bucket and heading to the sea to fill it. "The music is so loud it's disorientating them. The little ones haven't got a chance."

There were no man-made lights along our coast road, and the three of us worked in near silence for almost an hour waiting for the National Parks people or the lifeguards to arrive from down the coast, the light from our torches swinging backward and forward as we walked down to the sea and back again, trying to keep the beast wet. We were as quiet as possible. A whale's size gives a misleading impression of its robustness. In reality it is as easy to lose the life of this vast creature as it is to lose that of a fair-ground goldfish.

"Come on, baby boy," whispered Liza, kneeling in the sand periodically to stroke its head. "Hang on in there while we get you a stretcher. Your mum's out there, wait-ing for you."

We suspected this was true. Every half an hour or so we heard a distant splash, bounc-ing off the pine-covered hills behind the main stretch — the sound perhaps of her searching the seas, judging how close she could come. It was heartbreaking to listen to that mother's anguish. I tried to block my ears to it as we moved around each other. I was afraid that the mother, in her desperation, would beach herself.

Three times Greg called up on his phone, and once I drove up the road, trying to raise the lifeguards. But it was past midnight before the National Parks and Wildlife rangers reached us. Communications had apparently broken down; the wrong location had been reported; someone else had vanished with the only available stretcher. Liza barely heard their explanation, saying, "Look, we need to get him out into the water. Quickly. We know his mother's still out there."

"We'll try and float him," they said, and rolled the baby onto the dolphin stretcher. Then, grunting with the effort, they walked it into the shallows, apparently heedless of the unforgiving cold of the waves. Standing on the shore, I watched as they discussed whether to try to put him on one of the boats and take him out to his mother, but the National Parks man said he wasn't sure that the calf was strong enough to survive the upheaval, let alone swim. And they were fearful that the mother would feel threatened by the boat, and leave the area.

"If we can stabilize him," someone was muttering, "we might be able to get him further out to the bay . . ."

They rocked the calf gently, helping it recover its water balance, which it would have lost during its time on the shore. After an hour or so, they went deeper, Liza and Greg now submerged to their chests, neither wearing a wet suit, shivering as they urged the little creature to swim toward its mother. Liza's teeth were chattering and I was chilled too.

Still the baby didn't move.

"Okay, we won't push him off," said one of the men, when they had given up hope of him swimming. "We'll just stand here for a bit and let him work out where he is while he's supported. Perhaps he needs a little more time to orient himself."

Even half elevated by water a baby whale is awesomely heavy. From the shore, Yoshi at my side, I watched as the four of them stood, Liza's thin shoulders braced against the weight, and whispered words of encouragement to the calf, trying to will it into swimming back to its mother.

By that time it was getting on for two a.m. and it was obvious to us all that the calf was in a bad way. It seemed exhausted; its breathing was irregular, its eye closing periodically. Perhaps it had been sick before, I thought. Perhaps its mother knew this but still couldn't let it go.

I don't know how long they stood there. The night took on a weird, timeless quality, the hours creeping along in a fug of cold, muttered conversations and growing despair. Two cars came past, lured by the sight of torchlight on the beach. One was full of giggling young people who got out and offered to help. We thanked them and sent them away — the last thing the poor creature needed was a load of drunken teenagers careering about the place. At one point Yoshi and I made coffee on the berthed *Moby One,* then she and Lance stepped in so that each helper could break for fifteen minutes and warm themselves with a hot drink. But the night dragged, and I borrowed a jacket to go on top of the one I was already wearing because somehow the bones of the old chill that much deeper.

Then we heard it: a terrible, faint sound from out at sea, a strange keening and lowing, the rare sound of whalesong above water.

"It's his mother!" cried Liza. "She's calling him."

Yoshi shook her head. "The females don't

sing," she said. "It's far more likely to be a male."

"How many times have you heard whale-song with your head above water?" Liza demanded. "It's the mother, I know it."

Yoshi didn't push the point. Eventually she said, "There have been studies that showed a singer accompanying the mother and child at a distance. Like an escort. He may have been looking out for them."

"Doesn't seem to have done this little fellow much good," said one of the National Parks men, as we sat on the damp sand. "He doesn't seem to have the energy to fight."

Next to me, Liza shook her head. Her fingers were blue with cold. "He's got to. He's just disorientated. If we give him long enough, he might work out where his mother is. That he can hear her must count for something."

But none of us was quite sure how much that little calf could hear now. To me the poor thing looked half dead, and he was now visibly battling for breath. I was no longer sure who they were holding it in the water for. By then I was barely able to stay on my feet; while I have a robust constitution, I'm too old to stay up all night, and found that when I sat down, as Yoshi kept telling me to do, I would drift off briefly, brought to by the urgent discussions a few feet away.

For that is the worst thing when a whale beaches: it is as if they have chosen to die, and we humans, uncomprehending, merely prolong their agony by fighting it. Every time one is saved, every time one swims triumphantly out to sea, it makes us more certain of our actions, more sure that we should only ever fight to save them. But what if sometimes we should leave well alone? What if the baby needed to go? And if we had left him alone, would the mother have come and nudged him back into the water herself? I had heard of it happening. The idea that we might have contributed to the animal's distress was too awful to dwell on and I closed my mind to it, trying to think instead of domestic minutiae — Hannah's sports shoes, a broken kettle, the last time I did my accounts. Occasionally, I suspect, I drifted into sleep.

Finally, as the sun broke over the headland, casting a pale blue light over our little group on the sand, I jolted properly awake as one of the National Parks guys announced that there was no hope. "We should euthanize," he said, rubbing his eyes. "Leave it any longer and we'll risk the mother coming in and beaching herself."

"But he's still alive," said Liza. The pale light revealed her to be gray and exhausted. She kept shivering in her wet clothes, but refused to change into the dry ones offered by Yoshi, because they'd only get wet when she went in again. "Surely while there's life . . ."

Greg placed his arm around her shoulders and squeezed. His eyes were rimmed with red, and his face was dark with stubble. "We've done everything we can, Liza. We can't risk the mother too."

"But he's not actually sick!" she cried. "It's just those bloody boats. If we can get him out to his mother, he'll be okay."

"No, he won't." The National Parks man laid a hand on the baby's back. "We've had him here for eight hours, we've walked him into deeper water and back to the shallows, and he's barely moved. He's too young to rear, and he's too frail to get back out there. If we take him deeper he'll drown, and that's not something I'm prepared to be part of. I'm sorry, guys, but he's not going anywhere."

"It's a bad business," said Lance. Yoshi, drawn under his arm, had begun to cry — I was fighting tears myself.

"Half an hour more," Liza pleaded, her hands smoothing the baby's skin. "Just half an hour more. If we can just get him back to his mother . . . Look, she'd know if he wasn't going to make it? Right? She'd have left him by now."

I had to look away. I couldn't bear what I heard in her voice. The man headed for his truck. "His mother's not going to help him now. I'm sorry."

"Let him die close to her, then," Liza pleaded. "Don't let him die alone. We can take him out to be close to her."

"I can't do that. Even if the trip didn't traumatize him, there's no guarantee that she'd let us anywhere near. We might stress her even more."

I left then, to be with Hannah when she woke for school, and partly to escape a scene I found unbearable. I'm glad I didn't see the two injections go in, and the National Parks man's anguish as both failed to send the baby to sleep. It took him a further twenty minutes to find a gun, but Yoshi told me afterward that before they had placed the barrel to the baby whale's head the poor little creature let out a quiet, gurgling breath and died. They had all wept then, shivering in the morning mist. Even the big National Parks guy, who said it had been his second beaching in a fortnight.

But, in Yoshi's words, Liza had lost it. She

had sobbed so hard that she had almost hyperventilated, and Greg had held on to her for fear that she was not herself. She had half waded into the water, her arms outstretched, crying out an apology to the mother, as if she, personally, had failed. She had cried so hard as they covered the body with a tarpaulin, protecting it from the curious gaze of passersby, that the National Parks men had asked Lance, on the quiet, if she was, you know, all right.

It was then, Yoshi said, that Liza had calmed down a little. Greg had given her a large brandy — he had a bottle in the glove compartment of his truck. While Lance and Yoshi took a restorative tot, she had sunk several more. And then, after a few more still, as the sun rose over Silver Bay, illuminating the body on the beach and the blameless beauty around it, as the cries of what we all hoped had not been its mother faded away, Liza had climbed unsteadily into the truck and headed off to Greg's.

NINE:
MIKE

Curse that jet lag. It was just after six a.m. and I was uncomfortably awake, thinking about the conversation I had just had with Dennis in England, trying to tell myself I wasn't feeling the things I was pretty sure I shouldn't be feeling.

I didn't need to guess what had happened. I had woken shortly after four, and lain awake for some time, my thoughts humming malevolently in the dark. Eventually I got up, discovered that the hotel was still empty, but for myself and Hannah, and wandered through the deserted rooms. Finally I came back to mine with a pair of Kathleen's binoculars and focused them out of the side of the bay window. I could just make out the flickering of torchlight, the occasional illumination of the scene on the beach by someone's headlights. In flashing pools of light I had watched Greg and the other whalechasers wade in and out of the water and, some time later, I had recognized — from the color of her jacket — Liza seated on the sand, and two guys talking beside what looked like a tarpaulin.

I cursed the jet lag and told myself that it was possible to regain it even if you'd been sleeping perfectly well for more than a week. At that point I had drawn the curtain, made some coffee and fought the urge to look out again. There is something compelling about life-or-death drama, even when it involves an animal. But for me the compulsion to look always brought with it a slight queasiness, as if being so interested in it was indicative of something deficient in my character, something exploitative and cold.

Besides, being able to watch other people unseen made me think of secrets, things I had not told Vanessa . . . things that still threatened to swell and engulf me with the evidence of my duplicity. In Silver Bay, for the most part, I had managed to forget my own actions, losing them in distance and different time zones, and because I now felt, half the time, as if I were living someone else's life. But in the silent hours before dawn there were no distractions. There was little way of escaping the truth about myself.

Then, before I could ponder these and other such matters of the small hours any longer, Dennis had rung, apparently heedless of the time difference, explosive with barely suppressed fury at his enforced bedridden state and insisted on me detailing every conversation, every step I had taken toward the progression of the development. He was hard to reassure at the best of times, but nigh on impossible when he was in this mood. In the office, when he was like this, we would disappear to imaginary meetings and lie low until, like a hurricane, he had blown himself out. A man of extremes, for ninety percent of the time he could be the most generous, upbeat character, the kind of person who makes you want to be a better version of yourself, who makes you perform beyond what you had believed was your reach. This was one of the reasons I wanted to work for and with him. But for the remainder he could be simply bloody.

"Have you secured the planning permission?" he demanded.

"It doesn't work that quickly here." I twisted my pen in my fingers, wondering why this man, who was allegedly not that much more than my partner, my equal, could bring me out in an adolescent sweat even at a distance of twelve thousand miles. "I told you so before I came."

"You know that's not what I want to hear. I need it to be a done deal, Mike."

"There may be a few problems with . . . the ecological side of things."

"What the hell does that mean?"

"The watersports might . . . be considered to impact negatively on the local sea life."

"It's a bay!" he spluttered. "It's a bay that's held ships, oyster beds, speedboats, you name it. Has done for a hundred years. How can our fun and games off one tiny bit of shoreline be thought to affect anything?"

"We may get a bit of resistance from the whale-watchers."

"Whale-watchers? What are they, a load of Greenpeace-loving lentil-eaters?"

"They're the most important tourism attraction in the bay."

"So what the hell do they do day in, day out?"

I stared at the receiver. "Um, watch whales? . . ."

"My point exactly. And what the hell do they watch the whales in?"

"Boats."

"Yachts? Rowboats?"

"Motorboats." I could see where he was going.

When I looked out of the window again everyone, even the whale, was gone.

205

At around six I heard the screen door, and arrived at the bottom of the stairs to find Kathleen peeling off her wet coat in the hall. In the pale glow of the morning light, she looked done in, somehow older and frailer than she had twelve hours earlier, her movements muddied by exhaustion. Liza wasn't behind her.

"Let me take your coat," I said.

She brushed me aside. "Don't fuss," she said, and from her tone I guessed the fate of the baby whale. "Where's Hannah?"

"Still asleep." It was more than could be said for Liza's dog, who had scratched at the door and whined from the moment they had left.

Kathleen nodded. "Thank you," she said. She was stooped. It was the first time I had seen her as an old woman. "I'm going to make a pot of tea. Do you want some?"

I guessed that the death of the baby whale was unusual enough to have shaken her, although I was surprised that someone renowned for killing a shark could feel such grief for another sea creature. And all the while I was pondering this, sitting at the kitchen table because Kathleen had insisted on making the tea herself, I realized I was half waiting for the sound of the door, for Liza's oilskin to swish against the wall as she came in and dropped her keys into the bowl on the hall table.

"Poor bloody creature," she said, when she finally sat down. "Didn't have a chance. We should have shot it at the beginning."

I drank two mugs of tea before I had the courage to say anything. In the end, I tried to sound casual. I observed that Liza had obviously decided to go out early on *Ishmael,* and almost before the words had left my mouth Kathleen gave me a look that suggested there was no point in either of us pretending. "She's with Greg," she said.

The words hung in the air.

"I didn't realize they were an item." My voice sounded high and false.

"They're not," she said wearily. And then, apparently apropos of nothing, "She took the calf dying very personally."

There was a lengthy silence, during which I eyed my empty mug and tried not to let my thoughts stray. "But surely there wasn't anything she could have done," I said. It was a platitude. I couldn't understand how a dead whale meant she had to sleep with Greg.

"Look, Mike, Liza lost a child five years ago, just before she came to live here. This is her way of dealing with it." She dropped her voice, pulled her mug closer to her and took a sip of tea. Her hands, I noticed, were large and workmanlike, not soft and gentle like my mother's. "Unfortunately it means that once or twice a year that poor fool thinks he has a hope."

While I was digesting this news, she stood up, using her palms as leverage, and announced through a barely suppressed yawn that she had better get Hannah up. Her abrupt change of subject told me she didn't want to discuss the matter any further. The light flooding through the kitchen window made her skin seem washed out, a far cry from her usual ruddiness. I wondered what she'd been through, down on the beach. It was easy to forget how old she was.

"I'll drive her to school if you want," I said. "I've got nothing else planned." Suddenly I knew I needed a task to stop me thinking. I wanted Hannah's cheerful chatter about the pop charts, technology lessons and school dinners. I wanted to be going somewhere in my car. I wanted to get out of this house. "Kathleen, did you hear me? I'll take her."

"You sure?" The look of gratitude as I went for my keys told me just how tired Kathleen Whittier Mostyn, legendary game fisher and apparently tireless hostess, really was.

■ ■ ■ ■

It is entirely possible that on paper I appear, as my sister would say, to be more of a player than I am. In fact, during the four years of my relationship with Vanessa, until the night with Tina, I had never so much as kissed another girl. That's not to say I haven't thought about it — I'm only human — but until the night of the office celebration, the idea of cheating on Vanessa had seemed so far from possible, let alone likely, that even as I held Tina's slim, hard body to me, as her hands burrowed urgently down the front of my trousers, some part of me wanted to laugh out loud at the ridiculous idea that it was happening at all.

I met Vanessa Beaker at Beaker Holdings, while she filled a temporary position in the marketing department and, although many people have suspected differently, we had been dating for several weeks before I discovered the significance of her surname. When I found out who she was, I considered ending the relationship; I really wanted my job, had identified the way my career might progress within the company. The possibility of jeopardizing it over a relationship I was unsure about seemed not worth the risk.

But I had bargained without my new girlfriend. She told me not to be ridiculous, informed her father of our relationship in front of me, adding that whether we stayed together or not was no concern of his, then announced to me afterward that she knew I was The One. Then she gave me the kind of smile that said the possibility that such a statement might alarm me was not even worth considering.

And I suppose I hardly did consider it. My sister Monica said I was lazy in relationships; I was happy for attractive women to chase me, and had had to end a relationship myself only once. Vanessa was pretty, sometimes almost beautiful, happy, confident and clever. She told me she loved me every day, although even if she hadn't I would have known it because she fussed over me at home, had an uncomplicated appetite for sex, and spent endless amounts of time and energy worrying about my appearance and well-being. I didn't mind: it saved me having to. And I trusted Vanessa's opinion. She was clever, as I've said, and she had her father's aptitude for business.

I didn't know why I had to defend my relationship to my sister, but I did. Frequently. She said Vanessa was too "jolly hockey sticks." She said I'd probably marry anyone who made the same efforts as Vanessa, who made my life that easy, anyone at all. She said I had never been truly in love because I have never been hurt. I told her that her version of relationships all sounded more like masochism to me.

My sister hadn't had a relationship in fifteen months. She said she was getting to the age when eligible men found her "too complicated."

"What do you want?" she said, when I telephoned her.

"Hello, sister dear. I've missed you," I said. "How's life on the other side of the planet? How's your career-breaking deal shaping up?"

"Are you ringing me to tell me you're emigrating? Are you going to pay for me to visit? Buy me a club-class ticket and I'll tell Mum and Dad for you."

I heard a cigarette being lit. In the background a television burbled and I glanced at my watch, calculating what time in the evening it was at home. "I thought you'd given up," I said.

"I have," she said, exhaling noisily. "Must be something wrong with the phone line. So, what do you want?"

The truth was, I didn't know. "Just to talk to someone, I guess."

That threw her. I'd never before expressed an emotional need to my sister.

"You okay?"

"Yeah, fine. Just . . . just had an odd night. A baby whale died outside the hotel and it . . . threw me a little."

"Wow. A baby whale? Did someone kill it?"

"Not exactly. It beached itself."

"Okay. I've heard of that. Weird." I heard her drag on the cigarette. "Did you get pictures? Might make an interesting feature."

"Take off the hack head, Monica."

"Don't be so precious. So what, were you all trying to get it back in the water?"

"Not me personally."

"Didn't want to get those designer trousers dirty, huh?"

Suddenly I felt irritated by her singular inability ever to be nice and straightforward with me instead of smart and sarcastic. "We're not fourteen anymore, in case you hadn't noticed," I wanted to yell. But I just said, "Oh, forget it. I'd better go."

"Hey — hey — okay, Mike. Sorry."

"Look, we'll speak another time." I should have rung Vanessa. But I knew why I hadn't.

212

"Mike, don't be angry. I'm sorry, all right? What . . . what was it you wanted to say?"

But that was it: I didn't know. I sat there for almost five minutes before I realized I really didn't know.

I spied her walking down the coast road half an hour after I had returned from dropping off Hannah, the dog yapping for joy at her return. She was evidently exhausted and very pale, and the legs of her jeans were wet and sandy. When she saw me sitting at the beach end of the jetty, her expression didn't change but she stopped a few feet away from me on the sand, one hand raised against the morning sun. She teetered a little, and I wondered if she was slightly drunk. I looked at her differently now, knowing what I knew. It was as if Liza McCullen had acquired another dimension.

"You want to drive to the market with me?"

Silhouetted as she was, I could barely see her face. "You're driving?"

"I guess you could drive me, if you've mastered the gear change on that Holden. Kathleen's too tired to go grocery shopping today, and she needs sleep."

I figured it was as close to an invitation as I was going to get. I went inside to get my car keys.

To the British eye, Australian super-markets are a cornucopia, strange yet famil-iar, with an abundance of brightly colored fruit and vegetables punctuated by alien delights such as Violet Crumbles and Green's Pancake Shake. I didn't have much to do with the food shopping at home; either Vanessa organized it or, on her in-structions, I hit "repeat order list" on our Internet shopping site and it was delivered, neatly packed in color-coded bags marked "Freezer," "Fridge" and "Larder" — as if anyone in London had a larder. But as we walked around the cavernous interior of the Australian supermarket I enjoyed studying these new foods, found myself repeatedly calculating the cost in sterling — as if I had an idea how much the British equivalent cost.

Liza marched up and down the aisles, lob-bing items into the oversized trolley with the confidence of someone who performed this task regularly. You would not have guessed from the dexterity and swiftness of her movements that she had been up all night.

"Anything you want in particular?" she called over her shoulder. "Assuming you're staying a bit longer." There was no hint in her voice as to whether that made the slightest difference to her.

"I'm easy," I said, putting a packet of crackers back onto the shelf, and thought of the myriad ways in which that statement was true.

When she came to pay, I noticed that she had to rifle in her pockets for enough cash — crumpled notes, cents in various denominations — to make up the full amount. I made as if to interrupt, but her warning glance kept my hand in my pocket, where it rested on my wallet. I pretended I had been fumbling for a handkerchief and blew my nose so ostentatiously that the woman behind me backed away in horror.

As I watched, I found myself piecing things together, considering what now made sense. Her inability to let her surviving child out on the water. Her melancholy. Perhaps the child had drowned. Perhaps it had been a baby. Perhaps she had lost a husband at the same time. I realized how few questions I had asked her. How few, come to think of it, I had ever asked anyone. For all I knew Dennis Beaker might have a second family. Tina Kennedy might have left a convent two years previously. I had always taken people at face value. Now, suddenly, I wondered what I might have missed.

Liza McCullen had had a child who died. She was three years younger than me, and suddenly, next to her, I felt as if I had the life experience and self-knowledge of an amoeba.

We had been on the road for almost twenty minutes before we spoke again.

We passed the council offices, and I thought about the development, and my conversation with Dennis. I thought about something Kathleen had told me a few days earlier: that the only reason the area around Silver Bay had developed from bush at all was because Allied soldiers had built a base there. She could remember a time when there had been only her hotel, a few houses and a general store. She said this with some satisfaction, as if she had preferred it. I knew I should have said something by then. Part of it, I guess, was cowardice. I knew how she — any of them — was likely to respond. I liked them. And the thought of them not liking me . . . got to me.

And by then, after Liza, the distress flares and the baby whale, I was no longer convinced of the plan's rightness as we had envisaged it. There must be a way, I thought, to tie in the two sets of needs — those of our proposed hotel and those of the whalechasers. Until I had worked it out, though, I didn't want to discuss it with anyone. Not Liza or Kathleen. Or Dennis, no matter how angry he became over my supposed obfuscation. I sat in the driver's seat, trying to concentrate on the road, acutely aware of Liza beside me. The way she twisted her hair with her right hand when her thoughts took her somewhere far from where she sat.

I kept thinking of things to say, but I didn't want to give her the chance to retreat into polite conversation. I felt we had passed that stage. I felt, oddly, as if I was owed an explanation. And I kept thinking of the way Greg would grin at me that evening, drop thinly veiled references to their night together, as if he had been proven right in warning me off. I have met men like him in every walk of life: charismatic, loud, childlike in their determination to be the center of attention. It's incomprehensible to me how they invariably attract the nicest women, and usually end up treating them badly. I imagined him sitting next to Liza on the bench, laying a proprietorial arm around her shoulders, believing, as Kathleen said, that he had a chance. But perhaps he had more of one than she thought. Who knew what lay behind the choices of the human heart? Liza had liked him enough to go to bed with him, after all. More than once.

But why him? Why that drunken, philandering, beer-swilling loser?

We were halfway up the coast road, the hotel in sight, before she spoke. Two boats were moored at Whale Jetty: *Moby One* and *Ishmael.* I knew them both now by sight, which gave me an odd sense of satisfaction. The sun, high in the sky, glinted off the blue water behind them and the dense pines that covered the hills were an unnatural lush green. Every time I had looked at this setting, I had imagined it in the printed images of a brochure.

"I guess you know what happened last night," she said, without looking at me.

"None of my business," I said.

"No," she agreed, "it's not."

I indicated left and headed slowly up the track to the hotel, wishing suddenly that we were not so close to home. The car's clock said, unbelievably, that it was lunchtime. I felt as though I'd already lived a whole day.

When she spoke again, her voice was measured. "I've known Greg a long time. He . . . well, I know him well enough to know that it doesn't matter for him. That it doesn't have to mean anything."

I pulled into the car park. We sat in silence

as the engine cooled, ticking its way into immobility, as we pondered the weighty realization that she had deemed it necessary to say anything to me at all.

"Your aunt told me about your child. I'm sorry."

Her head snapped around. Her eyes, I saw, were red-rimmed. It might have been lack of sleep, or the result of endless tears. "She shouldn't have."

I didn't know what to say.

So I leaned forward, took Liza McCullen's exhausted, beautiful face in my hands and kissed her. God only knows why. The really surprising thing was that she kissed me back.

Ten:
Hannah

Lara took me out on her boat. It was called *Baby Dreamer* and it had a pram bow, and a thwart, the name for the bench that went across the middle, and it was rigged as a Bermudan sloop with a mainsail and a jib, which looked like two triangles, one smaller than the other, and she had a little flag — a burgee — that told her which way the wind was blowing.

She taught me how to tack and jibe, the most important things in sailing, and to do these you have to use the rudder, the sails and the weight of the crew all at once. Lara and I had to shift our weight from one side of the boat to the other, which made us giggle, and Lara sometimes pretended she was falling in, but I never panicked because I knew she was joking.

I didn't tell Mum. But Lara's mum knew — she watched from their house — and I wore her spare life jacket. My mum never says much to the other mums, so I guessed I was pretty safe.

Everyone in Lara's family sails. She has been sailing since she was a baby, and in her front room there's a picture of her, still wearing a diaper, with her fat little hands on a tiller and someone else's holding her around the tummy. She can remember sleeping on their yacht when she was really little and her mum said she was such a bad sleeper now because she got too used to being rocked to sleep by the water.

Lara has done a course at Salamander Bay and knows how to do all the points of sailing. These are all the different angles on which your boat can meet the wind, including a head-to-wind, which can send you drifting backward, and a beam reach, which is the one that helps you go fastest. She said that when my mum agrees to let me use *Hannah's Glory* we can go and do the course at Salamander Bay, where they make you practice things like sailing with one sail, or sailing without a centerboard. They run it in the school holidays and it's quite cool if you bring your own boat, instead of having to take turns in the school one. I had asked Mum once about Greg's dinghy, since my party, and she just said a flat no, in the way that meant she wasn't going to discuss it.

But Auntie K said to leave it with her, and if we were clever about it, Mum would come around. She said it was like fishing: you had to learn to be quiet and patient to reel in what you wanted.

It was quite warm, even on the water, and we just wore our fleeces. Lara's mum made us wear our life jackets the whole time, just in case, and they kept us quite warm, so we didn't need jackets. The sea was calm and we were allowed to go between the two nearest buoys and left up the coast as long as we didn't go out as far as the shipping lane. Lara always does what her mum says. She said her dad knew someone who had strayed into the shipping lane and nearly got sucked under a steel container ship because they weren't looking where they were going.

The dolphins came out to see us near the point. We had stopped for a moment to get out our chocolate and I recognized Brolly and Brolly's baby from the pictures on *Moby One,* and I showed Lara her dorsal fin, which was the exact shape of underneath an umbrella. Her baby was so cute that Lara nearly cried. We were pretty sure they knew it was us — they didn't always go up to the whalechasers, but this was the third time I had been out with Lara and the dolphins always came to us. They always look like they're smiling. We spent about an hour just sitting out there by the point, talking to them and watching them play. Brolly's baby had grown about six inches since I last saw her and Brolly came up close enough to the boat for us to stroke her nose, even though she must have known we didn't have any fish. I couldn't resist touching her, even though Yoshi said we must never encourage the dolphins to come too close in case they thought all humans would be nice to them. She told me that last year, for no reason, someone had stabbed a dolphin to death down the coast. They just went out on a jet-ski and stabbed it with a knife. I cried, because I kept thinking of that poor dolphin swimming up to the bike with its lovely smiley face, thinking it had made a new friend. In the end I cried so hard that Yoshi had to go and get Mum to stop me.

Dolphins were Letty's favorite animals. She had four on pieces of different-colored crystal on her dressing table that she got for her fifth birthday. I used to rearrange them and she got cross because I'd been in her stuff. We used to fight quite a lot, because she was only fourteen months younger than me and Mum said we were like peas in a pod. Sometimes I still think about when we used to fight and I feel really bad because if I'd known what was going to happen to her I would have tried to be nice to her every day. I say "try" because it's quite hard to be nice to someone every day. Even my mum gets on my nerves sometimes but I'm always nice to her because I know she's still sad, and because I'm all she has left. I still have the crystal dolphins. One looks a bit like Brolly, so I called her Brolly and I've made the smallest one of the others her baby even though it isn't really the right size. But I keep them in a box now because they're precious. And because having them out just brings everything back.

Lara said, picking them up very carefully, "Do you think about your sister a lot?"

I was under my bed trying to find something in a magazine that I wanted to show her, so I don't think she could see me nodding. "I don't really talk about her because Mum gets too upset," I said, as I backed out, trying not to hit my head, "but I still miss her." I couldn't really say more than that. It still felt too difficult.

"I hate my sister," she said. "She's a witch. I'd love to be an only."

I couldn't explain it properly to her — but I'll always have a sister. Letty not being alive anymore doesn't make me an only, just half of what I was.

On Thursday Mum asked me to take Mike his breakfast for the third time in a week.

"Can't you do it?" I said. "I haven't done my hair yet." It was really annoying as I like to put my hair in plaits before school and if you lose your rhythm as you're doing it they go all lumpy in the middle. Auntie K said her old fingers were too stiff to do plaits, and Mum never cares what her hair looks like so there's only me who can do it.

"No," she said. Like, that was that. And she left his tray on the step outside my room.

She was being quite weird. I didn't know if it was because she didn't like him but she won't sit out in the evenings anymore and the few times when she did she ignored him, even though he sat out every night like he was waiting for her. I told Lara it was quite childish, really, like some of the girls in our class who pretend you aren't there even though you're standing right in front of them.

"Are you cross with Mike?" I asked Mum in the end.

She was a bit shocked. "No — why do you ask?"

"You *look* cross with him."

She started to fiddle with her hair. "I'm

not cross, sweetheart. I just don't think it's a good idea to get too close to the guests," she said. Later I heard her and Auntie K talking in the kitchen, when they thought I was watching telly. The whalechasers were outside and Mum wouldn't go and sit with them, even though they really needed to talk about whether to raise ticket prices. Fuel costs had gone up again. They were always on about fuel costs.

"I don't understand why you're getting yourself so worked up about everything," Auntie K was saying.

"Who says I'm worked up?"

"That chip out of my dinner-plate?"

I heard the plate go down on the surface, and Mum's muttered "Sorry."

"Liza, love, you can't hide forever."

"Why? We're happy, aren't we? We do okay?"

Aunt Kathleen didn't say anything.

"I can't, okay? It's just not a good idea."

"And Greg is?"

Greg doesn't like Mike. He called him a "sonofabitch" when Auntie Kathleen was talking to him and he thought nobody could hear.

Mum's voice was all stressed when she said, "I just think it's better all around if Hannah and I steer clear of getting . . .

involved." Then she went out. And my aunt made that snorting noise with her nose.

I looked up "involved" in the dictionary. It said, "participating in a romantic or sexual relationship/complicated or difficult to follow." I showed it to Auntie K to see which one it was, but she stuck her finger on both and said that about summed it up.

At school, they were talking about the school trip. Sometimes it felt like they talked about nothing else, even though it was months and months away and sometimes our teacher said if we didn't pull our fingers out no one would be going. We were all outside sitting on the long bench in the yard and Katie Taylor asked me if I was coming, and I said I might not be. I didn't want to say anything as she's the kind who twists everything you say, so of course she stood there in front of everyone and said, "Why? Haven't you got enough money?"

"It's not because of money," I said, and went pink because I couldn't say what it was.

"Why, then? Everyone else in our year is coming." As usual, she had two pink patches of skin next to her ears because her mum pulls her hair too tight into her clips. Lara reckons that's why she's always mean.

"Not everyone," said Lara.

"Everyone except the nerds."

"I'm not coming because we're going somewhere else," I said. I spoke before I'd thought about what I was saying. "We're going on a trip."

Lara nodded, as if she'd known about it for ages.

"Back to England?"

"Maybe. Or we might go to the Northern Territory."

"So you don't even know where?"

"Look, her mum hasn't decided yet," said Lara. She can put on this voice that says not to mess with her. "Don't be such a stickybeak, Katie. It's none of your business where they go."

Later, Lara put her arm through mine when we walked back to hers. My mum was picking me up from there after tea, like she did every Tuesday, and Lara always said it was funny because I liked her house best, just like she said she liked mine. I like the way her family is all noisy and happy even when they're shouting at each other and I like the way her dad's always teasing her, rubbing the soles of her bare feet on his bristly chin and calling her "Kitten." Sometimes I think about him when Lance calls me "Squirt" but it isn't the same. I'd never have a cuddle with Lance the way Lara does with her dad. When Lara's dad once grabbed my feet and rubbed them on his chin I felt embarrassed, like everyone was pretending to include me because I don't have a dad of my own. Lara said she liked it at mine because no one went in your room and through your stuff, and the way Auntie K gives us the key to the Whalechasers Museum and lets us wander around in there without watching what we're up to. Auntie K knew we wouldn't wreck anything, she told us, because we were such good girls. The best girls she knew. I haven't told her about the time Lara nicked one of her mum's cigarettes and we smoked it in the corner behind *Maui II* until we felt sick.

"Hannah," Lara said, when we were at the bottom of her street, and her voice was really kind, like she wanted to show me how much she was still my friend. "Is it really about money? The reason why you can't come to New Zealand?"

I chewed my nail. "It's a bit complicated."

"You're my best friend," she said. "I wouldn't tell anyone, whatever it is."

"I know." I squeezed her arm. I really would have liked to talk to her about it. But I still wasn't always sure about it myself. All I knew was what Mum had told me — that we couldn't ever leave Australia and that I mustn't talk to anyone about that. Or tell them why.

And the next day Katie Taylor started going on about it again. She said I couldn't come because the Silver Bay Hotel was broke. Then she said she reckoned it was Auntie K who'd killed the baby whale, just like she'd killed the shark, because it had been in the paper then and everyone knew. She said if I had a dad perhaps I'd be able to join in more school trips, then asked me what his name was, because she knew I couldn't say, and then she laughed in that really sly way until Lara went up to her and gave her a shove. Katie grabbed her hand and bent her fingers back and they had a full-on fight in the yard until Mrs. Sherborne came and broke it up.

"She's a stupid bitch," said Lara to me, as we walked off to the cloakroom. She was spitting on the floor because some of Katie's hair had ended up in her mouth. "Don't pay her any attention." But that was the thing: suddenly I didn't feel mad with Katie, or any of her stupid mates, I felt mad with my mum. Because all I wanted was to do what everyone else did. I get good marks and I never talk about what I'm not supposed to talk about and I don't even talk about Letty half the time when I want to because I'm not allowed to hurt anyone's feelings. So if we could get the money for a trip to New Zealand, like Auntie K said, and absolutely everyone in my class was going — even David Dobbs, who everyone knows still wets his bed and has a mum who takes things from shops without paying — why was it always me who got left out? Why was I the one who always had to say no?

If you don't count where we came from, I'm the only person in my whole class who has never been further than the Blue Mountains.

I was still angry when I got home. Mum picked me up and I almost said something but she was so busy thinking about something else that she didn't notice how quiet I was. And then I remembered that we still had this horrible family staying, with two boys who looked at me like I was stupid. And that made me really mad too.

"Do you have any homework?" she said, when we pulled up outside the hotel. Milly was chewing Mum's torch in the back and I had known all the way back but hadn't stopped her.

"No," I said, then climbed out of the car before she could check. I knew she was looking at me, but Katie's words were still in my ears and I wanted to be in my room by myself for a while.

When I was going up the stairs I saw that Mike's door was open. He was on the phone and I hovered for a minute, not sure whether I should wait for him to finish.

I think he felt me there because he spun round. "An S94. Yup, that's it. And he said that should improve our chances a hundred percent." He glanced at me. "Okay — can't talk now, Dennis. I'll ring you back." Then he put down the phone and smiled a great big smile at me. "Hello there. How are you doing?"

"Terrible," I said, dropping my bag on the floor. "I hate everyone." I surprised myself, saying that. I don't normally say that sort of thing. But it made me feel better.

He didn't try to shush me, or tell me I didn't really feel like that, which is what my aunt usually does, like I don't even know what I'm feeling. He just nodded. "I have days like that."

"Is today?"

He frowned. "Is today what?"

"One of those days. Terrible. A terrible day."

He thought for a minute, then shook his head. I thought, as he grinned, that he was almost as handsome as Greg.

"No," he said. "Most days are pretty good at the moment. Here," he motioned at me to sit down, "would one of these cheer you up? I've made it my mission to try every Australian biscuit there is."

When he pulled open his drawer, I saw he had all my favorites: Iced Vo-Vos, Anzacs, Chocolate Tim Tams and Arnott's Mint Slices. "You'll get fat," I warned him.

"Nope. I go running most mornings," he said. "I have a good metabolism. And, besides, people worry far too much about all that stuff."

He made himself some tea, then sat on the leather chair and I sat at his desk and he let me go on his computer. He showed me a program that lets you change pictures, so just for fun we pulled up another picture of Auntie K and the shark and we drew a big smile on its face, and then I did another where I gave Auntie K a mustache and a pair of really big feet, and had her holding a sign and I wrote in it, "Shark Lady Toothpaste — For a Brighter Smile."

Just as I was finishing, I felt him looking at me. You can do that, you know, make someone turn around if you stare at them hard enough. I felt like he was staring at the back of my head so I spun around really fast and he was. "Did you have a brother or a sister?" he said. "The one who died, I mean."

I was so shocked to hear someone say it out loud that I nearly spat out my Chocolate Tim Tam. No grown-up talks about Letty. Not straight out like that. Auntie K has this kind of pained look whenever I say her name, like it's too much to bear, and Mum's so sad when I talk about her that I don't like to.

"A sister," I said, after a minute. "Her name was Letty." Then, when he didn't seem horrified, or look at me like I should be quiet, I said, "She died when she was five, in a car crash."

He shrugged a bit. "That's really tough," he said. "I'm sorry."

Suddenly I really wanted to cry. No one has ever said that to me. No one has ever thought about what it was like for me to lose my sister, or said that it might have been horrible for me. No one asks me if I miss her, or whether any of it feels like it was my fault. It's like, because I'm young, my feelings don't matter. I've heard them, they say, "The young bounce back. She'll heal." They say, "Thank goodness she can't remember too much." And, "It's the worst thing you can imagine, to lose a child." But they never say, "Poor Hannah, losing her favorite person in the whole world." They never say, "Okay, Hannah. Let's talk about Letty. Let's talk about all the things you miss about her, and all the things that make you sad." But I didn't feel I could say that to him: it's locked too deep inside, somewhere I've learned it's best to keep hidden. So when the tears came I pretended I was upset about the school trip and I told him about Katie Taylor teasing me, and about the money and how I was the only person in my whole class who couldn't go. And before long it had worked so well that I'd managed not to think about Letty, just about the school trip and how awful it would be when everyone went off to New Zealand without me and that made me cry.

Mike handed me his handkerchief and pretended to be interested in something outside while I pulled myself together. He sat quietly until I had stopped sniffing and then he leaned forward, looked me straight in the eye, and said, "Okay, Hannah Mc-Cullen. I'm going to make you a business proposition."

Mike Dormer asked me to take photographs around the bay. He went to the shop and bought three disposable cameras and said he would pay me a dollar for every good shot I could take. He said that when he went home his friends would want to know what he'd been up to and he wasn't much of a photographer so I should take pictures of all around the bay so that he could show them where he'd been and all the nicest spots. Then he asked me to write him a list of all the things that were good about my school, and about Silver Bay, and all the things that would improve it. "Like the fact that our bus broke down and we haven't got a new one? Or that our library is still in mobile buildings?"

"Exactly like that," he said, handing me a pad of paper. "Not who you like at school, or that stupid girl who teased you, but a project. A bit of proper research."

He said he would pay me a good salary, depending on how well I did. "But I want a really professional job," he said. "Not some fobbed-off piece of nonsense. Do you think you're up to it?"

I nodded, because I was excited at the idea of earning some money. Mike said if I worked hard enough there was no reason whatsoever why I shouldn't be able to afford to go to New Zealand with my friends.

"But how long are you staying?" I asked him. I was trying to work out how much time I had to earn the money and whether, if I showed Mum I had enough, she'd feel she couldn't say no. And he said his departure date was one of life's imponderables, and I almost asked him what that meant but I didn't want him to think I was stupid, so I just nodded again, like I do when Yoshi starts talking about stuff I don't understand.

Then I showed Auntie K the pictures we had doctored of her and the shark and she raised her eyes and said God in Heaven was never going to let her forget it.

The weird thing about that night was that I felt happy. If I'd gone straight to my room, like I'd planned, I know I would have been sad all night, but we had a good time, almost like it was a party.

The guests had gone out for the night, so I didn't have to look at those freckly boys with their stupid stares every time I walked past the lounge. Lance had had a win on the horses — he called them gee-gees — and bought everyone pizza in a great big stack of boxes. He told Auntie Kathleen that for once she should put her feet up, and Mike might be her guest but he was part of the ruddy furniture now so she didn't have to worry about him. And Mike had this little smile like he didn't want anyone to see but he was pleased to be part of the furniture, and then he let me eat all the salami off the top of his pizza because it's my favorite.

Richard and Tom from the other *Moby* came to join us and said they'd seen a pod of five whales out by Break Nose Island that afternoon, and they'd had an American tourist who had been so happy to see them that he'd given them a fifty-dollar tip each. And then Mr. Gaines stopped by with some wine that Auntie Kathleen said was far too good for the likes of us, but she opened both bottles anyway, and they started on about the Old Days, which is what they talk about a lot when they're together.

Greg wasn't there. The others said he hadn't been out on his boat for four days. Auntie K said breaking up with someone could do that to you, and that some people found it harder than others. I asked her where he was, and she said probably at the bottom of a bottle somewhere. The first time she ever said that to me I thought it was really funny because there was no bottle big enough in the whole of Australia to fit a grown man in, especially Greg, who is quite tall.

It was a cold evening, but all the burners were lit and we were squashed up on the bench, apart from Lance and Yoshi who were together on the big chair, and Auntie Kathleen and Mr. Gaines who were on two wicker chairs with cushions, because Auntie Kathleen said at their age they deserved a little comfort. Mum was sitting on the other side of me and when I finished my drink I told her about Mike's business proposition and her face did that thing it does when she's about to stop me doing something and my pizza went all dry in my mouth.

"Paying her money? You're paying her to take photographs?"

Mike took a sip of his wine. "You think I should give her money for nothing?"

"You're as bad as Greg," she said, not in a good way.

"I'm nothing like Greg. And you know it."

"Don't use her, Mike," she whispered, as if I couldn't hear. "Don't use her to try to get close to me, because it won't work."

But Mike didn't look bothered. "I'm not doing it for you. I'm doing it because Hannah is an exceptionally nice kid and I need some jobs done. If I hadn't asked her, I'd only have had to ask someone else and, frankly, I'd rather work with Hannah."

He bit off a great big piece of his pizza and when he spoke again his mouth was full. I tried not to think about being an exceptionally nice kid. I thought I might be getting a bit of a crush on Mike.

"Anyway," he said, as he chewed, "you're

very presumptuous. Who says I want to get close to you?"

There was a short silence as Mum looked at him quite sharply. Then I saw her mouth quiver, like she didn't really want to smile but couldn't help it, and I relaxed because if she was going to stop me earning the money she would have said so there and then.

She kept staring at her fingers, like she was thinking about something. "What are these photographs for?" she said.

Mike licked his fingers. "I can't tell you that. Commercial privilege. Hannah, not a word," he said. But he was smiling too.

"She's a good photographer," she said.

"She should be. She's charging me way above the market rate."

"How much are you paying her?"

"That's privileged information too." He winked at me. "If you're saying you'd like to undercut your own daughter, I'd be happy to hear what you can offer."

I didn't understand what they were talking about, but they seemed happy so I stopped worrying. I was trying to work out if I could steal some of Mike's beer without Mum noticing.

"So how long *are* you staying?" she asked.

Just as he was about to answer we saw

headlights appear along the coast road. We were quiet as they drew closer, trying to see who it was — Greg's truck has fog lights on the front, so we knew it wasn't him. "It'll be the bookies," said Mr. Gaines, leaning toward Lance, "come to tell you your last horse has just finished its race." And Lance, whose mouth was full, raised his beer bottle to him, like a salute.

But it was a taxi. As it pulled up at the bottom, Auntie Kathleen got out from behind the table, muttering that there was no rest for the wicked. "I've got no food left," she said. "I hope they don't want feeding."

"Well?" said Mum, turning to Mike. "You haven't answered my question."

I was waiting too, because I wanted to know. But Auntie Kathleen, who was walking back up the drive with someone's suitcase, distracted me. Behind her was a girl, quite young with very straight blonde hair and a soft pink cardigan wrapped around her shoulders. She was wearing high-heeled shoes with sequins, like she was going to a party, and as she walked the lights from the hotel made them sparkle. Auntie K came up to him, eyebrows raised, and dropped the suitcase in front of him. "Someone to see you," she said.

"Dad gave me the time off," the girl said. I felt Mike stand up beside me. I heard the sharp intake of his breath. "I've come to give you a hand. I thought we could have our honeymoon early."

ELEVEN:
MIKE

It was weird. You think of all the ways you're meant to greet your lover after a long separation — the slo-mo running together, the endless kisses, the desperate holding and touching. It's like there's an accepted protocol for big reunions, a kind of emotional outpouring, an affirmation of what you mean to each other. And all I felt when I saw Vanessa was this weird sensation I used to get when I was a kid, like when you're at a friend's house and your mum comes to get you before you're ready.

I felt guilty for the absence of what I knew she'd expected — what I might have expected of myself — and she picked up on it straight away. Like I said, she's not stupid, my girlfriend.

"I thought you'd be glad," she said, as we lay next to each other later that night. That was the other weird thing: we weren't touching.

"I am glad," I said. "It's just been difficult here . . . I've been so locked into work that I've deliberately not thought about anything to do with home."

"Evidently," she said drily.

I closed my eyes in the dark. "I've never been great with surprises. You know that. I was bound to disappoint you."

Her silence told me she agreed with me on that point at least.

In truth it had probably been the most awkward twenty minutes of our entire relationship. She had stood there in front of the whalechasers, dressed like something from a fashion magazine, gazing from one person to another as she grasped the magnitude of her mistake, her carefully prepared smile fading. Kathleen had gone inside to fetch her a drink. Beside me, Hannah had taken advantage of the diversion to swig surreptitiously from someone's beer bottle. Mr. Gaines had made a show of offering her his chair, brushing the cushion ostentatiously as if she were even more of an exoticism than she was. And all the time, Lance had joked about me being a dark horse, going on about it so long that I had seen Vanessa's confidence waver, and watched her start calculating how small a presence in my life she had been while I was in Australia.

And Liza had sat on my other side. Her face had been a Japanese mask, her eyes coolly registering this unforeseen element. I had wanted to take her aside, to explain, but it had been impossible. After about ten minutes, and a cool but cordial introduction, she shook hands with Vanessa and announced that everyone should excuse her but she and Hannah had to go in as Hannah had to get ready for school the next day.

I felt her presence at the other end of that corridor like something radioactive.

So, several hours later, I felt vaguely resentful, and guilty for it. It was strange having Vanessa in that room: it had become so completely mine that she was a reminder from another life. I had become used to its spare aesthetic, and found the freedom to live without the usual accoutrements of home actually liberating. Having Vanessa there, with her matching suitcases, her endless shoes, the rows of unguents and ointments — her very presence — changed the balance of things. It reminded me of my life in London. It made me wonder whether I had been as happy there as I'd believed.

I felt mean even thinking it. I turned onto my side, and put my hand on Vanessa's stomach, which was covered with something silky. "Look," I said, trying to reassure her, "it's just been a bit odd, with them not knowing about the plans. I guess you being here makes it a little more complicated."

"You seem to have got yourself quite . . . involved," she said.

I lay very still, trying to gauge what she meant.

Then she spoke again: "I suppose it's such a small place that it's impossible not to. Get to know the people, I mean."

"It's not . . ." I faltered ". . . your average executive hotel."

"I gathered that."

"It's very much a family-run thing."

"They seem nice."

"They are. It's very different from what I'm used to — what we're used to." I was glad she couldn't see my face.

"You looked . . . at home." She shifted beside me, making the bed creak. "It felt really weird walking up to you in the middle of all those people, with your jeans and your fisherman's jacket or whatever it is. I felt like a real outsider. Even with you."

She sat up and swung her legs over the side of the bed, so that her back was toward me. In the dark I could just see her outline and that her hair was messed up because she had been lying down, which made me feel oddly tender toward her. I didn't often see Vanessa with messy hair.

"It's been so odd without you," she said.

I lay back against the pillows. "I wouldn't have come out here if your dad hadn't had his accident."

"It's only been three and a half weeks, but it felt like years." I saw her head tilt. "I thought you'd ring more often."

"It's night here when it's day there — you know that."

"You could have rung me any time." Her perfume was potent. Until now the room had smelt of salt air.

"It's business, Ness. You know what it's like. You know what I'm like."

She turned away. "I do. I'm sorry. I don't know what's wrong with me. I just felt a bit . . ."

"It's the jet lag," I said, a bit shaken by her uncharacteristic wobble. Vanessa was sure of everything. It was one of the things I liked most about her. "I felt odd for days after I arrived." The idea that I could shake her was worse. I've never felt responsible for Vanessa's happiness — I didn't like the idea that I might be more responsible for it than I'd known.

I reached for her, to persuade her to lie down, thinking that perhaps if we made love we'd start to feel a little less like strangers. But she eluded me and, in a fluid movement, rose and walked around the bed to the window. The moon was high and the night clear so you could see the whole bay. The sea glinted like something magical, the lights from distant boats sending little ladders of illumination toward us across the inky waves, while around the bay the shadowy hills were dark with secrets.

"It's beautiful," she said quietly. "You said it was."

"You're beautiful," I said. She was like something in a film, silhouetted against the moonlight, the curves of her body faintly visible through the filmy fabric.

It's okay, I told myself silently. If I can feel like this about her it's okay. The other thing was an aberration.

She turned half toward me. This is the woman who is going to be my wife, I told myself. This is the woman I will love until I die. She looked at me, and I had a sudden sense of hope that it would all be fine.

"So, where are we with the planning permission?" she asked.

As I told Vanessa, there had been a few difficulties with the development plan. The previous day I had spent hours in the council planning department, going through the various forms that needed filling in, meeting the relevant officers. Over the previous weeks, I had reached Mr. Reilly — on the highest rung of the planning ladder. I liked him, a tall, freckled man whose expression suggested he had seen pretty well every kind of application there was. I had gone in quietly, had made clear that we were happy to consider modifying our plans in whatever ways he thought might be necessary. I had deferred to him, conscious that I didn't want him to see us as simply a foreign interest keen to exploit his area. Which, I suppose, was what we were.

To some extent, my approach had paid off. Over various meetings, he had said he liked the design, the employment opportunities and the potential for regeneration in a traditionally less than economically buoyant area. He liked the domino effects for local shops and traders, and I had emphasized the positive impact of similar developments on the local economy, using examples I had gleaned from other resorts along the east Australian coast. The architecture was in keeping with the area. The materials were to be sourced locally. The tourist office had expressed its approval. I had begun to put in place a website about the development that local people would be able to access, should they have any questions about it, or want to be considered for employment if it came off. He raised a wry eyebrow at this, as if I might have pushed my luck a little. But, he admitted, I had done my homework.

What he didn't like, as I had feared, was the development's potential impact on the environment. It wasn't just the noise and disruption of the building process, especially in an area so close to the national parks, he said, but people in Silver Bay had strong opinions about restriction of their waters. He said that a previous attempt to introduce a pearl farm to a nearby bay had met with a barrage of opposition and the development had been canceled.

"The difference between our development and theirs," I said, "is that the employment and other benefits are stronger."

Mr. Reilly was no fool. "To some extent," he said, "but we've seen this kind of thing before, and you can't tell me you'll be plowing the profits back into the community. This is backed by venture capitalists — British venture capitalists. They'll be wanting to see their return, right? You'll be in the hands of shareholders. It's not some community service you're proposing."

I gestured toward the plans. "Mr. Reilly,

you know as well as I do that you can't stop progress. This is a prime area of Australian waterfront, the perfect environment for families wanting to come on holiday — Australian families. All we want to do is facilitate that."

He sighed, steepled his fingers, then pointed at the document. "Mike — can I call you Mike? You need to understand that everything has changed here in the last couple of years. Yes, the proposed development falls within the envelope of what is considered acceptable, but there are other considerations we now have to take into account. Like, how are you going to minimize the environmental impact? You've not yet given me a reassuring answer. This area has a growing awareness of its whale and dolphin population, and people around here don't want to do anything to harm them. On a purely economic level, they're a growing tourist attraction in themselves."

"We're not like the pearl fishery. We wouldn't be marking off huge areas of the waterfront," I said.

"But you'd still be making some of it unusable."

"It would only be with the same activities that tourists normally take part in, nothing large-scale or controversial."

"But that's it. We don't get those kind of tourists around here — not in Silver Bay, anyway. They might swim, paddle out in a dinghy, but wetbikes, jet- or waterskiing are much noisier, much more intrusive."

"Mr. Reilly, you know as well as I do that in a place like this development is only a matter of time. If it's not us, it'll be some other corporation."

He put down his pen, and looked at me with a mixture of belligerence and sympathy. "Look, mate, we're all for development around here, anything that will help the local community. We know we need the employment and the infrastructure. But our sea creatures, our wildlife, are not an afterthought. We're not like European cities — build first, worry about the environment later. We don't separate the two. And you won't win over this town unless you can sort out the environmental stuff."

"That's fine, Mr. Reilly," I said, pulling my papers together. "Very commendable. But I'd have more sympathy with your argument if this week I hadn't watched two whales bullied half to death by tourists in disco boats, which didn't seem to be policed by anyone in your area. It's all very well for you to tell me that my development's going to have a negative impact — but the threat to the whales is already out there, far worse than anything we're proposing. And, as far as I can see, no one is doing anything about it. What we're suggesting is a limited development. We're willing to be as sympathetic as we can be to environmental concerns, to take expert advice and to be licensed, if necessary. But you can't tell me your area's a model for environmental excellence because I saw that dead baby whale, saw what prompted its death. I've been out whale-watching and, I hate to say it, that's an intrusion in itself."

"You don't know that."

"And you don't know whether a few water-skiers are really going to affect a whale migration that's gone on for centuries. There's got to be consistency about this."

"I'll discuss it," he said. "But don't be surprised if it goes to a public inquiry. People are getting wind of these plans, and a few are already antsy."

I had arrived home in a foul mood and rung Dennis, perversely glad when I worked out the time difference and discovered how long he had been asleep. After I'd outlined the results of my meeting, I was disconcerted to find that he could spring into life from a deep sleep with virtually no sluggish

in-between. It was as if he had been processing it all as he slept. "It's complicated,
Dennis. I can't pretend it's not. But I've
had a radical thought. What if . . . we shut
down the watersports angle, made it more
of a spa experience? We could really go for
it, make it a *Vogue*-type thing. Where
celebrities go."

"But the watersports are its bloody
Unique Selling Point," Dennis barked.
"That's why the venture capitalists are
interested. It's *meant* to be about sport,
about keeping fit. It's about a total body
experience, targeting men as much as
women. A luxury leisure experience. Is this
the bloody whale crusties again? What have
they said?"

"They've not said anything. They still
don't know."

"So what's your bloody problem?"

"I want this to work on all levels."

"You're not making sense."

"Dennis, we'd have a lot easier ride from
the planners if there was no risk of anything
happening to the sea creatures."

"We'd have a lot easier ride from the planners if you did your job properly and
stressed what a fantastic opportunity it is
for a depressed area, how much money
everyone stands to make."

"It's not just about money —"

"It's *always* about money."

"Okay. But it's just that when you're out here, you also get a sense of the . . ." I ran a hand through my hair ". . . the importance of the whales."

There was a pause before he spoke again. "The. Importance. Of. The. Whales."

I braced myself.

"Mike, this is not what I expect to hear from you. This is not what I promoted you for. This is not what I *want* to hear when I'm stuck on my arse in England waiting for news of a one-hundred-and-thirty-million-pound luxury-hotel development that you've still not secured the planning permission for even though you've been in Australia three weeks. Now, we need the permissions secured, and we need them superfast. We have to start building in a matter of months. So, you talk to your bloody crusty whale friends and go sing your whalesong, throw some money at Mr. Reilly or get his picture taken with some Lithuanian lap dancer — whatever it takes! — but come back to me in the next forty-eight hours with a concrete plan I can present to Vallance Equity when they turn up on Monday. Okay? Or the whales won't be the only things blubbering."

He took a deep, shaking breath. I was glad

that so many thousands of miles separated us. "Look, you wanted to be a partner — prove you're up to it. Or, even though I love you like a son, you may find your arse imprinted with my metaphorical left boot. Along with your employment prospects. You get me?"

It certainly didn't need spelling out anymore clearly than that. I sat back in my chair, shut my eyes and thought about everything I'd worked for over the past years, everything I'd looked forward to becoming. Then I thought of what Hannah had told me about her school bus. The lack of a library. "Okay . . ." I said. "There's one possible way through this. Do you remember me mentioning a thing called an S94?"

As Mr. Reilly had explained it to me, it worked like this: for every tourist development in the Silver Bay area, the council generally expected a fifty percent financial contribution from the developers toward the extra strain on local services — roads, car parking, recreational facilities, firefighting and emergency services, that kind of thing. It was not unfamiliar to me: we had come across similar provisions in other developments, and I had found there was usually some clause, as there was in the case of Silver Bay, that allowed for a waiver if the development was deemed of sufficient benefit to the community. I had usually wangled it on the basis of my research. Dennis had also achieved it — but hinted at palms being greased and companies receiving lucrative building contracts. "More than one way to skin a cat," he liked to say, smacking his hands together. And everyone had their price.

The council document was a thorough piece of research, detailing not just the population projection for the area, but the cost of all the amenities likely to be needed to accommodate it. I began to plow through them, calculating the cost to our development, trying to highlight those that would have the most favorable impact on the public.

Continuing growth in the development of Tourist Accommodation, which is occurring over the whole council area, as well as the traditional coastal fringe, will create an increase in demand for the provision of council facilities . . . the level of demand on the facilities varies with the category and stay time at the Tourist Accommodation provided, but there is an increase in demand, over that of the permanent population . . .

I had sat up staring at the paper, thinking. But studying the S94 document, I had seen that we could turn this one on its head: what if our company offered over and above the contribution level, and brought with it, for example, a new library for the Silver Bay School or a new school bus, or a regeneration of the Whalechasers Museum?

During our meeting, Mr. Reilly had worn the expression of a man well used to hearing it all before. He had probably had many such approaches over the years, and turned down as many as he had approved. But Beaker Holdings would not, like most developers, try to provide the minimum material public benefit to build its resort. Instead it would show itself to be a model for responsible development. It would provide over and above what was needed; it would be generous and imaginative and, with luck, we could use this development as a model for the next. It is fair to say that local-government projected spending does not generally make the most exciting reading in the world, but that afternoon, before Hannah had come upstairs and disturbed me, I had been as excited by a municipal financial document as it's possible to be.

Vanessa slept till after eleven the next morning. I lay beside her for some time after daybreak, glancing at her face, watched her shifting unconsciously under the sheet. Eventually, when my thoughts became too complicated, I got out of bed without waking her. Some time after seven thirty, I crept downstairs, let myself out and ran five miles along the coast road and back, enjoying the damp chill of the morning air, the sense of quiet and isolation that only running provides.

I ran longer and harder than I generally do, shedding layers of clothing as I went, but did not feel noticeably more exhausted. I needed the physical effort, the time to think. As I ran along the dirt track that split the pavement from the beach, I pictured the new resort, perhaps some low-cost housing to accommodate the staff. Australia, I had discovered, had the same problem as England with housing affordability. Perhaps we could offer some watersports-related shops and cafés. Maybe, if the returns were great enough, a medical center. As I headed back, I tried not to look at the Silver Bay Hotel. If the development were to go ahead it would be at best overshadowed, at worst demolished.

Twice, people whose faces I now recognized — dog-walkers, fishermen — lifted a hand in greeting, and as I waved back, I wondered what they would think of my plans. To them I was not the English stranger, the fish out of water, the proposed fiancé, the stickybeak, the thief of other men's women. As I ran through a list of urgent phone calls I had to make — to Dennis, to the financial department, to Mr. Reilly to arrange another meeting — I thought again about those waving people and asked myself, Who the hell *are* they waving at?

Somewhere along the Silver Bay coast road I had had a revelation. For months I had been obsessed with this development, had thought about it only in terms of what it meant to my career and my company. Now I had been confronted with the potential cost. And I saw that my first concerns were no longer money and ambition, but something infinitely more difficult: successful compromise. I wanted Kathleen and Liza to be as happy with this outcome as the flint-eyed venture capitalists. I wanted the whales and dolphins to continue their lives, unaffected by it. Or, at least, as unaffected by it as any creature can be when it lives in close proximity to man. I hadn't worked it out yet, but with my head full of conservation areas and commemorative museums I felt I might at last be grasping toward something.

I returned at eight thirty, wet with sweat, brain numbed with effort, half hoping I could fetch myself breakfast without bumping into anyone. I had timed my return, I am ashamed to say, to coincide with Liza and Hannah's school run and it was my best chance of finding an empty house.

But Kathleen was still sitting at the kitchen table, her own breakfast long finished, her gray hair tied back and a dark blue sweater announcing the arrival of winter. She had set me a place, with coffee and cereal. Another place setting sat ostentatiously beside it. "Kept that one quiet," she observed, from behind her newspaper, as I sat down.

How could I tell her it was as if I had forgotten?

TWELVE:
GREG

You'd never have noticed the scar on Liza McCullen's face if you hadn't been right up close to her, never run your hand down her cheek and pushed her hair behind her ear. It was pretty faded now — a good few years old, I reckoned — about an inch and a half of slightly raised pearl-white skin, a little jaggedy as if she'd never had it fixed up properly when she hurt herself. Half the time she wore her old baseball cap so that that part of her face was always in shadow. When the hat was off, her hair was always in strands around her face, whipped by the wind out of her ponytail. When she laughed, you could barely notice it because of the creases the sea and the sun had blown into the corners of her eyes.

But I saw it. And even without the scar you'd have known there was something a bit off-key about Liza.

The first time I met her she was like a

ghost. This may sound a bit fancy, but I swear that you could almost see through her. She was like sea mist, like she wanted to vaporize into air. "This is my niece," said Kathleen, as we all waited for our beer one afternoon — like, that was all that would be said about the arrival of someone most of us had never even heard existed. "And this is her daughter, Hannah. From England. They'll be staying."

I said g'day — a couple of the other whale-chasers echoed me — and Liza nodded this weird hello, not looking anyone in the eye. She was about as done in by jet lag as it's possible to be. I'd seen the kid a couple of days before, hanging on to Kathleen's hand, and I'd guessed she belonged to one of the guests. It was a bit of a shock to discover not just that she was Kathleen's family but that someone else had been there all along. I checked her out a little (she was blonde and leggy — just my type) but there was nothing much to her then. She was pale with big old dark circles around her eyes and her hair hanging in curtains around her face. I was more curious than, you know, interested.

But Hannah — I loved Hannah the moment I saw her, and I'm pretty sure she liked me too. She stood there, tucked behind Kathleen, with those big brown eyes as wide as a possum's, and she looked like if anyone said boo! to her she'd fall over and die of fright. So I knelt right down — she was a tiny kid then — and I said, "G'day, Hannah. Did your auntie Kathleen tell you what's right outside your room?"

Kathleen looked sharp at me, like I was about to say the bogeyman or something. I ignored her, and carried on: "Dolphins. In the water out there in the bay. Smartest, most playful creatures you can imagine. If you look hard enough out of your window, I betcha you'll see them. And you know what? They're that smart they'll probably stick a nose up to check you out too."

"The bay's full of them," said Kathleen.

"You ever seen a dolphin up close?"

She shook her little head. But I had her attention.

"Beautiful they are. They play with us when we take the boats out. Jump around, swim underneath. Just as clever as you or me. Nosy, but. They'll come and see what we're doing. There's pods of them that have lived in this bay thirty, forty years. Isn't that right, Kathleen?"

The old lady nodded.

"If you want, I'll take you out to see them," I said.

"No," came a voice.

I stood up. Kathleen's niece had come to life.

"No," she said, her jaw set tight. "She can't go out on the water."

"I'm safe as houses," I said. "You ask Kathleen. Been doing dolphin tours for nearly fifteen years. Hell — me and the *Moby*s are the longest-running operators here, next to Kathleen. And the kids always wear life jackets. You tell her, Kathleen."

But Kathleen didn't seem quite like herself. "Everyone needs a little time to settle in. Then we'll think about nice things for Hannah to do. There's no rush."

There was a weird silence. Liza was staring at me, as if daring me to suggest any other trips. It was as if I'd suggested doing something terrible to the little girl. Kathleen smiled at me, like an apology. She seemed about as out of her depth as I'd ever seen her.

I'm a simple bloke, not the kind to dig my way into a mess. I decided to make it an early night with the missus. That, of course, was in the days before she was out giving it up to her fitness instructor.

"Good to meet you, Hannah. You keep an eye out for those dolphins, now," I said to her, tipping my cap, and she gave me a little smile that wiped out everything else around me. Liza McCullen already seemed to have forgotten I was there.

"Hey, Greggy. You seen this?"

I was sitting in MacIver's Seafood Bar and Grill, a five-minute walk up the path from Whale Jetty, trying to shift my sore head with a pie and a coffee. I figured it might work as a cross between breakfast, which I had missed, and lunch, which I rarely ate. It had hardly been worth going home; I had left the bar after a lock-in with Del, the owner, some time after two that morning, and virtually retraced my footsteps there as soon as I could get myself out of the shower.

The bar was quiet, the sun still casting long shadows over the bay, the stiff winter breeze keeping what remained of the tourists away from the front, so he walked over and sat down, shoving the newspaper toward me across the table.

"What?" I was having trouble focusing.

"The front page. About this big old development in Silver Bay."

"What are you talking about?" I squinted, pulled the paper toward me and scanned the front-page story under the headline "Major Tourist Boost For Town." It said that a multimillion-dollar development had been approved for the land along the bay from Kathleen's. A major international corporation had got planning permission for the development after an unprecedented series of offers to safeguard the nature of the town and the sea life around it.

Vallance Equity, the financiers behind the plan, have put forward a proposal that includes a new Museum of Whales to raise awareness of Port Stephens's sea creatures among tourists, whale-friendly watersports, with all instruction including whale safeguards, and a series of add-on benefits, including funding for a new library and a school bus for Silver Bay Elementary School.

"We're hoping that this is just the beginning of a fruitful partnership with the local community," said Dennis Beaker of Beaker Holdings, one of the British-based developers. "We want to take the relationship further to provide a benchmark for responsible building in the area."

Mayor of Silver Bay Don Brown said: "We deliberated long and hard about the appropriateness of this development. But after a lengthy planning process we are happy to welcome both the employment and infrastructure benefits that the new hotel complex will bring. But most of all we welcome the company's responsible and thoughtful attitude toward our waters."

" 'And the sizable bribe I've got stuffed in my back pocket,' " mocked Del. "Kathleen know about this?"

"Dunno, mate. I've — I've not been down there for a few days."

"Well," said Del, "I guess she'll know now." He slung his tea towel over his shoulder and waddled back toward the grill, where a burger was sending sparks up into the extractor fan.

" 'Whale-friendly watersports'?" I said. "What the Sam Hill are 'whale-friendly watersports'?"

"Perhaps they're going to teach them synchronized swimming," Del chuckled, "or train them to pull water-skiers."

My brain had started to clear. "This is a bloody disaster," I said, reading on. "They've bought up the old Bullen place and the water around it."

Del said nothing, flipping his burgers. I kept reading. "We'll need permission to get the boats out next. I can't believe what I'm seeing."

"Greg, you can't say the town doesn't need the business."

"You reckon?" I suddenly saw the Bar and Grill through the eyes of a visitor. The linoleum had been unchanged for the fifteen years I had lived in Silver Bay, the tables and chairs more comfortable than stylish. But that was how we liked it. How I liked it.

Later I walked down to the ticket booth. Leonie, a student, was manning it for the winter. You could usually find some dolphin-mad teenager to work there for a pittance. "You've got four this afternoon," she said, waving a docket, "a family of six for Wednesday morning, and a two for Friday, but I've told them I'll have to confirm that because the forecast's not so good."

I nodded, barely seeing her.

"Oh, Greg," she said, "Liza's coming up this afternoon. She wants to talk to you and all the other guys about this development thing. I think she's a bit worried."

"She's not the only one," I said. I lit a cigarette and went to sit in my truck.

The first time Liza McCullen and I went to bed she was so drunk that, to this day, I'm not sure that she remembered afterward what we'd done at all. It was about a year after she'd got here. She'd warmed up a bit — less a tropical warmth than a kind of

Arctic thaw, I always say — but she was still pretty cool with everyone. Not a great one for conversation. She'd started going out with Kathleen on *Ishmael.* Kathleen was showing her the ropes while the little one was at school, and the more time she spent on the water the happier she got. I made a few jokes about her being competition and all, but Kathleen gave me the eye until I made some Shark Lady crack. Then she'd ask me why I couldn't go and spend my measly dollars in some other bar. I think she was joking.

By then Liza would talk to me a bit. She'd sit out some nights with me and the other whalechasers — Ned Durrikin and that French girl with the mustache were running *Moby Two* — and chat a little — "Hi," "Yes," or "Thank you" — it was like getting blood out of a stone.

I used to crack jokes at her all the time. By then she'd kind of got to me — I like to make a girl laugh — it bugged me that some nights I could barely raise a smile. I'd been working on her so hard that, if I'm truthful, it was probably about that time that Suzanne got fed up. I'd stay all night outside Kathleen's, drinking a few, and before you knew it I'd be home drunk and Suzanne would be sitting there with a face like a smacked arse, the dinner so charred you could have drawn pictures with it.

But that night you could tell something was different. Liza hadn't come out, and Kathleen was tight-lipped and said she was staying in the house. So I went in, and sat down where I found her in the kitchen. I didn't say anything about the fact that she was checking out some photograph because when I came in she shoved it into her jacket pocket, like she didn't want anyone to see, and her eyes were all red, like she'd been crying. For once in my life I managed to keep my big gob shut because I had a feeling like something was different and, if I was careful, it might work to my advantage.

Then, after she'd sat there for a few minutes, and I'd tried not to shift about on my chair (I've hated sitting still since I was a nipper), she looked up at me, her big eyes so sad they made even me want to weep, and said, "Greg, will you help me get drunk? I mean, really drunk?"

"Well, now," I said. I slapped my knees. "No man more qualified in the whole of Silver Bay." Without a word to Kathleen, we walked down the track, got into my truck and drove to Del's, where she sat and knocked back Jim Beam like it was going out of fashion.

We left after the bar shut, and by this stage she was so far gone she could barely stand. She was not a silly drunk, like Suzanne, who would sing and get fresh, which, I'd tell her, just wasn't pretty in a woman, or even an angry drunk. She acted like whatever was getting to her was eating at her from the inside.

"Not drunk enough," she mumbled, as I shoved her into the truck. "Need some more drink."

"The bars are shut now," I said. "I don't think there's one open this side of Newcastle." I'd had a few myself, but there's something about watching someone who's really out to drink them that puts you off getting too drunk.

"Kathleen's," she said. "We'll go back and drink at Kathleen's."

I didn't imagine the old Shark Lady would be too happy at the thought of us raiding her bar in the small hours but, hell, it wasn't my decision.

It was still hot enough that your clothes stuck to you and we sat outside with our beer. In the moonlight I could see the sweat glistening on her skin. Everything felt odd that night, like the atmosphere was charged, like anything could happen. It was the kind of night where you get a sudden storm at sea. I listened to the waves breaking on the beach, and the crickets, and tried not to think about the girl next to me, swigging hard at her beer. I remember that at some point we had taken our shoes off, and it was someone's idea to go paddling. I remember her laughing so hysterically that I couldn't be sure if she was actually crying. And then, as she lost her balance under the jetty, she kind of fell against me and I still remember the taste of her lips as she reached for mine — Jim Beam and desperation, I told myself. Not a pretty mix.

Not that that stopped me.

The second time was about six months later. Suzanne and I had split up for a while, and she was staying with her sister in New-castle. Liza had got even more drunk and I'd had to hold back her hair while she was sick before she was together enough to come back in the truck. Didn't stop her finishing a bottle of Mr. Gaines's finest shi-raz at mine. She was a strange one, though — stone-cold sober every night of the week, but now and then it was as if she'd decided to knock herself out cold. That night I woke up in the small hours to find her weeping in bed beside me. She had her back to me, her shoulders were shaking and her hands over her face.

"Did I hurt you?" I was half groggy with sleep. You don't like to find a girl weeping after you've given her one, you know what I mean? "Liza? What's the matter, love?"

Then, as I touched her shoulder, I realized she was asleep. It freaked me out a little, so I called to her, then shook her.

"What?" she said. And then, as she looked around the room, "Oh, God, where am I?"

"You were crying," I said, "in your sleep. I thought . . . I thought it was me."

She was already out of bed, reaching for her jeans. Honest, if I hadn't been so drunk myself it would have been insulting. "Hey, hey, hold your horses. You don't have to go anywhere. I just wanted to make sure you were okay." I saw the white flash of her brassiere as she hooked it over her arms.

"It's nothing to do with you. Greg, I'm sorry, I've got to go."

She was like a man. She was like me when I used to go out drinking, before I met Suzanne, and wake up with someone I'd have gnawed my arm off to get away from.

Ten minutes after she'd left I realized she didn't have her car. But by the time I got downstairs she was long gone. I reckoned she must have run halfway down the coast road to get home. She would do that, like she had no fear. ("Why should she?" said

Kathleen, cryptically, when I asked. "The worst has already happened.")

The next day, when I sat down beside her on the bench, she behaved like nothing had gone on.

Four more times she had done this to me. Not once had we been together when she was sober. If I was less of a looker I reckon I'd have been a bit worried.

I guess I should have got pissed off, but you couldn't with Liza. There was something about her. She was not like anyone else I knew.

When she finally told me about the baby, she was sober. And she told me not to say a word. She wouldn't answer questions. Didn't even tell me how the little one died. She just told me because I'd got mad and asked her point-blank why the hell she had to get so drunk to go to bed with me.

"I don't get drunk to go to bed with you," she said. "I get drunk to forget. Going to bed with you is a by-product of that." As straight as you like, as if none of it would hurt my feelings. "And don't go asking Hannah about it." She looked like she regretted telling me already, which was a bit much. "I don't want you stirring things up. She doesn't need reminding."

"Jeez, you've got a poor opinion of me," I said.

"No, I'm just careful." She closed her hands into two tight fists. "These days I'm just careful."

Del was happy to host the meeting — he knew he'd get a few extra all-day breakfasts out of it — but he'd told me straight beforehand that he didn't oppose the development. Sited where he was, within a few feet of it, he said, wiping his hands on his apron, he stood to make a killing. Like the kind of clientele they were talking about would stop by an old greasebucket like MacIver's for lunch. I knew I wasn't going to sway the old bugger, but I guessed correctly that guilt might make him good for a bacon roll and, as the time approached, I sat outside and ate it, washed down with a good strong coffee.

I had put the word around, and a few local hotel owners, fishermen, the whalechasers, people who were likely to be affected by it all, were coming. We sat and stood outside MacIver's, waiting for people to straggle in. A few clutched copies of the newspaper. Some murmured to each other, while a few chatted normally, as if the town weren't about to be changed completely.

I didn't talk to Liza when she got there, and she didn't seem in a hurry to talk to me. But I waved at Hannah, who came over and sat next to me. "Your boat's still in the lockup," I said quietly, because I wanted to see her smile.

"Will all the dolphins move away?" she said.

Kathleen had arrived, and put a hand on her shoulder. "I'm sure they've seen worse than this," she said. "In the war we had warships in the bay, bombers going overhead, submarines . . . but we still had dolphins. Don't you worry."

"They're smart, aren't they? They'll know to keep out of everyone's way."

"Smarter than most people around here," said Kathleen. I didn't like the way she looked sideways at me when she said that.

Lance got up and began to speak. We'd agreed he'd be better at all that stuff — I was never one for public speaking and we all knew Liza would have died rather than put her face about. He said he appreciated that the development would have some economic benefits for the town, but the watersports school would run the risk of destroying the town's one area for tourist growth: the whales and dolphins. "I appreciate a lot of you guys won't care one way or the other, but this is the one thing that marks out Silver Bay from a lot of the other destinations, and most of you will know that when the tourists come out on our boats, they'll often stop off in the cafés or shops on the way home. Or they'll stay in your hotels and motels."

There was a murmur of agreement.

"This thing is foreign money," he said. "Yes, there will be a few jobs, but you can bet your life the profits won't stick around in Silver Bay. Not even in New South Wales. Foreign investment means returns to foreigners. And, besides, we don't even know the full nature of this development. If it has its own cafés and bars, well, hell, you guys will lose as much as you gain."

"It might boost the winter trade, but," came a voice from the back.

"At what cost? If the whales and dolphins go, there isn't going to be any winter trade," said Lance. "Be honest. How many people would come here in June, July, August if it wasn't for Whale Jetty? Huh?"

There was silence.

Beside me Hannah was reading the newspaper. I swear that kid's getting so grown up it'll be two ticks before she's driving. "Greg," she said, frowning.

"What is it, sweetheart?" I whispered.

"You want me to get you something to eat?"

"That's Mike's company." Her little finger was on a bit of the print. "Beaker Holdings. That's the one that has his picture on their website."

It took me a minute or two to work out what she was saying, and a little longer to work out what that meant. "Beaker Holdings," I read. "You sure, sweetheart?"

"I remembered it because it was like a bird beak. Does that mean Mike's bought Silver Bay?"

I could barely see straight for the rest of that meeting. I just about held it together while Lance organized a petition. I managed to raise my hand when they voted to call up the planning guy and register a complaint. And then, as everyone drifted away, I asked Kathleen if she knew whether Mike was at the hotel.

"He's in his room," she said. "I think his girlfriend's gone shopping." She sniffed. "She likes shopping." She looked up at me. "Greg? You okay?"

"Can you get Liza?" I said, trying to keep the edge from my voice in front of the little one. "There's something you need to know."

It took eighteen months for me to get Liza McCullen into bed and nearly two years

279

more for her to trust me enough to tell me about her daughter.

That was why I couldn't believe it when, the day after the whale calf died, I drove up to the hotel to bring her keys, which she'd left at mine in her usual hurry to get home. It's why I haven't been back to the hotel since — because the image still burned in my imagination, tormented me no matter how many beers I poured down my throat: her sitting in the car park of the Silver Bay Hotel, soon after she'd got out of my bed, bold as brass, held tight in the arms of that Englishman.

As it turned out, he was sitting in the kitchen — where only Kathleen's family ever goes, like he had some kind of rights over the place. When we appeared in the doorway he looked up. He had been reading an old guide book and was wearing a smart shirt. Just the sight of him in that space made me want to smack him.

It took him a second or two to register. But Liza didn't give him any more than that. She slammed the newspaper onto the kitchen table.

"That how you do your research, is it?"

He looked at the headline and actually went white. I've never seen it happen before, but the color ran out of him so fast that I almost found myself looking down in case a puddle of blood was leaking on to the floor.

"Sit in our hotel for the best part of a month making friends, asking questions, chatting up my daughter, and all the while you're planning to ruin us?"

He stared at the front page.

"Of all people — of all people! Knowing what you knew, how could you, Mike? How could you do that?"

By God, I'd never seen her so mad. She was electric, fizzing. Her hair almost stood on end.

He stood up. "Liza, let me explain —"

"Explain? Explain what? That you came here pretending to be on holiday and all the while you've been plotting and planning with the bloody council to destroy us?"

"It's not going to destroy you or the whales. I've been working on putting all these safeguards in place."

She laughed then, a hollow, crazy sound. I have to admit she was a little scary at this point.

"Safeguards, safeguards. How is a bloody watersports park bang in the middle of our waters any kind of safeguard? There'll be speedboats whizzing around pulling skiers, jet-skis, you name it. Do you know what this is going to do to the whales?"

"How is it worse than what you do? It's just boat engines. They'll know to steer clear of the migration path. There will be rules. Advisories."

"Rules? What the hell do you know? You think an eighteen-year-old boy with a jet-ski wants to talk about rules?" She was shaking with rage. "You watched us try to save that baby whale, and now you can stand there and say your bloody watersports park won't affect anything? Worse, you got my daughter to tell you what was most needed so you could suck up to the planning department and win them over."

"I thought it might be something good," he protested. "She said they were things they needed."

"They were things *you* needed to get the bloody planning department on your side. You're sick, you know that? Sick."

"It's not my decision," he said helplessly. "I've been doing my best to make this thing work for everybody."

"You've been doing your best to line your pockets," I said. I moved a step closer to him, and I saw him square, as if he were preparing himself for a blow.

Liza turned back, tearful now. She shook her head and said bitterly, "You know . . .

everything you said you were is a lie. *Every-thing.*"

That was the first time he looked angry. "No," he said urgently, reaching out a hand. "Not everything. I wanted to talk to you. I still want to talk but —"

She brushed him off as if he was toxic. "You really think there's *anything* you have to say that I'd want to hear?"

"I'm sorry. I wanted to say something about the development," he continued, "but I had to get it worked out first. Once I realized what the whales meant to you guys, I wanted to find a way to keep everyone happy."

"Well, congratu-bloody-lations," she spat. "I hope you're happy, because this thing's going to destroy us, and it'll destroy the whales. But, hey, as long as your investors get a good return, I'm glad you're happy."

I offered to hit him then.

"Oh, don't be such a bloody fool," she said, and with a dismissive wave that seemed to include both of us, she pushed past me and out of the kitchen.

A girl was standing in the hallway, blonde with expensive clothes and a diddy little handbag held close to her chest. She stood back to let Liza pass. "Is everything okay?" she said. Another Brit. This must be the girlfriend, I thought. Too good for the likes of him.

"I'll have you, mate," I said to him, pointing my finger into his face. "Don't think any of this is going to be forgotten."

"Oh, calm down, Greg," said Kathleen, wearily, and pushed me out of the kitchen. Like it was my bloody fault. Like any of it was my bloody fault.

"Vanessa, perhaps you'd like to come in and sit down. I'll make a pot of tea."

THIRTEEN:
KATHLEEN

Newcastle Observer, 11 April 1939

The largest gray nurse shark ever caught in New South Wales has been landed in a fishing community north of Port Stephens — by a 17-year-old girl.

Miss Kathleen Whittier Mostyn, daughter of Angus Mostyn, proprietor of the Silver Bay Hotel, hauled in the creature on Wednesday afternoon out in waters near Break Nose Island. She landed it unaided from a small sculling craft while her father had briefly returned to the hotel to fetch some provisions.

He said: "I was genuinely shocked when Kathleen showed me her catch. The first thing we did was bring it into shore and call up the appropriate authorities, as it was my guess that she had broken some kind of record."

A fisheries spokesman confirmed it was the largest shark of its kind ever netted in the area. "This is a considerable achievement for a young lady," said Mr. Saul Thompson. "The shark would have been difficult to land even by a proper game fisherman."

The shark has already become a considerable attraction, with local game fishermen and sightseers travelling some distances to see the creature. Mr. Mostyn plans to have it mounted and placed in the hotel as a record of his daughter's estimable catch. "We just have to find a wall strong enough," he joked.

The hotel staff say bookings have trebled since news broke of Miss Mostyn's prize, and the record is sure to add to the area's growing reputation as a fine place for game fishing.

I dusted the glass frame and put the yellowing newspaper cutting back against the wall, alongside the photographs of the stuffed shark. The taxidermy itself hadn't been particularly successful — I suspected my father had been in such a hurry to put it on show that he had not had it done by anyone of genuine skill — and the creature had fallen apart when it was moved from the hotel into the museum, stuffing oozing from the seams around the fins and along the joint of the tail. Eventually we admitted defeat and put it out with the bins. I watched out of the window with amusement on the day the bin men came.

It didn't help that it had been handled by pretty much every visitor who ever walked in. There was something about a stuffed shark that made people want to touch it. Perhaps it was the frisson of knowing that in normal circumstances they wouldn't be that close to one without amputation or death following hard behind. Perhaps it gave them some strange sense of power. Perhaps we all harbor a perverse need to get close to things that might destroy us.

I looked away deliberately from the photographs and ran the duster lightly over the other objects and curios, seeing the museum through the eyes of the kind of tourist who would be interested in a top-of-the-range watersports park. Or, as the newspaper had put it, a "proper" Museum of Whales and Dolphins. I had not had a visitor in ten days. Perhaps I couldn't blame them, I thought, carefully placing a harpoon back on its hooks. This was increasingly less a museum than a bunch of old fishbones in a rackety shed. I was only keeping it going because of my father.

They were all up at the hotel, sitting

outside, loudly discussing their ideas to fight the planning decision over beer and chips. I hadn't wanted to be among them, didn't want to feign sympathy for as yet uncommitted crimes against free creatures of the sea. My own feelings, my own reservations, were quite different from theirs.

I heard the door creak and turned. Mike Dormer was there. It was hard to see his face, as he stood against the light, so I beckoned to him.

"I haven't been in here before," he said, glancing around as his eyes adjusted to the darkness. His hands were shoved deep in his pockets, his normally straight-backed posture stooped and apologetic.

"Nope," I agreed. "You haven't."

He walked around slowly, staring up at the beams, from which hung old lines, nets and buoys, whaler's overalls from the 1930s. He seemed interested in everything in a way genuine visitors rarely were.

"I recognize this picture," he said, stopping in front of the newspaper cutting.

"Yes, well . . . One thing we do know about you, Mike, is that you certainly do your research."

It came out harder than I'd intended, but I was tired and I still felt unbalanced because I'd had him under my roof for so long yet failed to get the measure of him.

"I'm sorry," he said. "I deserved that."

I sniffed, and began to dust the souvenirs on the trestle table, next to the old till. They seemed tacky and pathetic all of a sudden: whale key-rings, dolphins suspended in plastic balls, postcards and tea towels featuring grinning sea creatures. Children's gifts. What was the point when no children came here anymore?

"Look, Kathleen, I know you might not want to talk to me right now but I do have to say something to you. It's important to me that you understand."

"Oh, I understand, all right."

"No, you don't. I wanted to say something," he said. "Really. I came out here expecting it to be a straightforward development job. I thought I'd be in and out, that I was building in an area that no one would be fussed about. Once I realized that wasn't the case, I was trying to work out a solution that would keep my boss happy in England and you lot happy out here. I needed to find out as much as I could."

"You could have shared that with us. We might have been able to contribute something. Especially since I've lived in the area for seventy-odd years."

"I know that now." I noted with a weird

satisfaction that his shoes had become very scuffed. "But once I got to know you all it was impossible."

"Especially Liza," I said. Call it a wild guess.

"Yes," he said. "Yes, and Liza."

"Well, Mike, for a quiet man you've made a big impact around here." I kept polishing, not sure what else to do with myself. I didn't want to stand there in front of him. We were silent for a few minutes, as I worked with my back to him. I sensed him staring at me.

"Anyway," he said, coughing, "I appreciate that this probably changes things. I've been ringing around. There's a place up the coast that will have me — us. We'll go this afternoon. I just wanted to say how sorry I was, and that if there's anything I can do to — well, to mitigate the effects of this development, you should let me know."

I paused, my duster raised in my hand, and turned to him. My voice, when it came, sounded unusually loud in the cavernous space. "How do you mitigate killing off a seventy-year-old family business, Mike?" I asked.

He looked shattered then, as I'd guessed he would.

"You know what? I don't really give a fig

about the hotel, no matter what you might think. Buildings as such don't hold a great deal of importance for me, and this one's been falling down for years. I'm not even that fussed about the bay. And the whales and the dolphins, I'm hoping that the busybodies who look out for them now will see they're okay."

I shifted my weight, passed my duster into the other hand. "But there's something you should know, Mike Dormer. When you destroy this place, you destroy Hannah's safety. This is the one place she can be in all the world where she doesn't have to worry, where she can grow up safe and untouched. I can't explain more than that, but you should know it. Your actions will have an impact on our little girl. And for that I can't forgive you."

"But — but why would you have to leave here?"

"How can we afford to live in a hotel with no customers?"

"Who says you'll have no customers? Your hotel is completely different from what's planned. There'll always be customers for a place like yours."

"When there are a hundred and fifty rooms with en suites and satellite television next door? And winter three-for-two offers and a heated pool indoors? I don't think so. The one thing we had going for us here was isolation. The kind of people who came here wanted to be in the middle of nowhere. They wanted to be able to hear the sea at night and the whisper of the grass on the dunes and nothing else. They didn't want to hear karaoke night in the Humpback Lounge, and the sound of forty-eight cars reversing in and out of the car park on their way to the subsidized buffet. Come on, Mike, you deal in hard figures, in commercial research. You tell me how an operation like this stays afloat."

He made as if to speak, then mutely shook his head.

"Go back to your masters, Mike. Tell them you've done their bidding. You've sealed the deal, or whatever it is you City types say."

I was close to tears and this made me so furious that I had to start dusting again, so he couldn't see my face. Seventy-six years old and about to cry like an adolescent girl. But I couldn't help it. Every time I thought about Liza and Hannah disappearing, about them having to settle somewhere far from here, having to start over, I got short of breath.

I had half expected him to leave, I'd had my back to him for so long. But when I turned he was still there, still staring at the floor, still thinking.

At last he raised his head. "I'll get it changed," he said. "I'm not sure how, Kathleen, but I'll put it right."

I must have looked disbelieving because he took a step toward me. "I promise you, Kathleen. I'll put it right."

Then he turned on his heel, hands deep in his pockets, and walked back up the path toward the house.

The following day I dropped Hannah at school, then took the inland road to see Nino Gaines. He was one of the few people with whom I could have an honest discussion about money. Trying to convey to Liza how little there was would have made her even more anxious, and I had always taken pains to disguise how little her whale-watching trips offset the costs of running our household.

"So, how much have you got?" We were sitting in his office. From the window I could see the rows of vines, bare now, like battalions of barren twigs under an unusually gray sky. Behind him there were books on wine and a framed poster of the first supermarket promotion that had included his shiraz. I liked Nino's office: it spoke of healthy business, innovation and success, despite his advanced years.

I scribbled some figures on the pad in front of me and shoved it toward him. It may sound daft but I was brought up to think it rude to discuss money, and even at my age I find it difficult to say out loud. "That's the pretax profits. And that's the rough turnover. We get by. But if I had to put on a new roof, or anything like it, I'd have to sell the boat."

"That tight, eh?"

"That tight."

Nino was pretty surprised. I think until that point he had assumed that, because my father was the big name in the area when we'd first met, I must still be sitting on some sizable nest egg. But, as I explained to him, it was fifty years since the hotel's heyday. And ten years since the Silver Bay had had anything like a constant stream of guests. Taxes, building repairs and the cost of looking after two extra people — one of whom required an endless supply of shoes, books and clothes — had put paid to what little I had set aside.

Nino took a gulp of his tea. Earlier, Frank had brought us a tray, complete with a plate of biscuits. That he had placed these on a lace doily made me cast a new look at Nino's remaining single son, although Nino seemed to believe the decorative touch was for my benefit.

"Do you want me to invest in the hotel so you could do a bit of renovation? Smarten up the rooms? Put in some satellite TV? I've had a good few years. I'd be glad to sink a few quid into something new." He grinned. "Diversification. That's what the old accountant says I should focus on. You could be my diversification."

"What's the point, Nino? You know as well as I do, once that monster goes up by the jetty, we'll be little better than a shed at the end of their garden."

"Can you not survive on the whale-watching money? Surely Liza will be going out more often, with more people around. Perhaps you could invest in another boat. Get someone to run it for you."

"But that's just it. She won't stay if there are more people. She — she gets nervous. She needs to be somewhere quiet." The words sounded feeble even to me. I had long since stopped trying to justify the apparent enigma that was my niece.

We sat quietly, as Nino digested this. I finished my tea and placed the cup on the tray. Then he leaned forward over the desk. "Okay, Kate. You know I've never stuck my nose in, but I'm going to ask you now." His voice dropped. "What the hell is Liza running from?"

It was then that the tears came and I realized, in horror, that I couldn't stop them. The sobs wrenched my chest and shoulders as if I were suspended on jerking strings. I don't think I've cried like that since I was a child, but I couldn't stop. I wanted so badly to protect my girls, but Mike Dormer and his idiotic, deceitful plans had brought home to me how vulnerable they were. How easily our supposed sanctuary at the end of the bay could become so much matchwood.

When I had composed myself a little I looked at him.

His smile was sympathetic, his eyes concerned. "Can't tell me, huh?"

I put my head into my hands.

"I guess it must be something pretty bad or you wouldn't be so shook up."

"You mustn't think badly of her," I mumbled, through my fingers. A soft, worn handkerchief was thrust into them, and I mopped inelegantly at my eyes. "No one has suffered more than she has."

"Don't you go fretting. I know what I've seen of your girls, and I know there isn't a malicious hair on either of their heads. I won't ask again, Kate. I just thought telling someone . . . whatever it is . . . might offer you a bit of relief."

I reached out then, and took his strong old hand. He held mine tightly, his huge knuckles atop mine, and I took great comfort from it, more than I had guessed I might.

We sat there for some minutes, listening to the ticking of his mantelpiece clock, me feeling the alien warmth of his skin absorbed by my own hand. I realized I didn't want to go home. I didn't have the strength to reassure Liza, who was almost manic with anxiety. I didn't want to be nice to Mike Dormer and his fashion-plate girlfriend, and think of what they had done to me. I didn't even want to have to calculate their bill. I just wanted to sit in the still room, in the silent valley, and have someone look after me.

"You could come here." His voice was gentle.

"I can't, Nino."

"Why not?"

"I told you. I can't leave the girls."

"I meant you and the girls. Why not? Plenty of room. Close enough for Hannah to stay at her school, if you didn't mind a bit of driving. Look at this big old house. These rooms would love to see youngsters again. The only thing keeping Frank here is that he doesn't want to leave me alone."

I said nothing. My head was swimming.

"Come and live with me. We can set it up however you want — you in your own room or . . ."

He was gazing at me intently and, in his heavy-lidded eyes, I could see an echo of the cocky young airman of fifty years previously. "I won't ask you again. But it would make us both happy, I know. And I'd help to protect the girls from whatever it is you're so worried about. Hell, I'm in the middle of bloody nowhere, you know that. Even the ruddy mailman can't find us half the time."

I laughed, despite myself. As I said before, Nino Gaines has always been able to do that to me.

Then his hold on my hand became tighter. "I know you love me, Kathleen." When I said nothing, he continued, "I still remember that night. Every minute of it. And I know what it meant."

My head jerked up. "Don't talk about that night," I snapped.

"Is that why you won't marry me? Is it because you feel guilty? Jeez, Kate, it was one night twenty years ago. Loads of husbands have behaved worse. It was one night — one night we agreed wouldn't be repeated."

I shook my head.

"And we didn't, did we? I was a good husband to Jean and you know it."

Oh, I knew it. I'd spent more than half my life thinking about it.

"Then why? Jean told me — Jesus, with her dying words — she told me that she wanted me to be happy. She as good as told me that we should be together. What the hell is stopping us? What the hell is stopping you?"

I had to get up to leave. I shook my hand at him, the other pressed over my mouth as I made my way unsteadily toward my car.

I couldn't tell him — I couldn't tell him the truth. That what Jean had told him was a message, all right, but it was a message for me. She was telling me through him that she'd known — that for all those years afterward she'd known. And that woman understood that knowing this would fill me with guilt for the rest of my days. Jean Gaines had known both of us better than Nino thought.

That night I didn't go out to the crews. Guessing correctly that their indignation would fuel a long evening, I let Liza serve them and pleaded a headache. Then I sat in my little office at the back of the kitchen, where I worked out the guest accounts, and stared at the years of ledgers, the accounts that charted the hotel's history. The years from 1946 to 1960 were fat binders, telling in the width of their spines the hotel's popularity. Occasionally I would open them and look at the parchment-like bills for sides of beef, imported brandy and cigars, evidence of celebrations for a good day's catch. My father had kept every last receipt, a habit I have carried with me. That was when the seas were full, the lounge area was loud with laughter and our lives were simple, our chief concern to celebrate the end of war and our new prosperity afterward.

The spine of last year's book was less than half an inch wide. I ran my hand along the row of leatherbound volumes, letting my fingertips register by touch the diminishing widths. Then I looked up at the photograph of my mother and father, solemn in their wedding clothes as they stared down at me. I wondered what they would have thought of my predicament. Nino had told me I could probably sell this place to the hotel people; that, given the right negotiator, I could argue the price up. Maybe get enough to start somewhere new. But I was too old for house-hunting, too old to cram what

remained of my life into a boxy little bunga-
low. I didn't want to have to find my way
around new medical centers and super-
markets, make polite conversation with new
neighbors. My life was in these walls, these
books. Everything that had ever meant
anything to me stood in this place. As I
gazed at those books I realized I needed this
house more than I had admitted.

I'm not a drinker, but that night I reached
into the drawer of my father's desk, opened
his old silver hip flask and allowed myself a
tot of whisky.

It was almost a quarter past ten when Liza
knocked on the door. "How's your head?"
she said, closing it behind her.

"Fine." I closed the accounts book, hoping I looked as if I'd been working. It didn't
hurt. But I did. Everything about me felt
weary.

"Mike Dormer has just walked in and
gone straight upstairs. He acted like he's
not going anywhere. I thought you should
probably have a word."

"I said he could stay," I told her quietly,
rising from my seat to place the book back
on the shelf.

"You did what?"

"You heard."

"But why? We don't want him anywhere

near us."

I didn't look at her. I didn't need to — I could tell from her appalled tone that her face would be pink with anger. "He's paid up to the end of the month."

"So give him his money back."

"You think I can throw that sort of money away?" I snapped at her. "I'm charging him three times as much as anyone else."

"The money's not the issue, Kathleen."

"Yes, it is, Liza. The money *is* the issue. Because we're going to need every last penny, and that means every last guest who wants to stay here is going to get a welcome from me, even if it makes my darned blood curdle to do it."

She was shocked. "But think of what he's done," she said.

"Two hundred and fifty dollars a night, Liza, that's what I'm thinking. More for the girlfriend's meals. You tell me how else we're going to make that kind of money."

"The whale crews. They're out there every night."

"How much money do you think I make off them? A couple of cents per bottle of beer. A dollar or so per meal. You really think I could charge proper money when I know half of them are living on free biscuits? For goodness' sake, haven't you noticed that half the time Yoshi doesn't have the money to pay us at all?"

"But he's going to destroy us. And you're going to let him sit up there in your best room while it happens."

"What's done is done, Liza. Whether that hotel goes ahead or not is out of our hands. All we need to think about is making the most of our income while we still have one."

"And bugger the principles?"

"We can't afford principles, Liza, and that's the truth. Not if we want to keep Hannah in school shoes."

I knew what she was really saying, what neither of us could bear to say out loud. How could I willingly harbor the man who had broken what remained of her heart? How could I put her through the ache of having to watch him and that girl float around her home, flaunting their relationship?

We glared at each other. I felt breathless, and put out a hand to steady myself. Her lips were tight with hurt and indignation. "You know what, Kathleen? I really don't understand you sometimes."

"Well, you don't have to understand," I said curtly, making as if to tidy my desk. "You just get on with your business and let me run my hotel."

I don't think we'd had a cross word in the five years she had lived here, and I could tell it had shaken us both. I felt that hip flask calling to me, but I wouldn't take it out in front of her: I didn't want her to take an example from me and get drunk herself in case it led to another catastrophic encounter with Greg.

In the end she turned sharply and left, bristling, without a word.

I bit my tongue. I couldn't tell her the truth behind my decision, because I knew she'd disagree: she'd react badly even to the merest suggestion of what I suspected to be true. Because it wasn't just about money. It was because I understood, more than anyone realized, how that young man had got into the situation he had. More importantly, it was about bait. And despite everything that had happened, my gut told me that keeping Mike Dormer close to us was going to be our best chance of survival.

Fourteen:
Mike

The dog-walkers had stopped waving to me. The first morning I ran past them, I assumed they hadn't seen me. Perhaps my woolen hat was pulled too far down over my face. I'd got used to our little morning exchanges, and had found myself looking out for familiar faces. But on the second morning when I lifted my hand in greeting and they turned away their faces, I realized that not only was I no longer anonymous but, in parts of Silver Bay, I was now public enemy number one.

The same was true at the local garage, when I pulled in for fuel, at the supermarket checkout and in the little seafood café by the jetty when I sat down and tried to order coffee. It took nearly forty minutes and several reminders to arrive at my table.

Vanessa was bullish. "Oh, you're always going to ruffle a few feathers," she said dismissively. "Remember that school development in east London? The people in the flats opposite were funny about it until they discovered how much it would push up the value of their properties."

But that had been different, I wanted to say to her. I didn't care what those people thought of me. And, besides, Vanessa wasn't having to confront Liza, who managed to behave both as if I were no longer in existence and treat me with a kind of icy resentment.

On the one occasion I had found her alone in the kitchen — Vanessa had been upstairs — I had said, "I've told your aunt. I'm going to try and stop it. I'm sorry."

The look she gave me stopped me in my tracks. "Sorry about what, Mike? That you've been living here under false pretenses, that you're about to ruin us, or that you're a duplicitous sh—"

"You told me you didn't want a relationship."

"You didn't tell me you were already in one." As soon as she said this her expression closed, as if she felt she had given too much away. But I knew what she had felt. I had rerun that moment in the car as if it were on a spool tape inside my head. I could have recited word for word what we had said to each other. Then I was reminded of my own duplicity on so many levels, and at that point I usually rang Dennis or found some administrative task to do with the development. That's the beauty of business: it's a refuge of myriad practical problems. You always know where you stand with it.

I told Vanessa why I thought the development was no longer right as the plans stood. She didn't believe me, so I took her out on *Moby One* with several tourists and showed her the dolphins. Yoshi and Lance were courteous, but I felt an almost physical discomfort at the lack of good-humored conversation, and I missed Lance's caustic insults. I was no longer one of them. I knew it and so did they.

That sense of silent disapproval followed me around the bay until I was convinced that even the Korean tourists on the top deck knew what I was responsible for. "I might as well stick a harpoon in my hand and label myself 'whale-killer,' " I said, when the silence became too much.

Vanessa told me I was being oversensitive. "Why should you care what they think?" she said. "In a few days you'll never have to see any of them again."

"I care because I want to get this right," I said. "And I think we can get it right. Ethically and commercially." I knew it was vital to have Vanessa on my side if we were to convince Dennis to alter the plans.

"Ethical business, eh?" She raised an eyebrow, but she didn't write it off as an idea.

Then, as if in answer to my prayers, the seas opened. Yoshi's voice came over the PA system, lifted with excitement as it always was in the presence of a whale. "Ladies and gentlemen," she said, "if you look out of your portside windows — that's left for those who don't know — you can just make out a humpback. She might be headed toward us, so we're going to turn off the engines and hope she comes close."

There was a swell of excited chatter on the top deck. I pulled my scarf up around my face and pointed to where I'd caught sight of a blow. I watched Vanessa's face, knowing that this moment might be crucial, praying that the whale would know what was good for it and impress her.

Then, as if on cue, it breached not forty feet away from us, its huge, prehistoric head turning as it splashed back into the water. Like me, she couldn't help gasping, and her face softened with a child-like joy. For a moment, I saw in her the girl I had loved before I had come here. I took her hand and squeezed it. She squeezed mine back.

"You see what I mean?" I said. "You see how this is impossible?"

"But the planning's going through," she said, when she could tear her gaze away. "You made it."

"I can't live with myself," I said. "I've seen what can happen and I don't want to feel responsible for spoiling something here."

We stood and watched as the whale breached again, further away this time, then disappeared under the waves, no longer diverted by curiosity, compelled to continue its journey north. The tourists around us hung over the rails, hoping it might re-emerge, then drifted back to the plastic chairs and benches, chattering and comparing images on their cameras. I thought of Lance, below us in the cockpit, breathing a sigh of relief at another whale-watching trip successfully completed. Perhaps he and Yoshi would be discussing the animal's movements, chatting on the radio to the other boats as they worked out where to go next. If Vanessa gets it, I thought, we have a chance of making this thing work.

I stood and let my eyes run 360 degrees around me, taking in the distant coastline, the series of small, uninhabited islands that stood like sentries to the greater expanse of land. Above us birds swooped and dived, and I tried to remember what the crews had previously told me: ospreys, gannets, white-breasted sea eagles. Around us the sea rose and fell, glinting on one side, darker and apparently less amenable on the other. I no longer felt alien out here. Despite their lack of money, their insecure lifestyle and, their diet of cheap biscuits, I envied the whale-chasers.

It was then that Vanessa spoke. Her hat was pulled low over her eyes so it was difficult for me to see her face. "Mike?"

I turned to her. She was wearing the diamond earrings I had bought her for her thirtieth birthday.

"I know something's gone on," she said carefully. "I know I've lost a bit of you. But I'm going to pretend that none of this has happened, I'm going to pretend that you and I are still okay, and that this is some kind of weird reaction to the shock that you're getting married."

My heart skipped a beat. "Nessa," I said, "nothing happened —" but she waved a hand to stop me.

She looked at me, and I hated myself for the hurt in her eyes.

"I don't want you to explain," she said. "I don't want you to feel you have to tell me anything. If you think we can be okay, that you can love me and be faithful to me, I just want us to carry on as we were. I want us to get married, forget this and get on with our lives."

The engines started up again. I felt the vibrations under my feet and then, as the boat swung around, the wind picked up and Lance started to say something over the PA system so I wasn't sure if she said anything else.

She turned back to the sea, pulled her collar up around her jaw. "Okay?" she said. And then again: "Okay?"

"Okay," I said, and stepped forward. She let me hug her. Like I said, she's a clever woman, my girlfriend.

In the five days that remained before we traveled back to Sydney, Vanessa and I spent most of our time locked in our room. We were not engaged in the kind of liaison I suspected Kathleen and Liza imagined, but hunched over my laptop, working out how to alter the plans in a way that would satisfy her father and the venture capitalists. It was not an easy task.

"If we can get the USP, we can crack it," she said. I thanked God that she had marketing skills. "Without the watersports, the whales are the USP. We just have to work out a way of involving them that isn't going to alienate all of the whale-watching people. That means not setting up our own operation, which would be my immediate choice. There has to be some other way of making the sea creatures accessible." She had got onto the National Parks and Wildlife people to talk to them about the dolphins, but they had said they wouldn't encourage tourists to have greater contact with the animals than they already allowed.

"Perhaps something radical. Some kind of platform at the mouth of the bay, with an undersea viewing area."

"Too expensive. And the shipping people would probably object. We could build a new jetty with a restaurant on top and a viewing area below."

"What are you really going to see that close to land?" She sucked the end of her pen. "We could try to work out some radical new spa idea."

"Your dad didn't like the spa thing."

"Or we could scrap the plans altogether and find another site. I can't see a way of using the hotel in its present form without the watersports. There's just nothing else to mark it out from what's available. Not for the luxury market."

"Tennis?" I said. "Horseriding?"

"A new site," she said. "We've got five days to find a new waterfront site for a one-hundred-and-thirty-million pound development." We looked at each other and started to laugh: saying it out loud made it sound even more ridiculous than it actually was.

But Vanessa Beaker wasn't her father's daughter for nothing. Within an hour of us deciding that that was the way forward, she had hit the phones with Kathleen's old phone book, and within four hours she had spoken to probably every land agent between Cairns and Melbourne.

"Can you e-mail me some pictures?" Between calls on my own phone, I heard the same request time and time again, then the other questions.

"Can you tell me, are the waters designated a protected area?"

"Do you have sea mammals or other indigenous creatures that are likely to be affected by a development?"

"Would they be interested in selling?"

"Might they be up for negotiation?"

By the end of the second day we had earmarked two possible sites. One was an existing hotel development an hour south of Brisbane. Its plus points included its own protected bay, which had been used without complaint for watersports. But it wasn't half as beautiful as Silver Bay, and the area was already thick with five-star hotels. The other, half an hour from Bundaberg, was more accessible but almost a third again in price.

"Dad's not going to like that," she said, then smiled brightly at me. "But everything's doable, right? If we try hard enough? I mean, look what we've achieved already."

"You," I said fondly, pushing her hair back from her face, "are a star."

"Don't you forget it," she said. Perhaps I imagined the edge to her voice.

That night we made love for the first time since she had come to Silver Bay. Given our previous physical appetite for each other, I can't explain what had happened until that point — but the atmosphere had been too odd. Neither of us had felt our old confidence in the other's response. We had hidden this insecurity under declarations of exhaustion, of too much wine. We had professed ourselves riveted by our books. I had found myself oddly conscious of the hotel's thin walls.

We had gone out to eat in the town, and walked back slowly along the bay holding hands. The wine, the moonlight, and the fact that I might have saved Silver Bay from the fate I had almost inflicted on it conspired to smooth over the strange resistance I felt when Vanessa and I now held each other.

I had nearly messed it up, I told myself, as we strolled along silently, but not quite. We would save this development, we would save the whales and we would save our relationship. We understood new things about each other. I had been given a second chance.

In my room we had left the light off and removed our clothes wordlessly, as if we had determined by telepathy that tonight was the one. We moved closer to each other, me focusing on the voluptuous beauty of Vanessa's silhouette, my mind locked only on physical sensation as we lay down on the old bed, skin on skin, her hands skillfully searching for me, her mouth emitting little gasps of pleasure. I ran my hands over her breasts, her skin. I buried my face in her hair. I remembered the scent of her, the feel of her, the familiar way her curves felt under my fingertips. And finally I plunged into her, forgetting everything, allowing myself the despairing gasp of release.

And afterward we lay quiet as something heavy and melancholy settled in the dark around us.

"You okay?" I said, reaching across her for her hand.

"Fine," she said, after a pause. "Lovely."

I stared up into the dark, listening to the waves breaking on the sand, the distant sound of a car door closing and the revving of an engine, thinking about what the core of me knew had been missing. Thinking about what I had lost.

We left on the Saturday. I went downstairs early and settled up with Kathleen. I paid her half in cash, guessing that would be more useful to her than credit cards. "I'll be in touch," I said. "Things are happening fast. Really."

She looked at me steadily. "I hope so," she said. She stuffed the money into a tin under the desk without counting it. I hoped that meant that, in some small way, she trusted me again. I felt buoyant with relief, and the confidence that something good could happen.

"Is — is Liza around?" I asked, when I realized she wasn't going to volunteer.

"She's out on *Ishmael*," she said.

"Say good-bye to her for me." I tried not to sound as awkward as I felt. I was acutely aware of Vanessa, who had come down the stairs and was now behind me.

Kathleen said nothing, but shook Vanessa's hand. "Good-bye," she said. "I wish you luck with the wedding."

There was more than one way you could interpret that, I thought, as I went upstairs for the bags, and none reflected well on me. I would have gone straight back down, but as I passed the family corridor, I heard music. Hannah was still there. She had barely spoken to me since the development had come to light and, more than anything, that child's silence had convinced me of my failure.

I stood at the door and knocked. Eventually she opened it, a burst of music filling the air behind her.

"I thought I'd say good-bye," I said.

She didn't answer.

"Oh . . . and I came to give you this." I held out an envelope. "Your wages. The pictures were very good."

She glanced at it. Her voice, when she spoke, held the faintest hint of an apology. "My mum says I'm not allowed to accept your money."

"Okay," I said, trying to look less disconcerted than I felt. "Well, I'm going to leave it on the hall table, and if you really aren't allowed to take it I hope you'll give it to a charity for the dolphins. I know you love them."

I could hear Vanessa's mobile phone going off downstairs, and nodded, as if that were my excuse to leave.

Hannah stood in the doorway, studying me. "Why did you lie to us, Mike?"

I took a step back toward her. "I don't know," I said. "I probably made a big mistake, and I'm trying to put it right."

She looked down.

"Grown-ups make mistakes too," I said. "But I'm trying to put it right. I hope you . . . I hope you believe me."

She raised her head and on her face I saw suddenly that she had learned this lesson long ago, that what I had done had merely reinforced her sense of adult fallibility, of our ability to sabotage her own blameless life.

We stood still for a moment, the City hot shot and the little girl. I took a breath, and then, almost as if by instinct, I held out a hand. After the longest pause she shook it.

"What about your phone?" she called suddenly, as I paused at the top of the stairs. "We've still got your phone."

"Keep it," I said, grateful for the chance to offer her something, anything, that might redeem me in her eyes. "Do something good with it, Hannah. Really."

Vanessa was already waiting in the Holden. She was wearing what she had described as her traveling outfit — a suit in a non-crease fabric, with a clean shirt and a cashmere cardigan at the top of her duffel bag, ready for her to change into before we hit Heathrow. I had asked, with some amusement, whom she was intending to meet, and she had told me that just because I no longer cared about my appearance it didn't mean she had to give up and become a slob too. I think this was aimed at my jeans, which I had taken to wearing most days. They were comfortably worn in now, and somehow putting on a suit for a flight seemed excessive.

"So long, then," said Kathleen, her arms folded, as she saw us to the Holden. She was a pretty different Kathleen from the one who had welcomed me five weeks previously.

"So long," I said. I didn't try to shake her hand. Something about the steely cross of her arms told me it would be a pointless gesture. "I won't let you down, Kathleen," I said quietly, and she tipped her head back, as if that was as much as she was prepared to grant me.

She had told me Liza was out on *Ishmael.*

Part of me thought that perhaps it would be for the best if I never saw her again. As she had said, what could I possibly have to say that she would want to hear?

But then, as we headed down the road and passed Whale Jetty, I looked in the rearview mirror. A thin blonde woman stood at the end, her silhouette clearly outlined against the glistening sea. Her hands were shoved deep in her pockets, her dog at her feet. She was watching our white car as we drove slowly but surely away down the coast road.

The flight back was as much of a pleasure as a twenty-four-hour flight ever is. We sat beside each other, bickered about correct terminals, swapped unwanted items from our trays of food, and watched several films, none of which I can remember, but I was grateful for the distraction. At some point I slept, and when I woke, I was dimly aware of Vanessa going through a list of figures next to me. I was thankful again for her willingness to back me.

We landed at almost six in the morning, but by the time we had made it through Passport Control it was nearly seven.

Heathrow was crowded, chaotic and gray, even at that hour and at the height of what was loosely described as summer. Everyone feels bad when they get back from abroad, I told myself, rubbing at the crick in my neck as we headed for the baggage carousel. It's one of the certainties of travel, like delays and inedible airline food.

Predictably, the luggage was late. An announcement, in unapologetic tones, revealed that because of staff shortages there was only one team of baggage handlers for the four flights that had arrived in the past hour, and added, with masterly understatement, that we should "expect a slight delay."

"I could murder for a coffee," said Vanessa. "There must be a shop somewhere."

"I need to find a loo," I said. She looked exhausted, even with her carefully refreshed hair and makeup. She never slept well on flights. "The coffee shops don't start till after Customs. You watch for the bags."

I walked away, more swiftly than exhaustion should have allowed. Over the past month I had got used to being alone, and spending a week joined at the hip to Vanessa, working and sleeping with hardly a minute's break, had been hard. It had been made harder given that few people wanted to talk to us anymore, so that socializing, or sitting out with the whalechasers, had been almost impossible. I had not been tempted to try

321

— I was afraid that Greg, with his simmering volatility, would confront Vanessa with what he guessed to be true. We had survived the unspoken; I was not convinced that we could manage such equanimity if the truth were laid out in front of us.

The short walk across the squeaking Heathrow linoleum was the first time I had been by myself for eight days, and it felt like a relief. I have done the right thing, I told myself, feeling bad about such disloyal thoughts. I am about to do the right thing.

I returned a few minutes later, my face still damp from where I had stuck it under the tap. As I drew closer I could see that the baggage carousel was revolving. Oddly, Vanessa had not collected our luggage although I could see it traveling its lonely, squeaking path along the conveyor belt.

"You must be tired," I said, bolting for the cases.

But when I turned back, hauling the cases effortfully behind me — my girlfriend did not understand the concept of traveling light — Vanessa was looking at her mobile phone. "Not your dad," I said wearily. "Not already." Couldn't he even give us time to go home and grab a shower? I was dreading what I knew would be a confrontational meeting, even with Vanessa present, and felt

I needed a short time to brace myself.

"No," she said, her face uncharacteristically pale. "No, it's your phone. It's a text. From Tina." Then, thrusting the message under my nose, she walked out of the airport, leaving what remained of her baggage slowly traveling around the carousel.

The next time I saw her was almost twenty-eight hours later, when I arrived at the office for the crunch meeting with Dennis. He was on his feet, and with his restored physical mobility came a kind of mad sharpening of his energies. "What's going on, boyo?" he kept saying, grabbing at my folder of planning letters. "What's going on?"

The office had felt alien to me, the City so loud and crowded that I could not convince myself it was purely jet lag that had disorientated me. When I closed my eyes I could see the serene horizon of Silver Bay. When I opened them I saw gray pavements, filthy gutters, the number 141 bus belching purple fumes. And the office. Beaker Holdings, once more familiar to me than my own home, now seemed monolithic and forbidding. I hesitated outside, telling myself that jet lag had thrown me in Australia, and was likely to throw me again, even in England.

And then there was Dennis, and I had no chance to think of anything at all.

"What's going on, then? Feeling good about your big coup? The VCs are happy boys, I can tell you. Happy as pigs in the proverbial." His time immobilized had brought him extra weight, and he was oversized, florid, compared to the lean, wind-whipped figures with whom I had spent the past month.

"You look like crap," he said. "Let's organize some coffee. I'll get one of the girls to go out and get us some. Not that instant swill they make here."

In the brief moments after he left the boardroom, I sat down next to Vanessa. She had failed resolutely to meet my eye, and was now sitting in front of a blank notepad. She was wearing what she called her power suit.

"I'm sorry," I murmured. "It's not what it seems. Really. Meet me afterward and I can explain."

"Not what it seems," she said, doodling on the pad. "That little welcome home seemed pretty self-explanatory to me."

"Nessa, please. You wouldn't answer my calls. At least give me five minutes. After this. Five minutes."

"Okay," she said eventually.

"Great. Thank you." I squeezed her arm, then braced myself for the task ahead.

He listened carefully as I outlined what I had done while I had been out there. He and Darren, our accountant, and Ed, the head of projects, scribbled notes as I outlined my considerations with regard to the ecological impact. I told them why I had been wrong to go for the S94 option, and why the planning process could still backfire on us if it went to a public inquiry, as it had with the pearl farm.

"The upshot," I said, "is that while I think the idea of our development, the idea of its USP —" here I glanced at Vanessa "— is still the right one, our existing plan is wrong for all the following reasons." I handed them the pages I had photocopied that morning: the list of alternative sites and the breakdown of incurred costs that altering our proposal would take. "We have already identified the new sites, have spoken with the local agents, and I think, having done the research, that these are by far the better options in terms of both potential adverse publicity and in terms of our new, added USP, which is that of responsible, community-friendly development."

I gestured toward the table. "Vanessa has

been out with me. She's seen these creatures in the flesh, she's seen the whales' habitat, and the strength of feeling about them. She's in agreement that the best way forward for this company is either of the two alternative options. I know there will be time penalties, I know we'll have to sell the existing site, but I believe that if you were to take me along to Vallance, I could swing them around to the same way of thinking."

"Bloody hell," said Dennis, studying the figures. "That's some change you're proposing." He sucked his teeth, flicked through the two bottom pieces of paper. "That's going to cost almost twenty percent of the total budget."

He had not, I noted hopefully, dismissed it all out of hand. "But we lose the costs of the S94 by building on an existing site. If you look at column three, you'll see there is very little in the final figures. This is a less risky option. Really."

"Less risky, eh?" Dennis turned to Vanessa. "Ditch the whole thing, eh? You really think we should move the whole development to this second site?"

She looked at him, and then she turned slowly to me. Her eyes were cold. "No," she said. "I've considered this carefully. I think we should go ahead with what we've got."

FIFTEEN:
LIZA

I saw a whale today, one of the last of the season. She came right up to the boat with her calf and they sat there starboard side in the clear blue water, looking at us, as if they had nothing better to do in all the world. She was closer than she should have been, close enough for me to see each little cut of the mother's "fingerprint," the pattern on her tail fluke, close enough to see the calf lie still and happy, half protected under the belly of its mother. The customers were thrilled — they squealed, took pictures and video footage, and said aloud it was an experience that had changed their lives, something they would never forget. They said they'd heard I had a way of finding the whales, and now that they'd seen it was true, they'd recommend me to all their friends. But I couldn't smile. I wanted to shout at the whale to take her baby far from here. I kept seeing that calf, washed up on the shore, covered with tarpaulin. I didn't want her to trust us like she did.

I suppose I shouldn't have been shocked at what Mike had done. But I was. I'd really thought that, after everything I'd been through, I could spot someone like him a mile off. And the knowledge that I'd failed gnawed away at me, woke me up from what little sleep I ever had. It sat over me and mocked me when I woke, joined the chorus of other voices that told me much of what I had ever done was wrong.

I suppose the raw anger I carried with me in those early days was directed at myself; for what had been my stupidity. For allowing myself to sleepwalk us all into danger. And, perhaps, for allowing myself to think, even briefly, that my life might be allowed to take a different course from the one I have long since resigned myself to.

But I was angry with pretty much everyone; with Mike for lying to us, with the planners for considering his proposal without considering the whales, with Kathleen for letting him stay on so that I'd had to live with his perfumed accomplice floating around my house flashing her engagement ring and pretending none of it mattered, and then with Greg for — well, for being such an idiot. He was around every day, half furious with me, half wanting my forgiveness. We seemed to end up shouting at each other every time we met. I think we were both all over the place for a while, and neither of us had the energy to be kind.

I don't know why — I hadn't felt like that for some time — but for several days during that first week while Mike and his girlfriend remained in the hotel it had been an effort to get myself out of bed. Then he had gone. And somehow that didn't make it any better.

Hannah had picked up on it. She had told me, a little defiantly, that Mike had paid her for her photographs, showed me the brown envelope packed with notes, and before I could say a word she had announced that she was donating the money to the National Parks to help rescue stranded sea creatures. She had spoken to them, she said, and there was enough to buy another dolphin stretcher and some over. How could I refuse her? I knew there was some small part of my daughter that wanted to defend Mike, and for that I hated him even more.

She seemed low. She had stopped asking about the New Zealand trip and spent a lot of time in her room. When I asked if anything was the matter she told me, very politely, that she was fine, in a way that let me know my presence wasn't wanted. I missed my daughter, though. At night, when she still crept into my room, I held on to her sleeping form as if I was making up for all the times in the day when she no longer chose to be near me. So, all in all, we were a disjointed household that winter. The whalechasers often stayed away in the evenings, as if sitting out together gave them too acute a sense of what might be lost. Yoshi, Lance told me, smoking furiously, was thinking of resuming her academic career. Greg's ex had finally relinquished her claim on *Suzanne,* but he didn't behave as if this was any great victory. I think that, having stopped scrapping with her about the boat, he had had the head space to think about what he had lost, and introspection didn't suit him.

The demolition of the Bullen place went ahead at the end of August. Overnight, wire fencing went up around it, contractors from out of town, with their team of great yellow prehistoric machines, came and clawed it to pieces. Less than seventy-two hours later the fencing was gone and there was nothing left but a dug-out patch of disturbed earth where the old house and sheds had been. When I steered in and out of the bay it looked like a great scar on the land, a mournful O of protest.

To add to the despondent mood, the skies were unusually gray and soulless. A seaside town enveloped by gray is a place with the joy vacuumed out. Guest numbers had fallen, the local motels dropped their rates to recapture the weekend trade. We all put our heads down against the wind and tried not to think about any of it too hard. And all the while those boats kept circling. It was as if they had heard about the hotel complex and decided it was open season. Twice I was out by Break Nose Island and those triple-deckers came thudding along the coastline, full of drunks, deafening the ocean with their music. Ironically, one was describing itself in the local paper as providing "all the excitement of a whale-watching trip." After I had rung the paper and told them exactly what I thought of them for carrying the advertisement, Kathleen told me baldly that if I carried on like that I'd give myself an ulcer.

She seemed oddly reconciled to our fate. Either way, since our discussion in her office that night we didn't talk much about it. I didn't understand why she was so willing to let Mike off the hook, and she didn't enlighten me. Night after night Kathleen lay at her end of the house, and I lay awake in my little room at the end of the corridor, listening to the sea and wondering how long I would still be able to hear that sound before, inevitably, Hannah and I were forced to pack our bags and move on.

At the start of September the council offices announced there would be a planning inquiry and everyone would be allowed to have their say. Few in Silver Bay held out much hope that our say would make a difference: in previous years we had seen many such developments in and around the various bays, and nine times in ten they went ahead in the face of the fiercest local opposition. Given the amount of supposed benefits Mike's company was offering, I couldn't see that this inquiry would pay any more than lip service to our views.

And, besides, the opposition was far from straightforward. It had become an issue that divided the town: there were those who accused us whalechasers of dramatizing the whales' plight; a greater number who didn't seem to care much one way or the other; and some pointed out that what we did was an intrusion in itself. It was hard to refute that, especially when we were faced with the fact that other boats, with less rigorous codes of behavior, increasingly treated our waters as their own. The café owners and boutique managers had an interest in a bigger, busier town and, while it sounds unlikely, I had some sympathy for them. We all had to earn a living and I knew more than most that some seasons were harder than others.

Then there were the whalechasers, the fishermen and those who simply enjoyed the presence of the dolphins and the whales, and others who didn't want to see our quiet bay become loud and lively, like so many places that people like us would pay good money to avoid. But it felt as if we were the quieter of the voices. It felt as if we were unlikely to be heard.

The newspapers covered the debate with what seemed unhealthy relish (it was the best story they'd had since the great pub fire of '84). They withstood the accusations of bias that flew from both sides, and repeatedly called on the planners, developers and council officers to justify and rejustify their position until I guessed even they were sick of the sound of their own voices. Twice I saw Mike's name mentioned and, despite myself, read what he had said. Both times he talked about compromise. Both times I heard his voice in my head as clearly as if he'd spoken and wondered how someone could say so much and mean so little, at the same time.

Let me tell you something about hump-backs. The first time I saw one I was a child of eight. I was on holiday, out fishing with my aunt Kathleen and my mother, who didn't like fishing but didn't want me in the boat alone with my aunt. Her big sister Kathleen, she said jokingly, was liable to forget everything if faced with the challenge of a large fish, and she didn't want me plop-ping over the edge while Kathleen reeled one in. I suspect now that she had just wanted an excuse to spend time with her sister — by then they had lived on separate continents for several years, and the distance hurt them both.

I loved those holidays. I loved the sense of safety, of my own immersion within a fam-ily I had not been aware I had. I didn't have a father in England; my mother called Ray McCullen "careless," and my aunt called him something a little spicier, until my mother shook her head, as if it were some-thing that shouldn't be said in front of me. It certainly wasn't to be mentioned in front of anyone else. I was brought up by women, by my mother in England and, when we were sent the money, by Aunt Kathleen and my grandmother in Australia. Kathleen's mother, my grandmother, was a shadowy sort, as indistinct a memory as Kathleen was a sharp one. She was the kind of woman who had no interests, who cooked and raised a family, and then, once those duties had been discharged, seemed a little lost. A woman of her time, Kathleen would say. My few memories of her stem from my two visits as a child, and are of a benign, distant presence in the back rooms of the hotel, lost to television soaps or asking me questions ill suited to my age.

Kathleen, said everyone old enough to remember, was her father's daughter. She was always doing something, gutting fish or sneaking me into the empty Whalechasers Museum, which, to a child of eight, seemed the height of freedom. My mother, a good fifteen years younger, always seemed the more mature of the two, dressed to the nines with immaculate hair and makeup. Kathleen, with her worn trousers and unbrushed hair, her salty language and her shark tales, was a revelation to me. Her godlike status was sealed on our second visit when she took me out fishing with my mother, and we were joined by an unexpected visitor.

She had been carefully explaining the different flies in her little fabric roll and attaching them to her line when, not ten feet from us, making no sound except the gentle breaking of the waters, a huge black-and-white head surfaced. My breath lodged in my throat and my heart was thumping so hard that I thought the terrifying creature would hear it.

"Aunt Kathleen," I whispered. My mother was asleep on a berth, her lipsticked mouth slightly open. I remember wondering fleetingly whether it was preferable to be asleep when you were killed so you wouldn't know what had happened.

"Wh-what's that?"

I honestly thought we were about to be eaten. I could see what I thought were its teeth and its huge, assessing eye. I had seen the old engravings of malevolent sea creatures, had seen the broken-backed *Maui II* in the museum, testament to nature's fury with man. This huge creature appeared to be weighing us up, as if we were some tempting seaborne morsel.

But my aunt just glanced behind her, then turned back to her bait. "That, sweetie, is just a humpback. Pay it no attention, it's just being nosy. It'll go soon enough."

She paid it no more heed than a seagull. And, sure enough, some minutes later, the huge head slid back beneath the waves and the whale was gone.

And this is what I love about them: despite their might, their muscular power, their fearsome appearance, they are among the most benign creatures. They come to look, and then they go. If they don't like you, their signals are pretty clear. If they think the dolphins are getting a little too much attention from our passengers, they will occasionally come partway into the bay and jealously divert them. There is often a child-like element to their behavior, a mischievousness. It is as if they cannot resist discovering what's going on.

Many years ago the early whalers referred to humpbacks as the "merry whale" for the way they performed — and when I began working the boat trips five years ago I discovered the nickname held true. One day I would call up the other whalechasers on the radio and find a whale swimming upside down on the surface, one flipper waving. The next I would come across one launching fully out of the water with a 360-degree breach, like an oversized ballerina pirouetting for the sheer joy of it.

I'm pretty sure I could never be described as "merry," but Kathleen once told me she suspected I felt such a bond with the whales because they are solitary creatures. There is no male-female bond — not a lasting one, anyway. The male plays no parenting role to speak of. She didn't add that the females are not monogamous — by then she hardly needed to — but they are admirable mothers. I have seen a humpback risk beaching itself to nudge her baby into deeper water. I have heard the songs of love, and loss, breaking into the silence of the deepest parts of the ocean, and I have cried with them. In those songs you hear all the joy and pain of any mother's happiness held captive by their baby's heart.

After Letty died, there was a period when I thought I would never be happy again. There is nothing redemptive about the loss of a child, no lessons of value it can teach you. It is too big, too overwhelming, too black to articulate. It is a bleak, overwhelming physical pain, shocking in its intensity, and every time you think you might have moved forward an inch it swells back, like a tidal wave, to drown you again.

If you can blame yourself for that child's death, the days when you can get your head above water are even fewer. I had trouble, in those early days, remembering that I had two daughters. I can thank Hannah for my existence now, but in the weeks after we got here I was so lost that I had nothing to give her. No reassurance, no physical comfort, no love. I was locked somewhere untouchable, my nerve endings seared with pain, and it was a place so ugly I half think I wanted to protect her from coming too close.

That was when I saw the sea as my one opportunity for release. I eyed it not as a thing of beauty, of reassuring permanence, but as an alcoholic views a secret stash of whisky: savoring the fact that it was there and the potential for relief that it promised. Because there was no relief from Letty's absence, not from the moment I woke or during my disjointed, nightmare-filled sleep. I felt her resting against me, smelt the honey scent of her hair and woke screaming when I realized the truth of where she lay. I heard her voice in the silence, my head echoed with the last wrenching screams of our separation. There was a hole in my arms where her weight should have been, which, despite the presence of my other daughter, grew into an abyss.

Kathleen is no fool. She must have guessed my intentions when I expressed interest in that boat. My depression insulated me from the idea that I might be transparent. One afternoon, when the two of us dropped anchor around the heads, she secured *Ishmael,* turned away and said, with a bite in her voice, "Go on, then."

I had stared at her back. It was a bright afternoon, and I remember thinking absently that she wasn't wearing sun cream. "Go on what?"

"Jump. That's what you're planning, isn't it?"

I had thought I was numb to feeling, but it was as if she had kicked me in the stomach.

She turned, and fixed me with a gimlet stare. "You'll excuse me if I don't look. I don't want to have to lie to your daughter about what happened to her mother. If I don't look I can pretend you fell overboard."

I let out a coughing sound then. Air kept expelling itself in little gasps from my chest, and I couldn't speak.

"That little girl has been through too much," Kathleen continued. "If she knows you didn't love her enough to stay here for her, it will finish her off. So, if you're going to do it, do it now while my back's turned. I don't want to spend the next six months living on my nerves, wondering how I'm going to protect her from it."

I found myself shaking my head. I couldn't speak, but my head moved slowly from side to side, as if I was telling her, telling myself, even, that I wasn't going to do what she had predicted. That somehow I was making a decision to live. And even as my body made that decision for me, some small part of my mind was thinking, But how do I live? How is it possible to exist with so much pain? For a moment the prospect of having to go on, with all that inside me, seemed overwhelming.

It was then that we saw them. Seven whales, their bodies slick with seawater as they rose and fell around Kathleen's boat. There was a kind of graceful rhythm to their movements, a flowing continuity that told us of their journey. After circling the boat, they dived. Each emerged briefly, then vanished below the waves.

As a spectacle, then, it diverted me from the most despairing thoughts I have ever had. But later, when we returned home and I took my poor living, grieving child in my arms, I saw that, although I was skeptical about "signs," there had been a message in what I had seen. It was to do with life, death and cycles, the insignificance of things, perhaps the knowledge that everything will pass. One day I will be reunited with my Letty again, although I no longer expect to choose when that will be.

If there is a God, Hannah tells me sometimes, when we are alone in the dark, He will understand. He will know that I am a good person. And I hold my daughter close to me and think that possibly, just possibly, her mere existence is proof that that might be true.

Since that day on the boat, I have never had a problem with finding the humpbacks — Kathleen always said I could smell them and, odd as it sounded, there was some truth in it. I just seemed to know where they were. I followed my nose, and although it often seemed an impossibility, staring at those waves in the hope that one would metamorphose into a nose or a fin, nine times out of ten they would show for me.

But toward the end of that winter something odd happened. At first it was the slapping. When a whale is sending a warning, either to humans or other whales, it engages in "the peduncle slap," thrashing the water with the flukes of its tail or, occasionally, just slapping the surface, its tail flat side down, sending out a noise that reverberates for miles. We don't see it often — we try not to upset the whales — but suddenly I seemed to see it in all of the few that surfaced.

Then, at least two weeks earlier than they

should have done according to migration patterns, they disappeared. Perhaps it was the extra boat traffic; perhaps they had sensed somehow that things were changing, and chose not to grace us with their presence. Either way those of us who operated off Whale Jetty gradually found it harder to locate them — even at a time when they should have been surfacing at a rate of two or three a trip. At first we hardly liked to admit it to each other — it was a mark of honor to be able to find the whales, and only those like Mitchell Dray hung off everyone else's coattails. When we got talking, each of us discovered that our experience was not unique. By mid-September, things had got so bad that both the *Moby*s switched temporarily to dolphin trips around the bay. It was less lucrative, but it meant less disappointment for the customers and, more importantly, fewer refunds.

Then the dolphins seemed to disappear too. There were so few some days that we knew them by sight, and were conscious of the risk of harassing them. As we headed for October I was the only boat still going out every day, more in hope than expectation. The seas, dark and swaying around me, seemed alien, even on the brighter days. I felt the whales' absence, as I felt the absence of all those things I've loved. I couldn't believe so many sea creatures would just leave us, that they would change the behavior of centuries at whim. And grieved by the past weeks' events, perhaps a little unhinged by loss, I found myself yelling at them one day when I had gone out alone. I stood, holding the wheel, my voice bouncing off the waves, ignored by the creatures who perhaps swam beneath me, hiding themselves from an increasingly unfriendly world.

"What the hell am I meant to do?" I shouted, until Milly stood up on the bridge and whined with uneasiness. But I knew that somehow it was my fault, that I had failed the creatures of the sea, as I had failed my children. And my question disappeared, caught and carried away on the wind: "What the hell am I meant to do?"

At four p.m. on the last Thursday in September John John rang to say Mr. Gaines had suffered a heart attack. My aunt Kathleen was a tough woman. They didn't call her Shark Lady for nothing. It was the first time I had ever seen her cry.

SIXTEEN:
MIKE

Monica's guest bedroom was a guest bedroom in only the loosest of senses. It was
not remotely geared up for guests, and was
a bedroom only in that, along with the
fourteen cardboard boxes, two electric
guitars, a mountain bike, forty-nine pairs of
shoes, a 1960s pine chest of drawers, framed
posters of various rock groups I had never
heard of and my childhood train set, it
contained a camp-bed.

"I'll clear you a space," she had promised,
when I had concluded that it made no
financial sense for me to stay long-term in a
hotel and had tentatively mentioned moving in. But in Monica's world that didn't
mean clearing some boxes, or even transfer-
ring the bike to the communal hallway, but
instead shifting a trash bag or two of clothes
so that there was room, just about, for the
camp-bed to open out on the floor.

There I lay, night after night, the springs

digging through the foam mattress into my back, the leathery scent of my sister's old shoes permeating the dusty room as, like some penitent, I considered the mess I had made of what had seemed at the time a rather good life.

I had an ex-fiancée whose hatred of me was only exceeded by her determination single-handedly to propel the new hotel I didn't want into existence. I had no home, since she had informed me in a typed letter that the very least she expected was that I should allow her to buy out my half; the same went for the car. She had promised me a market rate, although I hadn't bothered to check what that might be and had merely agreed. It seemed pretty irrelevant now, and if it made her feel better to score a few thousand off me, then I was happy to let her.

I had a dead-man-walking role at work where, although I had retained my position as partner, I was no longer consulted on any of the remaining deals, let alone deferred to, even by the secretaries. At the moment Vanessa had contradicted me at the Silver Bay project meeting, my authority had been fatally undermined. I found that there were crucial "meetings" at the pub to which I had somehow not been invited, messages for me that were somehow diverted to other people. Dennis ignored me. Even Tina, perhaps scenting my diminished status, no longer found me attractive. All of which left me with two choices: fight to hold on to my job, trampling over anyone who stood in my way, in order to become, again, a Big Swinging Dick in the office, as Dennis so elegantly put it, or leave, and take what remained of my reputation to a rival developer. I had the appetite for neither.

Worst of all, I sat in at the meetings with Vallance, read the copied-in documentation and watched, at a distance of several thousand miles, the slow but steady progress of the project that would ruin Silver Bay, and the lives of those at the Silver Bay Hotel. The site was restored, the derelict Bullen property already bulldozed. There was a planning inquiry, which, we were assured, should go through "on a nod and a wink." I knew that Dennis was only holding me in position because of Vallance — if he lost such a key member of his team at this crucial moment they would look twice.

I also knew that to survive professionally beyond this deal I had to sharpen up. But I was immobilized, unable to apply my old analytical rigor to the state of my career, paralyzed by indecision and guilt.

And night after night I lay sleepless on the camp-bed, surrounded by the detritus of someone else's life, waiting for my own to make sense again.

One thing was clear: Vanessa had released me at the moment she had said she wanted the development to go ahead. When she had looked at me every last atom of love was gone, and I was sobered by the depth of her enmity.

"Bloody hell. You can't blame her." Monica handed me a glass of wine. One of the many conditions of my stay with her was that I had to put together the flat-pack chest of drawers she had bought several weekends ago, so I was seated amid piles of MDF and clear plastic bags with too few screws. In the interests of effective engineering, I should have stopped drinking several glasses earlier.

I got through quite a lot that month — in fact, I was drunk much of the time. Not that anyone would have guessed. I was not like Greg, loud, obstreperous, demanding. I was a subtle drunk. The third double whisky slipped down discreetly. The glass of wine turned into a bottle and a half. It was not that I had an addictive personality, but breakups are not suited to male patterns of behavior. We do not have groups of friends to prop us up and endlessly analyze our former partner's actions. We do not go in for aromatherapy baths and scented candles to "pamper ourselves" or read inspirational stories in magazines to feel better. We go to the pub or sit alone in front of the television with a drink or two.

"I don't blame her," I said. "I know it's all down to me."

"My brother the serial shagger, eh? Watch that screw — you're about to lose it."

"I'm not a serial shagger."

"Snogger." She giggled. "Serial snogger, then." I couldn't help laughing too. It sounded so ridiculous.

"There," she said, pointing her cigarette at me. She was seated cross-legged on a rug. "There — you see? You can't have loved her that much or you'd be devastated. Told you I was right."

"You have no heart," I accused.

But perhaps she *was* right. I felt bad, admittedly, and guilty, and a bit horrible, but I knew I wasn't drinking because I'd lost Vanessa. I was drinking because I no longer knew who I was. I had not just lost material things — the flat, the car, my position at Beaker Holdings — but the things I thought defined me: my analytical skills, my drive, my strategic focus for deals. My hunger. I was not sure I liked the elements of my character that had revealed themselves to me recently.

And I was drinking because one thought hung over all the others: that I had inadvertently destroyed the lives of three people who had no facilities with which to fight back. "What do I do, Monica? How can I stop it happening?" I dropped the screwdriver on to the floor beside me.

"Why does it matter?" she asked, picking it up, and studying the instructions. "You lose your job if it doesn't."

I stared at the pieces of wood in front of me, which didn't even look like wood, then at the tiny, chaotic flat, where the sound of traffic penetrated the walls. I felt homesick.

"Because it just does," I said.

"Mikey, what the hell went on out there? You went out as Billy Big Shot and came back a bloody mess."

So I told her. I told her everything. And the odd thing was that in saying the words, I realized what was going on. It took me two hours and several more glasses of wine, but I sat with my sister, in her cramped, untidy flat in Stockwell, and talked into the small hours. I told her about Kathleen and the hotel, Hannah, Liza and the whalechasers, and as I spoke, their faces came alive to me, and I felt briefly as if I were back there in the wide open space with just the sound of the sea in my ears and the salt breeze on my skin. I told her about Letty's death and the baby whale, and the sound I'd heard when Liza had dropped the microphone into the water. And when I got to the part where I had watched the thin, blonde figure recede in my rearview mirror, I understood. "I'm in love," I said. The words had just slipped out. I sat back, dazed, against the sofa, and said them again. "God. I'm in love."

"Hallelujah," said my sister, stubbing out her cigarette. "Can I go to bed now? I've been waiting for you to work that out since you got here."

When Dennis Beaker yawned, he made the same sound as a large dog does when you meet it first thing in the morning. It was a genuine sound, impossible to reproduce, which was odd, because I knew that yawning was a tactic he used to considerable effect when underlings or rival firms were making presentations, or when someone was attempting to say something he didn't want to hear. Which was often.

He leaned back now, in his leather chair, and yawned so widely that I could count the number of amalgam fillings in his upper jaw. "Sorry, Mike. What did you say you wanted?"

I stood in front of him, and said evenly, "I quit." I had planned a speech, refined it through several hours of sleeplessness, but when it came to it those two words were all I wanted to say.

"What?"

"I've put it in a letter. I'm giving notice."

Dennis's yawn stopped abruptly. He looked at me from under lowered brows, then leaned back in his seat. "Don't be ridiculous," he said. "We've got the Carter deal lined up for spring. You've babysat that from the start."

I shrugged. "I don't care about the Carter deal," I said. "I'm hoping you'll let me go immediately. I'm happy to forgo my salary."

"Don't piss me about, Mikey boy. I haven't got time."

"I'm deadly serious."

"I'll talk to you this afternoon. Go on, get lost. I'm waiting for a call from Tokyo."

"I won't be here."

At that point he saw I was serious. He looked irritated, as if I were trying something on. "Is this about money? I've told you you'll get a salary review in January."

"It's not money."

"And we're bringing in better private health insurance as part of the package. Much wider cover. Plastic surgery, if you fancy it. You won't even need to pay contributions."

My shirt collar was uncomfortable, and I fought the urge to pull off my tie and loosen it.

"Is this about Vanessa? You think I'm trying to force you out?"

"You want me to go, but it's not about Vanessa. Look . . . I know you don't want me to leave while Vallance are wobbling."

"Who says Vallance are wobbling?"

"I'm not stupid, Dennis. I read the signs."

He picked up his pen. He let his gaze travel around the room as if he were considering something. Finally it settled on me and he gave a grudging nod. "Oh, sit down, for God's sake. You're making the place look untidy."

London was not beautiful that autumn: the skies sat low, threatening and sulky, and the rain came down in sheets, creeping up my trousers from the uneven pavements where it collected in puddles. Sometimes the clouds seemed so close to the tops of the buildings that I felt almost claustrophobic. But it might, I thought, looking out of the window, have been almost any season for the amount of time I spent outside. In winter months I occasionally brought an overcoat, and in summer I might wear a lighter shirt, but closeted day after day between double glazing and air-conditioning, ferried to and from work by tube or taxi, years could pass without my needing to adapt at all.

I sat. Outside, I could hear car horns and some kind of altercation. Normally Dennis loved a good scrap, and would stop whatever he was doing to peer outside. But now he studied his hands. Waiting, thinking.

"Look, Dennis, I'm sorry about Vanessa," I said, at last, into the silence. "I never wanted to hurt her."

His demeanor changed then. His shoulders unbraced themselves, and he leaned toward me, his expression briefly softening. "She'll get over it," he said. "She'll find someone better. I should be madder at you, given that she's my daughter, but I'm well aware that Tina's a minx. Nearly headed down that road a couple of times myself. It's only because Vanessa's mother has pretty well all our assets in her name that I haven't dared." He chuckled. "Plus she's told me she'd have my bollocks for paperweights."

He let out a huge sigh, and chucked his

pen across the desk at me. "Bloody hell, Mike. How has it come to this?"

I caught it, and placed it back on the desk in front of him. "I can't be part of this development, Dennis. I told you."

"For a few effing fish?"

"It's not just the whales. It's everything. We'll be . . . ruining people's lives."

"It's never bothered you before."

"Perhaps it should have."

"You can't protect people from progress. You know that."

"Who says this is progress? Anyway, some people need protection."

"It's a ruddy hotel, Mike, not a nuclear-waste plant."

"Might as well be, for the effect it's going to have."

I could tell he couldn't quite believe what he was hearing. He shook his head, dug a few black crosshatches on to his telephone pad. Then he looked at me. "Don't do this, Mike. I admit I've kept you out of the loop since you got back, but you'd turned into such a bloody pious git. I can't trust you if you're not a hundred percent with me."

"I am with you, Dennis, just not with this development."

"You know we're too far down the road to back up now."

"We're not. We'd earmarked two other sites. Both are viable, you know they are."

"They're more expensive."

"Not if we offset the costs of the S94. I've been through it."

"It's going ahead, whether you like it or not." He was apologetic rather than bullish, and I saw suddenly that this was not about business: it was about Vanessa. He could forgive me, but to undermine his daughter publicly was asking too much. "I'm sorry, Mike. But it's going ahead as planned."

I shook my head regretfully. "Then I have to quit." I rose from my chair, and held out my hand. "I'm really sorry, Dennis. More sorry than you know."

When he didn't shake my hand, I walked toward the door.

His voice, lifted in exasperation, followed me: "This is effing ridiculous. You can't ruin a bloody good career for a few fish. Come on, boyo. We're mates, aren't we? We can get past this."

I hesitated by the door. Oddly, I heard reflected in his voice what I felt — an almost greater regret than I had experienced in splitting with Vanessa. "I'm sorry," I said.

As I opened it he spoke again: "You're not going to fight me on this, Mike." It was a question as much as a statement. "You go if you have to, but don't try to fuck up my deal."

I'd hoped he wouldn't ask. "I can't sit by and watch it go ahead," I said, swallowing hard.

"I'll screw you, if I have to." He nodded, to make sure I'd got the message.

"I know."

"I'll shitbag you all over the City. You'll never get a job anywhere decent again."

"I know."

"Don't expect me to hold back. You know what I can do."

I nodded. More than most, I knew.

We stared at each other.

"Oh, *bollocks.*" Dennis stepped forward and enveloped me in a bear hug, until Tina's voice came over the intercom, announcing that his call from Tokyo had come through.

I met Monica in a bar a short walk from her newspaper's offices. She had nipped out for a drink, but said she'd be returning to her desk until late that evening, trying to follow up a story. Still mulling over my meeting with Dennis, I had asked her, more out of politeness than genuine interest, what it was about, and she had muttered something vague about farming fraud and EU subsidies, then looked rather cross. "I hate stories that involve finance," she muttered. "You spend weeks trying to understand the figures, and when you run it nobody cares because there's no human interest in it."

"Want me to help?" I said. "I'm not a forensic accountant, but I can find my way across a spreadsheet."

She seemed a little taken aback. "I might." Her face lit up with a brief smile. "If I get stuck I'll bring some home, and you can take a look."

I had to admit that one of the unexpected benefits of my collapsed personal life was that my sister and I had discovered, to our mutual surprise, that we liked each other. I still thought her overly sarcastic, ambitious and chaotic, and that her taste in men was appalling. But now I understood that inse- curity lay beneath the sarcasm, and that at least some of her ambition stemmed from having an elder brother who appeared to have scaled the career ladder effortlessly, and parents who, I saw with some shame, had used that success relentlessly and unthinkingly against her. I suspected now that she would have liked a boyfriend more than she was prepared to acknowledge, and that the longer she lived by herself, the less likely she was to leave room for one. If we stayed close, if we were able to leave this particular door open, I would have that conversation with her. One day.

"Did you bring the pictures?"

I reached into my pocket and handed over the little paper folder. She began to flick through them, head down as she tilted them toward the light. "I've been thinking about this, and the best hope you have is in publicity. You reckon Vallance are nervous of bad publicity so what you have to do is get an effective figurehead to oppose the scheme, one spokesman, and then you need to work on two levels, local and national."

"Meaning what?"

"On the local level, leaflets, posters, local newspapers. Try to create a groundswell of opposition. On the national, or even international level, you need a couple of well-placed features that might get you some telly coverage. Maybe get some wildlife experts involved, or use some new research. You should be able to find some. Isn't there a whale-conservation society who can help you?"

I began to scribble some of this down. This was a Monica I had never met before, and her knowledge was valuable. "Whale-conservation society," I murmured. "Dolphins too?"

She held up one of the pictures Hannah

had taken, of Liza standing on Whale Jetty. She was tilting her head, smiling directly at the camera, the way she often smiled at her daughter — brimful of warmth and love. Her hair, unusually, was loose, and the dog was gazing at her adoringly. I knew how it felt.

"That her?"

I nodded, temporarily silenced.

"She's pretty. Looks a bit like that wildlife girl on telly."

I had no idea who she was talking about.

She thrust the pictures back at me, and tapped that one, now resting on the top. "You'll have to get her to step up. Make her the figurehead of the campaign. She looks good, and most people will be expecting some crusty do-gooder. I could probably get her a feature or two. Put her and the old lady together and you've got a better chance. Maybe you could try and get something like Relative Values in the *Sunday Times*. Didn't you say there were old newspaper reports about her?"

"I think I can get them off the Internet."

"If she hasn't been written about since then it might make a piece. Did I mention local radio? Oh, Christ. Look, first and foremost you need a press release, something to send out to all the news organizations with your contact details clearly marked. And then, bruv, you need to get tough. You need to come out fighting."

"Me?"

She looked up at me.

"I was asking how *they* could do it."

"You're not helping?"

"Well, I'll do what I can from here."

My sister's face was suffused with disappointment.

The barman asked if either of us wanted a refill, and for a minute she appeared not to have heard him. Then she glanced at her watch and declined. "And he doesn't want one either," she added, nodding at me.

"I don't?"

"You said you loved her," she said accusingly, when he had gone.

"Doesn't mean she loves me," I said, taking the last swig of my drink. "In fact, I have it on fairly good authority that she hates my guts."

My sister raised her eyebrows in a way that transported me to a time when we were children. It was a gesture that spoke of the uselessness of boys, of her eminent superiority. It told me that, yet again, I had got it wrong, and that this was probably only to be expected. As I had then, I wanted to wrestle her to the ground and sit on her, to stop her doing it and prove who was boss.

But, irritatingly, this time I had to accept she was right. She sat back on the bar stool and folded her arms. "Mikey, what the hell are you sitting here for?"

"Because I'm a stupid bloke who can't make a decision to save his life?"

My sister shook her head.

"Oh, no," she said, and grinned. "You made a decision. You're just too stupid to realize it."

For the first time in my adult life, I didn't shop around for flights. I didn't compare legroom against cost, weigh up the benefits of frequent-flyer miles against the quality of the airline's meals. I booked the first available seat on a flight to Sydney. Then, before I could think too hard about it, I packed a suitcase of essentials and my sister drove me to the airport.

"This is a good thing," she said, straightening my jacket, almost fondly, as we stood outside at the drop-off point. "Really. A good thing."

"She won't talk to me," I said.

"Then for once in your life, Mikey boy, you're going to have to work at it."

During that flight I became steadily more nervous. When it stopped to refuel in Hong

Kong, I was jittery in a way that couldn't be explained purely by the time change. I kept trying to think of what I would say when I saw her, but every conversation opener was inadequate. In fact, my presence would be inadequate. With Monica several thousand miles behind me, my vague dreams of an impassioned reunion dissipated like jet-fuel trails in a clear sky.

I had not done what I had promised Kathleen I would do, which was to stop the development. If anything, it was now moving forward with greater speed than ever. Despite my feelings for Liza, I was still the duplicitous pig she had identified: if Tina had not sent that incriminating text, would I have split with Vanessa? I could fool myself that it would have happened anyway, but I seemed so out of touch with my own feelings that I couldn't claim it as an absolute truth.

The murmured words I had rehearsed for Liza were drowned by different voices. I heard Hannah's, with the clarity of a silver bell: "Mike, why did you lie to us?," then her mother telling me accusingly that everything I had said, everything I had been, was a lie. I thought about Vanessa's bleak expression when she had seen the message on my mobile phone, and knew that I wanted never to inflict that kind of pain on anyone again.

Sitting on that flight, headed east, I discovered before the end of the first in-flight movie that I had no idea what I was doing. It was unlikely that Kathleen and Liza would want my help, even if I had known what I should do to oppose the development. Few people left in the town would welcome me. I was not even sure where I would stay.

I drank a lot on the flight, despite what my sister had said to me, partly because it was the only way I could relax, and partly because sipping wine was something to do with my hands. I dipped in and out of fitful sleep, and felt the knots in my stomach accumulate in proportion to the miles that the plane traveled toward its destination.

Some thirty hours later, I got out of the rental car that I had driven to Silver Bay from Sydney, stood up in the bright sunlight, and fought an almost overwhelming urge to climb back into the car and drive back to the airport.

The only time I saw my mother cry was when she threw a cherished porcelain shepherdess at my father's head. It broke, of course — no fragile ornament could have survived such a trajectory. But after it smashed, she slumped to the floor, cradling the pieces and weeping as if she had come across the scene of some terrible accident. I remember standing in the doorway and feeling shocked by my mother's uncharacteristic show of desperation, yet repelled by it. My father, his temple bloodied, had been standing by the sofa, and said nothing. As if he accepted that it had been his fault.

He had a small engineering firm, which my parents had run on hippieish lines, allowing everyone a say and doing their best to share profits. Surprisingly, for ten years it had worked quite well. It grew, my parents became more ambitious, and decided to open a second plant about an hour away. We would move too — and as all their money was plowed back into the business they had been delighted to find a large country house available for a knock-down rent, due to its general state of disrepair. The hot-water system was eccentric and half of the rooms were too damp to live in, but this was in the days when unmodernized houses like this were not unusual, and central heating not a necessity. My sister and I loved it. We spent five years roaming the woods, setting up camps in the unused wings of the house, not really minding as the damp spread and the number of habitable rooms shrank commensurately. My parents were too preoccupied with the business to do much more than the bare minimum of repairs.

Eventually the owners announced that they would not renew the following year's contract. No great disaster, my father observed. It was probably time we bought our own place.

Then they were alerted to the small print on the lease. My father had signed up to a "renew and repair" clause. He had agreed to restore the house to a condition it had not known for several decades. "Don't be ridiculous," my father protested. "The house was barely habitable when we moved in." But the solicitor just pointed to the print. My father should have read the contract, he said. He should have taken pictures and agreed the property's initial condition. He could not argue with what was there in black and white. The solicitor read out an estimated sum for renovations, and my parents knew that they were ruined. The shepherdess figurine was the first casualty.

My sister and I were moved to an unfriendly school, forced to share a bedroom in a grim maisonette, and for years there were no holidays other than in borrowed caravans at cheap seaside towns. For years I held up that porcelain ornament as a symbol of what happened when you fell foul of sharp practice, when you were not on top of the deal, when you believed that people had a natural tendency to play fair. Now I saw things differently. My father had rebuilt his business into an ultimately more successful company, run on more efficient lines. My sister and I were probably more resilient, and more ambitious, because of our early brush with loss.

My parents were still together. The shepherdess, painfully glued together, was still on the mantelpiece. "It showed us what was important," my mother would say, touching the cracks fondly.

It sounds stupid, but it was only now that I realized she was not talking about reading the small print.

I knocked three times on the back door before I caught sight of the note. "Lance/Yoshi: Help yourselves, we are at the hospital. Back soon. Please write down what you take in the book. L."

I held it for a minute, feeling winded to have her little note in my hands, then looked down to the jetty. There were no boats except *Ishmael,* and as it was only a quarter past ten in the morning, it was possible that Liza and Kathleen would be gone for some hours. I sat down on one of the empty benches for a few minutes, then walked to MacIver's Seafood Bar and Grill and ordered a coffee. My body didn't want coffee — it told me it was late at night still, contrary to what my eyes could see. I drank only half of it, letting the remainder stain a dark brown ring around the inside of the pale blue cup as it cooled.

"You the English guy?"

The owner, a large man in a grubby apron, was staring at me.

"Yes," I said. There was no point in asking which English guy he meant.

"The guy from the development company, right? The one that was in the paper?"

"I've just come in for a quiet coffee. If you want to pick a fight about the development, I'll leave, if you don't mind."

I put my wallet into my pocket and reached for my case.

"You won't get a fight from me, mate," he said, picking up a plate and drying it with a tea towel even filthier than his apron. "I'm looking forward to it. Glad of the extra business."

I said nothing.

"Not everyone's against it, you know, no matter what the papers are saying. There's plenty like me who think the town needs a bit of investment."

I must have looked disbelieving because he continued, walking over and sitting down heavily at the other side of my table. "I've got a lot of respect for the whale guys — Greg's an old mate of mine — but, strewth, I reckon they make a big deal about these old whales. Those big fish have been swimming past this bay for a million years and a few little jet-bikes ain't going to make any difference to that. Oh, sure, they might quiet off for a while, but they'll be back."

"Quiet off?"

He jerked a thumb toward the jetty. "Oh, they're all moaning, saying they've already gone. Like the fish know what's coming. I ask you!"

"Who's gone?" I was having trouble keeping up with the conversation.

"The whales. There's none showing. They've had to shut down the whale-watching early and now they're just going around the bay to see the dolphins. I don't reckon it makes a big difference to their profits. They can do two dolphin trips in the time it takes to do one whale trip. I don't know what they're complaining about."

I sat there for a while, digesting this. Then I turned to him. "You wouldn't serve me a drink, would you?" I had a feeling that the next conversation I had would require of me rather more Dutch courage.

He raised his bulk from the table, both hands resting like fat hams in front of me as he levered himself upright. "Mate, I reckon you guys are about to do me a big favor. This one's on the house."

It took me almost an hour to make it back up the coast road to the Silver Bay Hotel. I had run it several times in less than ten minutes. Normally it would have taken twenty to walk. But the jet lag had combined unhappily with the several large Scotches that my new best friend Del of MacIver's Seafood Bar and Grill had pressed on me, and despite the elegantly discreet curve of the coastline it was difficult to maintain a straight line. A few times I sat down on my case and thought hard about how best to continue my journey. The hotel was there, within spitting distance, but somehow kept moving away from me, like a mirage in the desert. Once I thought of having a paddle in the sea — the water looked inviting, and it was a lot warmer than when I had last been here — but for some dim reason it was important that I looked smart. Besides, I could no longer remember how to remove my shoes.

Twice when I had got up I had remembered some minutes later that I had left my case in the sand, and had had to go for it, with all the handle-missing and toppling over that that now apparently entailed. I had sand everywhere, in my nose, my hair and my shoes, but I kept a tight hold of my wallet, holding it out in front of me so that I could keep an eye on it at all times. My parents had always impressed upon me the need to hang on to your wallet when in a strange country.

When I made it to the hotel I felt an almost euphoric sense of achievement, tempered only by the fact that I could no longer remember why it had been so important to get there. I dropped my case outside the door, then gazed at the note, which swam around in front of me. I snatched at it vaguely a few times, in an attempt to make it stay still.

Then, suddenly immeasurably weary, I decided I needed a lie-down. The wooden benches were too narrow — I wasn't sure whether I could actually sit on them, let alone lie down on one — and the sand, at this end of the beach, was pebbly. I could just make out the invitingly dim interior of the Whalechasers Museum a short distance away and stumbled toward it. I would grab forty winks in there, and when I woke I would remember what the hell I was meant to be doing here.

I woke to the sound of shouting. At first it had been part of my dream — I was on an airplane, and the stewardess was trying to wake everybody up because until we all flapped our wings the thing would not rise off the ground. Gradually, through the fog of jet lag and whisky, I became aware that even as the stewardess evaporated, the shouting was louder, and her grip on my arm was uncomfortably tight.

"Let go," I murmured, trying to shift away from her. "I don't want any peanuts."

But then as my eyes opened and grew accustomed to the light, I realized I knew the face. Standing above me, her yellow oilskin flapping like the wings of some great bird, was Liza McCullen. And she was shouting at me: "I don't believe it! Like, this is all we need — Mike bloody Dormer turning up here drunk. You stink, do you know that? You stink of whisky. And what the hell do you think you're doing just coming in here like you own the place?"

I closed my eyes again slowly, feeling a strange calm descend on me. The weird thing was that, just before I did, I could have sworn I saw Kathleen smiling behind her.

Seventeen: Kathleen

He told me I should "step up." He told me he had discussed it with his sister, who was a journalist and knew about such things, and that I could be the main focus of a feature on "The Shark Lady Trying to Save the Whales," or some such. He said that publicity was the best chance we had of increasing opposition to the development and that it had to spread wider than this town, given that so many people seemed not to care much one way or the other.

I told him I didn't want to stir all that up again and that I certainly didn't want to feature in any newspapers. He looked at me like I was insane. "It would bring a lot of publicity. Helpful publicity," he said.

"It might interest a few local people but there's only so much interest a seventy-five-year-old woman who once caught a shark can generate. Better just let all that be."

"I thought you were seventy-six."

I shot Hannah a look that would have stopped me in my tracks, had I been her age. But the young seem so much less mindful of such things, these days.

"Kathleen, I told you I would fix this, and I'm doing my best. But we have to have a strategy and, believe me, this is the only strategy available to us at the moment."

Mike had had three days to recover his equilibrium, and although he still looked tired, he had regained that peculiar self-containment, the professionalism, that had characterized his early days here. If anything, he had become more serious since his return. He had come back to save us, he had announced, with some fervor, when we stumbled across him in the Whalechasers Museum. It's hard to take a man seriously, even a longed-for savior, I'd told him afterward, when he's lying drunk on the floor with wet shoes and seaweed up his nose. He appeared to have taken this to heart.

"Really. I've had specialist media advice on this." He was wearing an ironed shirt. It was as if he thought this might make us take him seriously.

"Mike, I know you mean well, and I'm touched you saw fit to come back to help us. But I've told you, I don't want to dredge up all that Shark Lady business again. It's been the bane of my life, and I don't want the attention."

"I thought you might be proud of it."

"Shows how little you know."

"You should be proud of it," said Hannah, cheerfully. She had been surprisingly pleased to see Mike — certainly more so than her mother. "I'd be proud of killing a shark."

"I don't think killing is ever something to be proud of," I muttered.

"Well, then, use the death of that shark to help the whales." Mike nodded at me.

"I'm not going to be the Shark Lady again. I have enough on my plate without stirring all that up." I pursed my lips, and hoped he'd leave it there.

"Liza then," he said. She had been doing her best to ignore him, her head buried in the newspaper. But she was, I noted, in the kitchen, rather than her bedroom or on board *Ishmael,* her traditional places of retreat.

"Liza what?" she said, not looking up from the paper.

"You'd make a great figurehead for the campaign."

"Why?"

"Well . . . there aren't many female skippers. And you know a lot about whales. You're . . ." here he had the grace to cough and flush ". . . you're a good-looking woman. I've been told how it all works and —"

"No," she said abruptly.

I stood very still at the sink, wondering what she would say next.

After a moment she added, a little defensively, "I don't want — Hannah exposed to . . . all that."

"I don't mind," said Hannah. "I'd like to be in the paper."

"It's the only way to stop the development," Mike said. "You have to galvanize as much support as you can. Once people know what's —"

"No."

He stared at her. "Why are you being so stubborn?"

"I'm not."

"I thought you'd do anything for the whales."

"Don't you dare tell me what I should be doing for the whales." Liza folded up her newspaper and slammed it down on the table. "If it hadn't been for you, none of this would have happened and we wouldn't be in this bloody mess."

"Liza —" I began.

"You really believe that?" he interrupted. "You really think this area would have been untouched forever?"

"No — but it wouldn't have happened yet. We would have had more time . . ." Her voice tailed away.

"What do you mean, 'more time'?"

The little room went quiet. Hannah glanced up, then down at her homework.

Liza looked at me and shook her head, a delicate, discreet movement.

Mike caught it and I saw it register on his face as disappointment. I started to tidy away the empty cups, as a kind of distraction. Both Mike and Liza handed theirs to me, as if grateful for it.

"Look," he said, finally, "one of you is going to have to do something. You two are the best chance we've got to stop this development, and at the moment even that chance is pretty slim. I'll do everything I can to help you — and, believe me, I can't do more than I already am doing — but you have to cut me a little slack."

"No," said Liza. "You might as well get this straight, Mike. Neither Hannah nor I will appear in any publicity. I'll do anything else you suggest, but I won't do that. So there's no point you going on about it."

With that, she got up and left the kitchen,

Milly following tight at her heels.

"So what are you going to do?" he called after her. "Fire rockets at all the jet-skiers like you did with the boats?"

Hannah gathered up her things from the table, gave Mike an apologetic smile and followed her mother.

I heard him sigh deeply.

"Mike, I'll think about it," I said, more to be kind than out of genuine intention. He was so disappointed, I had to say something. He gazed after Liza's departing back like a starving man whose last meal has been whipped away from him, and his feelings were so obvious that I looked away.

"Right," he said. "On with Plan B, then." He gave me a lopsided grin and flipped a new sheet of paper. "I just have to work out what Plan B is."

I discovered pretty quickly that Mike had given up everything to come back to Silver Bay. He admitted he no longer had a job, or a girlfriend, or apparently even an address. "I can pay, though," he said, when he asked for his old room back. "My bank balance is . . . Well, I don't need to worry about money."

He seemed oddly changed by his month away. The slickness had disappeared, and a new uncertainty had crept in. He tended to ask, rather than state, and his emotions sat more obviously on the surface, no longer masked by a deceptively bland shell. He also drank more, so I took pains to remark on it, which brought him up short. "Is it that bad?" he asked quietly. "I guess I've tried not to think about it."

"Perfectly understandable," I said, "as a short-term measure."

He got the picture. I found the new Mike Dormer rather more endearing. It was one of the reasons I had allowed him to stay. One of the few I was prepared to confide in Liza.

Meanwhile, every disco boat, every two-bit operator who had once seen an oversized sardine and now described itself as an eco-tour, found their way into what our crews had considered their waters. It was as if they were sizing us up, trying to work out how far they could impinge on our business. The coast guard told me there had been talk of extending Whale Jetty, so that others could move in. Twice the disco boats had come as far as our bay, and Lance had complained to the National Parks and Wildlife Service, blaming them for the disappearance of the whales. The official line was that perhaps migration patterns were changing, that perhaps global warming was shifting either the timing or the distance of the migration. The whalechasers didn't buy it — Yoshi had spoken to some of her old academic friends and they thought it was likely to be something more local. The dolphins were still occasionally visible in the bay, but I wondered if they felt bullied, the focus of so much daily attention because they were now the only thing for the passengers to see. For every pod there were now two or three boats a session stopping nearby, the tourists leaning overboard with their cameras.

Perhaps because she was so distracted by the plight of the whales and — although she would not admit it — Mike's return, I persuaded Liza to agree to Hannah having sailing lessons. I took her to the first, with her friend, at Salamander Bay, and when I saw her out on the water I saw, with a start, that it couldn't have been the first time she had negotiated her way alone in a dinghy. She confessed afterward, with a grin, that I was right, and we agreed that it was probably best not to tell her mother.

"Do you think she'll let me take out *Hannah's Glory*?" she said, as we drove home, the dog drooling happily over her shoulder. "When the teachers say I'm good enough?"

"Don't let that dog take your sandwich," I said, pushing at Milly's nose.

It had been a beautiful day, but clouds were moving in from the west, a dark forbidding line. "I don't know, sweetie. I think we should just take it one step at a time."

"Greg says she won't — just to get up his nose."

"He told you that?"

"I heard him say it to Lance. They didn't know I was listening."

I'd have words with young Greg. "What your mum thinks about Greg has nothing to do with it," I said. "You'll get your boat. But, as I said, you have to be patient."

I slowed down on the coast road to say g'day to old Mr. Henderson, returning on his bicycle from the fish market. When I turned back to Hannah she was staring out of the window. "Can you change the name of a boat?" she said, gazing at something in the distance.

"Why?"

"I thought I might change the name of mine. Once I'm allowed to take it out."

"It can be done," I said. I was half thinking about what I could cook for dinner that night. I was no longer sure how many whale-chasers I could expect. I should have asked Mr. Henderson what was on special at the market. "You might not want to change it, though — there's some say it's unlucky."

"I'm going to call it *Darling Letty.*"

I braked so hard the dog nearly fell into my lap.

For a moment neither of us spoke, and then Hannah's eyes widened. "Can't I even say her name?" she cried.

I pulled the car over, raising a hand in apology to the van that had had to brake suddenly behind me. When it had disappeared I turned in my seat and stroked her cheek, trying to appear less rattled than I felt. "Sweetie, you can say whatever you like. I'm sorry. You just gave me a start."

"She's my sister," she said, her eyes filling with tears. "She was *my sister.* And I want to be allowed to talk about her sometimes."

"I know you do." The dog was clambering into her lap, whining. She hated anyone to cry.

"I thought if my boat had her name I could say it whenever I wanted without everyone going all weird."

I stared at my great-niece and wished there was something, anything, I could say that would alleviate what I now knew she had been hiding.

"I want to talk about her without Mum

looking like she's going to collapse or something."

"It's a lovely idea, a really smart one, Hannah, but I'm not sure that's ever going to happen. Not for a long time yet."

When we got home, I climbed slowly up to my room and pulled out the drawer where I kept the picture of Liza with her two little girls. The edges are a little uneven, where I'd cut that man out with a little too much resolve. Liza thought the only way to protect them all was to bury Letty, I knew. It was the only way she herself could continue to live, and the two of them could exist safely.

But it wasn't as simple as that. They couldn't bury Letty then, and they couldn't bury her now.

And trying to pretend otherwise was no kind of living at all.

Every afternoon I visited Nino Gaines. I brushed his hair, brought him freshly laundered pajamas and, when I felt brave enough, I even gave him a shave — not out of sentiment, you understand, but because there wasn't anyone else to do it. Okay, so Frank might have been able to, or John John, or perhaps John John's wife, but the young are busy. They have their own lives to lead. So I volunteered, and sat there for a few hours every day and read him the bits I thought he would enjoy from the newspaper and occasionally berated the nurses on his behalf.

I had to come. I reckoned he hated it in there by himself, his nostrils filled with the smell of disinfectant, his strong old body hooked up to bleeping monitors, and tubes that fed him God only knows what. Nino Gaines was built for the outdoors: he had strode up and down the lines of his vines like a colossus, occasionally removing his hat as he stooped to take a closer look at this or that grape, muttering about bloom or acidity. I tried not to see him as he was now: too large for the hospital bed, but somehow diminished. It was clear he was not asleep, no matter how hard I tried to convince myself that he was.

His family were happy for me to stay; they came and left food that moldered beside his bed. They brought photographs, in case he opened his eyes, and music, in case he could hear. They whispered together, held his hand and talked in huddles with the doctors about prognoses and medication, reassured by the EEGs, which said that his brain was working fine. I could have told them that. I talked to him: about the vineyard, how Frank had said the first buds of this year's growth were about to show through, and that some supermarket buyer had made a special trip to see him all the way from Perth because he'd heard how good his wines were and wanted to stock them. I told him about the planning inquiry, which had received an unprecedented number of public objections, including a whole folderful from the children of the Silver Bay Elementary School who had deemed their whales more important to them than a smart new school bus. I told him about Mike and the hours he spent alone in his room on the telephone, doing what he could to stop the development. I told Nino about my sneaking affection for the young man, despite what he had brought to bear on us, and about the watchfulness in Mike's eyes that seemed to me a reflection of what he expected of himself as much as anyone else, and the way that when they alighted on my niece I felt I might have done the right thing in letting him stay.

And I told him about the disappearing whales and the poor, beleaguered dolphins, and about my niece, who seemed so rattled by Mike Dormer's reappearance in her life that she didn't know what to do with herself. She was busy and she was not busy.

She went out by herself on *Ishmael* and came back in a worse mood than when she had left. She ignored Mike at every meal, then scolded her daughter if she did the same. She was furious with both of us for allowing him to stay at the hotel. She swore she had no feelings for him — and when I finally told her she couldn't see what was in front of her face she had the temerity to use the words "pot and kettle" at me.

But she was a fool and Nino Gaines was an older fool. He lay there uncharacteristically still, the tubes flowing in and out of him. He said nothing, did nothing, just let me pour my troubles into him as if he hadn't a care in the world. Sometimes I left feeling hopeful. Sometimes his immobility made me mad. One day the nurse caught me shouting, "Wake up!" at him with such ferocity that she threatened to get the doctor.

But when I was by myself in that little room, and I lowered my cheek onto the back of his old hand — the one without the cannula fed under the near-transparent skin — it was only Nino Gaines who could feel the wet of my tears.

It rained all afternoon, as I had guessed, and by nightfall it turned into a storm. It was what my father would have called an old-fashioned storm, while my mother would mutter that it was no different from any other storm. I understood what he meant, though — it was no-nonsense, biblical weather with thunderclaps that made your teeth rattle, and sparked lightning strikes out at sea, like a wet-season storm in Darwin. When I got back from the hospital I called up the coast guard, and he said we needn't worry too much — we're always wary of the waterspouts, tornadoes over water, that look like God's finger pointing from the heavens, but behave like the hand of the devil — because the worst of it had already passed. I closed the shutters, built up the log fire and Liza, Hannah and I sat in front of the television, Hannah glued to some program she liked, Liza and I locked in our own thoughts as the wind rattled around us and the lights flickered, just to remind us that we were still at God's mercy. At around a quarter past six, I heard noise in the hall, and stepped out to find Yoshi, Lance and Greg shedding their oilskins, bringing with them the cold damp air, their skin shining with rain.

"You all right if we stop with you for a bit, Kathleen? Thought we'd have a drink before we set off home." Lance apologized for the puddle his feet had left on the floor.

"You've been out all this time in this weather? Are you mad?"

"Someone didn't check the weather reports," said Yoshi, glancing at Lance. "We thought we'd go out a bit further, head around the coast toward Kagoorie Island, in case there were any whales around there, and it came on awful sudden."

"It's okay, we didn't have any passengers," said Greg. "Waves were a bit sloppy coming back, but. Winds were against us all the way. Anyway, we weren't out on the water all this time — we've been securing all the boats. Gave *Ishmael* an extra knot or two."

"You'd better come in and sit down," I said. "Hannah, move up. I'll put on some soup." I fussed as if they were an inconvenience, but I was pleased to have them there. The hotel had been empty lately and their presence was reassuring.

"Did you find any?" Liza put down her newspaper.

"Not a sign." Yoshi fumbled in her pocket and brought out a comb. "Something odd's going on, Liza, I tell you. No dolphins today, either. If they go we're all in trouble."

"Go where?" Hannah lifted her head.

Liza shot Yoshi a warning look, but it was too late. "The dolphins are hiding out somewhere while the weather improves," Liza said firmly. "They'll be back soon."

"They're probably sheltering by the rocks," said Hannah. "I think they hide in that little cove."

"More than likely, Squirt," said Lance. "God, that tastes good," he said, as he took his first swig of a beer.

Yoshi leaned around the door frame toward the kitchen. "Actually, Kathleen, can I have a cup of tea? I need warming up."

I relaxed a little when I realized the worst of the storm had passed. Since I was a girl I've counted the seconds between thunderclaps and flashes of lightning, calculating how many miles away the storm is. It was only now I was sure that the worst was headed back out to sea that I could concentrate on the conversation around me. I still remember the storm of '48 when two cruising ships were wrecked on our shores, and my father and the other men spent half the night out in the waters picking up survivors. They collected the dead too, but I had not discovered that until years later when my mother confessed the bodies had lain in the museum until the authorities could take them away.

Greg had sat down next to Liza. He muttered something to her, and she nodded vaguely. Then his eyes narrowed. "What the hell is he doing here?" he said sharply.

Mike stood in the doorway, holding a sheaf of papers, a little taken aback to find so many people in the lounge.

"Paying his way, Greg, just like anyone else." I hadn't told Greg about Mike's return. I'd figured he'd find out eventually with no input from me, and that it was none of his business.

As I looked now at Liza's studied indifference, I guessed she had reasoned the same.

Greg made as if to say more, but something in my expression must have stilled him. He gave an audible harrumph and settled into the sofa beside Liza.

Mike walked over to me. "The phone lines appear to have gone down," he said quietly. "I can't get an Internet connection."

"They often do in heavy rain," I said. "Sit tight, and they'll be back later. The rain won't last all night."

"What are you doing? Trying to ruin some more businesses?"

"Leave it, Greg," Liza snapped.

"Why are you defending him? How can you even have him sit here, given what he's done?" Greg's voice had risen to an unattractive whine, and he glared at Mike.

"I'm not defending him."

"You should have slung him out on his ear."

"If it was any of your business —" Liza began.

"I'm trying to clear up the mess," said Mike. "Okay? I'm no longer attached to Beaker Holdings. I want to get the development stopped."

"Yeah, you say that —"

"What the hell do you mean?"

Greg looked at me. "How do you know he's not a plant?"

The idea had never occurred to me.

"His company must know there's opposition brewing. What's to stop them sending him here to suss out what's going on?"

Mike took a step toward him, his voice lowered. "Are you calling me a liar?"

I held my breath, feeling the atmosphere start to spin.

Greg's English accent was mocking: *"Are you calling me a liar?"*

"I've had just about enough of —"

"Yes, I'm calling you a liar. And howsabout deceiver, cheating, stinking penpusher, spiv—"

It was Greg who threw the first punch, his left fist slicing through the air to catch Mike a glancing blow to the side of his head. He stumbled and Greg swung his fist again, but

Lance stepped between them, blocking it with an audible grunt. Mike squared up immediately, fists raised. "Back off!" Lance shouted, swinging around and pushing Mike backward, inadvertently knocking over a side table. "For heaven's sake, back off!"

My heart was thumping so hard I felt almost dizzy. I froze as my room shrank around the men. There seemed to be furniture crashing and people shouting everywhere.

Mike lifted his hand to his face, saw blood on his fingers, and lunged forward. "You bastard —"

Yoshi screamed.

"Stop it! You're pathetic, the pair of you." Liza, on her feet between them, threw up her hands. "Get out! You hear me? I won't have this in my house. I won't have it." She was pushing at Greg, trying to eject him from the living room.

"What the hell did *I* do?" he yelled, as she and Lance maneuvered him toward the kitchen.

"I don't have to take this crap from you!" Mike shouted.

It was only when they were in separate rooms that my breathing slowed.

"Jesus Christ," said Lance, stepping back into the room. "Jesus Christ." Mike shook off his arm and began mopping at his cheekbone with a handkerchief. As he stooped to right the side table, I could hear the sound of my niece and Greg engaged in a shouting match in the kitchen.

It was then I noticed Hannah. She was huddled in a corner of the settee, clutching Milly. "Sweetie," I said, trying to make my own voice steady, "it's okay. It's just the storm making everyone cranky."

"They're not going to fight again, are they?" Her brown eyes were wide with fear. "Please don't let them fight."

I glanced up and Mike was staring at her, horrified by the effect on her of what had happened.

"Hannah, it's okay," he said. "Nothing to be frightened of."

She was staring at him as if she didn't know him anymore.

"Really," he said, kneeling down. "I'm sorry. I just lost my temper for a moment, but it was nothing serious."

She didn't look convinced, and recoiled from him.

"It's fine now. Really," he added.

"I'm not stupid," she whispered, her face both furious and fearful.

We all looked at each other.

"Look," he said, "I'll show you." As I held

her to me, he stood up and went toward the kitchen. "Greg?" he called, and I felt her flinch in my arms.

"Greg?" He disappeared. A second later they both appeared in the doorway. "Look," he said, holding out a hand — I could tell that that gesture half killed him, "we're mates, really. Like Kathleen said, the storm just made us a little cranky."

"Yeah," said Greg, as he took the hand and shook it, "nothing to be frightened of. Sorry, love."

She looked at me, then at her mother. Liza's smile seemed to reassure her.

"Really. We'll go now." Mike tried to raise a smile. "I'm sorry, okay?"

"Me too," said Greg. "I'll be headed off now. And, Liza," he said to her meaningfully, "you know where I am."

I could tell she wanted to say something but the telephone started to ring. She strode past him into the hall to answer it.

"Kathleen. Hannah." Greg was deflated now. "I'm real sorry. I wouldn't frighten you for the world, sweetie. You know that . . ." I squeezed Hannah's shoulders, but she still didn't seem to want to respond.

Suddenly Liza was back in the room, her oilskin already half on. The argument was forgotten. "That was Tom," she said, voice tight. "He says there's ghost nets drifting into the bay."

Eighteen:
Mike

The room was a blur of activity. I stood in the midst of it, my handkerchief pressed to my bloodied face, wanting to ask what a ghost net was, but it was as if they were marching to a drumbeat I couldn't hear.

"I'll come out with you," Kathleen was telling Liza, pulling on her gloves. "I'll steer while you cut."

Yoshi already had her jacket on. "Has someone rung the coast guard?" she was asking.

Lance had a mobile phone pressed to his ear. "Signal's down."

"You stay here, lovey," said Liza, to Hannah.

"No," said Hannah, her previous fragility forgotten. "I want to help."

Liza's face was stern. "No. You stay here. It's not safe."

"But I want to help —"

"Then stay here, and when the lines are

back up, field the calls. Ring the National Parks, the whales and dolphins people, anyone you can think of. Get them to send out as many people as they can, okay? The numbers are in the book on the hall table." She knelt and looked her daughter straight in the eye. "It's very important that you do that, Hannah. We're going to need as many people as possible."

Hannah seemed mollified. "Okay."

Kathleen came back into the room, oilskin on, a large flashlight under her arm. "I've put the wet suits in the back of the car. Spare flashlight . . . Has everyone got cutters?"

Greg pulled his woolen hat low over his head. "I've got a spare pair in my lockup. I'll run down and get them. Lance, give us a lift down — we'll be quicker."

I looked at Liza, feeling as I had when I'd first come here: an outsider, useless. "What can I do?" I said. I wanted to talk to her in private, to apologize for mine and Greg's stupidity, to find a way to be of some use, but she was already somewhere else.

"Stay here," she said, glancing at Hannah. "Best that there's someone in the house. And don't let the dog out. How's the weather looking, Kathleen?" She tucked her hair into her hat, and peered outside.

"Been prettier," said Kathleen, "but there's not a lot we can do about that. Okay, let's go. We'll keep in touch by radio."

As they trooped out Hannah explained that vast fishing nets, some many miles long, with floats at the top and weights at the bottom, had drifted into the bay. Labeled "walls of death," they had been declared illegal in Australian waters, but as a result many had been dumped overboard or had torn away from their ship and floated along until, weighed down by the bodies of those sea creatures they had caught and killed, they sank to the seabed. "We learned about them at school," she said, "but I never thought they'd come here." She bit her lip. "I hope our dolphins'll be okay."

"I'm sure your mum and the others will do everything they can to make sure they're fine," I said. "Come on — haven't you got some calls to make?"

The lines were back up, the mobile signals restored. I made myself a cup of tea while I listened to Hannah leaving urgent messages on answerphones and occasionally talking to someone who might have been an authority. She was astonishingly poised, I thought, for an eleven-year-old. Then again, I had never met an eleven-year-old who knew as much about dolphins as she did.

Outside, the thunder and lightning had moved on, but the rain beat down mercilessly, sending rivers down the panes and hammering an insistent tattoo on the flat roof of the porch. I put another couple of logs on the fire, then paced the kitchen, watching the dog's eyes flicker from me to the door and back again.

"You get them?" I said, when Hannah came in.

"Most of them," she said. "I think the coast guard must be out already. I wish I was helping." She peered out wistfully through the rain-spattered window.

"You are — someone has to make the calls."

"Not proper help. You're getting a bruise." She pointed to the side of my face.

"Serves me right." I grinned.

Hannah reached out for the dog, who lifted her nose. "I looked out of the window upstairs and there are loads of boats in the bay with their lights on."

"There," I said. "I told you they'd be okay. Everyone's out helping."

But she didn't seem to hear me.

It was then that I heard a shrill sound from upstairs — my mobile phone. "Back in a sec," I said, and leapt up the stairs two at a time, wondering fleetingly if it was Liza.

She might have tried to call while Hannah was on the telephone.

But when I reached my room and scrabbled in my pocket the little screen told a different story. I gazed at the name, at the flashing backlight, then flipped the button. "Hello?"

There was a pause.

"Vanessa?"

"Mike."

I looked out of the window at the dark night, just able, through the rain, to see the lights of the boats illuminating the inky black. I had no idea what to say.

"I heard you quit," she said. She sounded as if she might be next door.

I sat down on the leather chair. "A week ago. I — ah — didn't work any notice." It already felt another lifetime ago.

"I've been off," she said. "I didn't know. Dad didn't tell me."

"I would have called," I said, "but —"

"Yes."

There was a long silence.

"I didn't want to go in," she said, "not with you and — and her still there."

I dropped my head into my palm and took a deep breath. "I'm so sorry, Ness."

There was another silence. I felt the hurt in it, and was crushed.

"I wanted to tell you . . . it was stupid and — and you deserved better. But you should know that it was only once and I regretted it more than I can say. Really."

More silence. I guessed she was digesting this.

"Why did you quit?"

I frowned. "What do you mean?"

"Did Dad make you go? Because I never meant you to lose your job. I mean, I know I went against you at that meeting . . . but I just wanted to — I just felt so —"

"It wasn't your dad," I said. "It was my own decision. I thought it would be . . . best, you know, given . . ." I was distracted by the sound of the dog barking. "In fact he asked me to stay."

"I'm glad," she said. "It's been worrying me. Mike?"

"Mm?" The dog sounded as if she was at the front door. I wondered if I should go down but I knew that if she kept barking I wouldn't hear a word Vanessa said. And it was important to me that we squared this. "Vanessa, I —"

"What's that noise?"

The dog was scrabbling at something now, whining. I stood up and went to my door. I wondered if one of the whalechasers was trying to get back in. But the door was rarely locked.

"The dog," I said absently.

"You don't have a dog," she said.

"Not my dog." I held my hand over the phone. "Hannah?"

"Where are you?" she said.

I hesitated.

"Mike?"

"I'm in Australia," I said.

A stunned silence has a different quality from any other, I realized at that moment. It stretches, takes on greater weight, then implodes under the weight of unspoken questions.

"Australia?" she said weakly.

"I had to come back," I said, craning over the banister now. "I told you I thought this development was a mistake, Ness, and I'm here to try to put it right. I've got to go — there's things going on here — and I'm sorry, okay? I'm sorry for everything. I've got to go." I switched off my phone and ran downstairs. Milly was hurling herself at the front door, barking feverishly.

"Hannah?" I said, sticking my head around the kitchen door, hoping she might tell me what was going on.

But she was not in the kitchen or the living room. She was not in her bedroom, or any of the other rooms upstairs. She was not by the phone in the hallway. I was still so disorientated by my conversation with Vanessa that it took me longer than it should have to grasp that neither was her jacket.

I stared at the empty peg, then at the dog, who was still barking, glancing around at me as if I should be doing something. My heart sank.

"Oh, Christ," I said, and grabbed an oilskin jacket. Then I fumbled for the lead and attached it to Milly's collar. "Okay, old girl," I said, opening the door. "Show me where she's gone."

The worst of the storm might have passed, but the rain still bore down in solid unforgiving sheets, drowning sound, sending rivers over my feet as I splashed down the coast path after Milly. I didn't think I'd ever experienced rain like that before — it fell into my mouth as I shouted Hannah's name, had saturated my jeans and shoes within seconds. Only my upper half was dry, protected by the oilskin.

Milly strained at the lead, her whole body a shining missile, hampered only by my own lack of speed on the unlit path. "Steady!" I shouted, but the word was carried away on the wind. I ran through the dark, trying to remember the location of the potholes, and saw trucks arriving by the jetty, their headlights blurred by the moisture in the air. In the bay, as I drew closer, I could see the lights of the boats, maybe a hundred feet apart, bobbing as they struggled against the waves. I couldn't make out clearly what they were doing.

"Hannah!" I yelled, knowing it was pointless. I prayed that Milly knew who she was looking for, and that she wouldn't lead me to Liza.

The dog skidded to a halt by some large sheds — the lockups where some of the whalechasers stored their gear. Several doors were open, as if the crews had been in too much of a hurry to get out onto the water to think about protecting their belongings, and Milly skidded into one, her paws scrabbling on the concrete floor.

I hesitated in the sudden quiet, the wet lead slipping through my fingers, and tried to get my bearings. "Hannah?" I yelled. The rain thrummed dully on the flat roof and fell in ceaseless streams through cracks in the guttering. A low-wattage bulb hung from the middle of the ceiling, and I could just make out a contour map of what looked like sea depths on the wall. There were various plastic canisters, wooden crates full of tools and, lined up against the opposite wall, ropes, buoys and rolls of canvas. I could smell fuel.

"Hannah?"

I stared at the framed license on the wall. Greg Donohoe. This was Greg's lockup. In that brief moment of stillness I remembered a snatched conversation I had once heard about a little boat that was out of bounds. A boat that lived in Greg's lockup.

"Oh, Christ," I said, into the too-vacant space around me, and grabbed a flashlight as Milly, perhaps coming to the same conclusion, bolted for the waterfront.

I ran, my fingers locked around the dog's lead, trying to fight rising panic as I drew close to the sea and saw the conditions that the boats were working in. Heavy waves crashed onto the beach, clawing and pounding at the shore, the bastard cousins of those I had jogged past happily on many bright mornings. Out in the bay, perhaps half a mile to sea, boats bobbed and engines whined, trying to maintain position, and now I heard voices, lifted briefly above the noise of the rain. I scanned the horizon, trying to wipe water from my eyes, and the dog strained at my legs. I had no idea where the child might be in that inky blackness, but I could see that even the experienced adult crews were struggling in that water.

"Hannah!" I yelled.

I ran toward the jetty, the thin beam of the torch scanning the ground in front of me. A hundred feet back I found two men pushing a small motorboat toward the water. Both were wearing life jackets. I could barely make out their faces. "I need your help," I gasped. "There's a child, a girl — I think she's gone out on the water."

"What?" One of the men stepped forward, and I recognized him as a dog-walker I had met during my previous stay. "You're going to have to shout, mate. I can't hear you."

"A girl." I gestured toward the bay. "I think she might have taken a dinghy out by herself. She's only a kid."

The two men looked at each other, then at the boat. "Grab a jacket," one shouted. I couldn't think where to leave the dog, so I shoved her in too, and helped them push it out onto the water.

"Hannah McCullen," I yelled, as the engine roared into life. "Little girl from the hotel." The other gestured to me to point the flashlight out to sea. As I grabbed the side with my other hand, trying to hang on, he took his own light and hooked it onto the front of the boat, scanning the waves.

If I hadn't been so concerned for Hannah's safety, I would have been afraid. I have always tended to avoid risky situations, and as the boat bounced off the waves, then hit them with a smack, jarring me, I would rather have been anywhere in the world than out on that sea.

"See anything?" the man in the blue cap yelled. I shook my head. I was shivering now, which made it hard to keep Milly wedged safely between my legs. I tied her lead to the side rail — I had to focus on finding Hannah.

"Got to watch out for the nets," one shouted. "If we get the propeller caught up we're really stuck."

I worked out their plan — to start at the jetty end and do a sweep of the bay taking in all of the boats we could see, making sure she was not among them. I sat braced against the side, stomach lurching as we negotiated the waves, my flashlight beam swinging out, showing nothing but the dark, churning waters beneath us. As we drew closer to the other boats it seemed that half of Silver Bay had turned out in huge cruisers and little motorboats. I caught sight of bodies in wet suits, others in oilskins handing down shears. They didn't notice us. They were focused on their own task, and trying to keep their boats stable.

"It's a bugger of a size," yelled one of the men. I assumed he was talking about the net, but I couldn't see it. We plowed on through the waves, up to the next boat. Hannah was not there. I wondered whether I'd got it wrong — perhaps the little boat no longer lived in Greg's lockup. Perhaps she was still at home and I had misunderstood. But then I remembered Milly's reaction: her face was tense and watchful, and I decided to trust her. I couldn't risk believing that Hannah was not out there.

As we passed the sixth or seventh boat, and headed for the mouth of the bay, I became aware of the ghost nets. We passed between one of the *Moby*s and another cruiser and, with the greater illumination their lights shed, I glimpsed what looked like a tangled web, just visible at the top of the floodlit waves. In it I could see unidentifiable shapes, and struggled to work out what it was I was seeing.

Then Milly barked, great anxious gulps, and I heard screaming.

The dog sprang up, straining at her lead. I swung my flashlight, and shouted to the men, "Cut the engine!" As it stalled, I could hear Hannah — a thin, terrified shriek. As the men started the engine and steered toward my pointing arm, I saw, briefly illuminated by my weak beam, a little boat rocking dangerously, a small figure clinging to its side.

"Hannah!" I shouted, and the motorboat swung toward her, its engine almost drowned by the noise the dog was making. "Hannah!" The boat's light was on her then, and I could see her clearly: her face contorted with fear, her hands gripping the side, her hair plastered over her face as the rain beat down on her.

"It's okay!" I shouted, but I wasn't sure if she could hear.

"Help me!" she was sobbing. "The nets are all caught up in my rudder. I can't move."

"It's okay, sweetheart." I wiped rain out of my eyes. "We're coming." I turned as I felt the engine slow beneath me. "Closer!" I yelled to the men. "We've got to get closer!"

One swore loudly. "I can't go any nearer," he yelled. "We'll get stuck in the nets ourselves. I'll radio the lifeboat."

"Can we throw her a rope?"

"If her rudder's caught in the nets it won't help her."

Hannah's scream as a huge swell hit galvanized me. "I'll get her," I shouted, kicking off my shoes.

"You sure you'll be okay?"

"What the hell else are we going to do?"

One man handed me a pair of cutters as I pulled off my jacket. The other was hauling the front of my life jacket together, securing the ties. "Just watch you don't get caught in the nets yourself," he shouted. "I'll try to keep the light on you. Swim where I'm pointing it, okay? Follow the beam."

Even with the life jacket the force and cold of the sea struck me like a blow. I gasped as another wave crashed over me, saltwater stinging my eyes. I fought my way to the surface and squinted toward the light, trying to work out which direction I should be headed. I looped the cutters round my wrist, and then, as another wave hit me, began to swim.

She can have only been thirty or forty feet away, but that swim was the most arduous I have ever undertaken. The waves and current pulled me away from her, and the sound of her cries kept disappearing as my head was swamped by the swell. I took a breath when I could, stuck my head down and plowed toward where I thought she was, hearing the cries of the men behind me, Hannah's own cries growing gradually louder. There was no time to be afraid. I became a thing, hauling each arm in turn out of the dragging water, riding each

411

oncoming wave, telling myself that with each stroke I was, against visible evidence, getting closer to the little boat.

I was about ten feet away when I saw that she was wearing a life jacket, for which I thanked God. "Hannah!" I yelled, as she hung over the side toward me. "You'll have to swim."

And then I saw it. As the beam of the men's boat swung round, stronger, perhaps closer than it had been before, the swell lifted the net wrapped around Hannah's rudder, and suddenly, illuminated in the dark water, I saw something I shall never forget. Caught up in the fine filaments of the tangled net, visible only for the briefest moment, the bodies of fish, seabirds, pieces of creatures that might have died weeks previously, all suspended in the near-invisible web, the floating wall of death. I saw, in that instant, a baby turtle, a huge gull — an albatross, perhaps — its feathers half torn away, and worse, near the surface, a dolphin, its eye open, its body bound tight in netting. I am no expert when it comes to sea creatures, but I knew it was alive. And Hannah, hanging over the edge, had seen it too. I heard her piercing scream, and then, as I reached for the side of the boat, I saw in her huge eyes the reflected horror of what

I, too, had seen. I reached up a hand, praying with a shudder that my limbs were not going to come into contact with the rotting bodies below.

"Hannah!" I yelled. "You've got to swim. Come on."

The light swung away from us, then back again. For a millisecond I saw her face, still fixed on the water, drained of color. She was sobbing hard, lost to me, paralyzed by what she now knew to be beneath her.

"Hannah!" I pleaded. I couldn't climb up to her: my limbs were too cold and there was nothing for me to hang on to.

"Hannah!" I drew up my leg involuntarily as I felt it bump against something.

Then, over the rain, my yelling and Milly barking behind us, I caught her wail of despair: *"Brolly!"*

It was, I hope, the closest I will ever come to a vision of hell.

Hannah's hand reached toward me, and as I turned, perhaps fifty feet of that ghost net was illuminated again with its grisly, helpless haul. I thought, with a chill, of its sheer length, of the number of creatures dying silently below, of the whalechasers and crew trying to cut the living away.

"You've got to get her out!" Hannah was screaming. "You've got to!"

"Hannah, we've got to get to the boat!" I shouted.

But she was near-hysterical. "Cut her free! Please, Mike. Cut her free!"

There wasn't any time to debate. I took a deep breath and, when the light swung around again, I grasped the cutters and ducked under the water.

The most surprising thing was the silence. After the noise and wind and rain and Hannah's screaming, I felt a strange relief at being away from all the chaos. Then the looming shape of the trapped dolphin swayed into view and I lunged for it, realizing as I did so how easily my own limbs might be trapped in that net, how easily I might be dragged down. I swung at the net with the cutters, trying to keep a purchase as the surprising weight of the ghost net pulled it away. I cut, and as I wrestled with the net, I felt the nylon filaments give. The dolphin twisted, perhaps frightened out of its deathly torpor by this new threat. As the light dipped and swooped upon us I saw that the animal was bleeding, that its dorsal fin had been almost sliced away, that its skin was cut where it had fought against the fibers. I had to keep closing my eyes as the corpses of the dead kept rising up to meet me, the net swirling, threatening to make

414

me part of that terrifying haul.

"Mike!"

I heard, at a distance, Hannah's muffled wail. And then, suddenly, I had cut through the last of the net and the dolphin fled, wavering, into the murky dark, heading toward what I hoped was open water.

I broke the surface, my mouth a huge retching O of relief. "Hannah!" I shouted, holding up the cutters. Finally, her face white with fear, she slipped over the edge of the boat and into my arms, pressing her face against mine so that she didn't have to see any more of what surrounded us.

After she had established that I had cut the dolphin free she said nothing during the trip back to shore. She asked, her mouth pressed to my ear, if I had seen a baby, and when I said no, she buried her face in Milly's wet neck.

I held her close to me as we bucked and dipped back across the waves, and tried not to shiver too violently, but the looks I exchanged with the two men told me everything I needed to know about how lucky we had been.

Liza was already running toward us when we arrived at the jetty. She was wearing a wet suit, and her eyes were dark with fear.

She didn't even see me, so desperate was she to grab her daughter to her.

"I'm sorry, Mum," Hannah was crying, her frozen, bloodless arms wound tightly around her mother's neck. "I just wanted to help them."

"I know you did, darling. I know . . ."

"But Brolly . . ." Hannah began to sob violently. "I saw . . ."

Liza grabbed the blanket that was held toward her, wrapped her daughter in it and rocked her gently on her haunches as if she were much younger than eleven. A small crowd had gathered, standing on the dark sand, illuminated by car headlights. "Oh, Hannah," she kept saying, and what I heard in her broken voice nearly felled me.

"I'm so sorry, Liza," I said, when she finally looked up. I was shaking hard, despite the blanket someone had placed around my own shoulders. "I was only upstairs five minutes and —"

She shook her head mutely, and in the dark I found it impossible to say whether she was excusing me, or warning me not to come closer, perhaps shaking her head in disbelief at the unbelievable folly of a man who couldn't keep an eye on an eleven-year-old girl for fifteen minutes.

"I reckon the little boat's a goner," said

someone. "Nets are all wrapped around her rudder. I wouldn't be surprised if she goes down."

"I don't care about the boat." Liza's face was pressed to her daughter's. And then, as Hannah cried harder: "It's okay, baby, you're safe now." It was hard to tell whether she was comforting Hannah or herself.

I stared at them, wishing I could envelop them in my arms. I felt again the dragging sensation I had noticed when I was pulling against the net, as I grasped that I had sabotaged my last chance with Liza, and what my lack of watchfulness had almost cost her.

I felt something catch in my chest, and dropped my head. Then someone shouted that one of the larger boats was caught in the net, and several people headed back down the beach toward the jetty.

A woman I didn't know handed me a mug of sweet tea. It scalded my mouth, but I didn't care. Then Kathleen appeared behind me. "We'd better get you back," she said, laying a gnarled hand on my shoulder.

Suddenly Greg was running toward us, through the dark. "Liza?" he was shouting. "Liza?" His voice was full of fear. "I just heard. Is Hannah okay?" There was something proprietorial in that fear, and for once

I felt sympathetic, rather than indignant.

"I'm sorry," I said again, into the blackness, hoping Liza would hear me. Then, flanked by people I didn't know, I turned and walked slowly up the path toward the hotel.

It was almost one in the morning before I began to feel warm again. Kathleen had forbidden me the steaming bath I craved, but had plied me with hot tea until I had to plead with her to stop. She had built up the fire in my room — in the fireplace I had assumed was merely decorative — and as I shivered under several duvets, she brought up a concoction of her own, which included hot lemon, honey, something spicy and an equal measure of brandy. "You can't take any chances," she said, tucking me in as if I were a child. "You'd be surprised at what being in seas like that can do to you."

"How's Hannah?" I asked as, having placed another log on the fire, she made to leave the room.

"Sleeping," she said, brushing nonexistent dust from her trousers. "Little mite's exhausted. But she's okay. She got the same treatment you did — bar the brandy."

"She was . . . pretty shocked by what she saw."

Kathleen's face was briefly grim. "Not a sight I'd wish on anyone," she said, "but we did what we could. They freed a whale, you know, by the Hillman place. And they're still going. What that net would have taken if the boys hadn't spotted it . . ."

I saw again that murky water, those floating bodies, and tried, as I had for the past hours, to push it all away. I wondered whether Liza was still out there, launching herself into those wild seas to destroy the nets.

"Kathleen," I said quietly. "I'm so sorry —"

But she cut me off. "You need rest," she said firmly. "Really. Burrow down and get some sleep." And, finally, weary to my bones, I obeyed.

When I heard the noise I could not be sure whether I had been asleep for hours or minutes. Years of London living had made me alert to any unexpected nocturnal sound, and I propped myself on an elbow in my bed, blinking into the dark, still spinning in the strange space between dreams and reality.

For a moment I couldn't remember where I was, and then the dying red embers of the fire reminded me. I sat upright, the layers of bedclothes dropping from me, my eyes adjusting to the dark.

Someone was standing by my bed.

"Wha—"

Liza McCullen leaned forward and placed a finger on my lips. "Don't say anything," she murmured.

I wondered, briefly, whether I was still dreaming. I could hardly make out her silhouette in the blackened room. But my dreams had been fitful and horrifying; full of choking water and the bodies of the lost. Here, in the warm darkness, I could smell the sea on her, feel the faint grittiness of the salt on her skin as her hand met mine. And then, as she moved closer, I could feel her breath, the shocking, numbing softness of her lips on mine.

"Liza," I said, but could not be sure whether her name was flooding my thoughts or I had spoken it aloud. *Liza.*

She slid wordlessly into the bed beside me, her limbs still chilled and damp from the night air. Her fingers traced my face, rested briefly on the bruises wrought by Greg, then wound themselves into my hair. She kissed me with a ferocity that incapacitated me. I felt her delicate weight on me, the sudden cool of her skin against mine as she pulled her shirt over her head, heard the distant crackle of flames. Then, my thoughts jumbling, I stopped her. I took her face in my hands, trying to see her, trying to gauge what storm I was entering now. "Liza," I said. "I don't understand."

She paused above me. I could sense, rather than see, that she was looking at me. "Thank you," she whispered. "Thank you for bringing my daughter back to me."

She was electric. It was as if every fiber of her pulsed with energy, as if she was some force of nature undammed, a genie let out of a bottle. For weeks I had imagined this, had thought of myself making tender love to this sad girl, kissing away her melancholy. But here, wrapped around me, was someone I had not anticipated: she was greedy, encompassing, alive. Her body was as lithe as that of an eel, and she moved against me as relentlessly as waves. The ease with which she gave herself up to me was humbling. Is this a thank-you? I wanted to ask, in my few remaining moments of lucidity. A reaction to the shock of the evening? Somewhere deep in the recesses of my memory I recalled Kathleen's words: that Liza took the death of sea creatures hard. "And then, twice a year, that poor fool thinks he's got a chance." I made to speak, and then, as Liza's lips melted into me, as her skin warmed and then burned fiercely against mine, and I finally felt heat grow within me, I was incapable of speech, or of thinking anything at all.

When I woke, the bed was empty. Even before I was awake enough to think with any clarity, I realized I had known that would be the case. I blinked hard in the dawn light, allowing the events of the previous night to seep slowly into me.

She had let me in. I had looked into those iridescent eyes and I had seen into her soul. And when she had let me in, she had allowed me to be the man I had always wanted to be with her, the man I had waited all my life to become. Strong, certain, filled with passion — not some pale imitation of love. Someone who could protect her, cherish her, bring her joy through sheer force of will. I felt as if I had aged twenty years. I felt like a boy. I felt I could demolish buildings with my bare hands.

As my eyes adjusted to the light, and I pushed myself upright, I was unsure whether to feel elation at what I had been given or melancholy that it had already been taken from me.

I had been so sure that I would wake alone that it was several minutes before I saw that

I was not the only person in the room. Liza was sitting in the leather chair, which she had pulled toward the window. She was in her jeans, and her knees were pulled up to her chin, her arms wrapped around them. I glanced at my watch. It was a quarter past five.

I gazed at her, wanting to watch her forever, knowing that when she guessed I was awake I would have to hide that fact. I felt an unexpected pang of empathy with Greg: I, too, knew now what it was like to love someone unreachable.

"Good morning," I said quietly. Please don't pull back too far, I told her silently. Please don't make it obvious that you regret this.

She turned slowly. Her eyes met mine, and I observed that wherever her thoughts were they were far from me. How could that be, I wondered, when I felt as if her body was etched on my own? That her blood now ran through my veins?

"Mike," she said, "you say you know about publicity."

I stumbled mentally, trying to keep up. "Uh-huh," I said.

"What if someone who had done something really bad owned up to it? Something nobody had known about. That would generate publicity, wouldn't it?"

I ran a hand through my hair. "Sorry," I began. "I don't follow . . ."

"I'll tell you how Letty died," she said, her voice soft, but as clear as a bell, "and you can tell me who that will save."

NINETEEN:
LIZA

Nitrazepam — Mogadon, by its commercial name. Forty-two pills in a bottle. Pills to help me sleep. Perfectly legitimate, perfectly understandable, given my history of postnatal depression and the stresses of bringing up a young family. The doctor had been happy to give them to me. In fact, he had paid little attention, so gratified was he to be confronted by someone to whose problems there was a simple solution. He had known me for some time. Had seen me through a pregnancy. He knew my mother-in-law, the baby's father, where I came from. "I need to get some proper sleep," I said. "Just for a little while. I know I'll be able to cope better."

He had handed me the prescription without a moment's hesitation, then turned back to his screen to prepare himself for his next patient. Moments later I stood in the car park of the pharmacy gazing at the label on the bottle in my hand. Gazing at the warnings it contained. Sleeping pills. Takers of life, in the wrong circumstances. When I held them, I felt a strange, hollow excitement. They would give me back my life.

When I began my life in Australia — my real life, rather than the period in which I had merely existed — Kathleen persuaded me to see her doctor and ask for something to help me sleep. I was still plagued with nightmares to the extent that sometimes I was afraid to lay my head on the pillow. In sleep I would see Letty's terrified face, hear her screaming my name, and I prayed for oblivion. The first remedy the Australian doctor offered was those pills, albeit under a different name. When I registered what they were, on the prescription he offered me, I took a faltering step toward him and passed out cold.

I was told by people who knew no better that I came from a broken home, but it never felt broken to me. I never felt the lack of a father: my mother was enough parent for anyone, blessed with an indomitable spirit, fierce with maternal love and pride, determined that I should escape her own mistakes with a decent education. She shepherded and chivvied me, scolded and adored me, and even though we were patently neither a rich nor a conventional family I never felt the lack of anything. Even by childhood standards I sensed that my lot was a good one. My mother worked incessantly, low-paid part-time work that kept me close by her. Often she worked as I slept, and now I wonder how she managed to raise a smile — and a cooked meal — for me at breakfast.

We lived in a cottage in an area that was half suburban sprawl, half village a little way out of London, rented to Mum by a woman she had once worked for. I had twenty-odd friends within half a mile of my house and the freedom within that half-mile to do pretty well what I wanted. Twice, during my childhood, we flew to Australia, which made me an expert among my peers on global matters. One day, Mum promised me, we'd go and live there with Aunt Kathleen. But I don't think she wanted to be close to my grandparents. She never had much good to say about them. And when my grandfather died she found other reasons — her latest job, my schooling, a man she had grown fond of — not to uproot and move to the other side of the world.

And then it was too late. My mum's cancer was shockingly efficient. She had lost weight — a source of pride, then concern when she discovered it was not due solely to her careful monitoring of calories. The latest "nice man" — a divorcé who lived an hour away by train — found excuses not to visit and then, as the treatment became messy and unpleasant, as her emotional demands grew greater — melted away. Perhaps stung by his disappearance, independent to the last, she did not tell Kathleen she was dying. I found out afterward she had sent a letter that would arrive after her death. In it, she told Kathleen I was not to be pressured to go to Australia but asked her to be there for me wherever I wanted to be. It was the one badly judged decision of her maternal career.

There is never a good age at which to lose your mother, but my seventeen-year-old self was spectacularly ill prepared to face life alone. I watched my proud, glamorous mother shrink, then diminish. I saw her appetite for life disappear, buried in morphine and confusion. At first I did my best to care for her, and then, as the nurses took over and I understood what she had not been brave enough to tell me, I withdrew. I told myself it was not happening, and as my mother's friends whispered behind their hands at how brave, how capable I was, I sat at home alone, stared at the pitiless bills, and wished I had a life that belonged to anyone but myself.

My mother died one dark, painful night in November. I was with her, and told her she should stop apologizing, that I would be fine, that I knew I was loved. "There's money in my blue bag," she told me hoarsely, in one of her last moments of lucidity. "Use it to go to Kathleen. She'll look after you." But when I looked, there was less than a hundred pounds — not enough to get me to Scotland, let alone Australia. I suspect pride kept me from telling Kathleen of my plight. Perhaps predictably I went off the rails. I left school and got a job stacking shelves, then discovered that this would not keep me in my mother's house. The rent arrears built up until my mother's friend told me, apologetically, that she could not afford for me to stay. She offered me a position as a live-in nanny, and was relieved when I told her I was going to stay with a friend.

My life became chaotic. I sold bits of my mother's jewelry, although what little she'd had was worth barely enough to keep me in food. I lived in a squat, discovered nightclubs and worked as a barmaid, trying to ensure that I was drunk enough when I left each night that I didn't have to think about how lonely I was when I got home. For a while I was a Goth, and when I was twenty-one I got pregnant by one of the many men who passed through that squat in Victoria, a giant of a man whose last name I never knew but who made a great lentil stew, stroked my hair and called me "baby" on one of the nights when I had enough money to get very, very drunk.

Once I realized I was pregnant, everything changed. I don't know if it was hormones, or just the inheritance of my mother's good sense, but a self-preservation instinct took over. I thought of what I had avoided thinking about for four years, and what my mother would have said if she could see where I was. I never considered getting rid of the baby. I was glad that I would have a family of my own once again, someone who was linked to me by blood.

So, I stripped my hair of its violent dyes, got a job working as a mother's help, and when Hannah was born, I was employed by friends of that family in a picture-framing shop. They were happy for me to work until half past one when I had to pick up Hannah from nursery. I wrote to Kathleen occasionally, and sent her photographs, and she always wrote back promptly, enclosing a few pounds "to buy something for the baby," telling me she was proud of me for the life I had created for myself. It was not an easy life, or a financially stable one, but it was fairly happy. I think, as Kathleen used to tell me, my mother would have been pleased to see it. Then one day Steven Villiers came in and asked for a molded gilt frame with a dark green mount for a print he had bought. And my life, as I had created it, changed forever.

I was lonely, you see. I was lucky, I knew, to have a family who were prepared to tolerate me and a baby, but I used to watch them around the kitchen table, joking with each other in front of the television, the children's feet prodding their benign, grubby-sweatered father. I even envied their arguments. I would have loved someone to argue with.

As I watched Hannah turn from a mewing, downy kitten into a beaming, affectionate toddler, I wanted the same for her. I wanted her to have a father who would love her and swing her around by her hands in a garden, carry her on his shoulders and complain, good-humoredly, about her diapers. I wanted to have someone I could talk to about her, someone who might have an opinion on whether I was feeding her the right things for her age, who might think about schools or shoes.

I had soon found that men were not interested in women with babies — the men I knew, anyway. They were not interested in why you couldn't meet them at the pub in the evening, why you suggested the park at Sunday lunchtime. They didn't see the charms of my beautiful, fair-haired girl, just the restrictions she imposed on me. So when Steven Villiers bumped into me outside the supermarket and not only did not eye Hannah like she was something infectious, but offered to push the buggy for me, so that I could manage my shopping more easily on the short walk home, was it really any surprise that I was lost?

He reminded me at first of the father of the family I lived with. He had the same shabby-expensive way of dressing. But that was the only similarity. Steven was compact, but gave the impression of height. He had a kind of inbuilt authority, one of those people who make you stand back slightly without quite understanding why. He was surprisingly old never to have married — a fact he put down, while looking me straight in the eye, to never having met the right person. He lived with his mother in a beautiful house at Virginia Water, the sort you see in expensive property magazines, with huge, neatly clipped hedges and a bathroom for every bedroom. He was surprised when I expressed awe at what he possessed — he was the kind of man who assumed his life was the norm, and never bothered to inquire further.

Given his background, his assets, I was unsure for a long time what he saw in me. I wore clothes from charity shops. I was no longer wild-looking, but there was no way I could have been confused with the kind of sleek, moneyed girls he had grown up with. I had nothing to offer. When I look at photographs from that period, I now know a little better. I was beautiful. I had a kind of unworldliness, despite my situation, that men found appealing. I was without friends or support and therefore malleable. I was still emotionally giddy from my daughter's birth, anxious to see love everywhere, to bestow what I felt for her on everyone around me. I thought he was a savior, and everything I said and did would have convinced him of that. It was probably how he saw himself then.

The first time I went to bed with him I lay in his arms afterward and I told him of my life, of the mistakes I had made, while he held me close, kissed the top of my head and told me I was safe. There is something remarkably seductive, if you have been alone and vulnerable, in hearing you are safe. He said he was meant to be with me, that he thought I was his mission. I was so grateful, so besotted, that I saw nothing worrying in that statement.

Six weeks after we met he asked me to marry him. I moved in with him and his mother. My clothes became more conventional — he took me shopping — and my hair was tidier, which was more fitting in the fiancée of that kind of man. I took a new pride in my housekeeping skills, slowly adapting under the terse tutelage of my prospective mother-in-law. There were hiccups, but Hannah and I learned together how to live under that roof. I had grown up, I told myself. I enjoyed the challenge of fitting in.

Then, some four months later, I discovered I was pregnant. Initially Steven was shocked, but quite quickly delighted. Letty was born as it grew light on the morning of 16 April, and I thanked God, as Hannah and Steven cooed over her, that I finally had a family of my own. A proper family.

Letty was not the most beautiful of babies — in fact, she resembled a shar-pei for several months longer than she should have

— but she was the most adored. I used to watch Steven's uncomplicated love for her, her grandmother's affectionate fussing, and wish it had been the same for Hannah. As a baby, Letty was as sweet-natured and sunny as they come.

Perhaps it was sleep deprivation, or just the moment-to-moment nature of life with a new baby, but it wasn't until several months after Letty's birth that I realized Steven hardly noticed Hannah. Until then I had told myself he loved her, that his occasional thoughtlessness toward her was a male thing, rather than deliberate omission. I had little to go on, you see. Having been brought up by my mother, and seen so little of my grandfather, I wasn't familiar with the ways of men. Steven was a good provider — as his mother was always telling me — he knew about discipline and routines, and if Hannah frustrated him with her two-year-old tantrums and her faddiness about food, was it any surprise that he sent her to bed? Letty was so adorable — was it any surprise that fairly often, Hannah's own behavior was seen as wanting?

I tell myself now that I was blinded by the demands of new motherhood. That one sees what one wants to see. But in my heart I should have known. I should have grasped earlier that my daughter's increasing silence was not solely the result of adapting to a new sibling. I should have seen that my mother-in-law and Steven had become harsher with her, their criticisms more openly expressed. Mostly I should have guessed it from that woman's attitude.

She never forgave me for saddling her son — a senior manager with prospects — with a child who wasn't his. She didn't like the fact that I had no history, as she called it. Oh, she was polite enough to start with, but she was one of those bridge-playing women, the ones with blue helmet hair and Jaeger cardigans, and everything I was screamed irresponsibility and fecklessness at her, whether I was making a lentil stew (hippie food) or letting Hannah sleep with me when she was two.

She dared not say anything at first, when Steven and I were locked in our bubble of new love. She had led him to believe that he was the head of the family since his own father had died, and now found that she had painted herself into a corner because he would not discuss my supposed faults. Until Letty was born, when I could not meet their standards. Then my inability to cope with two small children in the manner Steven and she expected was gradually

436

revealed. As the toys spread across the floors, and our beds remained unmade until the afternoon, my clothes wore epaulettes of baby milk and Hannah screamed in a corner over some supposed misdemeanor, my mother-in-law discovered she could say and do whatever she liked.

Once, before it got too bad, I dared to ask Steven whether we might find somewhere of our own, whether we might be happier by ourselves, but the look he gave me was withering. "You can barely get those girls dressed by yourself," he said, "let alone run a house. Do you think you'd last five minutes without my mother?"

Looking back now, I find it hard to identify myself as that creature. In Kathleen's pictures, from which Steven was long removed, I see a strange, lost girl with hair that wasn't like hers and weird, docile clothes. Her eyes display a fearful determination not to recognize what she had got herself into. What was the alternative, after all? I had nothing — no home, no money, no support. I had two infant daughters and a man who was a father to them, prepared to forgive me for the mess I had made of my life. I had a mother-in-law who was prepared to tolerate me in her beautiful house, even though it was far beyond anything I had known. My domestic skills weren't up to much and, frankly, my manners often let them down, especially since Steven had been elected to the local council and his career at the bank was taking off.

You don't understand how easy it is to be ground down, if you haven't been there. With his mother's help, over the years, Steven gradually grew to acknowledge my faults. Our wedding was spoken of rarely, then never. Hannah learned to close her mouth while she ate, and that the better she behaved the less likely she was to be scolded. I learned that if you wore long sleeves the mothers at playgroup would stop remarking on your bruises.

I had grown up believing that that kind of thing only happened in the most desperate houses. I thought it was about poverty, and lack of education. With Steven, I learned that it was about my own inadequacy, my failure to repay the trust he had placed in me, my inability to make myself look half-way decent and, when it was really bad, my uselessness in bed.

The first time he hurt me I was so shocked I assumed it had been an accident. We were upstairs and the girls were crying, fighting over some cheap plastic toy. I had been so distracted by them that I had forgotten the iron, which was burning through his shirt. He had come into the room, furious at the noise, yelled at the girls, and then, when he saw the shirt, he cuffed me, as if I were a dog.

"Ow!" I exclaimed. "That hurt!" He turned to me with an expression of disbelief on his face, as if I hadn't understood it was meant to. And as I stood, holding my throbbing ear, he walked briskly downstairs, as if nothing had happened.

He apologized later, blamed work stress or something like it, but sometimes I think that that first time was a tipping point for him. That once he had crossed the line, it was easier to cross it again. Sometimes we went months with nothing happening, but there were times when almost anything I did — peeling potatoes wastefully, not polishing shoes — prompted a fist or a hard hand. Never a fight — he was too clever for that — just enough to tell me who was boss.

By the time I realized what I had to do I was a shadowy creature, a woman who had learned it was best not to offer an opinion, answer back or draw attention to myself, that scars fade quickly, even if their memory lingers. But then I looked at my daughter's face on the day he hit her, hard, for failing to take her shoes off before she reached the pale green hall carpet, and my resolve began to return.

I began to stash money. I would ask for an amount to buy a coat for Letty — knowing he could refuse his daughter nothing — then would show off something immaculate I had bought from the charity shop, pocketing the difference. I squirreled away money from the supermarket shopping. I was good at living on little, having done it for years. And they suspected nothing, because I had become such a downtrodden thing.

By then I hated him. The fog of my depression lifted, and I saw clearly what had happened to me. I saw his coldness, his arrogance, his blind ambition. I saw his determination to ensure my elder daughter knew she was a second-class citizen in his house, even at the tender age of six. I saw that other families did not live like we did and, finally, that his class, his background and financial position did not prevent what he was doing from being abuse. I saw, with relief, that my daughters loved each other regardless, that their tenderness, games and bickering were those of every other set of siblings. I saw Letty's plump brown arms linked casually around her sister's neck, heard her high, lisping voice telling Hannah stories about what she had done at play-

440

school, begging her to "pretty up" her hair; I saw Hannah, at night, snuggled in with Letty as she read her a story, their blonde hair entwined, their nighties a pastel tangle. He had not poisoned them yet.

But seeing the truth of my situation did not help me — I could leave with Hannah, I thought, and they would barely care. (Half the time he told me I was a waste of space anyway.) But they would never hand over Letty. In one argument, when I had threatened to leave with them both, he had laughed at me. "What kind of judge is going to let you look after my daughter?" he said. "Look at what you have to offer, Elizabeth. Look at your history — squats and goodness knows what — your lack of education or prospects, and then look at what she'll get with me. You wouldn't have a bloody hope."

I suspect he was sleeping with someone else by then. His physical demands on me were far fewer — a source of relief. He had a schizophrenic attitude toward me. If I dressed nicely he told me I was ugly, if I approached him with affection, that I was a turnoff. If another man looked at me, even if I was dressed simply in jeans and a loose shirt, he held my face tightly between his hands and told me that no other man would ever lay a hand on me. On the night when his work colleague made an admiring comment about my legs he forced himself on me so that I could barely walk the next day.

What kept me going was the money mounting up in the lining of my green coat. The hours in which they thought I spent mindlessly ironing or washing up or sitting with the girls in the park, but in which I sat, the peaceful expression on my face belying my burning intent, plotting escape.

They were creatures of habit. Every Tuesday and Thursday she would play bridge. For years, on Thursday and Friday evenings he "went to his club" — a euphemism for the other woman — and on Saturdays he played golf. I cherished those Thursday evenings, when I knew I had a few precious hours alone with the girls to laugh, run around, be silly and remember who I was before the sound of a key in the door could leave me silent and cowed.

Then, one Thursday, Steven came back early and found the letter I was writing to Kathleen, telling her the truth about what he had done to me. After his initial rage was spent, I suspect he told his mother I was not to be left alone: after that, whenever I was in the house, so was one of them. And whenever I went out, they would find a reason to take Letty to the park, or keep her at home. From that point I was never alone with my two girls. I think he knew by then he was losing control; that letter to Kathleen (thank goodness I hadn't addressed it) had shocked him, not only because it showed I might have the courage to tell someone what he had done, but because it laid his actions bare, in print, and they were not pretty. Until then I think he had convinced himself that his behavior was reasonable, that his beatings were an inevitable consequence of my failures. To see the cruel words, the split lips and broken fingers in print, to see his actions for what they were — the behavior of a bully — must have been unconscionable for him.

I bided my time. I had become patient. I just needed to get to Kathleen. I could work out everything else from there. Her home was a mirage I hugged to myself on the nights when the darkness of my life was overwhelming. He knew only that I had a distant aunt. He had no idea where she lived.

By the time I had worked out a plan and a date for its execution, I was so nervous that I was surprised they couldn't see it. I hadn't been able to eat properly for weeks. The knot in my stomach made me clumsy, the endless reworking of plans in my head made me forgetful so they both tutted about my general uselessness and warned Hannah that if she didn't buck her ideas up she'd end up like me. If the girls knew something was up, they didn't show it. Thankfully, children tend to live in the moment. I watched their games, their private conversations, the absent way they ate their fish fingers, and imagined them in Australia, running down Whale Jetty. Then I offered silent prayers to God that He would grant them that freedom. I wanted them to be free, strong, independent, happy. I wanted that for myself — but by then I had hardly any idea who I actually was.

"Your daughter needs a haircut," he said that morning. "We're having a family photograph taken for my council election leaflet on Saturday. Please try to make sure that you and she are halfway presentable. Make sure your blue dress is clean." He kissed my cheek — a cold, formal peck, for his mother's benefit, I guessed. As much as she disliked me, she would have disliked his affair even more.

"Will you be back for supper?" I said, trying to keep my voice light and unconcerned.

He looked irritated to be asked. "I've got a meeting tonight," he said, "but I'll be home before Mother goes out."

I barely remember that day now, except that it rained heavily, and that the girls, stuck indoors, squabbled. It was the school holidays and having Hannah at home all the time had irritated my mother-in-law so much that she'd got one of her "headaches." She warned me that if I couldn't keep the noise down I'd have Steven to answer to. I remember smiling my apology and hoping the headache heralded a tumor.

I must have checked the passports every half hour. They and the tickets were safe in the lining of my coat. While that woman slept, I packed two duffel bags with the bare essentials so that a cursory glance in the children's drawers would not suggest we had gone. At one point Hannah came up to ask what I was doing — when she opened the bedroom door my heart beat so fast I thought it would bounce clean out of my chest. I placed my finger to my lips, trying to keep my face free of anxiety, and told her to go downstairs, that I had a surprise planned, but it would only work if she kept it a secret.

"Are we going on holiday?" she said, and I fought the urge to clap my hand over her mouth.

"Something like that. A little adventure," I

whispered. "Go downstairs now, Hannah, and don't say anything to Letty. It's very important."

She opened her mouth to speak, but I almost shoved her out of the door. "Go on now, Hannah. We mustn't wake Granny Villiers or Daddy will be cross." It was a cheap shot, but I was desperate.

Hannah didn't need telling twice: she left my room and, as silently as I could, I put the bags under the bed in the spare room.

He was late that evening, as I'd suspected he would be. Thursday evening was his night for seeing "her," I had guessed, and my mother-in-law grew increasingly agitated after he missed the time he had agreed to come home.

"He's going to make me late for bridge," she said bad-temperedly, for the eighteenth time, staring out at the wet driveway. I said nothing. I had long learned that that was the safest way.

Then, miraculously, she stood up. "I can't wait any longer," she said. "Tell Steven I had to go. And make sure that casserole doesn't burn. You've got it on too high a heat."

I think the casserole reassured her: in some perverse way she reasoned that I wasn't likely to go anywhere if food was cooking.

"Have a nice time," I said, keeping my features as bland as possible. She looked at me a little sharply, so I busied myself with plates, as if I was laying the table.

"Don't forget there's bread to warm in the oven," she said. And then, with a swish of her coat, she was gone. I stood in the kitchen with the girls chatting at my feet about some game they were playing and freedom was so close it tasted metallic in my mouth.

As her car left the drive, I ran upstairs and grabbed the pills from their hiding-place in the wardrobe. I came down, and while the girls watched a video, I broke several capsules into a glass, then added some wine, stirred and tasted it. The drug was undetectable. I poured some more, then broke in four more capsules, just to be sure. I tasted it again — with luck, if I made the casserole spicy enough, he would taste noth-ing. It was almost half past seven.

He would eat, fall into a deep sleep, and I would have several hours before she came home. Several hours in which to get to nearby Heathrow in his car. To board a plane. Her Thursday sessions could go on as late as eleven thirty or even midnight. With luck, by the time she got home, he would still be asleep and we might already be in the air. It was a good plan. A near-perfect plan.

I started as I heard Steven's car pull up in the drive, and tried to quell the butterflies in my stomach. I had never before prayed for him to come home sooner rather than later. The smile I had on my face as his key turned in the lock was as close to genuine as I had worn in years.

"Elizabeth," he said —

Mike was holding my hands. "It's all right," he said, his eyes kind. "It's all right."

My breath was coming in deep jags, tears streaming down my face. "I can't —" I shook my head at him. "I can't —" My chest was so tight I could barely breathe. I gulped air, and my lungs inflated with a painful gasp.

I felt his arms surround me. "You don't have to say anything," he murmured, into my ear. "You don't have to tell me any-thing."

"Letty — I —"

He held me then. He held me without say-ing anything and let me fall apart. And he never moved. He just sat, his face pressed to mine so tightly that his skin must have absorbed my tears. His arms stayed locked around me. Tight enough to comfort. Loose enough to reassure me of my freedom.

"Mum?"

Hannah stood in the doorway, still in her nightdress. She looked from me to Mike and back again. Her hair was still matted from sleep.

Her presence brought me back from the brink. I pulled away from Mike and wiped my eyes. My beautiful daughter, my beautiful, frightened, brave, living daughter.

"Why are you crying?" she whispered.

I wanted to tell her, but I wanted to protect her too. For years I haven't spoken about Letty in front of her. For years, not knowing how much she remembered, I've tried to shield her from the memory of that awful night, the night on which, because of what I did, our lives imploded.

"Hannah —" I reached out to touch her, and my voice stopped in my throat.

Mike's voice cut across the room, quiet and firm: "Letty," he said gently. "We're talking about Letty, Hannah." And as she stepped forward to take his outstretched fingers, my heart broke, overwhelmed not by the pain, or the memory of my poor lost daughter, but by the presence of so much love. Then, my hand pressed to my mouth, I had to run from the room.

Twenty:
Hannah

My mother didn't talk for almost two weeks after we came here. She just lay in her bed, like someone dead. Then for ages she drifted around, there but not quite there, as if she was a hole in a room. Aunt Kathleen looked after me, feeding me up, getting me to explain a bit about what had happened, holding me when I couldn't stop crying. When she decided I shouldn't be on my own, she got Lara around, and helped us bake cakes together, as if we were cooking up a friendship. As if she was trying to find me a substitute for Letty. And when I asked her what was going on with my mum, why she wouldn't come down and be with me, Auntie K just said: "You and your mum have suffered something unimaginable, Hannah, and she's not coping with it quite as well as you are. We have to give her a bit of time."

So she gave her some time, and a bit

more, and then I think she decided she'd had enough. "Your mum and I are going to have a little chat," she told me. "You and Lara stay here with Yoshi and mind the dog." I don't know what was said, but they went out on Auntie K's boat, and when they got back Mum looked less shadowy than she had done. She climbed out onto Whale Jetty, walked down to me and held me. I felt like it was the first time she'd actually seen me for ages. "I'm really sorry, Mum," I said, as the tears started. I could feel her bones through her shirt.

Her voice didn't sound the same. "Nothing to be sorry for, lovey. You did everything right. It was me who got it all wrong."

But I knew that if Letty and I hadn't had that argument in front of Steven . . . if Letty hadn't said that thing about not wanting to go on holiday . . . Suddenly I missed Letty so badly. I couldn't believe she wasn't alive anymore. "I want her to be here," I cried.

I felt a big sob catch in Mum's chest. She squeezed me tight. "Me too, lovey," she said softly. "Me too."

Mum had told me not to say anything. She had stood there in her room and said it was very important. But I'd been so excited at the thought of me, Mum and Letty going somewhere, the thought that we might have whole weeks of giggling and doing the things Granny Villiers didn't like. "I didn't mean to tell her," I whispered. Then my mother took my shoulders, and her eyes, when they met mine, were bright, bright blue, like the sky, her eyelashes all pointy, like stars, from her tears. "Your sister's death was not your fault, okay?" Her voice was fierce, almost like she was telling me off. But her eyes were kind. "Not one iota of this was your fault, Hannah. Not one. And now you need to forget that any of it ever happened."

A couple of weeks later, on a Monday evening, after I'd had my tea, we had a service for Letty. Out at sea. Just me, Mum, Aunt Kathleen and Milly. We went out on *Ishmael* to what Aunt Kathleen said was the prettiest spot in the whole of Australia, and while the dolphins bobbed around and the sun shone red and a few clouds drifted high in the sky Aunt Kathleen gave thanks for the life of Letty and said that even though we were on the other side of the world it was perfectly obvious to her where Letty's spirit was. I kept hoping a dolphin would swim up beside us, maybe poke its head up, as if it were a sign, but although I stared for ages, they didn't come any closer.

When we unpacked the second duffel bag,

Mum found Letty's crystal dolphins. She must have packed them really carefully, because not even their little fins were broken. She held one in her hand for a long, long time. Then she took a big breath and handed it to me. "You look after these," she said. "Keep them . . . keep them safe."

That was one of the last times we ever spoke about Letty.

And now it's just me, remembering things. Some things, like when me and Letty used to make camps in our bedroom, or when we used to run around in the garden and squirt the hose at each other, I try to keep in my head because I get worried that she's fading away and soon I won't remember her. I have two photographs of her in my drawer and if I didn't look at them every night I wouldn't remember how her face was, how her missing tooth looked when she smiled, the way she stroked her nose with her finger when she sucked her thumb, how she used to feel when she slept with me. And there are some things I'd like to forget. Like that night when Mum took me and Letty in her arms as soon as Granny Villiers had left and told us things were going to change. I think about the way I had found her packing our bags, and that I'd felt relieved that she'd even remembered my old flannel dog, Spike, which I couldn't sleep without, and that she had told me we mustn't say anything to Daddy or Granny because we were going to give them a surprise. And even though she thought I wasn't looking I saw when she hid the bags in the spare room. I remember the purply bruises I saw on her arms, a bit like the one I had when Steven was cross with me for getting felt-tip on the kitchen table and pulled me so hard off my stool that it hurt.

And I remember feeling so excited — a bit like I did before Christmas — that I had to say something to Letty, even though I told her it was a very important secret.

And then I remember we watched a video — *Pinocchio* — even though it wasn't a weekend, and that when Steven came home he smelt of drink but she had poured him a big glass of wine anyway and stood there smiling at him until he said she looked like an idiot. When she served up the supper, I could see her looking at him out of the corner of her eye as if she was waiting for something.

And then Letty and I had a stupid fight about crayons, because we both wanted the same green, which was much better than the browny-green, which never came out right on the paper, and I won because I was bigger and Letty started to cry and said she didn't want to go away, and Steven said, "Go where?" And he looked at Mum and they stared at each other for a few seconds. Then he pushed past her and went upstairs, and I heard him pulling out all the drawers. When he came back his face was so angry that I hid under the table, and pulled Letty with me. I heard him shouting, "Where are the passports?" and his voice had gone all slurry and I shut my eyes really tight and while they were shut there was lots of banging and Mum fell on the floor and hit her head and his hands reached under the table and I heard him pick up Letty, who was screaming and screaming, and he said she'd be going anywhere over his dead body, and his voice sounded like he was under water or something. I tried to grab Letty's hand but he pushed me really hard and he had her under his arm, like she was a sack of potatoes or something, and she was screaming and screaming. And then, as Mum woke up, I heard the sound of his car going down the drive, all the gravel spraying up, and Mum started crying, "Oh, my God, oh, my God," and she didn't even notice that her face was bleeding and I held on to her because I was scared of where he'd taken Letty.

I don't know how long we sat there.

I remember asking Mum where Letty was and she held me close to her and said, "They'll be back soon," but I wasn't sure if she believed it. I was afraid because I guessed that when Steven came back he was going to be really angry.

I think it was a few hours later that the phone rang. Mum was sitting, shaking, on the floor, and her head still had blood on it and I picked up the phone and it was Granny Villiers and her voice sounded strange. And she said, "Put your mother on, please," like I was a stranger. And then she started shouting at Mum because I could hear her voice down the phone and Mum went all gray and moaned and I held on to her legs to try to stop them shaking. And she kept saying, "What have I done? What have I done?" That was the longest night I remember. When it started to get light, I remember Mum waking me up. I'd fallen asleep on the floor and I was cold and stiff. She said, in a weird voice, that we had to go now. I said, "What about Letty?" and she said there had been an accident, that Steven had had a car crash and Letty was dead in the hospital, and it was all her fault, and her teeth chattered like she was swimming in a pool with the water too cold. I can't remember much after that — just being in a taxi, and then an airplane, and when I cried and said I didn't want to go, Mum said it was the only way she could protect me. I remember crying every time my mum went to the loo because I was frightened she would disappear, too, and I'd be left by myself. And then I remember Aunt Kathleen standing at the airport barrier and hugging me like she knew me, and telling me that everything was going to be all right, even though everything definitely wasn't. And all the time I wanted to say to Mum, "But how can we leave Letty?" What if she wasn't dead, and was in the hospital waiting for us? And even if she was dead we should have brought her with us, not left her all those miles away so that we couldn't put flowers on her grave and let her know we still loved her. But I didn't say anything. Because for a long, long time, my mum couldn't say anything at all.

This was what I told Mike, on the morning I caught him holding Mum's hands in his bedroom. This was what I told him, after she'd gone, even though I've never been able to tell that story to anyone, not even Auntie K, not with everything in it. But I told him, because I got the feeling that somehow things had changed, and that

Mum would think it was okay if Mike knew.
I have never seen a man cry before.

TWENTY-ONE:
MIKE

As the rest of Silver Bay slept late the following day, and the waters stilled under a clear blue sky, several miles away, in a gently humming room at the Port Summer Hospital, Nino Gaines woke up.

Kathleen had been sitting at the end of his bed, leaning heavily on the arm of a blue padded chair. She had gone straight there from tucking everyone in, explaining afterward that she had wanted to tell her oldest friend a little of what had happened that momentous night. As dawn broke, exhaustion caught up with her and she had dozed for a while, then sat reading the previous day's newspaper, occasionally aloud when she found something that might interest him. In this case, it was a report about a man they both knew who had set up a restaurant. "Be a bloody disaster," he croaked. So weary was she from the fright of Hannah's disappearance and the horror of the ghost nets that Kathleen Whittier Mostyn read on another two sentences before she realized what she'd heard.

He was frail, and a little disorientated, but underneath the white hospital gown and the myriad tubes and wires he was indubitably Nino Gaines, and for that, it seemed, the whole Silver Bay community was grateful. The doctors gave him a raft of examinations, most of which he complained were a "bloody waste of time," did brain scans and cardiograms, consulted their textbooks and finally pronounced him surprisingly well for a man of his age who had been unconscious for so many days. He was allowed to sit up, lost a few of the tubes that had punctured his arms, and the trickle of visitors swiftly turned into a torrent. Kathleen was allowed to sit at the end of his bed throughout, a privilege usually accorded only to a wife, as long as she didn't raise his blood pressure.

"Been raising my bloody blood pressure for more than fifty years," he told the nurses, in front of her. "Fat lot of good it's done me." And Kathleen beamed. She had not stopped beaming since.

A lucky few know their purpose in life from an early age. They recognize in themselves a vocation, whether it be religion, art, story-telling or the spearing of sacred cows. I finally learned my purpose in life on a clear dawn at the start of an Australian spring, when an eleven-year-old girl took my hand and trusted me with a secret. From that moment, I understood that every bit of my energy would be given to her protection and that of her mother.

When I think back to those few days after the ghost nets, I realize my feelings were almost schizophrenic. I was euphoric in that I was in love with Liza — in love for perhaps the first time — and finally able to express it freely. And she seemed to love me too. After they had told me about Letty, she had feared I would see her differently — as cavalier, deceitful or, at worst, as a murderer. I had found her in her room, sitting by the window, her face a mask of misery. And when I had managed to compose myself (Hannah had put her arms around me when I cried, a gesture I found almost unbearably moving) I went in, closed the door behind me, knelt down and put my arms around her, saying nothing, trusting in my presence to say it for me. A long time later, I understood why she had told me. "I don't think you should do it," I said.

She had lifted her head from my shoulder. "I've got to, Mike."

"You're punishing yourself for something that wasn't your fault. How could you know he'd react like that? How could you know he'd crash the car? You were a battered woman, for God's sake. You could say you were . . ." I struggled with the words ". . . temporarily insane. That's what they say in these cases. I've seen the news reports."

"I've got to do it." Her eyes, although swollen with tears, were clear with determination. "I as good as killed my own daughter. I may have killed her father too. I'll give myself up, and use the publicity to tell them what's going on out here."

"It might be a wasted gesture. A disastrous wasted gesture."

"So let me talk to this media person of yours. She'll know if it'll help."

"You don't understand, Liza. If all this is . . . as you say, you'll go to jail."

"You think I don't know that?"

"How will Hannah cope without you? Hasn't she lost enough already?"

She blew her nose. "Better she loses me for a few years while she's still got Kathleen. Then we can start again. I can start again. And maybe someone will listen."

I stood up and began to pace the floor. "This is wrong, Liza. What if it doesn't stop the development? People may sympathize, but it's far from conclusive that any one person's going to make a difference to whether this building goes ahead."

"What other chance have we got?"

And there she had it.

She held my hands. "Mike, for years I've lived a half-life. I've fooled myself, but it's been a half-life, full of fear. I don't want Hannah to grow up like that. I want her to be able to go where she wants, see who she wants to see. I want her to have a happy childhood, surrounded by people who love her. What kind of life is this for her?"

"A bloody good one," I protested, but she shook her head.

"She can't leave Australia. The moment they see her passport, they'll catch up with us. She can't even leave Silver Bay — it's the only place I feel sure we're out of the way."

She leaned forward. Her words came out perfectly formed, as if they had been softened, rounded in the tides of her head, over years and years. "It's like living with ghost nets," she said, "all that history . . . what I did, Letty, Steven . . . It may be thousands of miles away but it's all out there, waiting to catch up with me. Waiting to strangle me, to pull me down. Has been for years." She pushed her hair behind her ear and I caught sight of the little white scar. "If the development goes ahead, we'll have to move on," she said. "And wherever we go, it will all be drifting silently behind us."

I put my face in my hands. "This is all my fault. If I'd never come here . . . God, the position I've put you in —"

I felt her hand on my hair. "You weren't to know. If it wasn't you it would have been someone else eventually. I'm not naïve enough to think we could have stayed like this forever."

She swallowed. "So here it is. I've been going over it all night. If I hand myself in, I'll give Hannah her freedom and bring some attention to the whales. People will have to listen." She smiled at me tentatively. "And I'll be free. You've got to understand, Mike, that I need to be free of this too. As far as I ever can be."

I stared at her, feeling her already slipping from my grasp. Yet again, a million miles from me. "Do me a favor," I said, reaching for her again. "Don't do anything until I've spoken to someone."

The following evening, I called my sister. And forcing her on pain of death not to say anything to anyone, I told her, with as much detail as I could remember, what Liza had told me.

There was a long pause. "Jesus Christ, Mike, you do pick 'em," she said, her voice awed. Then, as I heard her scribbling: "This is legit, right? She's not making it up?"

I thought of Liza, shaking in my arms. "She's not making it up. Do you think it would be a story?"

"Are you kidding? The newsdesk would wet themselves."

"I need it —" I tried to get a grip on myself. "If we do this, Monica, I need it to be as sympathetic as possible to her case. I need people to understand how she ended up in such a position. If you knew her . . . if you knew what kind of person, what kind of mother she is . . ."

"You want *me* to write it?" My sister sounded incredulous.

"I don't trust anyone else."

There was a short silence.

"Thanks. Thanks, Mike. I . . ." She was distracted now, as if she was reading through her notes. "I reckon I could make it sympathetic. I'll have a chat with the lawyer here — no names, of course — but I'll get her view on the legal position. I don't want to write anything that may turn out to be sub judice . . . that might jeopardize any case that comes to court."

I stared at the receiver, hearing in those words the unwelcome truth of Liza's situation and what it might mean. "And you think . . . she could highlight the cause?"

"If she made it clear that the reason she was coming forward now was not just to put things right but to protect a load of baby whales people might be well disposed toward her. The public love all that whale stuff and, more importantly, they love an eccentric. Especially a pretty blonde one."

"If you did the interview yourself you could make sure it all came out right. That her words weren't twisted."

"I'm not going to stitch you up, Mike. I'm not that much of a reptile. But you must talk to her very carefully about whether she really wants to do this. Because if everything you've told me is true, I can't guarantee what'll happen to her once it's in the open. Other papers will pick it up and twist it — they'll take their own line on her. It's not going to look good that she ran away."

"Her youngest daughter was dead. She heard Steven was critically ill. She had to take steps to protect Hannah."

"But even if I and everyone else make her sound like a bloody angel she could still be arrested and end up in prison. Especially if this bloke — the ex-partner — died too. If the prosecution can prove that she gave him those pills knowing he'd been drinking, knowing he would get in his car, well, I hate to say this but that sounds like manslaughter at best."

"And murder at worst."

"I don't know. I'm not a crime correspondent. But let's not get ahead of ourselves. Spell out his name for me again. I'll see what I can find out and get back to you."

It would be nice to be able to say that, along with those of Nino Gaines, the fortunes of Silver Bay's other inhabitants began to look up, but that wasn't the case. The objections to the public inquiry, while lodged, were widely predicted to be disregarded. The newspapers began to talk of "when" the new development went up, rather than "if." And, as if to prove as much, billboards rose around the wire mesh of the demolition site promising "an exciting new investment opportunity of 2-, 3- and 4-bedroom holiday homes, part of a unique recreational experience."

I read the phrases I had proposed and felt sick. The gleaming, twelve-foot-high billboards looked out of place on the near-deserted stretch of beach, and highlighted the shabbiness of the Silver Bay Hotel, whose peeling paint and stripped weather-board now appeared a badge of pride. It stood next to the tarred barn as a silent sentinel to a lost age, when a hotel had been somewhere to escape to, just another place to be, not a unique, shiny recreational experience or investment opportunity.

One morning while I watched yet another people-mover pull up with a group of unidentified people, who got out and walked around with clipboards talking into phones, I turned to find Kathleen standing beside me. This must feel like an invasion to her, I thought. After a lifetime with just the sea for company, she had the prospect of a never-ending stream of strangers on her doorstep.

She said nothing, her weathered profile sharp as she eyed them. When she spoke, she kept looking straight ahead. "So, when do we need to start packing?" she said.

My stomach lurched. "It's not over yet, Kathleen," I said.

She said nothing.

"Even if we lose the battle over the development, there are lots of things we can do to minimize the impact on your hotel. I'll do a business plan. We could think of some ways to modernize —"

She put a hand on my arm, cutting me

off. "I've got a lot of respect for you, Mike Dormer. I'd have a whole lot more if I could bank on you to tell me the truth."

What could I say? Yoshi was in contact with the whales and dolphins organizations, who were trying to speed up a report they were compiling on the disruptive effect of sound on cetaceans. She had asked if there was anything they could include on the effects of motorboat or jet-ski engines. We had a petition with almost seventeen hundred signatures. We had a website that scored several hundred hits a day, and attracted messages of support from all over the globe. We had other whale-watching communities sending letters of objection to the council.

After school Hannah sat e-mailing other schools, trying to get other children involved. My computer was virtually hers now, and I spent as many hours as I could on the telephone, trying to persuade local townspeople to go against it. I had done as my sister suggested, and was trying to generate local and national attention. None of it had seemed to make any difference. Every time I stepped outside, that scarred area seemed the focus of renewed attention. There were more besuited people, more construction workers in hard hats. Advertisements had appeared in the local paper, promising not only the exciting new development but asking for local tradesmen to get in touch "and be part of the adventure." Two empty local shops had new for-sale signs, perhaps hoping to capitalize on their proximity.

I shook my head. "It's not over yet." I was trying to convince myself as much as anything.

She began to trudge heavily back up the path to the hotel. "Sure sounds like a fat lady's vocal cords to me," she called, over her shoulder.

As predicted, *Hannah's Glory* had gone down that night, swamped by the tall waves, its rudder entangled in the ghost nets. When I looked out to sea now I found the sheer emptiness of the waves above it overwhelming. The sea swallowed things whole, and it was as if they had never been. No little boat, no nets, no dying sea creatures. Nobody talked about the little boat, once its resting place on the seabed had been established. Greg, I think, still felt awkward about his unwitting part in Hannah's close shave, as did I. It was too easy to imagine her out there with it.

Then, apropos of nothing, Liza had announced over breakfast that she was going to find Hannah a boat.

"What?"

She didn't mention *Hannah's Glory.*

"I think you're old enough. I've asked Peter Sawyer to keep an eye out for one. A little cutter, like Lara's. But you're to take lessons. And if I ever catch you going out on the water without permission that will be it. No more boat, ever."

Hannah dropped her spoon with a clatter, leapt from her place at the table and threw her arms around her mother's neck. "I'll never go anywhere without telling you," she said. "I'll never do anything. I'll be really good. Oh, thank you, Mum."

Liza tried to make her face stern, as her daughter squeezed her, bouncing with pleasure. "I'm trusting you," she said.

Hannah nodded, eyes shining. "Can I call Lara and tell her?" she said.

"You'll see her at school in half an hour."

"Please." Her mother's hesitation was all the confirmation she needed. We heard her feet skipping joyfully down the hallway, then her high-pitched exclamations on the phone.

Liza looked down at her breakfast, as if she had been embarrassed by her volte-face. Kathleen and I were still staring at her. It is possible that my mouth had dropped open.

"She lives by the sea," Liza said. "She's got to learn some day."

"True enough," said Kathleen, turning back to the stove. "Peter will find her a good one."

"Besides," said Liza, her eyes briefly meeting mine, "it's only sensible. I might not always be here to watch out for her."

Liza and I had not talked about "us." Several weeks in I assumed there was an "us," even though by unspoken agreement we displayed no affection in front of Kathleen, Hannah or the whalechasers. The southern migration had begun, albeit a trickle, and sometimes, in the day, if I needed a break, I would go out on a trip with her, sitting on the deck of her boat, a silent assistant, and watch as she moved sure-footed around it. I liked the lilt in her voice when she told stories about the whales, the affectionate, offhand way that she rubbed Milly's ears as she steered, the joyous cry she still gave when she caught the familiar flume of water. I was acutely physically aware of her when she brushed past me, her sinuous movements as she spun the wheel or hung over the rails. I liked the way the boat became an extension of her, the way she was utterly at ease with every part of it. The protest, ironically, had made them all busy, with passengers morning and afternoon, but every time I went out with her it might have been just ourselves for all the notice I took of anyone else.

Except Hannah. I loved Hannah as an extension of the way I loved her mother. I also felt an overwhelming urge to protect her, to screen her from the kind of terrors she had already endured. And I understood what Liza had meant, and why she would have given up everything to keep her safe. Hannah knew about her mother and me and said nothing. But the way she grinned at me conspiratorially and occasionally snaked her hand into mine left me choked with pride at her tacit approval. If I ever had a child, I wanted one like Hannah. I wanted to stay in her life, if Liza would let me.

We had not mentioned love, but my every nerve ending throbbed with it, and I carried it in a cloud around me, like sea mist. The lifting in Liza's manner, her ready smiles, her blushes told me she felt it too. I didn't need to make her say it aloud, as Vanessa had prompted me. This woman, who had lost nearly everything, whose trust had been so violently betrayed, had allowed me access not just to her physical self but to her heart. Most nights she would pad silently down the corridor to my room, and in the dim light, I would peel back my bedcovers and let her in. When she touched my face with her fingertips, her expression serious and slightly disbelieving, I knew it mirrored my own.

I don't think I have ever been as happy as I was then; perhaps it was the anticipation of waiting for her to arrive, listening to her conversations downstairs with Kathleen and Hannah, hearing the bathroom door, the various goodnights, knowing that in a matter of hours, perhaps minutes, she would be mine. I don't know if Kathleen knew what was going on but she didn't miss much. She was preoccupied with Mr. Gaines, though, getting him out of hospital and helping restore his health. By then we all believed that happiness should be treasured if good fortune happened to blow it briefly your way.

And Liza was my good fortune. There wasn't a piece of her that I didn't marvel at. I loved her hair, the way it never quite lost the appearance of having been blown around at sea; I loved her skin, which seemed always to carry the faint tang of salt, the faint scars I now understood, the freckles that had come with her new life outside; I loved her eyes — opaque and reflective one minute, greedy and devouring in secret with me. When I made love to her I kept mine open, and locked on hers, and when I came I thought I'd drown in them. She was mine. I knew that, and I was profoundly grateful.

One night, when we lay talking quietly, she told me that having a child brought the most love and the most fear anyone could feel. I understood that now, because having found her, I couldn't contemplate losing her. I lay awake at night, watching her, trying to picture her in prison in a cold, gray country a million miles from here, surrounded by unfriendly faces. And the image wouldn't come. The two simply did not compute. She laughed at me when I used those words.

"I'll be okay," she said, burrowing into me, her arm across my chest.

I felt its weight like a blessing. "I can't imagine you away from the sea."

"I'm not a whale. I can survive out of water." I heard the smile in her voice.

For some reason I wasn't sure that was true. "I'll help take care of Hannah," I said. "If you want."

"I'm not expecting you to stay."

"I care about her."

"But I don't know how long I'll be gone."

"All the more reason for me to be here."

I could hear her breathing. When she next spoke there was a catch in her voice. "I don't want . . . I don't want Hannah to lose anyone else. I don't want her to get attached to you and then, a few years down the line, for you to realize it's too much for you. The waiting, I mean."

"You really think I would?"

"Sometimes it's hard to know what you might do." She paused. "I know more than most that you don't always behave as you'd expect. And this isn't a normal situation."

I lay there beside her, thinking about what she'd told me.

"I won't blame you," she said quietly, "if you want to leave when I do. You've been . . . a good friend to us."

"I'm not going anywhere," I said. And with those words a new atmosphere settled around us in the dark, a kind of permanence. I hadn't even thought about what I was going to say, but it was out there: a true reflection of myself, of what I felt. I took her hand, and my thumb traced her knuckles as her fingers tightened around mine.

Her voice broke: "Hannah will need as many friends as she can get."

Along the corridor Milly whined in her sleep, perhaps unable to rest until Liza returned to her room. I held her until I felt the moment pass. I knew she was forcing her daughter from her mind, already separating herself, in an attempt to do what was right. In those moments I ached for her, wishing that, somehow, I could take that pain for her.

"You don't have to do it," I said, for the hundredth time.

She silenced me with a kiss. "I know you find it hard to understand, but I feel like I'm finally doing something. For the first time in my life I'm taking control." I heard her brave smile in the darkness. "I'm at the helm."

"My skipper," I said. Holding her.

"Trying," she replied, and wrapped her legs around me with a sigh.

My sister rang at a quarter past three that morning. She'd never been any good with time differences. Liza stirred beside me, and I fumbled for my phone.

"Okay, you want the good news or the bad?"

I pushed myself on to my elbow. "I don't know," I said, half asleep. I rubbed my eyes. "Whatever."

"The good news is I've found him, and he's still alive. It took a bit of time because he's gone double-barreled — added his wife's name too. I think he's taken his wife's surname too. The old woman is dead, which helps, as there are fewer people who can corroborate his side of things. It means your girlfriend's not going to face a murder charge."

She paused as I digested this, trying to force the relief I wanted to feel.

"The bad news, Mike, is that he's a councilor. A respected member of his community. Married, as I said, two children, stable, blameless existence. Round Table, charitable efforts, you name it. A councilor with parliamentary ambitions. Every single newspaper report he features in has him shaking hands with some police chief or handing over a check to a good cause. None of that is going to make your girlfriend's case any easier at all."

TWENTY-TWO:
LIZA

Mike worked night and day to stop the development. Some nights he worked so late I thought he'd make himself ill. Kathleen would give me meals to take up to him, and I sat with him and did what I could, but I'm not good at dealing with people. Listening to him wheedle and charm, the authoritative way in which he laid things down as absolutes, made my head spin. He wasn't afraid to talk to anyone. Whoever answered the phone, he would ask for the next person above them, and if they gave him no satisfaction he'd go for the one after that. He had a great memory for figures — he threw statistics into conversation like he had them written down in front of him, and everyone he spoke to he warned of noise and pollution levels, of extra costs and reduced business elsewhere. He explained how business would be drawn away from local bars, restaurants and small hotels. He showed where the profits from this hotel would go, and it was not into Silver Bay.

Yet even that wasn't enough. He had persuaded Yoshi to get her academic mates to research the effects on whales of noise — but, as she said to me out of his earshot, these things took time. It wasn't as if you could stick a whale in a Petri dish and prod it to see how it reacted. The southern migration was under way, the whales returning to the Antarctic, and after November they wouldn't be in our waters for months, when it would be too late. He didn't seem to hear when I mentioned these things, just stuck his head down and hit the phones again.

I think he thought that if he could stop it by other means I wouldn't go to England and somehow everything would be all right. When I told him I'd go anyway, he told me I was a masochist. My greatest fear was that the "story," as he put it, wouldn't be enough to save them.

He had got petitions running on all the boats, and was trying to haul together a protest for when the architectural model went on view at the Blue Shoals Hotel. He was finding it hard going: many people saw the new hotel as a given now and were already planning ways to capitalize on its presence. Even among those who didn't want it you couldn't guarantee action. People in Silver Bay weren't the agitating kind. The sea does that to you: living so close to something over which you have no control can make you fatalistic.

Hannah was his greatest support. He had got her and Lara writing banners saying their school didn't want the money or the new facilities if they came as a result of the new development. They had created new petitions, rallied their classmates, even been on local radio talking about the different personalities of the bay's dolphins. When Kathleen and I heard Hannah's voice on our station we almost burst with pride. Mike had set her up with an e-mail account so that she could alert all the whale and dolphin societies she had found on the Internet. It had focused her attention nicely, stemmed her shock over the ghost nets. In the daytime, she seemed like a different person, more confident, enthusiastic, determined.

But more nights than not, she padded down the corridor to my room, just as she had when she was six, to hang on to me.

As soon as I could I told my daughter. One warm Friday afternoon after school I bought her an ice cream and we sat at the end of

Whale Jetty, letting tiny silver fish nibble our toes, while Milly drooled on our shoulders hopefully. The solicitor had told me that if I went back there would be a court case, and I'd have to explain what had happened. It was likely Hannah would be asked, too, and would have to tell them everything, just as she had told Mike, I said.

She sat there, her ice cream untouched. "Will I have to go back and live with Steven?" she asked.

Even the mention of his name made me go cold. "No, lovey. You'll stay with Kathleen. She's your closest blood relative after me." I thanked God, as I always have, that Steven and I had never married, that he had no rights over Hannah, at least.

"Will you go to prison?" she asked.

I would not lie to my daughter so I told her it was possible. But I added that if I was lucky the judge would find that I had been temporarily unbalanced, or something like it, so with luck I might get a short sentence, or even a suspended one.

That was what the solicitor had said, as Mike and I had sat in her office the previous day. Mike, grim-faced, had held my hand under the desk. "You do realize it wasn't her fault?" he had said to her repeatedly, as if it were she he had to convince.

Afterward it dawned on me that he had been testing the waters, trying to gauge what kind of reaction my tale would get if told elsewhere to less-sympathetic ears. She was a cold fish, despite the inflated fee Mike paid for her time. The most he could get out of her was an admission that the way things had worked out was "unfortunate." Then she had said it was not her role to pass judgment on what had happened, in a tone that suggested she already had.

The important thing, I told Hannah, forcing a smile, was that once it was over we would be free to get on with our lives. She would be able to go where she wanted, and we would talk about Letty and help the whales and dolphins. "Hey," I said, holding her shoulders, "you might even be able to go to New Zealand. That school trip you were talking about. How does that sound?"

I didn't see her expression at first. She was looking at the far side of the bay, turned away from me. When she turned back the depth of her horror shocked me. "I don't want to go to New Zealand," she said, her face crumpling. "I want you to stay with me."

She wasn't buying any of it. There was nothing but fear and desperation in her eyes, and I hated myself for putting them there.

"Everybody leaves me," she whispered.

"No, lovey, that's not —"

"And now you'll go and I'll have no one."

She cried for a while, and I dropped my ice cream and held her tight, trying not to cry with her. The truth was that the prospect of being separated from my daughter made me feel ill. When I held her now it was no longer casual, no longer pleasurable, but as if I was trying to imprint her on myself. When I looked at her I was trying to burn her image onto the backs of my eyelids. It was as if I was already preparing for the months? years? when I would not have the privilege of holding her close to me.

It was these and future losses that kept me awake at nights. The prospect of her going through the delicate adolescent years without me. There was no knowing who she would become. Would she forgive me? Would she forgive herself? I closed my eyes, breathing in the smell of her hair, scenting in it an echo of my lost Letty. When I realized I was teetering, I pulled back and allowed her to do the same.

She composed herself. My daughter's bravery and self-control were heartbreaking. She said sorry as she wiped her eyes with the ball of her palm. "I don't mean to cry," she said.

"It might feel bad now, but it's going to get better," I told her, trying to convey a certainty I wasn't sure I felt. "We can write to each other and speak on the phone and we'll be together again before you know it." A blade of seagrass had blown into her hair and I picked it out.

She sniffed.

"And, most importantly, whenever I talk about Letty, I'll make sure to talk about the whales. And the dolphins."

"You think that would stop the hotel?"

"It might. And that way her life and death might mean something good."

We sat there, staring out over the water, mulling over what I had said. Hannah was too polite to tell me what I knew to be true: that I was wrong, that nothing good could ever emerge from Letty's death. Then she turned to me. "Does she have a grave in England? Somewhere you can put flowers?"

I had to tell her I didn't know. I didn't even know whether my own daughter had been buried or cremated.

"Doesn't matter where Letty is," she said, perhaps seeing my discomfort, "because she's always here." She took my hand and pressed it to her heart. She didn't say the rest, but I saw it in her eyes, in her clenched jaw: *Just like you will be.* And I didn't know whether I should treat that as a promise or an accusation.

Kathleen was not one of society's great party-givers. In fact, it would be fair to say that, despite her trade, she was one of the least outgoing people I knew, happier alone in her kitchen or out on her boat than making small talk with guests or visitors. It was one of the reasons she and I understood each other so well. So, it was a bit of a surprise when, two days after Hannah and I had talked, she announced that when Nino Gaines came out of hospital she was going to throw a celebration. It would, she said, take place outside, so that he could smell the fresh air, see the sea and catch up with all his friends.

"Lance, you've no need to be catching flies. It's about time we had something to celebrate in this sorry little hole," she said, as the whalechasers were stunned momentarily into silence at the bleached tables.

"Anyway," she said, "if we can wheel him out now, they won't be dropping in on him at home bothering him at all hours for the next few weeks. Nothing to make a fellow feel unwell like a load of do-gooders on his doorstep."

Three days later, on an afternoon warm enough to hint of the summer to come, we were sitting out under carefully prepared canopies when Kathleen's car pulled up in front of the hotel and a back door opened. After a few moments Frank helped his father out.

"Welcome home!" we all shouted, and Hannah ran down the path to hug him. He was the closest she'd ever had to a grandfather.

He struggled a bit to straighten himself. He had lost weight — his shirt collar gaped around his neck — and he was frail, a little unsteady on his stick. He held on to the open car door with one hand, squinting at us from under his hat. "This sorry parade of humanity the best you could get to welcome me home, Kate? Ah, take me back to the hospital." He made as if to duck into the car again, and I couldn't help but smile.

"Ungrateful old sod," she said, hauling out his bag.

"You're meant to indulge me," he said. "I could keel over any minute."

"I'll make sure you do if you keep milking this," she said, and slammed her car door.

"You get to sit near me, Mr. Gaines," said Hannah, holding his free hand as he made his way slowly up the path. "It's a special chair."

"Hasn't got a bedpan in the bottom, has it?" he said, and Hannah giggled.

"I meant it's got all the cushions."

"Ah, that's all right then," he said.

He winked at me and I stepped forward to hug him. "We're glad to have you home, Nino," I said.

"Well, now, Liza, someone has to keep your aunt on her toes, right? Can't have her going to seed."

He was trying a little too hard, but I understood why. A man like Nino Gaines would find it hard to be treated as an invalid.

It was a glorious afternoon. The crews had taken time off and, by tacit agreement, no one discussed the development, or what might lie ahead. We chatted about the weather, the footie results, the awfulness of hospital food and the southern right someone had seen down past Elinor Island. We drank and watched Hannah, Lara and Milly tear up and down the sand, Lance and Yoshi dance to some of Hannah's music, and various fishermen, neighbors and distant relations of Nino stopped by to share a few beers. Mike sat beside me and, periodically, I felt his hand reach for mine under the table. Its gentleness and strength made my mind wander to places it shouldn't have gone at three thirty in the afternoon during a family party.

Look at me, I mused, when that thought occurred, and gazed surreptitiously at the man who had landed in my life and now sat beside me. Look at Hannah, Kathleen and Nino Gaines, at the whale crews, who had, over the years, given me more friendship and support than many people's blood relatives would. I had a family. Whatever happened, even though there would always be someone missing at the heart of it, I had a family. And that thought filled me with sudden happiness. Mike might have caught it, because he raised an eyebrow, as if in silent question. I smiled, and he lifted my hand to kiss my fingers in front of everyone.

Nino Gaines raised his own eyebrows at Kathleen. "How long did you say I was out?" he said.

"Don't ask," she said, waving a dismissive hand. "I can't keep up with these young people."

"Where's Greg?" Hannah asked, from the other end of the tables. "He said he'd be here by now."

"He was being mysterious this morning," said Kathleen. "I saw him at the fish market.

He said he was on a mission."

"Yeah? What was her name?" Nino pulled his hat down over his eyes and rested back in his chair. "God, it's good to be back here, Kate."

To my surprise, she leaned forward and kissed his forehead. "Good to have you back, you old fool," she said.

Before any of us could say anything, the whine of Greg's truck could be heard down the road and, as if on cue, he drove slowly up to the front of the hotel and ground to a halt. "Sorry to interrupt," he said, climbing out of the cab. He was wearing an ironed shirt and was clean-shaven — rare for Greg — and looked uncommonly pleased with himself. "I just thought you should all know — you might want to swing by my lockup in half an hour. It's kind of important."

"We're having a party, in case you hadn't noticed." Kathleen placed her hands on her hips. "And you were meant to be here two hours ago."

"Ah, I'm real sorry, Kathleen, but this is important."

"What's going on, Greg?" I said. He was trying to stop himself smiling, like a school-boy keeping a lid on some practical joke.

"Got something to show you," he said to me, ignoring Mike. This was not unusual:

since he had guessed we were an item, he had pretended Mike didn't exist. He gazed at his feet, then at Kathleen. "Yosh — you still fixed?"

I glanced at her. She nodded.

"Good. I got something to show you all. Good to see you back, Mr. Gaines. I'll be glad to crack open a couple of stubbies with you later." He tipped his cap and, with a definite swagger — even by Greg's swaggering standards — headed back to his truck, swung it around in a spray of dirt and made for his lockup.

"He been on the amber fluid again?" Nino stared after him.

Yoshi and Lance were exchanging a glance. They knew something, but it was obvious they weren't going to let us in on it. "You know Greg," Kathleen said, shrugging. "Never fails to surprise us."

Hannah was grinning widely, and my heart sank. I hoped it wasn't another boat.

We didn't have long to wait. Nino stayed up at the hotel with Hannah, but the rest of us strolled slowly down the sea path, enjoying the sun and watching, with mild surprise, the crowd swell outside Greg's lockup. There were reporters and photographers, I noticed, and wondered how it would feel to have the cameras trained on me. I had seen the films: would there be a scrum of journalists on the courtroom steps? Would I be hounded? I shivered, despite the warmth of the day, and tried to push the thought away.

"Yoshi?" I said, but she pretended not to hear me.

I had tried to get her to say something earlier but she had tapped her nose and Lance adopted a theatrically blank expression.

"I hope Nino's okay by himself," Kathleen fretted. "I don't like leaving him."

"He's probably enjoying five minutes' peace," said Mike. "He might be a little tired."

"You think I should go back?" she said.

"Hannah will fetch us if there's a problem." I nudged her. "He's having the time of his life. Happy as Larry."

"He does look good, doesn't he?" she said, gazing up the coast road to the distant hotel. And then, awkwardly, "Daft old fool."

Greg was standing in front of his lockup, smoking a cigarette. He was gazing at the crowd, as if he was waiting to ensure that everyone was there. A couple of times he exchanged a muttered joke with one of the fishermen near him. His truck was no longer outside.

I tried and failed again to work out what this might be about. It was uncharacteristic behavior, for sure.

Finally, he spat out his cigarette and ground it into the dirt with his heel. Then, he slid his key into the padlock and, with a grunt of effort, opened the two weather-beaten doors and flicked on the light. As we stared into the darkened interior, he whipped a tarpaulin off the back of his truck to reveal his prize: an enormous tiger shark, its eye still clear, its mouth slightly open in blank outrage, revealing angled, pointed teeth. There was an audible gasp. Even dead, immobile and trussed up on a winch, that creature was terrifying.

"Went out fishing early this morning," he said to the reporters, patting its skin. "Just to the mouth of the bay, like. You can often get a good catch there. I thought I had a blue marlin at first — but look at the bugger I hauled in on my line! Dragged me around the cockpit like you wouldn't believe. Tony, back it up!" he called, to the man in the cab. As he stepped aside, the truck reversed out into the light. A few cameras clicked.

"I've called you guys out because we've not had tigers this close before and I want to tell everyone in the bay to keep their kids out of the water. You can't trust these monsters not to come in. You know the tiger shark's a mean old bugger, and we've seen from the ruddy ghost nets that pretty well anything can get right in to shore."

He slapped the shark appreciatively.

"I brought it into the fish market and the guys there identified it and weighed it for me. I'm told it's not the only one that's been seen in our waters."

The sight of that shark sent a chill down my spine. I kept thinking of Mike and Hannah in that dark, churning water, of the things he told me had bumped against his legs.

It's possible he felt the same: he reached behind my back for my hand and squeezed it.

Yoshi stepped forward and began to reel off information to the reporters. "Tiger sharks," she said, "are known as the dustbins of the sea. This one may have been attracted into the bay by the ghost net and the sheer number of dead creatures attached to it. But that means there's a good chance this big guy wasn't alone, and others might be hanging around here for some considerable time. They feed on anything, fish, turtles, humans . . ." She let that word dangle long enough for people to glance at each other nervously. "But don't just ask me," she added. "The Department of Environment and Heritage will tell you that they're not great creatures to have around."

"We need shark nets," said someone in the crowd. "They've got them at other beaches."

"How are you going to have shark nets in a bay full of dolphins?" said Greg, sharply. "They trap whales too. There'll be shark nets in this bay over my dead body."

"That'd be right." Someone laughed.

"Sharks are smart," said Yoshi. "If we put them in the mouth of the bay they'll just swim over or around them. If you check out the figures, shark-death rates stay around the same whether the beaches have nets or not."

"I reckon you're making something out of nothing." I recognized one of the hoteliers. He wouldn't be happy, I knew, about this sort of publicity just as the spring season was about to take off. "Everyone knows you're more likely statistically to be hit by lightning than killed by a shark."

"You think this old fellow worried about statistics?" Greg leaned against the shark's torpedo body. "He probably reckoned he had a one in a million chance of swallowing someone's fishing line."

The crowd laughed.

"You want to watch out for the tigers, because they'll come close to shore to follow the sea turtles," said Yoshi, earnestly. "And they're persistent. They're not like the great whites — they'll keep coming back to chew up whatever they've taken a bite out of."

The hotelier shook his head. Greg saw him and raised his voice. "Fine, Alf," he said. "You go swimming, then. I just thought it was my duty to let you guys know what's out there."

"Shark attacks are on the increase," said Yoshi. "It's a well-known fact. There are some possible solutions. We can maybe mark off safe swimming areas with buoys and nets. I'm sure the coast guard can fix that up. They just won't be enormous."

"In the meantime, as I said," Greg had pulled his cap low over his eyes so that I couldn't see them, "I'd advise you to keep your ankle-biters out of the water. We'll alert the coast guard if we see any others in the bay, and the fishermen will do the same."

There was a murmur of concern. Several people turned away, mobile phones at their ears, and others moved closer to the truck, wanting to touch the shark. I thought about Hannah and the conversation we had had about me getting her a boat. I didn't think anyone would let their children take boats out around Silver Bay while there were sharks in the water. But telling her that after what I had promised wouldn't be easy. While I was mulling this over, Kathleen stepped forward and stared at the dead creature in the back of the van. "Shark, eh?" she said, frowning, her arms crossed across her chest.

"You'd know," said Greg, as he hoisted it up on the winch so that the photographers could get a better picture.

"Where did you say you —"

"This, gentlemen," Greg said, gesturing toward her before Kathleen could continue, "is the world-famous Shark Lady of Silver Bay, Kathleen Whittier Mostyn. This lady here caught an even bigger shark some half a century ago. Biggest gray nurse shark ever caught in New South Wales, wasn't it, Kathleen? How's that for a story, eh?"

Kathleen stared silently at him. The bald malevolence in her eye would have been enough to send me scuttling for shelter. She knew she'd been set up, and she didn't like it. But Greg rattled on regardless: "So, gentlemen, you see? Once again Silver Bay has a shark population. The wildlife people will be delighted, but I do want to warn our good citizens not to go swimming or windsurfing or, indeed, to take part in any kind of watersports without great caution while the threat of shark attack exists."

The press gathered around Kathleen, their notepads and microphones in front of her. Several flashbulbs went off. Greg continued to pose beside his shark. After the horror of the ghost nets, the local newspapers had their second good front-page story in a fortnight, and you could hear the delight in their questions.

"I forgot to add — this little beaut's for sale, if anyone fancies him," he called. "He's fresh as you like. Make a lovely bit of sushi."

"I thought you didn't get sharks and dolphins in the same place," Mike said, as he and I strolled back to the hotel. The afternoon was clear and bright, the sea glinting benignly in the distance. I had had a couple of beers, and had eaten an unusually large amount. Half a mile ahead I could make out Hannah and Lara, performing some dance routine for Nino Gaines, and collapsing, giggling, onto the sand. Occasionally, on days like this, I could convince myself that the world I inhabited was a good one.

"Sometimes I think the whole planet is topsy-turvy," I said, pushing my hair off my face and glancing up at him. I wanted to kiss him, then — I wanted to kiss him most of the time.

I must remember this, I told myself, and wished I could be like Mike's little mobile telephone, stacked full of moments that I could replay with perfect clarity far, far into the future.

"Don't go," said Mike that night. He was standing in the bathroom brushing his teeth, a towel wrapped around his waist, and I had walked in behind him to get a glass of water.

"Go where?" I said, sticking the glass under the tap. I had been thinking about the jobs I needed to do the following day. Stupid things I now had to think about, like making sure Hannah had enough school uniforms to last several seasons, signing over power of attorney, sorting out a joint account for me and Kathleen. The solicitor had said I would be wise to get all personal matters in place before I talked to anyone, and the list of things that needed sorting out made my head spin.

"Don't do this. It's madness. I've been thinking about it, and it's madness." His reflection was staring at me from the mirror, and the rigidity of his naked back told me the tension I had thought I saw in his face that evening had not been imagined.

He had hardly spoken for several hours, although Greg had been so garrulous and the whalechasers so drunk it would have been hard for him to get a word in edgeways. I had thought Greg, doing his best to bait him, had prompted it. "No offense, mate," he would say, after each barb, and Mike would smile tightly at him. Only I saw the tic in his jaw. We could still hear them downstairs, although Nino, the true focus of the party, had long gone home to bed.

I sighed. "Mike, I don't want to go through this now," I said. I wanted to enjoy the day for what it was, to savor it and go to bed in peace.

"Nothing's going to stop the development," he said, pausing to spit out toothpaste. "I know what Beaker's like. They see big money in this, and when Dennis Beaker sees money, nothing stops him. It's gone too far. And you're about to ruin your own life, and Hannah's, for no reason."

"What do you mean, no reason? Is mine and Hannah's peace of mind worth nothing?"

"But you're fine," he said. There was toothpaste on his chin, but something told me he wouldn't thank me for pointing it out. "You're both fine. Maybe you can't do everything you'd like to do — but, then, who can? Hannah's safe and happy, surrounded by people she loves. You're happy — the happiest I've ever seen you. This guy — Steven — is still alive and married with kids, which suggests that even he's happy. No one's going to recognize you, especially after all this time. We could be a couple, and stay here and . . . see how things go. Why risk all that for something you might not be able to pull off?"

"Mike, we've been through this a million times. It's our only hope for the whales. And I'm not talking about it now. Can't we just go to bed?"

"Why? Every time I mention it you say the same thing. What's wrong with now?"

"I'm tired."

"We're all tired. It's the human condition."

"Yes, well, I'm too tired to talk." I was irritated that he was speaking the truth. I didn't want to talk about it: talking about it made me dwell on what I was about to do, and I was afraid that if someone challenged me too hard my resolve might vanish.

Downstairs Greg had broken into song. I could hear the others cheering him, Lance's piercing whistle.

"It's not just you this affects."

"You think I don't know that?" I snapped.

"Hannah barely leaves your side. She was glued to you this evening."

I glared at him. "I don't need you to tell me anything about my daughter, thank you very much." My blood was up. I hated him for pointing that out. I hated him for seeing Hannah's fear.

"Well, someone's got to talk to you. You haven't even discussed it with Kathleen."

"I'll talk to Kathleen when I'm ready."

"You don't want to tell her because you know she'll say the same as I have. Have you thought about what prison really means?"

"Don't patronize me."

"Being locked up twenty-three hours a day? Being labeled a child-killer by other inmates? You think you could survive that?"

"I'm not talking about this now," I said, starting to gather up my clothes.

"If you can't cope with me saying those words, how are you going to cope with it in court? From the police? From people who want to hurt you? You think they'll care what really happened?"

"Why are you doing this to me?"

"Because I don't think you've thought it through. I don't think you know what you're letting yourself in for."

"I can look after myself."

"How do you know? You've never had to."

I squared up to him. "This is about Greg, isn't it?"

"It's got nothing to do with Greg. I want you to talk about —"

"It's all about Greg. He sat there and riled you all evening, which reminded you that you're not the only man I've ever been with." He sat down opposite me, his eyes closed as if that helped him not to hear me. But I carried on: "So now you're taking it out on me. Well, if you're going to pick a fight, I'm going to —"

"Run away again? You know what? I don't think this has anything to do with the whales anymore."

"What?"

"You're determined to punish yourself for Letty's death. This development has forced you to look at what happened, and now you feel the need to atone for it by sacrificing yourself."

Downstairs the singing had stopped. The window was open, but I no longer cared.

"And it's pointless. You've already paid for what happened, Liza. You've paid a million times."

"I want a clean slate. And we need to —"

"Save the whales. I know."

"Then why are you going on like this?"

"Because you're wrong. And you're doing it for the wrong reasons."

"Who the hell are you to judge my reasons?"

"I'm not judging you. But you need to think about this, Liza. You need to know that by —"

"*You* need to butt out of my business."

"— that by going through with this, you'll take Hannah down with you."

My blood ran cold. I couldn't believe he would attack me like that. If his words hadn't sunk into me, like a knife, I probably wouldn't have said what I did: "Who the hell landed us in this situation, Mike? You ask yourself that the next time you start judging me. As you said, we were fine here. We were happy. Well, if Hannah and I end up spending the next five years separated, you ask yourself whose bloody fault it really is."

There was silence, both inside and out. All that could be heard was the sea, and then, after a few moments, the low scrape of a chair as someone beneath us began quietly to collect glasses.

I stared at Mike's gray face, and wished I could take back what I'd said. "Mike —"

He held up his hand. "You're right," he said. "I'm sorry."

And I understood, with a painful lurch, the truth of it: that he hadn't wanted to hurt me. He just couldn't bear the thought of losing me.

TWENTY-THREE: MONICA

My brother's behavior had been pretty surprising over the past few months. At this time last year if you had offered me a bet on the progression of his life I would have said that by March he'd be married to Vanessa, she would be in the process of getting herself pregnant and he'd be sliding his way up the greasy pole of his property-development company. A smart flat, perhaps a new house, maybe a holiday home somewhere hot, another flash car, skiing, expensive restaurants, blah-blah-blah. The most radical thing Mike would do was change his aftershave, or maybe the color of his tie.

I no longer had the slightest idea where he'd be in March. He might be in Australia, or New Zealand, or boatbuilding in the Galapagos. He might be growing dreadlocks. He might be protecting a fugitive woman and her child, and saving the whales. When I told my parents the half of it (he'll have to forgive me, I couldn't resist) Dad nearly spat out his false teeth. "What do you mean he's left his job?" he spluttered, and I could hear Mum in the background telling him to think of his blood pressure. "How long is he planning to stay in Australia?" And then: "A *single mother*? What the hell happened to Vanessa?"

I had thought perhaps Mike was having an early midlife crisis, that maybe Liza really was his first love — people do weird things when they fall in love for the first time. Perhaps property development wasn't all it was cracked up to be.

And then he had rung me last week and told me this story. I can't lie. My first thought was not, as he put it, how do we protect her? It was too good a story: the battered girlfriend of a political wannabe who fled the country after accidentally killing their child. It had everything: violent crime, long-buried secrets, tragedy, a dead child, a beautiful blonde. It even had whales and dolphins, for God's sake. I told him all we needed was Skippy and we'd have a full deck. He didn't laugh.

Except it didn't add up. I looked at all of the guy's cuttings, even with the change of name. I cross-checked that information with every database I could find. I spent almost a week doing nothing but looking up the facts of the story, and irritating the hell out of my newsdesk because I couldn't tell them what I was doing. And it still didn't add up.

Twenty-Four:
Mike

Milly had gone into a decline. She hardly ate, and slept only sporadically. She was watchful, anxious and snappy, twice disgracing herself on *Ishmael* by baring her teeth at passengers, and once soiling the lounge carpet — an act of depression that even she had the good grace to seem embarrassed about. Everywhere that Liza went, she was glued to her heels, a little black-and-white shadow. With canine intuition, she had picked up on the fact that her mistress was planning to leave, and was afraid that if she dropped her vigil Liza might disappear.

I knew how she felt. The anxiety. The impotence. Since the night of the party, we no longer discussed Liza's plans. I worked harder, partly because that was the only way I could think of to stop her, and partly because I found it increasingly painful to be with her. I couldn't look at her, touch her, kiss her, without thinking of how it would feel to be without her. If you want to put it in crude financial terms, I couldn't make any more investment in something that was about to be withdrawn from me.

Kathleen evidently knew now what she planned — they had had a conversation — and her way of dealing with it, as with so much in her life, was merely to plow on, being practical. I hadn't talked to her about it — I didn't feel it was my place — but I saw her paying extra attention to Hannah, making plans for trips and special treats, and I knew she was engaged in her own form of preparation. Mr. Gaines came most days now, and while Hannah was at school the two could often be found at the kitchen table, in whispered conversation or peaceably reading the newspaper and listening to what they both still called the wireless. I was glad for them, glad that Kathleen would not face this alone, and a little envious, too, of their happiness. Liza deserved that kind of contentment, after everything that had happened, and instead she was about to be punished again.

She had forgiven me for my outburst. She was gentle with me, occasionally running a finger down the side of my face with sympathetic eyes. At night she was increasingly passionate, as if she, too, was determined to glean every last bit of happiness from what remained of our time together. Sometimes I had to tell her I couldn't — I felt too sad and angry about what would soon take place that I couldn't make it happen.

She never commented. She would just wrap her thin limbs around me, rest her face against the back of my neck and the two of us would lie, in the darkness, each knowing the other was awake, neither knowing what to say.

Several times she had asked when my sister was likely to call, when she was likely to do the interview. She tried to make her inquiries sound casual, but I knew she needed to set things in motion, to know exactly how much time she had left. I had stalled at first, then tried several times to reach Monica, but always I got her voice-mail. Each time we failed to speak I felt nothing but relief.

My despondency was not helped by the seemingly unstoppable momentum of the hotel development. I was running out of ideas and energy, and despite my best efforts, I hadn't managed to get a demonstration going on the day the architectural model went on display. The owner of the Blue Shoals Hotel rang to tell me that, sympathetic as he was to what I was doing, he "didn't want any trouble" as there was a christening party in the back room that lunchtime, and surely I understood. He sounded like a nice guy, and I didn't feel I could ruin a family's special day, so I called it off. Kathleen had laughed drily when I told her, and said some revolutionary I would have made. I didn't like to tell her that only a handful of people had shown interest in joining the demonstration as it was.

Liza was out on *Ishmael,* and Hannah was at school, so after I'd tried and failed to continue the fight from my desk, I had headed down to the Blue Shoals, relishing, despite myself, the bright blue sky, and the warm breeze. These days, with the onset of warmer weather, Silver Bay seemed the most beautiful place on earth. Its landscape had become familiar, the volcanic horizon restful to the eye, the rows of bungalows and holiday lets no longer jarring, the pie and bottle shops along the coast road now regular stopping-off points. Everything a person could need is in this small corner of the world, I thought. One of the few certainties I employed to console myself was that I had decided to stay. I would help Kathleen in her fight to keep afloat, and look after Hannah until Liza came home.

In the circumstances it felt like the least I could do.

I was the only person in Reception at the Blue Shoals. The receptionist, who might have recognized me, jerked her thumb toward the leg of the L-shaped foyer, and there, flanked by cardboard screens, which illustrated projected visitor numbers and benefits for the community, it sat in a Perspex case, around four feet by six, unnoticed.

It was exactly as I had pictured it. In fact, I realized, as I bent over, it was better. Its four buildings were situated elegantly around a series of courtyards and swimming pools. Its solar canopies mimicked the shape of the hills behind it. It was white and glossy, immaculate and expensive. Despite the weird stasis you get with architectural models, you could imagine the throngs of people around the pools, strolling back to their rooms after a day at the beach. The watersports area, which jutted far into the bay, was punctuated by little plastic boats and even two water-skiers, complete with foam trails. Whale Jetty was lined with expensive white yachts and catamarans. The sand was white and the buildings gleamed with whitewash and glass. The little pine trees climbed mountains behind it, and the sea was turquoise. It looked like somewhere you might like to fall into. It looked, I had to admit, like a little stretch of Paradise, and the business side of me couldn't help but feel a perverse admiration for my own skills. Then I looked down the miniature bay and saw that Kathleen's place and the Whalechasers Museum no longer existed. There was white sand, the headland and nothing else.

Anger built inside me again.

"Looks pretty good, doesn't it?"

I glanced up to see Mr. Reilly gazing at the Perspex case. He was wearing a short-sleeved shirt and his jacket was over his shoulder, as if he hadn't been prepared for the day's warmth. "You must be pretty pleased with yourself."

I straightened.

"I've been wondering where they got all the little figures," he said.

"There are specialist companies," I said curtly. "They make them to order."

"I've got a son who's obsessed with model railways," he continued, squatting down so that he could see it all at eye level. "I should get them to make him a few figures. He'd love it."

I said nothing. I was staring at the space where Kathleen's hotel should have been.

"Different when you see it in three-D, though," he observed. "I thought I could see it on the plans, but this brings it to life."

"It's a mistake," I said. "It's going to be a disaster for the area."

Mr. Reilly deflated slightly, stood up. "I'd heard you'd gone native. You surprise me, Mike, given how hard you fought for this place."

"I saw what you would lose," I said, "and I didn't want to be part of it."

"I don't believe we'll lose too much."

"Just your whales and dolphins."

"You're being a little dramatic, mate. Look, the coast guards have had a clamp-down on those disco boats. There's been none here for over ten days now. They've got the message."

"Until the building starts."

"Mike, there's no evidence that building onshore is going to stress the animals."

"But the watersports will."

"Beaker has promised to put some pretty tough regulations in place."

"You think an eighteen-year-old with a jet-ski cares about regulations? It's all cumulative, Mr. Reilly," I said. "It's all add-ing to the stresses on the whales."

"I'd have to disagree," he said. "At least two humpbacks have been spotted this week, which is about right for this late in the season. The whale-watchers are out again. Dolphins are there. Forgive me for saying this, but I don't really understand why you're so opposed to it."

We stood opposite each other, the great glass case between us. I wanted to hit him, which was unusual for me, and a pity, as I suspected in other circumstances I might have liked him. I took a deep breath and gestured toward the model. "Mr. Reilly, do me a favor. Tell me what you see when you look at this," I said.

He shoved his hands into his pockets. "Apart from the fact that I wouldn't mind staying there myself? I see employment. I see life in an area that's pretty short on it. I see a new bus and a brick-built library for the school, and I see commerce. I see opportunities." He smiled wryly at me. "You should know, Mike. It was you who got me to see those things."

"I'll tell you what I see," I said. "I see men who've had a beer too many skidding too fast around the bay in motorboats. I see dolphins injured by rudders when they can't get out of the way in time. I see disco boats trying to catch passing trade and too many dolphin-watchers, disorientated whales beaching themselves on that pristine white shore. I see what remains of the humpback migration moving many miles from here, perhaps losing numbers in the process, and the people who relied on them losing their jobs. And I see a bloody great hole where a family-run hotel, a place that has existed seventy-odd years, should be."

"There's no reason why the Silver Bay Hotel can't exist quite happily alongside the new development."

I pointed at the model. "They don't seem to think so."

"You can't expect them to include every local building."

"You a betting man, Mr. Reilly? You want to lay five hundred dollars that the Silver Bay will still be around a year after this thing goes up?"

We were silent for a minute. An elderly couple stood in the doorway of the hotel, glancing nervously at us. I realized I had been shouting. I had to get a grip. I was exhausted, and I was losing my perspective. Reilly nodded reassuringly at them, then turned back to me. "I gotta tell you, mate, you've surprised me. That's some about-turn," he said. But his voice was not unfriendly. "Tell me something, Mike. You're against the development now, but you must have seen the advantages once. There must have been a reason why you tried to sell it so hard. So you tell me now. When you came to me all those months ago, back when you wanted this thing, what did *you* see when you looked at this plan — truthfully, mind?"

I looked at this thing, at this unstoppable force, and my heart felt like lead. "Money," I said. "I saw money."

When I got back Hannah was in my room on the computer. The window was open, and bright sunlight streamed in onto the white-painted floorboards, showing up the faded colors of the Persian rug, and the sandy footprints my training shoes had walked in after my morning run. Outside, someone's car spewed music, a resounding, relentless thud, and a distant trail bike whined across the dunes. A light breeze passed from the open window to the door. I rarely shut my door now — there had been no guests for weeks, and Kathleen behaved as though I lived there. She wouldn't even take rent.

"Mike!" Hannah exclaimed. She spun around on the chair, beckoning me closer, and showed me an e-mail she said was from someone in Hawaii, who had fought off a similar development. "She's going to send us a list of the organizations who helped her," she said. "We might be able to get them to help us."

"That's great," I said, trying to sound positive. I wanted to sink my head into my hands. "Good work."

"Me and Lara have been e-mailing everyone. I mean *everyone*. Someone from the *South Bay Examiner* rang and wants to take our picture because of the petitions."

"What does your mother say?" I said.

"She said to ask you." She grinned. "I've made a list of everything we did today — it's in the blue file in the corner. I've got Hockey Club now, but I'll carry on when I get back. Are you still coming out with me and Mum?"

"Hmm?" I was thinking about Mr. Reilly. The planning inquiry would close in three days' time, he'd told me as he left the Blue Shoals. But he'd added that between ourselves, nothing had been submitted that was persuasive enough to change the panel's mind.

"Mum said we could all go out, the three of us, on *Ishmael* — remember?"

"Oh," I said, trying to smile. "Sure."

She pulled on her school cardigan and thrust a newspaper at me. "Did you see Auntie K's picture with the shark? She's raging. She says she's going to have Greg's guts for garters."

The headline said: "Shark Lady Warns of Tiger's Return." Underneath it, the photographer had caught Kathleen as she stepped toward Greg, her own expression almost as baleful as the dead shark's. Beside it, in inset, was the now familiar picture of her as a seventeen-year-old in a bathing suit.

"I've scanned it in. I've got to give that one back to Mr. Gaines, but he said not to let Auntie K know he'd bought a copy or she'll harpoon him. It's on your desktop if you want to read it, with two others, the *Sentinel* and the *Silver Bay Advertiser,* but their pictures aren't as good."

Poor Kathleen. She was right: she'd be haunted by that shark till her dying day.

I watched Hannah gather her things and, with a cheery wave, she was off down the stairs. She seemed to have blocked out her mother's imminent departure. Perhaps some things were too big to contemplate when you were eleven. Perhaps, like me, she was hoping for divine intervention.

I listened to her singsong voice as she and her friend made their way up the road. For the umpteenth time, I offered her a silent apology.

It was then that my mobile phone rang.

"Monica?" I checked my watch. It must be nearly two o'clock in the morning in England.

"How's it going?" said Vanessa.

My first fleeting thought was: Where the hell is my sister? My second was irritation. Vanessa would know very well that my opposition to the plans was coming to nothing.

"How's what going?"

"Life. Stuff. I wasn't talking about the development," she said.

"I'm fine," I said.

"I hear you're still in Australia," she said. "I spoke to your mother the other day."

"Still playing Canute," I said, "against the unstoppable tide."

There was a dull noise in the background at her end — and I had a sudden picture of our apartment, the sleek flat-screen television in the corner, the vast suede sofas, the expensive furnishings. I hadn't missed it.

"Dad's got a cuttings file," she said, "all the pieces you've placed about opposition to the development. He throws things at it daily."

"Why are you telling me?"

"I don't know. To let you know that what you're doing is not totally in vain."

"But it's not stopping him."

There was a brief silence.

"No," she conceded. "It's not."

Outside, a flock of parakeets had landed in a tree. I watched them, still with the jolt of surprise that something so vivid could live naturally in the wild.

"Tina left."

So what? I wanted to say, gazing out of the window.

I closed my eyes. I was so tired. During the day I spent my time wrestling with the immovable, my mind constantly turning over possible opportunities and loopholes, and at night I lay awake watching Liza, frightened to miss the last moments before she disappeared.

"I miss you," said Vanessa.

I said nothing.

"I've never seen you like this before, Mike. You've changed. You're stronger than I thought."

"So?"

"So . . . I've been thinking." She took a breath. "I can get him to stop. I know he'll listen to me."

The world seemed briefly to stop turning. "What?"

"If it means that much to you, I'll stop it. But I'm asking you — please — let's give it another try."

My breath, which had risen like a bubble, stalled briefly in my chest. "You and me?"

"We were a good team, weren't we?" She was uncertain, pleading. "We can be even better than I thought. You've made me understand that."

"Oh," I said quietly.

"You hurt me, Mike, I'm not going to deny that. But Dad says Tina was a trouble-maker, and I don't think you're the kind of person to deceive me intentionally. So . . . so I guess I don't want to lose what we had. We were a team. A great team."

I stared, unseeing, at the floor.

When I spoke, my mouth, suddenly dry, stuck on the words: "You're saying that if I come back to you, you'll stop the development."

"That's putting it very baldly. It's not a quid pro quo, Mike. But I miss you. I didn't understand what this meant to you so I want to put it right. And we could do some serious business with one of the alternatives."

"If we're together."

"Well, I'm hardly likely to go to all that trouble for someone I don't care about." She sounded exasperated. "Is it so hideous a prospect? Us giving it another go? The last time we spoke I thought . . ."

I shook my head, trying to clear my thoughts.

"Mike?"

"Vanessa, you've really . . . surprised me. Look — I've got to go out now, but let me ring you later. Okay? I'll ring you later. In the morning. Your time," I said, as she began to protest.

I ended the call and sat, my ears ringing. I had nowhere to go. Vanessa Beaker was the only person in the whole world capable of stopping the development.

In the end I made excuses. I told them I had a headache and I had to return some calls. That I had used two excuses where one would have been adequate immediately alerted Liza to the truth: that some other reason lay behind my decision not to go with them on our planned outing. As Hannah, disappointment naked in her face, pleaded with me to change my mind, her mother eyed me curiously and said nothing. I wondered afterward if she saw it as part of an emotional continuum: that I was choosing deliberately to separate from her in stages . . . that I was trying to protect myself.

"I'll see you both when you get back," I said, trying to sound casual.

"Whatever you want," Liza said. "We'll be a couple of hours." The dog was already on the bridge, pressed close to the two of them.

It wasn't what I wanted, but I needed to think. Liza and I were so attuned to each other's moods and thoughts that if she spent more than a few minutes in my company she would see straight through me. I waved at the boat as the engines powered up and it bounded over the waves and away from me. I kept waving until I could no longer see them. Then, as they disappeared around the head, I sat down on the sand, drew up my knees and placed my head on my hands, not caring if anyone could see me.

That was how I began the longest afternoon of my life. Then, unable to face the hotel, I got up and walked down the coast road, over the dunes, and lost myself for a couple of hours, not sure where I was headed, not really noticing my surroundings. I had to walk, because the idea of being still, with those thoughts, was worse.

I walked with my hands in my pockets and my head down. I nodded at those people who said g'day to me, and failed to meet the eye of those who didn't. My footsteps, even on the uneven terrain, became as regular and plodding as those of a packhorse. Without a hat, or a wallet, seemingly without purpose, I must have attracted a few curious glances, but if I did I didn't notice. Unused to the strength of even the spring sunshine, I got burned, and by the time I headed down through the pines and landed by the side of the Newcastle road, the skin on the bridge of my nose was tightening. I didn't feel heat or thirst or tiredness, despite my sleepless night. I walked and I thought, and every possible solution felt ruinous.

I, Michael Dormer, a man renowned for his acuity in decision-making, for his brilliant ability to weigh up the pros and cons of any situation and hit the right answer, now found that whichever way I turned the options made me want to sink to my knees, like a small boy, and howl. And the one person whose advice I could have asked, whose opinion I would have respected, was the one person I needed to protect from what I knew.

I was back on Whale Jetty when they returned. It must have looked as if I hadn't been away. I had allowed myself a couple of beers, and sat there, suddenly conscious that my jeans were scruffy and that I was holding a bottle. I would have liked to stick a cap on my head but suspected that if I did I might morph into Greg.

I watched *Ishmael* come around the headland, turning from a small white blob to a gently bouncing white cruiser. Its swimming nets were stretched across the boom, where Hannah must have been allowed to sit in the water to see the dolphins. As they came closer, I could see her, life jacket strapped around her, treading sure-footed on the deck in her swimsuit and shorts. Milly was standing up at the helm in front of Liza, already anticipating the return home with the same pleasure that, every morning, she looked forward to her journey onto water. They looked beautiful and joyous, and in other circumstances, the sight of them out on the water would have made my heart sing.

Hannah stood braced at the prow. She waved when she saw me, a huge windscreen-wiper of a wave that shifted her weight from one foot to the other. Her legs were thin, with the lean muscularity of prepubescence, and in their rare moments of elegance I saw her mother's.

"We saw Brolly!" she was shouting. As they grew closer, she yelled louder, to be heard above the noise of the engine and the slap of the waves against the hull. "She was fine! No cuts or anything. It wasn't her in

the nets, Mike. It wasn't her you cut free!
And guess what — she was with her baby!"
She was beaming — they both were, Liza
with a mother's pleasure at her daughter's
uncomplicated joy. I stood up, wishing suddenly that I had gone with them, that I
could have shared a simple outing full of
small happinesses.

There had been other adventures. They
had seen a humpback, although it hadn't
come close, and some really big sea turtles,
and they had fished out a piece of baleen
they had spotted near the sound, but Milly
had eaten part of it when they weren't looking. That and several biscuits.

"I do feel sorry for that other dolphin,"
said Hannah, jumping onto the jetty as her
mother maneuvered slowly in, the engine
grinding gently to a halt. "But you probably
saved it, didn't you, Mike? It would have
found its way out. And I'm so happy that
Brolly's okay. I'm sure she recognized me.
Mum let me sit in the boom nets and Brolly
stayed by the boat for *ages.*"

Liza leapt nimbly onto the jetty and began
to secure the boat with her rope. She had
her cap on, so at first I couldn't see her face.

"I couldn't believe it when I saw her,"
Hannah said breathlessly, hauling Milly up
and clutching the dog to her chest. "I

couldn't believe it."

"There. You see? Sometimes good things happen," Liza said, her face pink with the effort of tying the knots. "If we have faith."

I didn't answer her. I suspected Hannah's illuminated smile had made my decision for me, and I was no longer sure that she was right.

I slept alone in my own room that night — or, rather, I sat in the battered leather armchair until my thoughts were as twisted and frayed as Liza's bits of rope. I did not have to explain my reticence to Liza — Hannah's mood had taken a sudden downturn that evening, seemingly in inverse proportion to the highs of earlier in the day, and she spent the night in her mother's room. As I stared out of the black window at the fishing lights, I could hear her sobbing, heard Liza murmuring reassurance. In the early hours I got up to make myself a cup of tea and found Kathleen in the kitchen in her dressing gown. She looked at me, and shook her head. "It's tough on her," she said, and I wasn't sure which of them she was talking about.

They say that a mother is genetically programmed to want to stop the cry of their baby. Well, that night I would have done anything to stem Hannah's tears. In them I heard every bit of loss she had suffered, every loss that stood ahead of her, and while I have never thought of myself as particularly emotional, that night I felt wretched. Anyone not moved by them would have had a heart of lead.

When I finally slept, as it was getting light, she had been quiet for several hours. But I felt the fragility of her sleep, just as I felt Liza's presence down the corridor, and I knew that twenty feet away, behind the whitewashed wooden door, she was awake too.

The following morning, when she returned from the school run I was waiting for her in the car park. I had positioned myself against the back wall of the hotel where I could not be seen by anyone else.

"Hey, gorgeous," she called, as she reversed in. In her smile was the relief of seeing me alone after what had felt like a day's separation. "You're a sight for sore eyes." She climbed out of the car, and closed the door behind her.

"Walk with me," I said.

She blinked and looked at me suspiciously. "What's up?"

Neither of us had made a move toward the other. Normally I would have had her in my arms by now, would have been unable to resist that brief moment of solitude to pull her close to me, to feel her skin against mine.

"Mike?"

I forced my face into the most neutral expression I could manage. "I've got some news." I squared my shoulders. "I'm going to stop the development. I've — I've spoken to someone behind it, and I think I can persuade them to go elsewhere."

She lifted a hand to her brow, the better to see my face. Her own was bruised with tiredness, mauve shadows around her eyes.

"What?"

"I think I can stop it — I know I can."

She frowned. "The development will just stop? No more planning inquiry? Nothing? Just like that?"

I swallowed. "I think so."

"But — how?" A smile was playing on her lips, as if she daren't give it full vent until she knew what I was saying to be true.

"I don't want you to say anything to anyone until I've made sure. I'm going back to London."

"London?" The half-smile vanished.

"So you don't need to go, Liza," I said slowly. "You don't need to go anywhere."

She glanced at me, stared fixedly at her

feet, then out to sea. Anywhere but at me. "You know the development's only half of it now, Mike. I need a clean slate. I need to stop running."

"Then do it when Hannah's older. Tell the authorities when she doesn't need you so much. It'll keep."

She stood there and I watched every thought I had had flicker across her face, like clouds scudding across the sky. The possibility of not having to go was beyond relief. But I could tell that she'd mentally adjusted to the idea of leaving and was finding it hard to pull back. Finally she faced me. "What's going on, Mike?"

"I'm going to make sure you're safe," I said, "and that Hannah gets to grow up with her mother."

She stared at me for a long time, her eyes questioning. Then she must have realized that I wasn't smiling. Given what I had achieved, I should have been. And I knew what she was going to ask next. She kicked at a pebble. "Are you coming back? When you've done this thing?"

"Probably not," I said.

There it was, out in the open.

"I thought you wanted . . . I thought you wanted to be with us."

I said nothing. There was nothing I could say.

"You're not answering my question."

"I need you to trust me," I said.

"But you're not coming back. Whatever."

I shook my head.

I saw her jaw tighten. I knew she wanted to ask me how I could do this when I had told her I loved her. I knew she had a million questions, and she no longer knew the answer to the biggest one. I knew she wanted to ask me to stay. But she wanted to stay with her daughter more.

"Why won't you trust me enough to talk to me?" she said.

Because I can't make you choose, I told her silently. But I can carry that burden for you. "Do you always ask so many questions?" I said jokingly. But I didn't laugh. I stepped forward and held her, feeling her stiffen in my arms, and knew that my heart was broken.

Night falls swiftly in Silver Bay. And, as with any small town, it comes with a rhythm of its own: birds declare the end of day with increasing fervor, then fall silent; cars edge into driveways; children are called in, bouncing or dragging their feet, for their supper; somewhere in the distance a hysterical small dog barks, warning of the end of the world. In Silver Bay there were other layers of nightfall: the sound of pans clattering through the open kitchen window, the creaking of warped lockup doors, the hiss and grind of tires in sand down the coast road as the fishermen readied their boats, the grunting and good-natured shouting of those launching their vessels from the shore. And then, as the sun sank slowly behind the hills, the winking advent of the bay's lights, silence, and the occasional distant illumination of an oil tanker on the horizon, and then, finally, blackness. A blackness into which you can project almost anything: the song of an unseen whale, the beating of a heart, the endlessness of an unwanted future.

I watched it all as I sat in the leather armchair. And, given the momentous nature of what was about to happen, of what had already happened, my final conversation of that day was almost anticlimactic.

"Vanessa?"

She had picked up on the second ring. I gazed out of the window and then, perhaps more sharply than I'd intended, pulled down the blind.

"Mike . . ." She let out a long breath. "I wasn't sure when you'd call."

She sounded unsure of herself. I wondered how long she had been waiting. I had promised to call several hours previously, but had sat in the room, staring at the phone, my fingers refusing to hit the keys. "Mike?"

"You still want me?"

"Do you want me?"

I closed my eyes. "We've been through a lot," I said. "We've hurt each other. But I'll give it a go. I really will give it a go."

I was almost relieved when she didn't say anything.

"When's your flight home?" she said.

TWENTY-FIVE: MONICA

I didn't tell Mike I was going to do it: I was worried he'd tell me not to, that he just wanted me to do what we'd discussed, and stop fretting about the detail. I guessed he was royally pissed off with me — he'd left increasingly strident messages on my voice-mail and every time I switched on my mobile phone it seemed there was a missed-call alert from Australia. Last night he must have called a hundred times, warning me not to speak to anyone until I'd talked to him.

But I couldn't ring him back, not until at least some of this made sense. I couldn't talk to him until I understood what was going on. I'm not the greatest journalist in the world — I've never fooled myself that I'm much more than a jobbing hack — but I know when something odd's going on, and my blood was up. In one respect at least I'm like my brother: I'm thorough. So, on my one weekday off, I headed to Surrey, caught a cab from the station to the address I'd scribbled on a piece of paper, and shortly after ten I was standing outside a large house in Virginia Water.

"Nice place," the cabbie said, peering at it through the windscreen as he scribbled a receipt.

"Yes — I'm scouting locations for a porn film," I said. "Their rates are very good, apparently." I grinned as he drove off. Mike's girlfriend could have that one on me.

I soon saw that I wouldn't be able to check out the house as I'd planned: it was surrounded by high hedges, and was so far from the road that I would have drawn attention to myself walking up the long drive. I had wanted to take a quiet look, maybe glean some clues about its inhabitants, its history, work out what I was trying to find. Instead I stood at the bottom of the drive, half hidden by a tree, outside the five-bar gate, and waited.

It was a big mock-Tudor affair, with leaded windows, the kind of house I imagine accountants aspire to. (This may be a slur on either accountants or mock-Tudor houses — but I live in a two-bedroom flat above a burger bar and, according to my friends, have no taste.) The lawns and flowerbeds were tidy enough, even in October, to suggest a gardener's vigilant attention. Five or six bedrooms, I thought, staring at it from the roadside. At least three bathrooms. Lots of carpet and expensive curtains. A Volvo station wagon stood in the drive, and pricy wooden play equipment in the damp garden. I shivered, despite my thick coat. There was something cold about that house, despite its affluence, and I didn't think I was being fanciful. Mike had told me what had gone on inside it, and I couldn't help but imagine that young woman looking out at the drive as she tried to plot her escape.

Several cars drove by, their occupants turning to stare at me as they passed. It was not the kind of area where people tended to walk, so I stuck out like a sore thumb. As I was considering where to move to, I caught sight of a woman walking past an upstairs window: a flash of a pale sweater, short dark hair in a neat bob. It was probably the wife. I wondered what he had told her about his previous life. I wondered whether she, too, was planning her getaway, or whether he treated her well. Whether it was a marriage of equals. Then I thought of what Liza had told my brother and wondered whether love had blinded him to the possibility that she was lying to him. How else to explain any of this? How else to explain such huge holes in what she had described?

As I considered what to do next, a girl in a thick blue sweater and jeans came around the side of the house. She might have left the door open; from inside I could just hear the dull murmur of the radio, then the sound of a baby crying and being pacified. As I ducked back, she walked toward me, to the end of the drive, and made to pick up the post from the mailbox. I stepped out from behind the tree, trying to look as if I had just been passing. "Hello there. Is Mr. Villiers in?" I asked. My breath left little clouds of vapor in the air.

"If it's council business," she said, "he sees people on Fridays."

"Fridays."

She nodded.

"His office told me he'd be working from home today." I don't know why I lied. I thought perhaps if I could keep her talking I might find out a little more about him.

"He's in London," she said. "He's always in London on Thursday nights."

"Oh," I said. "I must have got it wrong. He's still at the bank, right?"

"Yes."

"I saw him in the newspaper. Quite an

important man, isn't he?"

She pulled the letters from the box and leafed through them. Then she looked at me. "I can give you his number, if you like."

I glanced at my notebook. "I have it, but thank you."

I could ask to come in, I thought. But I wouldn't know what to say to his wife. I had no backstory thought out, and until I knew how to present myself, there was no point. *Hello, Mrs. Villiers. I'm a journalist. Can you tell me if your husband — the pillar of the community — is actually a wife-beating sociopath? Is he a bullying, unfaithful control freak partly responsible for the death of his own child? Lovely curtains, by the way.*

"I'll ring his office. Thank you." I smiled, in a friendly, businesslike way, as if it were of no importance. I would go into the village and have a coffee. I could always come back, once I had worked out the best way to proceed. Perhaps the wife *was* the way forward. Perhaps I could pretend to be a local feature-writer, keen to do something on the Villiers family life. If I could get her by herself, over a cup of tea, there was no saying what she might admit to.

" 'Bye then."

" 'Bye."

The girl stood in front of me, not really

paying me any attention, and pushed her hair back behind her ear. Then as she began to walk slowly toward the house, I noticed she had a pronounced limp. And something funny happened to my heart.

I've heard that expression: the world just fell away. I hate cliché. In my writing I've always worked hard to steer away from it. Yet that was the only phrase that echoed through my head.

I put my bag on the pavement beside me, and stood very still, staring after her.

"Excuse me!" I called, not caring who heard me. "Excuse me!"

I shouted until she turned around and walked back slowly toward me.

"What?" she said, head tilted to one side. It was then that I saw it. And, for a moment, everything stopped.

"What . . . what's your name?" I asked.

TWENTY-SIX: KATHLEEN

I was making lunch for Hannah when I heard the door slam. That isn't unusual in this house, not with a dog, a near-teenager and guests who either seemingly hail from barns or leave the sea wind to close doors. But the ferocity with which my ancient portal hit the frame, then the agitated thumping of Mike — not a small man — leaping up several steps at a time made me curse gently. His feet sounded like the pounding of a battering ram. When he made it into his room he must have left the window open because that door banged noisily behind him too, sending a shudder through the house.

"We're not in need of demolition just yet," I yelled at the ceiling, wiping my hands on my apron. "You go through my floorboards, you'll be paying for 'em!"

We had the radio on so at first I couldn't make out what he was yelling, but we both paused at the commotion in his room.

"You think he's having another fight with someone?" said Hannah.

"You get on with your homework, Miss," I said. But I turned off the radio.

This is an old house, wood-built, a little rickety in places, so from the kitchen you can hear a lot of movement upstairs, and as Mike threw himself across the room and dragged the chair back from his desk I was moved to remark that that man had ants in his pants.

"Perhaps he got bit by a spider," she said, suddenly interested.

"Monica?" he was yelling into his phone. "Send it now. Send it *now.*"

Hannah and I exchanged a glance.

"That's his sister," she said quietly. And I thought, That's the journalist, and my peaceable mood dissolved.

I was making a cheese omelet, and whisked the eggs furiously, trying to lose the dark thread of my thoughts in domestic tasks. Since Liza had told me her plans, I had never cooked so hard, nor the hotel been so clean. Pity there were no other guests — they would have had a rare five-star service. I stuck my head down, and whisked until I had forgotten what I was thinking about and I had eggs so light they were ready to fly out of the bowl. It was several minutes before I noticed that since Mike's shout there had been no noise at all from upstairs. Not even the usual padding of his feet as he moved from desk to leather chair, or the creak as he lay down on his bed.

Once again Hannah was engrossed in her exercise book, but there was a quality to the silence that made me curious.

I took the pan off the heat and walked to the doorway. "Mike?" I called up the stairs. "Everything okay?"

Nothing.

"Mike?" I said, holding the banister and taking a step up.

"Kathleen," he said, and his voice was tremulous. "I think you'd better come up here."

As I entered the room he told me to sit down on the bed. In truth he was so pale, so unlike himself, that it was a couple of seconds before I agreed to do so. He moved toward me and squatted in front of me, like someone about to propose. Then he said those two little words, and as I heard them spoken aloud I felt the color drain from my face. Afterward he told me he was afraid I'd have a heart attack like Nino Gaines.

He was a fool, I thought, with the part of my mind still capable of functioning. Or a madman. We'd been harboring a madman all this time. "What the hell are you saying?" I asked, when my voice returned to me. "What kind of joke is this?" Suddenly I felt furious with him, and he waved a hand at me, telling me, uncharacteristically rudely, to shush, to wait while he opened his computer.

He stood up and, as I began to protest, scanned down a load of messages. Then, as I wondered whether I should try to leave the room, a little box opened on his screen and there she was. Unbelievably. In full color. Staring at us with a wary incomprehension that matched my own. And my hands began to tremble.

"This is the picture Monica took today. It looks like her, right?"

My mouth hung open and my hand was glued to my chest. I was unable to tear my eyes away from that face. And then, in halting sentences, he told me what his sister had told him.

"Hannah," I croaked. "You've got to get Hannah."

But Hannah must have become curious about what was going on upstairs because when I looked away from the screen she was already in the doorway, her pen still in her hand. Her eyes flickered from me to Mike and back again.

"Hannah, sweetheart," I said, lifting a trembling hand toward the computer. "I need you to look at something. I need you to tell me whether this — this looks like . . ."

"Letty." Hannah moved closer to the screen, lifted a finger and traced her sister's nose. *"Letty."*

"She's alive, sweetheart," I said, as the tears came. I couldn't speak properly for several minutes, and I felt Mike's hand on my shoulder. "God save us, she's alive." And I was afraid for Hannah, afraid that she would be feeling even more than the shock and disbelief I felt. My thoughts were in turmoil, my heart numbed by the sight of that child, whom I'd never known but whose life and death had hung over this house as surely as if she'd been my own. How on earth could we expect Hannah to cope with this?

But she was the only one of us not crying.

"I knew," she said, a great smile breaking across her face. "I knew she couldn't be dead, not like the sea creatures. She never *felt* dead." She turned back to the screen and traced the image again. They were so alike, it was as if she was staring into a mirror. It's hard to believe now that I could have doubted it.

Mike had gone to the window. He was rubbing the back of his head. "Those bastards," he was saying, forgetting Hannah's presence. "How can they have kept the truth from her for all those years? How could they do that to her? How could they do that to the *child*?"

The size of their deception had hit me too, and the language that emerged from my mouth I haven't heard since I was a wartime barmaid. "That bastard! That yellow-bellied, rat-eating son of a rabid dog! That . . . sh—"

"Shark?" suggested Mike, raising an eyebrow.

"Shark," I affirmed, glancing at Hannah. "Yes. Shark. I'd sure love to gut him like one."

"I'd shoot him," said Mike.

"Shooting's too good." I had a sudden image of Old Harry, my harpoon gun, mounted on the wall of the Whalechasers Museum, and had a thought that would have shocked those who knew me. I knew Mike's mind was headed the same way. Then Hannah spoke again. "I still have a sister," she announced, and the simple delight in her voice stopped us both. "Look! I have a sister." And as Hannah placed her own face beside that oversized image, so that we could both take in the reality of that statement, Mike and I turned to each other.

"Liza," we said, in unison.

We didn't know how to tell her. We didn't know how to give her this news. She was out on the boat and it was too huge, too shocking, to tell her over the radio. Yet we couldn't wait for her to come in. In the end we borrowed Sam Grady's cutter. With Mike and Hannah at the prow, and me at the tiller, we sailed out past the bay to Break Nose Island. The breeze was light, the seas gentle, and within minutes we were accompanied by pods of dolphins, the joyful arcs of their bodies echoing the mood on our boat. As we bounced across the waves, Hannah leaned over the edge and told them. "They know!" she said, laughing. "They've come because they know!" For once I didn't put her straight. Who was I to say how life worked? Who was I to say those creatures didn't know more about it than I did? I felt at that moment that nothing would surprise me.

And there she was, coming back in, standing at the helm with Milly beside her, looking forward already to coming ashore. She had a full boat, largely Taiwanese. The tourists leaned over the front rails, curious as to why we had approached, some still clutching their cameras, then snapping madly as they saw the dolphins in our wake.

As she spotted us and steered toward us, the sun was behind her and her hair looked as if it was on fire. "What's up?" she yelled, as we pulled alongside. She forgot to be mad about Hannah not wearing a life jacket: when she saw the three of us crammed into the little boat, she knew we couldn't be there for any ordinary reason.

I looked at Mike, who nodded at me, and I began to shout, but before I had even said the words, the tears were streaming down my face. My voice broke. It took several attempts, and Mike's proffered hanky, before I could make myself heard.

"She's alive, Liza. Letty's alive."

Liza looked from me to Mike and back again. Above us, two gulls wheeled and cried, mocking what I had said.

"It's true! Letty's alive! Mike's sister has seen her. She's really, really alive." I waved the picture that Mike had printed off, but the breeze whipped it around my hand and she was too far off to see it.

"Why are you saying this?" she said, her voice cracking with pain. She glanced back at the passengers, who were all watching the scene intently. The color had drained from her face. "What do you mean?"

Struggling to keep my balance, I unfurled the picture and held it above my head, in two hands, like a banner. "Look!" I shouted. "Look! They lied to you! The bastards lied to you! She never died in the car crash. Letty's alive, and she's coming home."

The tourists hushed, and a few of the Taiwanese, perhaps sensing the enormity of the occasion, began a spontaneous round of applause. We waited below, our faces alive with joy and expectation, and then, as the gulls flew off on some predetermined path, Liza turned her face briefly toward the sky and fainted clean away.

Mike said he'd never realized how much he loved his sister till that day. In a three-hour conversation, as Liza sat pressed up to him, still pale with shock, she told him how she had arranged to meet Steven Villiers at his office and, once there, cup of tea in hand, told him she was following up a story about a respected councilor who had deliberately told his girlfriend that her daughter was dead in order to separate them. A councilor who had systematically beaten his girlfriend until she left in fear of her life. A girlfriend who had kept photographs of her injuries and had them verified by a doctor. Okay, so Monica had lied about that bit, but she said her blood was up by then and she'd just wanted to be sure she would win. I liked the sound of Monica Dormer.

The shocking thing was how easily the Villiers man had caved in. He went very quiet, then said, "What do you want?" He had married, you see, and had two young sons, and when Monica told him that Letty would know, one way or the other, what he had done, she had thought, from his voice, that this was a conversation he had probably expected for some time. They struck a deal: restore the child to her mother, and this would remain a family matter. He agreed a little too readily; she had the impression that it wasn't the happiest of families.

This is the best part. He had known where Liza was for years — through his contacts in the police, probably, or some kind of private investigator. The irony was that he had wanted her to stay away from him as much as she had wanted to stay away. He said his mother had told Liza the child was dead, partly because at that point they thought it might be true, and partly out of spite. Then when they discovered that Liza had disappeared, they'd decided it might be useful to let her believe it, that it would be an easy way to have her out of their lives. She was a loose cannon, a threat to his career and his future, an obstacle to his happiness with the elegant, dark-haired Deborah. And they had what they wanted. He had the grace, she said, to look a little ashamed. He wanted proper access, he said, the kind of man who at least wants to behave as if he still has control of a situation, and Monica told him he could have his access — as much as his daughter wanted.

Then, accompanied by a lawyer and with a child psychologist at the ready (Mike's sister was a little afraid by then, never having dealt with children herself), they went to the house to tell Letty she was going on holiday. It was quick. We worried later that it was too quick, given the shock that the girl experienced on being told that her mother had not abandoned her, after all. But, sounding as unsure as Mike had ever heard her, Monica admitted that until they left the drive, she had been afraid Villiers would change his mind.

There were so many lies that Letty would have to learn to disbelieve, so many secrets. Mike's sister said she was a bright kid, that she wanted to know everything. It was nighttime there now, and they were letting her sleep, but in the morning, our evening, Monica would ring us and, after five years, Liza would be able to speak to her. Her younger daughter, her baby, risen from the dead.

I saw the light on in the Whalechasers Museum as I let Milly out for her last walk of the night, and I guessed pretty quickly who it might be. I don't bother locking it half the time — there's nothing of monetary value in it to steal, and Milly would let us know if strangers headed up here when they shouldn't.

Liza and Hannah were upstairs making their telephone call and they needed to be alone, so I grabbed a couple of beers and went out there. He was probably feeling like I was, a bit of a spare part. This was Hannah and Liza's time. We could be happy for them, overjoyed even, but in truth, not yet knowing Letty, we could only ever feel a fraction of what they did. Being in that house while that conversation was going on upstairs felt intrusive, like listening in on someone's love affair.

Besides, I was curious about what Liza had told me the previous day, before her whole world had changed again — about the possibility that the development might not go ahead. It was nothing certain, she said, and she was not meant to tell anyone until it was confirmed. But she said it was down to Mike and then, her face darkening, she said that he would be leaving for good tomorrow and after that she wouldn't say much at all.

He didn't hear me at first. He was sitting on one of *Maui II*'s rotten timbers, one hand resting on it, and his shoulders were stooped, as if he were carrying a great weight. Given what he had achieved, it seemed an odd stance.

Milly shot in past me, wagging her way to him, and he glanced up. "Oh. Hi," he said. He was almost directly under the strip-lights, and they cast long shadows on his face.

"Thought you might like this." I held out a beer to him. As he took it I sat down on the chair a few feet away and cracked one open myself.

"Not like you," he said.

"Nothing normal about today," I said.

We sat and drank in companionable silence. The barn doors were open, and through them, in the near dark, we could see the shoreline, the distant lights of people's cars, of fishermen's boats preparing for their night's work. The gentle, humdrum life of Silver Bay pottering on, as it had done for half a century. I still couldn't believe what I'd been told — that it was possible Mike could pull us back from the brink. I couldn't believe that we might be allowed to stand, undisturbed, for a little longer.

"Thank you," I said, quietly. "Thank you, Mike."

He looked up from his beer.

"For everything. I don't understand how you've done it all, but thank you."

His head dropped again then, and I knew something was wrong. The dark, contemplative expression on his face suggested that he was not out here to give Liza space: he was out here because he had needed to be alone.

I sat and waited. I've been around long enough to know you catch a hell of a lot more fish by keeping still and quiet.

"I don't want to leave," he said, "but it's the only way I can stop the development."

"I'm not sure I understand . . ."

"There was a choice . . . and I couldn't make it hers. She's had to make too many hard decisions already."

He was holding so much to him, I swear he could hardly move.

"I want you to know this, Kathleen. Whatever you might hear in the future, whatever you hear about me, it's important she knows she was loved." His eyes were burning into me. Their intensity made me a little uncomfortable.

"I don't want you to think badly of me," he said, choking, "but I made a promise . . ."

"You really can't tell me what any of this is about?"

He shook his head.

I didn't like to push him. Call me old-fashioned, but I think a man becomes physically uncomfortable if you make him talk too much about what he's feeling.

"Mike," I said finally, "you saved Liza. You saved both my girls. That's all I need to know."

"She'll be happy, right?" He wouldn't look at me now. I had a bad feeling about why that might be.

"She'll be okay. She'll have her girls."

He stood up and walked slowly around the room, his back to me. I realized then how sorry I was that he was going. Whatever wrongs he had done us, he had put right in spades and then some. I'm no great romantic — Lord knows, Nino Gaines could tell you that — but when it came to him and Liza I had hoped for a happy ending. I knew now that he was a decent human being and there are few enough around. I would have told him as much, but I wasn't sure who would be more embarrassed.

He stopped in front of my Shark Lady picture. When I sensed he might be a little more comfortable with proximity, I raised myself out of my chair and walked over to join him.

Still in my original frame, sepia-tinted and yellowed with age. Still flanked by my father, Mr. Brent Newhaven and their invisible wires. There I was, smiling into that camera, my seventeen-year-old bathing-suited self, preparing to pursue me through the rest of my days.

I took a deep breath. "I'll let you into a secret," I said. "I never caught that ruddy shark."

That got him. He faced me.

"Nope," I said. "My dad's partner caught it. Told me it would look better on the hotel, give us more publicity, if it came from me." I took another draft of my beer. "I hated lying. Hate it still. But I understand something now. If it hadn't happened, this hotel would never have survived the first five years."

"Or it could have been a six-storey development for the last twenty," Mike said wryly.

I turned the picture to the wall. "Sometimes," I said, "a lie is the way of least pain for everyone."

I placed my hand on Mike Dormer's arm, and waited until he felt able to look at me again. He nodded toward the door, as if we should go, and we glanced up at the house, where Liza's bedroom light still glowed in the dark.

"You know something? I've never seen a tiger shark in this bay. Never," I said, stepping out into the dark.

"Greg has," he said, as he made to close the doors behind us.

"You're not listening," said the Shark Lady.

TWENTY-SEVEN: MIKE

I had one and a half suitcases, and the empty space within them was so great that I could almost have fitted one inside the other. That space seemed to echo my state of mind. I would be the only passenger, I thought, who was likely to be penalized for underutilizing their weight allowance. Somehow, during my time here, I had shed half of my wardrobe so that all I wore now, day after day, was one of my two pairs of jeans, perhaps a T-shirt and shorts if it was a really warm day. Not a lot to show for such a seismic period in my life, I thought, as I placed them on my bed. I guessed I could buy my parents a hell of a lot of duty-free.

I was not taking my oilskin: somehow it was too bound up with being here, and I didn't want to look at it hanging up in the wrong surroundings. I was not taking my suits, which I had given to the Silver Bay charity shop. I didn't pack the T-shirt I'd been wearing when Liza first came into my bed, or the sweater I had lent her the night we had sat out by ourselves until two a.m., and which I secretly hoped she might want to keep. I was not taking my laptop: I had left it in the living room for Hannah, knowing it would be of more use to her. Besides, it might only be a matter of hours now until Letty returned to them, but I couldn't bear to separate Hannah and Liza from that pixellated image. It might sound odd, but it would have felt like tearing them apart all over again. They both sat in front of it for hours, talking, comparing Letty and Hannah's faces, considering the myriad different ways in which they had changed and not changed.

Liza was out on *Ishmael* — her last trip before they, too, left for the airport. I had hardly seen her since the previous day and wondered whether a quiet exit with no good-byes might be the best thing for both of us. I told myself that at least they would be occupied: this afternoon they would finish doing up Letty's room. Hannah had been allowed the day off school, and they had spent the previous evening painting and putting up new curtains, filling it with the kinds of things a ten-year-old girl might like, and arranging Letty's dolphins. Hannah was up there now, music blaring, pinning up posters that she would tear down in a fit of indecision. "Do you think they like this group in England? What do English girls like?" she would ask me anxiously, as if I were likely to have a clue. As if it were likely to make a difference.

I watched all this from a distance, half removed from their happiness, too consumed with the prospective loss of my own. They might miss me a little, but they had a far greater prize to contemplate, and a whole new life ahead. Only I was likely to shed tears tonight. I looked out at the little bay, at the distant mountains and at Silver Bay's scattered rooftops. I listened to the birdsong, to distant engines, to Hannah's music thumping above me, and felt as if I was being wrenched from my home. What was I going back to? To a woman I was not sure I could love in a city that now stifled me.

I thought of having to pick up the pieces of my old life, revisiting once-familiar bars and restaurants with braying City acquaintances, forcing my way through crowded streets, shoehorning myself into a new job in an anonymous office block. I thought of Dennis, who would doubtless convince me to return — and what was the alternative?

Then I pictured myself stuck on a train in a new suit, closing my eyes to imagine Hannah tearing down the beach with Milly at her heels. I thought of Vanessa's smile, her perfume and high-heeled shoes, our smart apartment, my sports car, the trappings of our former life, and knew, with a sick feeling, that it meant nothing. I wanted to be here. Every last atom of me wanted to be here.

The worst of it was that I still liked Vanessa. I still cared about her happiness. And I cared about my own integrity. For those reasons alone it was important that if she held true to her promise I should hold true to mine.

Those were the words I would repeat to myself silently several hundred times a day. Then I would visualize the months ahead, of lying awake at night, with Liza's face, her intermittent smile, her knowing, sideways glance, haunting me. I would imagine burying my face in the one T-shirt that might still carry her scent. I would make love to someone whose body did not instinctively fit my own.

Come on, I told myself sternly, as I walked briskly to the rental car to bring it to the front of the hotel. Liza had her girls, and I was about to secure their future. Two out of three was a pretty good strike rate for anyone. I reversed into the front space, then sat staring at the dashboard. I had finally mastered the weird gearstick and, as I turned off the ignition, that small fact bugged me more than anything.

My flight was not due until the following morning, but standing there, increasingly swamped by my thoughts, I decided I had to leave now. I would drive to the city and book a room in a hotel for the night. If I stayed an hour longer, my resolve might melt. It meant that I would not see my sister, that I would not witness the reunion, but I knew Monica would understand. If I stayed till tomorrow, if I fooled myself for five minutes that I was any part of that new family, I might not be able to do the thing I had promised.

I got out of the car, and turned to the road as I heard a familiar whine. Greg's pickup skidded into the driveway then shuddered to a halt, his bumper a few inches from mine, buoys and fishing nets colliding noisily with the back of the cab.

He climbed out, pulling the brim of his cap over his eyes. "I heard the news about the little one. Unbelievable. Unbe*liev*able."

"News travels fast," I said. But it was a platitude — Hannah had run to the jetty

563

the previous evening, to tell every one of the whalechasers individually. They didn't know the full circumstances, but they knew Liza had had a daughter in England who was to be returned to her, and they were astute enough not to look beyond what they had been told. Not obviously, anyway.

"Arriving tomorrow night, is she?"

I nodded. He pulled a packet of cigarettes from his pocket and lit one. "Good on you, mate. I can't pretend I like you but, strewth, I can't argue with someone who brings children back from the dead, eh?"

He took a deep drag of his cigarette. We both stared for a minute at Whale Jetty, where only Greg's boat remained.

"Thanks," I said, finally.

"Yeah. Well."

Behind us, in the hotel, a telephone rang. Probably some future guest. It would not be Monica — she had been in the air for several hours. Kathleen had offered to put her up for as long as she wanted to stay. It was the least she could do, she said, beaming, and I felt suddenly envious of my sister. Tomorrow night she would be sleeping in what I now thought of as my room. Silver Bay was about to be consigned to memory. A strange little period in my life that I would look back on wistfully; a series of what-ifs that I would not allow myself to consider too closely.

Thinking about my sister made me remember my cases, and I went inside to fetch them. When I carried them out, Greg was still leaning against his pickup. He looked down at my luggage, then up at me. "Going somewhere?"

"London," I said, swinging them into my open boot. I closed it with a thud.

"London, England?"

I didn't bother to respond.

"Staying long?"

I wanted to lie to him — but what would have been the point? He would know soon enough. "Yes."

A slight pause, a few calculations. "Not coming back?"

"No."

His face actually lit up. He was as transparent as a child. "Not coming back. Well, now, that's a shame. For you, I mean."

I heard him take another drag on his cigarette, heard the smile in his voice when he said, "I always thought you were an odd one, mate, and now I know I'm right."

"Quite the psychologist," I said, jaw tightening. I wished he would get lost.

"Leaving us all, eh? I'm sure you've made the right decision. Best to stick where you fit in, eh? And I'm sure Liza will get over it. She'll be a different character now, I reckon. A whole lot happier. And, well, you don't need to worry at all — I'll make sure she has enough . . . attention."

He raised an eyebrow at me, delight written all over his face. If it hadn't been that Hannah might be watching us I would have punched his stupid face in. I knew he half wanted it. He'd been spoiling for a fight with me for weeks. "If I remember rightly, Greg," I said quietly, "it wasn't you she was interested in."

He took a last drag of his cigarette and spat it into the dust. "Aw, mate," he said, "Liza and I go back a long way. I'm a big guy. As far as I'm concerned, you were just a distraction." He held his finger and thumb about a centimeter apart. "A little blip on the old radar."

For a moment, the gloves were off. It was as well that Kathleen emerged from the house. "Mike!" she called, her voice indignant. "What are you doing with your cases? I thought you weren't going till tomorrow?"

I tore my gaze from Greg and went toward her. "I'm — waiting for a call. Then I think I'll head off."

She stared at me. Then at Greg.

"Don't look at me," said Greg, grinning.

"I've done me best to tell him just how much he's wanted."

"You want to come in for a minute?" she asked me.

"Don't mind me." Greg shrugged.

"Never have yet."

I followed her into the front room.

"You can't leave now," she said, her hands on her hips. "You won't see Letty. You haven't said good-bye to anyone. Hell, I was going to do you a little party tonight."

"That's really kind of you, Kathleen, but I think it's best if I go."

"You not even going to hang on till Liza gets back? Say good-bye to her?"

"Best not."

She stared at me, and I wasn't sure whether it was sympathy or frustration in her face. "You really can't hang on? Just till after lunch?"

I tried to think clearly over the sound of Hannah's boombox, which was pumping out disco music upstairs, my heart still thumping with thwarted adrenaline. I could hear her singing, her reedy little voice breathless and faintly out of tune. I stepped forward and held out a hand. "Thanks for everything, Kathleen," I said. "If any calls come here for me this afternoon will you give them my mobile number? I'll call you as soon as I know for certain about the development."

She looked at my hand, then up at my face. I found it difficult to meet her eye. Then she hugged me, her old arms surprisingly strong as they held me to her. "You call me," she said, into my shoulder. "You don't get to disappear just like that. Doesn't have to be about the ruddy development. You call me."

I walked out of the room, out of the hotel and into my car before the pain in her voice could change my mind.

I had to drive slowly down the coast road, not because its surface was potholed and uneven but because there seemed to be something in both of my eyes and I couldn't see straight. When I got to Whale Jetty I stopped to wipe them, and found myself hoping against hope that I might see *Ishmael* coming around the head and into the bay, that I might, one last time, see the thin figure, the hair blowing under the cap and the dog, steering in. Just one little glance, before my life continued its own separate course on the other side of the world.

But there was only the glinting water, the strings of buoys that marked out the boating channels and, on the far side, the hillsides of pines stretching up to the blue sky.

I couldn't think about what she would say when she returned to find me gone. I hadn't even been able to write her a letter: telling her what I felt would have meant telling her the truth, and I couldn't do that. You've done the right thing, I told myself, heading back onto the coast road. For once in your life, you've done a good thing.

I had done the right thing so seldom that I didn't know whether the terrible sense of dread I felt was the right emotion to go with it.

I had been on the highway for almost twenty minutes when my mobile rang. I pulled onto the hard shoulder and rummaged in my jacket pocket.

"Mike? Paul Reilly. This is a courtesy call, really. I thought you should be the first to know that the development isn't going ahead."

She'd done it. I let out a long sigh, not sure whether it was with relief that Vanessa had done as she'd said, or resignation that I had to keep my side of the bargain.

"Well," I said, as a truck rumbled past, making the car tremble, "I know we differ on this, but I'm glad. Bundaberg really is the better option."

"Can't see it myself. I thought that development would have been a real asset to this area."

"You've got something rare here, Mr. Reilly," I said. "At some point you and the other half of Silver Bay will realize that."

"Pretty unusual for someone to pull the plug so late in the day. I mean, they were after putting the foundations down this week." His voice lifted in resignation. "But you can't argue with the money men."

"Beaker will have done their research," I said. "If they thought Bundaberg had the better margins, then —"

"Beaker? It wasn't Beaker."

"Sorry — what did you say?" The cars and trucks kept roaring past, sporadically drowning his words.

"It was the venture capitalists. The finance. They pulled the plug unless the site was changed."

"I don't understand."

"They got antsy about the shark, apparently. They heard about all the newspaper reports and warnings not to let people in the water and took fright." He sighed. "I guess from their point of view it's going to be pretty hard to sell watersports holidays to people if they think there are sharks but, really, I think they got it all out of proportion."

He sounded pretty disappointed.

"Seems British people hear the word 'shark' and all reason goes out the window," he added.

Why would Vanessa go to Vallance first? I wondered.

"You've surprised me, Mr. Reilly," I said, my mind working. "Thanks for the call. But if you'll excuse me, I need to speak to someone."

I sat for a moment, barely noticing the traffic that hurtled past. Then I reached into my briefcase for my laptop, realizing too late that it wasn't there. I stared at my bags, then wrenched the car back onto the highway and accelerated hard to the next exit.

"Dennis?"

"Michael? I wondered how long it would be before you rang, you old bastard. Rung to gloat, have you?" He sounded well lubricated — it would be almost eleven at night there and, knowing Dennis, he would have had a few. Or a few more than a few.

"You know that's not my style." I was driving while I was talking, and had to wedge my phone between ear and shoulder as I negotiated the roundabout back into

Silver Bay. As I headed toward the hotel, the car bounced over the potholes and I wondered absently how much I'd have to pay the rental company for busted suspension.

"No — I forgot you'd turned into Mother bloody Teresa. What do you want? Calling to beg for your old job back?"

I ignored him. "So where's it going?"

"Little town just outside Bundaberg." I heard him take a drink of something. "Be even better. VCs are happy, local council is a hundred percent behind us. We're using the same model. Heaps better tax breaks. To be honest, you did us a favor."

There was nobody outside the hotel. I walked through the front door, down the hallway and into the deserted lounge, my phone pressed to my ear, and made for my laptop. It was still where I'd left it. Upstairs, Hannah's music was still blaring. I doubted she'd noticed I'd gone.

"*I* did you a favor?"

"Freaking the VCs out, your lobbyist bombarding them with shark tales."

"My *lobbyist*?"

This was weird.

"Dennis — I —"

"What did you do? Hire some professional crusty from Greenpeace?" He dropped his voice. "Between you and me, I have to admit you did a good job, sending all those newspaper reports about sharks. I was pissed off at first — we had to work four days and nights straight through just to keep the deal on track and Vallance onboard — but, now I think about it, we wouldn't have made any money in shark-infested waters. Much better off up the coast. So, who was it? More importantly, how much did you pay them? I know professional agitators don't come cheap."

He hadn't mentioned Vanessa. While he was talking I'd opened my computer. I glanced down the record of e-mails sent, trying to work out what had happened.

"So, what's your next move, Mike?" he was saying. "Going to do this professionally? You know, I made good on my promise. No one will touch you in the City."

I sorted my outbox into recipients and found the e-mails that had been sent to Vallance. I opened one, noted the scanned newspaper attachments, and began to read.

"That said, boyo, if you're desperate for a job, I might be able to find a small opening. To do you a favor. Nothing like the same salary, you understand."

"Dear Sir," it began. "I am writing to let you know of the risk of shark attack at the new Silver Bay develupment . . ."

I did a double take, read on. And as I read I began to laugh.

"Mike?"

She had done what I had failed to do. She had done what I had thought was impossible.

"Mike?"

The music was louder. I heard the singing and, just for fun, I held the phone up to it.

"Mike?" he said again, when I put the phone back to my ear. "What the hell is that noise?"

"That, Dennis," I said, "is your professional agitator, your overpriced lobbyist, your reverser of multimillion-pound developments. Can you hear it?"

"What?" he was saying. "What are you going on about?"

"That," I said, laughing again, "is an eleven-year-old girl."

I had one more call to make and walked outside as I wanted to be assured of privacy. I stood for a moment before I dialed, breathing in the undisturbed scents that had been there for half a century, and would now remain, if lucky, for half a century more. But I didn't feel any sense of peace. Not yet.

"So, you did it, then," I said.

She caught her breath, as if she had half expected it to be someone else. "Mike," she said. "Yes. You heard. I told you I would."

"You certainly did."

"Oh, you know I always get what I want." She laughed, then began to talk about the apartment, how she had booked a table for the night of my return at a restaurant that it was near-impossible for mere mortals to enter. Her voice was light. She always spoke a little too fast when she was excited. "I've pulled a few strings, and we're eating at eight thirty. That should give you plenty of time for some sleep and a shower."

"How?"

"How did I get a table? Oh, you've just got to know the right —"

"How did you persuade your dad to turn everything round?"

"Oh, you know Dad. I can twist him around my little finger. Always could. So, are you still on the Qantas flight? I've taken time off to meet you. I think I've got the number written down."

"Must have been hard, though — him having convinced Vallance to go so far down the line."

"Well, I just . . ." She sounded vaguely irritated. "I went over the reasons you and I had discussed and by the end of it he saw sense. He listens to me, Mike, and we had the alternatives ready, as you know."

"How did Vallance take it?"

"Fine — look, can we talk about your flight?"

"No point."

"Don't you want picking up? I was going to bring you a surprise, but I can't resist telling you. It's the new Mazda two-seater. The one you ordered — I managed to get it off the dealers at the original price. You're going to love it."

"I'm not coming, Ness."

I heard a sharp intake of breath.

"What?"

"How long had you known when you rang me? I just checked the e-mails that went to Vallance from our end, and I guess you must have known for, oh, two or three days at least that the development was to be shifted."

She said nothing.

"So, you thought, I'll capitalize on this little opportunity and make myself out to be the great savior. Earn Mike's undying gratitude."

"It wasn't like that."

"Did you think I wouldn't find out that it wasn't down to you? Do you think I'm stupid?"

There was a long silence.

"I thought . . . by the time you found out we'd be happy and it wouldn't matter anymore."

"Our whole relationship would have been based on a lie."

"Oh, you're a fine one to talk about lies. You and Tina. You and that bloody development."

"You would have let me come all the way back, uproot my whole life, on a —"

"On a what? *Uproot your whole life?* Oh, don't make yourself out to be some great victim, Mike Dormer. You're the one who did *me* a wrong, if you remember."

"Which is why I'm not coming back."

"You know what? I didn't even know if I really wanted you back. I would have let you come back and chucked you out on your ear. You're worthless, Mike, a lying, worthless piece of nothing." She was raging now, the discovery of her duplicity having sent her over the edge. "I'm glad you know. I'm glad you found out. You saved me a bloody journey to the airport. And, frankly, I wouldn't touch you again if —"

"Good luck, Vanessa," I said icily, as her voice rose another octave. "All the best for the future."

My ears were ringing when I flipped my phone shut.

It was all over.

I stared at the little phone in my hand, then hurled it as hard as I could into the sea. It landed with a halfhearted splash thirty feet out. I watched the sea close over it, and felt such extreme emotion erupting inside me that it was all I could do not to roar.

"God!" I shouted, wanting to punch something. Wanting to turn cartwheels. *"God!"*

"I'm not sure he'll hear you," came a male voice from behind me. I spun around to see Kathleen and Mr. Gaines sitting at the end of the whalechasers' table. He was wearing a blue fleece and his bush hat, and they were watching me calmly.

"That was a very nice phone, you know," Kathleen told him. "This generation is so wasteful. They're all the same."

"Emotional too. We didn't do all that yelling in my day," said Mr. Gaines.

"I blame the hormones," said Kathleen. "I think they put them in the water."

I took a step toward them. "My room," I said, trying to slow my breathing. "Any chance . . . any chance I can keep it a little longer?"

"Reckon you'll have to check your books, Kate," Mr. Gaines said, leaning into her.

"I'll see if it's still available. We'll be getting busier now . . . now that we're the only hotel in the bay. I'm not normally a sticky-beak," she added, "but you *were* yelling some."

I stood there, my heart-rate slowing, grateful for the two gently mocking old people before me, and for the sun, the benign glinting blue of the bay, the prospect of creatures dancing joyfully unseen below the water. For the thought of a carefree young woman in a battered old cap out somewhere chasing whales.

Kathleen motioned to me to sit down and pushed a beer toward me.

I took my first delicious gulp. I loved this beer, I thought, as I lowered the cold bottle from my lips. I loved this hotel, this little bay. I loved the prospect of my future life, which was unfolding before me, with its reduced income, its cranky teenagers, bad-tempered dog and houseful of difficult women. I was unable quite to grasp the magnitude of what had happened.

Kathleen caught it. "You know," she said, after a few minutes, lifting a crepey hand to her forehead, "all sorts of people are pro-shark these days. They'll tell you that sharks are misunderstood. That they're the product of their environment." She curled a lip. "I say a shark is a shark. Never yet met one that wanted to be my friend."

"That'd be right." Mr. Gaines nodded in approval.

I leaned back in my seat and the three of us sat in silence for a while. Down the coast I could see the building site with the glossy boards, which would soon be redundant. I could hear the music upstairs in Hannah's room, the roar of a distant motorboat, the dull, conspiratorial whispering of the pines. I would stay here for as long as they would have me. The thought filled me with the closest thing to contentment I have yet known.

"Greg never caught that shark, did he?" I said.

Kathleen Whittier Mostyn, legendary Shark Lady, laughed, a short fierce bark of a laugh, and when she turned to face me there was a steely glint in her eye.

"One thing I've learned in my seventy-odd years, Mike. If a shark wants to bite you, as far as I'm concerned, you do whatever the hell you have to just to stay alive."

TWENTY-EIGHT: HANNAH

It takes three hours and twenty-eight minutes to drive from Silver Bay to Sydney airport, another twenty to find a decent parking space, and on top of that, in our case, four further lots of fifteen minutes' stopping time for me to be sick out of the back door with nerves. My tummy still gets me — it was like that every time I went out on a whale-watching trip — and I never could persuade Yoshi it wasn't seasickness. Auntie K knew. She told me every time that it didn't matter — while my head was in the gutter I heard her telling the others she'd brought eight plastic bags and four kitchen rolls in expectation — and Mike had set off an hour early, thanks to her warnings.

There were five of us in the car — Mike, Mum, Mr. Gaines, Auntie K and me. It wasn't our car, but Mr. Gaines's seven-seater, which we borrowed after Mike pointed out that Mum's car couldn't accommodate the one extra person coming home. A convoy of trucks, trailing bits of net and lines and probably smelling of fish, all pretending not to be there, was following us. Every time we stopped they stopped too, but none of them got out. They just sat and looked out of the window as if they were interested in anything but the girl with her head in the gutter. If it had been any other time I'd have wanted to die of embarrassment.

No one had wanted to come too close, knowing what my mum was like about her privacy, but everyone had wanted to be there. My mum didn't care. To be honest, I don't think she'd have noticed if the Queen of England had turned up to watch. For twenty-four hours she had hardly spoken, just stared at her watch and calculated and occasionally reached out to hold my hand. If Mike hadn't stopped her, I think she'd have moved into the arrivals lounge two days ago and waited there.

Mike's calculations were spot-on. Even with our extra stops we got there fifteen minutes before the flight arrived. "Fifteen," Mr. Gaines muttered, "of the longest minutes of our lives." At least twenty more, Mike calculated, for baggage and Passport

Control. And for every single one of them, there Mum stood, as still as anyone ever had, her hands gripping the rail, while we tried to make conversation around her, eyes on the gate. At one point she held my hand so tightly that my fingers went blue, and Mike had to get her to let go. Twice Mike went to the Qantas desk and came back to confirm that the plane had definitely not dropped out of the sky.

Finally, just as I thought I might be sick again, the first trickle of passengers from flight QA2032 came through. We stared in silence, each of us straining to see the distant figures through the swinging doors, trying to match that image with the one we had on a crumpled bit of paper. What if she didn't come? The thought popped into my head, and my heart filled with panic. What if she'd decided she wanted to stay with Steven? What if we stood there for hours and no one came? Worse, what if she came and we didn't recognize her?

And suddenly there she was. My sister, almost as tall as me, with Mum's bright blonde hair and a crooked nose like mine, holding tightly to Mike's sister's hand. She was wearing blue jeans and a pink hooded top, and walked with a limp, slowly as if part of her was still afraid of what she might find. Mike's sister saw us and waved, and even from that distance you could see the smile on her face was as big as a mile. She stopped for a minute and said something to Letty, and Letty nodded, her face toward us, and they began to walk faster.

We were all crying then, even before they had reached the barrier. My mother, silent beside me, had begun to shake. Aunt Kathleen was saying, "Thank God, oh, thank God," into a handkerchief and when I looked behind me Yoshi was crying into Greg's chest and even Mike, his arm around my shoulders, was gulping. But I was smiling as well as crying because I knew that sometimes there's more good in the world than you can possibly imagine and that everything was going to be all right.

And as Letty got close Mum ducked under the barrier and started to run, and as she ran she let out a sound I'd never heard before. She didn't care what anyone thought — she and my sister locked eyes and it was as if they were magnets, as if there was nothing in the world that could stop them moving toward each other. My mother grabbed her and pulled her in and Letty was sobbing and had hold of Mum's hair and the only way I can describe it is to say it was as if each of them had had a piece of themselves given back. I pushed through then, and I held on to them too, and then Aunt Kathleen, and Mike, and I was dimly aware of all the people watching who must have thought she was just another kid coming home. Except for the noise. The noise my mother made, as they sank to the floor, surrounded by all of us, wrapped in arms and kisses and tears.

Because the sound that came from my mother, as she rocked my sister in her arms, was long and grievous and strange, and spoke of all the love and pain in the world. It echoed through the great arrivals hall, and bounced off the shiny floor and off the walls, stopping people in their tracks, and causing them to peer around to see what it was. It was both terrifying and glorious. It sounded, Aunt Kathleen said afterward, exactly like the song of a humpbacked whale.

Epilogue: Kathleen

My name is Kathleen Whittier Gaines and I'm a seventy-six-year-old bride. Even to say those words makes me wince with the silliness of it all. Yes, he caught me in the end. He told me if he was going to kick the bucket he'd like to do it knowing I was nearby, and I figured that was not a lot to ask of a woman, not when she knew she had been loved by a man her whole life.

I don't live in the hotel anymore. Not full time, anyway. Nino and I couldn't quite agree on where to settle: he said he had to be near his vines, and I told him I wasn't going to spend the rest of my days inland. So we split our week between our two houses, and while the rest of Silver Bay thinks we're a pair of mad old coots, this is an arrangement that suits us both fine.

Mike and Liza live in the hotel, which is probably a little smarter and a little more welcoming than it was when I ran it alone.

Mike has fingers in other pies, interests that keep him busy and bring in some money, such as marketing Nino's wines, but I don't pay much heed, as long as we have a bottle or two of something nice on the tables in the evening. Every now and then Mike gets ideas about making more money, or increasing yields, or whatever the hell it is he talks about, and I disagree, and the rest of them nod and smile and wait quietly for him to blow himself out.

There will be other developments, and other threats, and we'll keep fighting. But now we do it without fear. Nino Gaines — or should I say my husband? — bought the old Bullen place. A wedding present for me, he said. A bit of security for the girls. I don't like to think too hard about how much he paid for it. He and Mike have ideas for the space. They occasionally go down together to the faded billboards and walk the land, but when it comes down to it, neither of them seems like they actually want to do anything. And I get on with doing what I always have, running a slightly ramshackle hotel at the end of the bay and getting a little fidgety if we have too many visitors.

Down the coast road, the southern migration is shaping up just fine. There are reports every day of pods, mothers and babies, and on the surface, passenger numbers are pretty well what they were at the same time last year. The whalechasers come and go, the occasional new face replacing the old, bringing the same salty tales, the same jokes and complaints to my benches each evening. Yoshi went back to Townsville to study whale conservation, promising to return, and Lance often talks about visiting her, but I doubt he will. Greg is courting — although that may be too delicate a word for it — a twenty-four-year-old barmaid from the RSL, and she seems to give him as good as she gets. He spends less time around the hotel, anyhow, and I can see that suits Mike fine.

And Letty thrives. She and Hannah hang on to each other as if it was five days they were separated, not five years. Several times I've found them sharing a bed, and made to move them, but Liza says not to bother. "Let them sleep," she says, looking at them entwined. "They'll want space from each other soon enough." When she speaks there's such a lightness in her voice that I can't believe she's the same woman.

The first few weeks were strange. We tiptoed around the child, afraid that this strange series of events, this sudden shift of circumstance would leave her shattered. For a long time she stayed glued to her mother, as if afraid that she would be ripped apart from her again, and in the end I took her down to the museum and showed her my harpoon and told her that anyone who thought they were coming near any of my girls would have Old Harry to answer to. She was a little surprised, but I think she was reassured. Nino tells me drily that there was probably a reason I never had children.

She was better once her father had called: he told her he was happy for her to stay here, and would allow all decisions to be hers. From that point on she slept properly — albeit in her sister's bed. And there it ends. Mike's sister, true to her word, never printed her story. Mike says it's actually a love story — not about him and Liza, although you only have to look at them laughing together to know that that's the case — but about Liza and her daughters. Sometimes, if he's teasing me, he says it's about me and Nino.

I tell him I don't see it that way. Look out at the sea for long enough, at its moods and frenzies, at its beauties and terrors, and you'll have all the stories you need — of love and danger, and about what life lands in your nets. And the fact that sometimes it's not your hand on the tiller, and you can do no more than trust that it'll all work out okay.

Almost every day now, if Liza doesn't have too many trips booked, they head out together on *Ishmael* to see the whales still making their way back to their feeding grounds. At first I thought it was Liza's way of creating a family, of binding them together, but soon I realized that they were as drawn to it as she was. It's not just about the creatures they see, they tell me. It's about what they don't. The girls like to watch the humpbacks disappear, enjoy the thought that, after some spectacular breach, there's a whole life beneath that they cannot see. Songs being sung into an abyss and lost forever, relationships being forged, babies being nurtured and loved. A world in which we and the mindless things we do to each other are unimportant.

At first Mike laughed at them for being fanciful, but now he shrugs and admits: what the hell does he know? What does any of us know? Stranger things have happened, especially in our little corner of the world.

And I watch the four of them now, running down Whale Jetty in the sunshine, and I think of my sister, and perhaps my father, who would have enjoyed a story like this. ("We thought you had company," I tell them, wherever they are. "But, boy, were we mistaken.") They would have understood that this story is about an elusive balance; about a truth we all struggle with whenever we're blessed enough to be visited by those creatures or, indeed, whenever we open our hearts — that sometimes you can damage something wonderful merely through proximity.

And that sometimes, Mike adds firmly, you don't have a choice. Not if you want to really live.

I never let him know, of course. I can't let him think he has it all his own way. But I have to say in this case, just in this case, I agree with him.

ABOUT THE AUTHOR

Jojo Moyes is the *New York Times* bestselling author of *One Plus One, The Girl You Left Behind, Me Before You, The Last Letter from Your Lover, Silver Bay,* and *The Ship of Brides.* Moyes writes for a variety of newspapers and magazines and is married to Charles Arthur, technology editor of *The Guardian.* They live with their three children on a farm in Essex, England.